The Sweetwater Point Motel

The Sweetwater Point Motel

PETER SAAB

GUILD PUBLISHING LONDON

THE SWEETWATER POINT MOTEL
First published in the United States of America
This edition published 1986 by
Book Club Associates
by arrangement with
Arlington Books (Publishers) Ltd
15—17 King Street St. James's
London SW1

© 1981 Peter Saab

Typeset in England by
Inforum Ltd Portsmouth
Printed and bound in England by
Billing & Sons Limited
Worcester

The belief in the supernatural source of evil is not necessary; men alone are quite capable of every wickedness.

Joseph Conrad

1

The English night was so cold, still, and without noise that when the telephone rang it was heard two fields away by a fox walking at the edge of a wood. It sounded five times before a light responded in an upstairs window of the house set a little apart from the others in the village. It continued ringing while Philip Burrows fumbled his way, cursing, down the stairs. He did not trust a phone in the bedroom; he might go back to sleep again. But, hell, why couldn't people arrange to be ill at a reasonable hour? It had been a late night and there was an early morning ahead of him. Hell!

Behind the telephone in the hall was a clock fitted into the wooden frame of a barometer. Through drooping eyes he saw that one said twenty past two and the other Very Cold. God, it was. He shivered in his pyjamas. Hell again. He picked up the receiver.

"Wenham 534," he recited with no enthusiasm. "Doctor Burrows."

The hurried American voice took him by surprise. "Phil?" asked the man. "Is that you, Phil?"

"Yes, Philip Burrows here."

"Phil, this is Andy Curtis, Edith's cousin. I'm calling from Charleston."

There was an edginess in his words. "Andy," Burrows frowned. "Yes? What's the trouble?"

"Phil, maybe I'm scared for nothing, but Edith and the girls haven't arrived. They should have gotten here days ago."

"Not there?" His voice came in a croak.

7

"We've heard nothing. Not a call. Nothing. I let it ride until now. But today I told the police."

Burrows sat down heavily on the low telephone stool. His shotgun was leaning against the wall and he nudged it as he sat. It began to slide down the wall. He caught it and put it upright again. "But it's . . . I can't believe it. I had a postcard yesterday. Wait—" He picked up the card from the hall stand. It showed the skyline of New York. "Andy," he continued. "It's postmarked January 6. How long does it take to drive to Charleston, for God's sake?"

"Three days even if you take it very easy. I'm sorry to call you in the middle of your night, Phil, but I'm getting real worried. We expected them a week ago." The voice seemed to be coming from somewhere beyond space.

"I don't know what to say, Andy," he said helplessly. "They could have done some sightseeing, but surely Edith would have telephoned you. She *should* have."

"Sure she would. That's what I mean."

"What did the police say?" For some reason he bent and held the stock of the gun. At daybreak he had planned to go duck shooting.

"The police took all the particulars. But I can't even give a good description. I haven't seen them for years, not since the girls were little kids. Adele is going crazy."

"Maybe they had an accident," muttered Burrows. He had not liked the idea of Edith driving in America. "But Edith drove in California when Gerald was alive. When they lived over there for that year."

"If there'd been an accident," Andy Curtis pointed out, "it would be on record. The cops would know. They had papers, passports, everything. I don't even know what model car they were renting. And I couldn't tell the police which hotel they were at in New York."

"The Randall Plaza," said Burrows looking again at the post-card. "Edith put it on the card."

"Randall Plaza. Right. I'll call them right now," said Andy. "Then I'll call you back. You'd better stay awake."

"Of course I will. What about the New York police?" asked Burrows. "Will your police at Charleston inform them?"

"They send these things out to all police departments, I guess," the American replied. "Just let me call the hotel and I'll get back to you right away. Jesus, I hope they're all right, Phil. Maybe we're getting all wound up for nothing."

"I sincerely hope so," said Burrows. "I'll wait until you ring."

Slowly he put the phone down. He was six feet one and weighed 185 pounds. He looked incongruous sitting on the small telephone stool in his striped pyjamas. He rubbed his eyes with his hands. No, it wasn't possible. Not *another* damned accident. His brother Gerald – Edith's husband – had been killed in a car crash and Philip Burrows had lost his wife Gwen in the same tragic incident two years ago. Although he had really lost Gwen long before that.

He walked through the house and then, abruptly conscious of the cold again, he went up to his bedroom, found his dressing gown and slippers and returned downstairs. There was an electric fire in the sitting room which he sometimes used as a consulting room if he saw patients at home. He pushed down the switch and stood in front of the fire, trying to think, while the increasing heat warmed, then burned, his legs. He grunted and moved away.

Walking into the adjoining room, he switched on the light, went to the bookcase, and took down an old and bulky atlas. It had scarcely been looked at since his school days. There was a dining table, slightly dusty because the room was hardly ever used now. He laid the atlas down with his customary heaviness causing a fusillade of dust. He checked the index and then turned the leaves until he came to a full-page map of the United States. Putting his little finger on New York he spanned it until his thumb was touching Charleston, South Carolina. He transferred the measurement to the scale at the foot of the page. It was eight hundred miles.

Picking up a pair of surgical tweezers from the bureau, he used them as a pointer as he traced the roads running south from New York to the Carolinas. The routes had probably changed by now and Edith, Abigail, and Kate Burrows could be anywhere. He jumped as the telephone rang again. He hurried into the hall and picked it up.

"Phil," said the American voice immediately. "Is that you, Phil?"

"Yes. What happened?"

"I checked with the hotel. They left on the day they said –

9

January 6. There are any number of car rental companies where they could have got the car. I'll check the big ones, Avis, Hertz, and so on. But it may take time. I don't know what else I can do."

Burrows said, "Listen, Andy. Give it till six tomorrow evening, your time. Let's wait as long as that." He was conscious of having made a firm decision and yet postponing action. "That's midnight here, right. Ring me then."

"Sure. If they get here before that I'll call you right away."

"Good." He waited. "Andy, do *you* think they're all right? I mean . . . you're *there*. I've never been to America."

The pause from the other end was longer. "I just don't know, Phil. They may be perfectly okay. But . . . ."

"But what?"

"This is a crazy country, Phil. Ninety-five percent of the people are good. You know, like everyone is *good* to an extent. But there's some real crazies. Freaks. Nuts like that. You just have to read the newspapers to see that. Right now maybe we shouldn't try to dream up too many explanations."

Burrows nodded as if the other man could see him. "All right," he said. "I'll expect your call tomorrow."

They said good-bye and he replaced the phone. "Oh Christ," he said to himself quietly, half blasphemy, half prayer. "How could three people just vanish?"

He did not sleep again that night, lying staring at the ceiling until the pallid winter day came over the top of his bedroom curtains. At five o'clock he telephoned to cancel his participation in the duck shoot. He said he had been dealing with an emergency all night. At ten o'clock he conducted his normal surgery and when the last patient had gone at noon he telephoned Inspector Harry Mead at the police station in Burrington, the nearest small town. They were old friends.

"Harry," he said, "can you spare me a few minutes? I've got a problem."

"I should think you've got a hangover after the dinner last night," said Mead jocularly. "Didn't get up to go shooting this morning, did you?"

"No, something else came up. Can I come over now?"

Mead detected the note in the voice. "Of course. Do you want to go to the pub or will the office do?"

"I'd prefer the office."

He drove there in ten minutes. Mead was behind his desk. The police inspector got up and, without asking, poured two measures of scotch. "What's the trouble, Phil?" he asked.

"You remember my sister-in-law, Edith—" began Burrows.

"Of course. I remember the accident."

"Well, ten days ago she went off to America with her two daughters. They went to New York and they were supposed to make their way down to South Carolina, to Charleston, to see a cousin and his wife. They've never arrived at his house. He rang me at two-thirty this morning. I can't think what to do."

The police inspector screwed up his face. "Ten days?" he said. "That's a long time for *three* people to be missing."

"Exactly. They left their hotel in New York on January 6 and they were supposed to be hiring a car to drive to Charleston."

"Do they know any people between New York and Charleston?" asked Mead.

"Apart from Andy and his wife I don't think Edith knows anyone in that part of the States. When she was there with my brother for a year they lived in California. All their friends are in the San Francisco area."

"But it's possible there might be someone she'd visit that you don't know about?"

Burrows looked up sharply. "It could be. But even if she did, you'd think she would have rung Andy."

Mead nodded. "As I remember her, she was a sensible sort of woman," he agreed. "What ages are the girls?"

"Abigail is seventeen and Kate is twelve." He looked carefully at Mead. "It doesn't seem credible."

"The cousin has reported it to the police, I take it?"

"Yes, but only yesterday. I wish he'd done it sooner but I suppose he didn't want to panic. But he can't even give proper descriptions. He hasn't seen them for years."

"You must get recent photographs over there," said Mead decisively. "Get them to me and I'll have them sent by wire."

Burrows regarded him hopefully. "Is there anything else you can do, Harry? How about Interpol and suchlike?"

"You could get the newspapers over there to cooperate. That's always the best way of circulating people's descriptions."

Burrows considered it. "I don't think so – yet," he said

11

eventually. "Edith would be mortified if it were all a false alarm and their photos were plastered all over the newspapers."

Mead regarded Burrows carefully. He had never been able to understand how a man like this could have lost his beautiful wife to a superficial brother. Carelessness, he supposed. With caution, he said, "You and your sister-in-law . . . What is your relationship like?"

"I'm very fond of Edith," nodded Burrows. "And the girls. After the car crash we leaned on each other a good deal. In fact, I'd asked her to marry me. At Christmas. But she wasn't sure. For various reasons. One of them was that she thought I wasn't sure either. She was going to tell me when she got back from America." He caught Mead's expression. "All right, I know what's going through your mind, Harry. Yes, I admit it, it *is* possible that she went to see somebody in America, some person I don't know about, some man she may have met in California when she was there with Gerald. It's a chance, I'll concede. But she'd hardly vanish into thin air, would she?"

"Why go in January?" asked Mead. "It's not much of a month for touring."

"She wanted the girls to go with her. Kate starts at a new school at Easter, and Abigail's going to secretarial college, and Edith thought she might be tempted to spend the money on a new car if she didn't go right away. It suited them all to go now and they thought it might be quieter on the roads and cheaper in hotels."

"I wonder what the weather has been like in that area," said Mead. "That might delay her."

Burrows looked down at his big hands. He said, "I telephoned the American Embassy in London this morning. Apart from notifying the police and the British Embassy in Washington they couldn't give me any further advice. They say the weather is good for the time of year. No snow, just rain and some fog. If Edith had been in a car accident it'd be known almost right away."

Mead ran his teeth together. "Photographs, descriptions, and that type of thing. That's all I can think of to do. I know it's not much, but it's all. And I wouldn't delay getting the American newspapers in on it."

"How do I do that? Ring the London offices, I suppose."

12

"There are American news agencies. Associated Press is one and there's United Press. Or there's Reuters, that might be as good. I'll find out from the press boys if you like."

Burrows still backed away from the suggestion. He remembered the newspapers from the time of the car crash. His wife and his brother in the car. Going where? And he and Edith knew nothing about their being together. "Leave it for a while," he said. "I don't want any misunderstanding."

"Right. You know best. But it's the best way of finding people. Better than all your police descriptions. Think about it."

Mead got up and poured them each another scotch. He handed the glass to Burrows and said, "It's probably all right, Phil. Just a fuss for nothing."

"God, I hope so. But ten days, Harry – that's a long time."

"The other thing you could do is to hire a private detective. They have some in America who specialise in missing persons. And it's a more concentrated thing than the police channels. Whatever the police do it's all computerised in the end. They'll just *watch* out, see if they turn up, but they won't *search*. They won't have the time. Too many people go missing. But a private man would search. It would be expensive, but it might be worth considering."

"I feel so impotent, Harry," Burrows said. "I hate the bloody helpless feeling. I think I ought to go myself."

He'd been brewing and drinking tea for an hour when the telephone rang again at midnight. "Phil," Andy said at once. "They haven't arrived here."

Burrows ran his free hand across his eyes. His face felt tired and rough. "I knew," he said hollowly. "You'd have called earlier otherwise."

"I've been at the police department half the day," said Curtis. "Jesus, those guys sure seem slow when it's something like this. They want a goddam dead body before they'll get off their arses." He realised what he had said and hesitated. "Well, not a body," he went on. "But something . . . this seems too tame for them. They always figure that any attractive female who disappears has gone off with some guy."

"There are three in this instance and one of them is twelve years old," put in Burrows sharply. It was almost as if he were blaming

13

Curtis. He immediately felt apologetic. "I didn't mean to sound like that, Andy," he said. "I'm very on edge, that's all."

"Sure," answered the American. "I'm strung out like hell myself. Adele wants to speak to you. She's right here."

Burrows was afraid that might happen. The woman was sobbing. "Oh God, Phil," she whimpered. "What's happened? There are some terrible things, Phil. Every day in the newspapers there are terrible things. And on television."

Almost by instinct he slipped into his doctor's manner. "Don't distress yourself, Adele," he said carefully. "Just try to keep calm. Maybe it's all right. Maybe we'll all be laughing at ourselves for fools tomorrow."

"Dear God, I hope so," she breathed. "The cops here don't seem to have half a brain between them. When we were there today they were laughing about some football game. They couldn't find out the time of day, Phil."

He remained the doctor. "Everything will be sorted out," he said. "Tell me, how are *your* children?" He had not meant the emphasis as it came out.

She seemed surprised at the question. "My kids?" she repeated. "Oh, they're just fine, Phil, thank you. Sometimes I wish I could get rid of them for a while." She had not intended it like that, and her own words sent her into further sobs. "I'll put Andy on again," she trembled. "Let's pray, Phil. Let's just pray that they're okay."

Her husband came back. "Sorry, Phil," he said. "She's really taking the whole thing bad. You see, we feel kind of . . . well, responsible, if you get me."

"I understand very well," said Burrows. He pulled himself together in the chair and attempted to sound business-like. "We've got to do some logical thinking, Andy," he said. "I've arranged through a police friend for the photographs and descriptions to be sent by wire to America, to the police, to the British Embassy in Washington and the British Consulate in New York. This friend – he's a police inspector – also suggested getting the newspapers to help."

At once he sensed the awkward silence on the far end of the line. Andy eventually said, "Yes, okay. We've got to do *anything* we can, Phil." He was going to say something more so Burrows waited. "It's just . . . well, you know I'm a lawyer tied up with

14

politics here . . . " went on the American. Then he said, "Oh hell, yes, *we've got to.*"

Suddenly Burrows had made up his mind. "You've got enough on your plate, Andy," he said. "I think I'd better come over. I can't just sit here."

The American's relief filled his voice. "I'd be very glad if you were over here, Phil," he replied. "I truly would. What will you do, come here to Charleston?"

"No, I think it had better be New York," decided Burrows. He was surprised how firm he felt. "That's the end to start from. Do you think I ought to retain a private detective?"

"You could," Curtis said doubtfully. "Maybe you ought to decide when you get over."

"Yes, I will," acknowledged Burrows. "I'll also make up my mind about the newspapers then. I'll get there first."

"I'll fly up to Kennedy to meet you," said Curtis. "Just let me know."

"Don't bother to do that," replied Burrows. "It's not going to help a lot and you'd have to leave your work and that sort of thing . . . "

"I really don't mind. I could fix things here."

"I think it's best that you stay there," said Burrows. "They may yet turn up in Charleston or there may be things to do at that end. I'll keep in touch by telephone. If we need to join up then I'll ask you."

He could tell that Curtis was relieved. "Well, if you're certain, Phil," he said carefully. "I've got a hell of a lot on at the office right now. But just call me and I'll be with you. When will you get here, do you think?"

"As soon as I can," Burrows said. "I can get the doctor in the next village to stand in for me here. I'll need a visa, I suppose. I'll just have to get one and come on over. I'll telephone when I'm there."

"Great," said Curtis. "I feel a whole lot better now."

"I wish I did," replied Burrows. "I'm a doctor, not a detective. I'll just have to learn, I suppose."

"Maybe doctors make good detectives," suggested Curtis.

"Let's hope this one does," muttered Burrows.

Curtis had been waiting to ask something. He needed to do so before replacing the phone. "Phil," he said unhappily, "there's

15

no reason – none that you know of – why Edith should have taken the girls and just . . . gone away? You know, planned it herself? Just felt that she wanted to get away and start afresh?"

"None," said Burrows firmly. Here it was again. "You're thinking back to the accident," he added.

"Well, it was a hell of a thing," said Curtis. "For both of you. You *and* Edith."

"It was," answered Burrows. "But it's two years now. I think we're both over it. As much as we'll ever be."

The American would not let it go immediately. "You see a lot of each other?" he asked. The awkwardness was heightened. "I guess you were sort of thrown together by what happened."

"On the contrary, for some time – about eight months – we didn't see each other. We avoided each other. Because of the circumstances. But since then we've started visiting. She lives only twenty miles away. And I was always very fond of the girls. In fact, since you ask, at Christmas I asked her to marry me."

The voice was surprised. "And she accepted?"

"She wanted time to consider it. To put it bluntly she didn't want just an alliance. It had to be a proper marriage."

"But there's no reason to suppose that this has happened because of that," said Andy. It was half a question. "I mean she wasn't upset or disturbed or anything?"

"Not at all. I've never seen Edith upset or disturbed, not in that way. Even at the time of the car crash she was very composed, whatever she felt inside. She's not the type to run away, Andy. She's a very remarkable woman."

Once he had replaced the telephone Burrows sat for three minutes trying to organise his thoughts. He looked up at the clock on the barometer. It was five minutes past midnight. The barometer still said Very Cold. Picking up the telephone again he dialled Harry Mead's number. A voice that was half smothered by blankets answered.

"Harry," Burrows began. "Sorry to call you like this but they've still not turned up, Edith and the girls. I've just heard from Charleston. I've decided to go over to see what I can do."

"When are you going?" asked Mead.

"Now. I'll get some things together and drive down to London right away. I'll get the first plane I can. I'll need a visa."

16

"Yes. I'll probably be able to help there. I'll call Scotland Yard. I'll ring you back and tell you what I've arranged."

"Thank you, Harry. I'm very grateful."

"It's no trouble. I should be back to you in about fifteen minutes."

"Right. Thanks."

Burrows immediately rang another number. A second sleepy voice answered. "Sandleford 892, Doctor Bryant here."

As concisely as he could Burrows explained the situation. He could hear Bryant coming more awake with each sentence. Eventually the other doctor said, "You've certainly got to go, Phil, and right now. Don't worry, I'll manage."

Burrows was grateful. He put the phone down and went up to the loft of his house. It was freezing there. He could hear an owl calling very close – it seemed almost at his ear – probably from the tree in his garden. A dog answered from a far distance across the winter night. There was a tough leather suitcase that had belonged to his father in one corner of the loft. It had stickers and labels from many countries and many years before. His father had been a traveller. It was grey with dust. He banged it against one of the low rafters to knock some of the dust off, then carried it down the steps onto the bedroom landing. His cleaning woman kept her dusters in a cupboard on the landing. He took one of them and wiped the outside of the case. In doing so he uncovered his dead father's handwriting on one of the labels. He stared at it for a moment then quickly took the case into the bedroom.

He had not undressed that night and now he changed into a blue suit and packed pyjamas, shirts, socks, and underwear into the leathery old case. As a strange afterthought he went downstairs, returned with the out-of-date atlas and attempted to put that in also. It would not fit so he discarded it.

Downstairs again he opened a bureau in the sitting room and took out his scarcely-used passport. He had been twice to France, to the fowling marshes of the Camargue and once to Italy when he and Gwen were first married. From a metal cashbox in the same place he took his cheque-book and thirty-four pounds in notes, silver, and copper all it contained. The telephone rang.

Burrows carried the suitcase and set it on the floor by the phone. "Phil, it's Harry," said the voice.

"I'm ready to go," said Burrows.

"About the visa. You'll have to go to the United States Embassy first thing in the morning. Don't go in the Visa Department entrance; go through the front door and ask for Mr. Killip. He's a visa man there, and he'll stamp the passport and so on without your having to wait. But you'll have to take a passport-sized picture of yourself. Get that taken at one of those booths. If you like I'll call Frank Wilson at the bank as soon as it's open and get him to arrange some money through his branch at London Airport."

"You're a friend, Harry," Burrows said quietly. "Christ knows how I'm going to make out."

"You'll be all right," Mead assured him. "Perhaps it's not a bad thing to be starting from scratch, in a way. Makes you more aware of things. Amateurs often make good detectives."

"Thanks, Harry. I'd better be going. I want to go to Edith's house on the way. I know where the key will be. They'll have some better photographs than the ones I gave to you."

The police inspector's attitude became strangely cautioning. "Do you have to?" he said. "Go to the house?"

"It's all right, isn't it? I'll get the photos, then lock up again."

Mead still sounded unhappy. "Be careful in there, Phil. Don't let the local coppers arrest you for breaking and entering."

Burrows was puzzled. "If they do, can I refer them to you?" he said, knowing that he would. "You can vouch for me."

"Well, yes. But it's a strange business, that's all. Sorry to sound so solemn, Phil, but if *they're* gone missing and you're rummaging around their house . . . Well, you may not understand, but as a copper, I can see complications . . . I *know* you, but just be careful, that's all. Over there in the States as well. Especially over there. You'd be surprised how easy it is to put yourself in the wrong."

In a dull voice Burrows said, "All right, Harry, I'll be careful."

Edith Burrows' house was in the village of Martinsford, twenty miles south of his own home. Burrows brought his snorting car out into the frosty night, loaded his belongings, and set out cautiously along the icy country roads. As the headlights swept along the black hedgerows and he pressed his tired face forward toward the windscreen, there came the full realisation of the enormity of the task and the journey ahead. A cat ran from the sheen of mist bordering the road and he braked and swerved before cursing it. His shoulders and arms ached. His eyelids kept lolling. He called himself a fool for not resting the previous evening.

Edith Burrows' house at Martinsford was cumbersome Victorian, saved from ugly solemnity by a beautiful garden. Now it loomed in front of him like a black railway station, the high pointed roof just discernible against the low, chill sky. He located the back door key in the garden shed where they had left it for the daily cleaner to feed the cat and collect their mail during their three-week absence. Mead's warning came back as he turned it in the lock. He felt like a burglar. The cat, asleep in a warm basket in the kitchen, yawned and eyed him suspiciously as he went through the door. He switched on the kitchen light and spoke to the cat. The light could attract attention, but at least it might be evidence of the legitimacy of his entering the place.

It was odd going in there like that, not knowing where Edith, Abigail, or young Kate were. He went into the sitting room, turned on the lights and stared around. It had always been a comfortably lived-in house, with plenty of cushions and rugs and oddments, a fire in the hearth all winter, and never formally tidy. Now the rooms looked as if they were set out for some sort of exhibition, like rooms in a museum might be. The comfort had gone, the colours looked stiff, the hearth clean and chill. The pictures and ornaments appeared to stare at him. He sat down in the big, cold fireside chair and held his tired face. God, where had they gone?

The icy sound of a remote church clock marking two roused him. He stood up conscious of the engulfing emptiness of the room. The fireplace gaped like a cold laugh. There was a Victorian bureau in the adjoining room and he remembered the silver frame with family photographs which stood on its top ledge. He walked in, put down the switch, and filled the room with empty light.

In the frame were separate portraits of Edith and her daughters, Edith composed, both the girls laughing. One other picture was smaller. It had been placed in the corner of the frame so that it almost hid Katy. His younger brother, Gerald, smiling. A shit, he thought fiercely, a real shit.

19

Sadly and awkwardly, Burrows took the three female pictures from the frame; opening the bureau he took an envelope to contain them. He put them in his pocket, then placed the silver frame with Gerald, now looking solitary through the glass, into the bureau and shut the lid.

He remained motionless by the bureau. Standing there only weeks before, Edith had given her studied reply to his difficult proposal of marriage. The room had been draped for Christmas and there was a small, rosy fire in the grate. She had stood, in an odd official sort of stance at the desk, as if in some manner it were a business discussion. She was only three inches shorter than his six feet one, her hair carefully set, her make-up deliberate, her nails pink and shapely. There was a pale gold watch on her lean wrist, a present from her husband on the final Christmas they had spent together. That was three years before. Burrows remembered feeling somehow unkempt standing near her. But his clumsily-presented suggestion of marriage had moved her. Her fingers reached and touched his forearm and she looked away toward the fire.

"You don't propose very easily do you, Phil?" she said in a sort of joke.

"I haven't had a lot of practice," he replied.

She turned back, leaned quietly and kissed him on the side of his mouth. Their arms contacted, but not the rest of their bodies. "We mustn't do it as an excuse," she said painstakingly. "Or is that the right word? What I'm trying to say is that we mustn't just get married because it's the *right* thing for us to do. The way out, if you like. Or . . . as a kind of revenge."

"I know," he nodded. "I've worked that out myself."

"No," she said. "We must not, whatever we do, marry just because we're left here, because we're the survivors. Or to get our own back." She sat thoughtfully on the edge of the polished round chair that went with the bureau. Her face became kind and she reached for his hands again. He could hear the voices of her daughters from some other part of the house. They had been riding and had just returned. "We wouldn't suit each other very well," she warned with a smile. "We've very different." The smile tightened. "The others were much more suited."

"It still hurts you, Edith," Burrows said, "doesn't it?"

"What about you?" she asked.

20

"It hurts." He looked away from her down at the dark wood of the bureau. His tone hardened. "I'll never understand how they got away with it – without us knowing. I was just careless, I suppose. I was too busy with my work and other things, shooting and suchlike."

She smiled and said, "You always were a bachelor, even when you were married to Gwen. You always *will* be, too. That's why we've *both* got to think about things now." She closed her eyes briefly. "Gerald and Gwen were very good at adultery," she shrugged. "That's why we didn't know. Perhaps I was careless, too."

Burrows realised that this was the first time they had talked about the matter privately and at length. At first nobody had wanted to discuss it and since then they had not been in close contact. "Perhaps it had not been going on very long," he suggested without conviction. "Perhaps we may be doing them an injustice. It would be nice to think of some good reason for them being in that car together. But I haven't been able to think of one."

"There isn't a good reason," she sighed. "Fifty miles away, both with packed suitcases, both having told lies. Your brother was supposed to be at the other end of the country. No. There's no benefit of the doubt because there *is* no doubt, I'm afraid." She left the bureau abruptly, and he saw that the discussion had upset her. She left him standing and went and looked out the window into the dull winter garden.

"Thank you for asking me, Phil," she said. "I'm very flattered."

"Will you then?" he said. "I mean, there's a lot we can do for each other and I'm . . . I'm very fond of you." She smiled at his diffidence. "And the girls like me, I think," he went on.

"I'm not sure it would be a good thing for you," said Edith quietly. "You don't know me as well as you think, Phil. I might well make a better sister-in-law, and a friend, than a wife. I'd be awful to you. I might try to stop you shooting innocent ducks." She laughed at his patent discomfiture and moved towards him slowly, but then with quicker steps. She looped her arms loosely about his broad neck. He could feel the wool of her dress sleeves against his jaw. His large hands rested on her waist. Edith regarded him genuinely. "Can I ask a favour?" she had said.

"Of course. Anything."

21

"Can I ask you to wait for my answer? Just a few weeks. Until I get back from the States. I want to talk to myself about it, if you know what I mean. It's just that I want to be fair to both of us. Will you?"

"If that's what you want to do," he said, "that's what you must do."

"As soon as I get back," she promised. They kissed each other lightly on the lips, the first time they had ever done so, and she drew away. The girls were in the hall outside.

"I'll wait for that," he had said. He remembered how she had smiled, standing in the spot which was now there, vacant, in front of him. Suddenly, alone as he was, a strong, almost glad feeling, grew in him. It was right that he was going. He would not fail again. He *had* to find them. Jesus Christ, he *would* find them. He'd been careless too long. Any bloody fool with half an eye could shoot duck.

The plane reached Kennedy Airport at five o'clock on a rainy evening. Burrows had wandered in and out of slumber throughout the flight. He was so exhausted he hardly noted the experience. Eventually he fell into a deep well of sleep only to be aroused within minutes, it seemed, by the announcement that they were descending to New York. An hour later he was in a dented yellow taxi going toward the piled lights that were Manhattan. He slumped in the worn seat while the cab bounced along the rough route to the Triborough Bridge, weary and low in spirit.

The driver crouched as if he were just as tired. He went at a pace through channels of rainwater, sending bow waves over the hood.

"You from London?" the driver eventually called back to him.

"Wenham, Northamptonshire," replied Burrows dully.

"Never heard of that," answered the man, apparently rousing himself by the conversation. "You sure come to some kind of lousy weather. But I guess you got to be used to rain."

"Winter is winter anywhere you go," answered Burrows. He said immediately, "If you were going to drive from New York to Charleston, which way would you go?"

The driver thought about it. Burrows pressed him: "Say you were going from the Randall Plaza Hotel, which way?" He suddenly saw the Empire State Building lit against the hanging clouds.

"Empire State Building," said the driver looking in the mirror and seeing his glance. "Gee, now, the Randall Plaza is about Forty-third and Lexington, right? You'd go through the tunnel, the Lincoln Tunnel see, or the Holland Tunnel. That means you're in Jersey. You want to get on the turnpike and head south. Interstate 95."

"What about other routes?"

"You got a choice. But Ninety-five's the best. There's even a route down the ocean, right down through Atlantic City, Virginia, and the Carolinas, but it ain't no way to travel, not this time of the year. There's bridges and roads right over the ocean and it gets goddam cold and wet. It's okay in the summer. I go that way myself when I take my vacation. I go fishing."

"Where's the police headquarters?" asked Burrows.

This time the man was surprised.

"The cops? There's police stations all over the city – they have precincts all over. But there's Police Plaza, Lower Manhatten, that's the main one, I guess. Headquarters. Do you want to go there instead of the hotel?"

"No, I'll go to the hotel first," answered Burrows tiredly. "I'll find it later."

"It's in the City Hall area," said the driver. "Big brick building. Been there just a few years." He waited a moment, then asked. "You got trouble?"

"Yes," admitted Burrows. He suddenly had the ridiculous notion that the man might be able to help. "I have some relatives who have gone missing over here. I've come to find them."

"Missing persons," whistled the driver with interest. He shook his head. "People do, they sure do. My own wife was missing. Just there one minute, vanished the next."

"Did you find her?" asked Burrows.

"No, never did. Didn't look too long."

Burrows regarded the rising spine of the bright, wet city becoming larger through the night. "How many people in New York?" he asked.

"Oh, I guess ten million," said the driver. "Nine or ten."

"That's a lot of people," breathed Burrows.

"A whole lot," nodded the driver. "And how, if you're looking for somebody."

2

At the Randall Plaza Hotel Burrows stood, patient and haggard, in the line of guests waiting to register. Eventually he reached the counter and leaned against it like a bar. The girl clerk hardly looked up. She was young but harassed. In her lapel she wore a badge which said, *I Love New York*. "Do you have a reservation?" she asked.

"No, I don't. But I have to stay at this hotel."

"That's no problem. We have rooms. Just fill in this slip. Which credit card?"

"I haven't got a credit card. I'm English." The illogicality of the statement only faintly occurred to him. "I'll pay in money."

"Cash," she wrote and said at the same time. "Nice to have somebody here with cash. It's something you don't see so much these days. How long will you be staying?"

"I don't know. Two or three days, I expect." He leaned closer. "Do you remember some people called Burrows coming here? English. Two weeks ago. Mother and two daughters."

The girl looked up sharply. "The people who are missing?" she said.

"That's them," said Burrows. He felt relieved that she had heard. "I'm a relative. I've come to find them."

"We had some police inquiries," she said dropping her voice. "I checked them into the hotel, your relatives, so that's how I know. But I don't recall them very clearly. We get a lot of people. Do you want to see the duty manager? Maybe you'd better."

"Yes, thank you. I will."

She picked up a desk phone and while she was waiting she said over her shoulder, "No news yet?"

"None at all." Burrows had an abrupt thought. "Could I have the same room?" he asked.

The girl had reached the duty manager. "Mr. Simonson, Kathy at reception. There's a gentleman from England here. About the Burrows family. That's right." She glanced down at the registration slip. "Doctor Burrows," she said into the mouthpiece. "Dr. Philip Burrows. Okay, I'll have him wait."

"I'll check on the room," she said to Burrows after replacing the phone. "The duty manager – it's Mr. Simonson – is on his way down to meet you."

Burrows nodded appreciatively. "You've been very kind," he said.

"That's okay. I guess you can use all the kindness you can get."

The duty manager appeared, a young dark man in a stiff suit and with a moustache two sizes too big for him. They shook hands and he directed Burrows back down the corridor to his office. He closed the door and they say down.

"You look pretty tired," he said. "Can I get you a drink?"

"Thanks but no," said Burrows. "I've got a lot to do. I must get on with it."

"I understand," nodded the American. "I would too. It's no good leaving it to the police."

"A drink would really send me off to sleep."

"Maybe that's what you should do," suggested the man kindly. "You're going to get nowhere fast in your state. Why don't you get a night's sleep and then start fresh tomorrow? You'll be better for it. You'll gain more than you'll lose. I could get you a sleeping pill."

Burrows smiled wryly. "I can't tell you the times I've prescribed sedatives and I've never had to take one myself. Never. But I think the time is coming when I'll need it. First I must get some things straight. I gather the police have already made inquiries here."

"Yes, an officer came from the Missing Person's Bureau." He looked at a note on a desk pad. "A Detective Draycott. We tried to help. Told him everything we knew."

"And what did that amount to?" asked Burrows.

"Not too much, I'm afraid. They just checked in. Two rooms. Mrs. Burrows in one and the girls in the other: 1313 and 1315. Adjoining. But nobody remembers very much about them. We get hundreds of guests through this hotel in two weeks. I didn't see them myself, or I ought to say I don't remember seeing them. The only person who really has any recollection, apart from Kathy you saw at the desk, and her memory is pretty faint. . . . The other person is the guy who works in the gift shop. He remembers talking to them because they were English and, as he says, real good-lookers."

"He noticed that, did he?" said Burrows with gratuitous suspicion.

The young man smiled seriously. "I wouldn't be too hurried in starting a list of suspects, Dr. Burrows," he pleaded. "This is an old guy with a war wound. He just liked talking to them, that's all. He couldn't kidnap a kitten."

"What did he remember?"

"Only that they were disappointed about the weather. It's been pretty bad here since Christmas, not even snow, just cold rain. They didn't feel inclined to do much sightseeing and they thought they would maybe rent a car and get on the road to the south. Gus, the guy in the gift shop, told everything to the detective. You haven't heard any news from the police?"

"Nothing," said Burrows. "I'm going to the bureau right away. That's the first stop. I'd better telephone them first."

Simonson said, "Do you have pictures of the lady and her daughters? Maybe I could see them. Might just jog my memory."

Burrows felt inside his jacket and brought out the envelope with the photographs. "There they are," he said handing them over one by one. "Edith Burrows, aged thirty-seven. Abigail Burrows, seventeen, Kate Burrows."

"I don't recall seeing them," said Simonson, shaking his head. "But they're certainly very attractive people. How old is the young one?"

"Twelve," said Burrows sadly. "Twelve years old."

"Jesus."

"That's one reason I've got to find them," said Burrows grimly.

"Listen," said the American seriously. "Just let me give you some advice, doctor. For God's sake get some sleep. It's going to be hopeless if you don't. You'll never be able to do anything. I'll get these pictures copied and circulated around all my staff. I'll have the house detective question everyone we can. I'll get a check made on the car rental agencies, although the police have presumably already done that. I'll call the Missing Person's Bureau and tell them you're coming in tomorrow morning. Maybe they close at night anyway. And I'll get you a drink. You sure look as though you could use it."

Burrows lifted his head. "I'll have the drink," he said. "Thank you. Then I'm going down to this Missing Person's Bureau. I'll sleep after that."

He and the duty manager left the office and walked into the lobby of the hotel. A loud man in a cowboy hat was slapping a porter on the back. Several Japanese were taking photographs of the reception desk. Simonson detached himself and spoke quickly to Kathy at the desk. He returned to the waiting Burrows and said, "The room Mrs. Burrows occupied is free. We'll check you in there."

"Good. Thank you," answered Burrows. His eyes were down to slits. He squeezed his knuckles against them. "I'll call the police from there," he added. "I just want to make some sort of start."

"Sure, sure," said the manager. He had taken the key. "I'll take you up myself." He motioned the porter to pick up Burrows' one suitcase. The man followed them to the lift.

"You're taking on a hell of an assignment," said the manager. "In a strange country. Have you been here before?"

"No, never," said Burrows dully.

Simonson shook his head. "It's going to be tough," he said. "Very, very tough."

They reached the floor and then the room. It was 1313, although the significance of the numbers escaped Burrows. Simonson wondered professionally why they had to have a room with that sort of number in the hotel. It was asking for trouble. He made a note to raise it with the company. He opened the door and pushed it. It swung in. In some hallucinatory way the Englishman almost expected to see Edith Jane Burrows standing there, turning to him with her calm smile.

But the room was as vacant and tidy as an unused tomb. The manager turned on all the lights from a switch at the door. He automatically went into the bathroom as if expecting somebody to be hidden there.

27

"Everything seems in order," he said inadequately.

Before Simonson left, he asked the telephone operator to place the Police Plaza call for Burrows. The young man turned and closed the door behind him. Burrows wandered after him toward the door and saw with a start the small security chain and double lock on the inside with its notice. "For your own safety and comfort please double lock this door and attack the security chain at all times when occupying the room." He stared at it, then slowly obeyed the instruction. What dangers could there be, he wondered, enclosed on the upper floor of a large hotel? The telephone rang. He hurried to the bed and picked it up. His free hand touched the bedspread and then the pillow. This is where Edith had slept.

"I have your party," said the operator. Her voice was gritty. "Just hold the line."

"Missing Person's Bureau." The man's voice was easier. "Detective Lomax."

Burrows swallowed. He said, "My name is Philip Burrows. I'm from England. I'm inquiring about Edith Jane Burrows, Abigail Burrows, and Kate Burrows, from England. You know about it, I think."

"Oh yes, sure," said the voice. "I'm sorry, but we don't have any news for you. They haven't shown up yet."

Burrows clenched his teeth. "I've come to *look* for them," he said.

"Gee, you're in New York! I thought this was an overseas call." The manner changed to the slightly incredulous. "You've come to *look for them*?"

"Yes," replied Burrows woodenly. "I'm coming right round to see you."

"It's all being handled, Mr. Burrows. Everything is being done."

Burrows detected the reproach. "I'm sure it is,' he said. "But I have a deeper interest, you understand. I just can't sit back and leave it to anybody else, not even the police."

There was a touch of annoyance in the reply: "You say your name is Burrows. Are you a relative? We like to deal with the next-of-kin, Mr. Burrows."

"I *am* next-of-kin," said Burrows. "And I'm a doctor. It's Dr. Burrows."

"Sure. Oh, I'm sorry. Well, if you want to come around here this late, then feel free. I'll be on duty until ten o'clock and I'll be glad to show you what we do, what we're doing in this case. In fact, because it's three females and because they're foreign, we've pulled out a lot of stops we wouldn't normally. Get in a cab and come over here. I'll be glad to see you."

"I'll be with you as soon as I can."

Burrows put the receiver down. "Three females," he muttered to himself. That's how impersonal it was. He went into the bathroom and sitting on the lavatory became aware of his profile reflected in the mirror. He looked white and black: white skin, black creases and black pouches under his eyes. With automatic professionalism he put out his tongue. It was yellow in the stark neon of the mirror light.

Back in the room he stood looking around. He made himself do so carefully, checking the location of everything. A dozen people had probably occupied this room since Edith Burrows had been there but he had some forlorn notion that she might have left some clue, some indication. Opening the drawers in the dressing table he lifted the lining paper and peered down into the recesses. Nothing. He did the same with the wardrobe, running his hand along the shelf above the clothes rack and not even finding dust. The curtains were drawn. He walked over and pulled the cord. They eased back and with a shock he found himself looking out over the amazing panorama of New York at night.

Lights everywhere, from sky to ground, burning and flashing brilliantly through the streaming rain. In the street below, cars moved on beams of yellow light, a million windows shone out, piled high against the sky. He stood, a solitary stranger, looking out on the immensity of it and a great, weary despair closed over him. He bowed his head, hardly able to contemplate more.

They called a taxi for him and he went off through the unremitting New York rain, hunched in the darkness of the uncomfortable seat, staring out at the wet lights that ran by the windows. The driver had trouble finding the Police Plaza, not the building itself but the street that led to it. In lower Manhattan the logically criss-crossed New York streets suddenly curl and entangle themselves like roots writhing in the bottom of a flower pot. "It's always the goddam same," grumbled the driver.

29

"Never find the cops when you want them. When you don't –
wham! They're there!"

Eventually he took the correct turn and Burrows paid him
under the heavy brow of a massive brick building rising like some
memorial from a platform of wide steps. In the main reception
area was a security desk where two black girls sat engrossed in
shaping their finger nails. Burrows regarded them through the
channel formed by his upturned overcoat collar. "I want Missing
Persons, if you please," he said deliberately. "Detective Lomax."

"Sure," said one of the girls. "Wait, please."

He waited while she called. The building was almost empty. A
janitor swept a floor in the distance.

"Doctor Burrows?" she asked. He nodded. She handed him a
cardboard badge bearing the number twelve. "It's on the twelfth
floor," she explained unhurriedly. "He'll meet you at the lift."

Tiredly, Burrows turned and went through another security
channel and into the lift. Already standing in there was a whey-
faced man, wearing a gun in a shoulder holster, and a young,
oily-skinned woman who was weeping quietly. They took no
notice of his entry. He pressed the button for twelve and they
went up together. "I don't know how," sobbed the woman into
her hands. "I just don't know how he did that. Not that."

"He found a way," said the policeman. At the eighth floor they
got out. When the doors closed Burrows kept staring at them as
though he might see through them into the dramas and miseries
of the place. Lomax, an anxious-looking man, wearing a red-
striped shirt, was waiting for him. "Doctor Burrows," he said as
they shook hands. "I'm Jim Lomax. I'm sorry you had to come
here at all."

"So am I," muttered Burrows.

"You look pretty exhausted."

"I'm very tired," admitted the Englishman. "But I had to
make this one call before I tried to rest. It may just be another case
to you, Mr. Lomax, something on the files, but it's different for
me."

Lomax went ahead of him into a wide open-plan office, bathed
in yellow light. There was a reception desk at which a youth was
laboriously cutting items out of newspapers. On the wall behind
him were posters bearing photographs and the words: "Wanted
for Terrorism." Lomax indicated a seat beside one of the dozen

desks in the room. The others were vacant. Burrows saw that the "Explosives and Bomb Squad Office" was next door. "It's never just another case, believe me," said Lomax. "In this department we just do our best. Have a cup of coffee."

Burrows nodded. "Thank you. I've brought some photographs. They're different from the others sent from England." He took the envelope with the pictures from his pocket and handed them to the American. He called over his shoulder. "Hi, Benny – get a couple of cups of coffee – and have these pictures copied. Okay?"

"Okay," responded the youth at the desk. He stopped clipping the newspapers and came over to take the envelope from Lomax. He went out of the room. "I hope I didn't seem unhelpful on the phone," said Lomax. "I sure didn't mean to be. But we get some strange customers in here, please believe me. People walking in here demanding we find their uncle who vanished twenty years ago. Within the hour, too! You say you're Mrs. Burrows' next-of-kin?"

"I'm not sure I am," Burrows replied. "She is my sister-in-law. She has a cousin in Charleston, South Carolina."

"Right," said Lomax looking in the folder on his desk. "That's Andrew Curtis."

"Yes, but he hardly knows them. He hasn't seen them for some years."

Lomax raised his eyes steadily. "And yet they came to America with the intention of visiting Mr. Curtis," he said. "A cousin they hardly know."

Burrows had not thought of it like that. "They came to tour. Andy Curtis was just a convenient point to make for. They planned to stay with him a few days and then return to New York and then home to England. There was no other reason to visit him." He paused and then added, "Not that I know of."

The coffee arrived in styrofoam cups and Burrows drank his gratefully. The detective continued to frown at the sheet before him. "Don't you think it was a strange time of the year for tourism?" he said without looking up. "It's a lot more fun in the summer."

"Obviously," replied Burrows. "But they took the opportunity while they could. There were jobs and school involved, for the girls, and they thought it might be difficult for them all to be

31

together at a later date. In any event they thought it would be cheaper and the roads quieter."

Lomax pointed to the document. "We've located the rent-a-car company, which wasn't easy because it wasn't one of the major people. It was a small concern in Newark, New Jersey, out of town."

"Why should she have done that?" asked Burrows, puzzled. The answer occurred to him immediately. "She probably didn't like the idea of driving in New York," he said. "She probably got the car outside the main city to make things easier."

"To cut the hassle," nodded Lomax. "That fits."

"What was the car?" asked Burrows. He took out a pen and his medical diary. He looked up directly at Lomax, almost a challenge. "You have a description of the car?"

Lomax hesitated as though thrown by the reversal of their roles. "Well, I guess I can tell you," he answered. "Red Ford Tempo, 1984. Number 345 PZY. New Jersey licence plate." He watched Burrows write it down. "She was a widow, right?" he asked pointedly.

Burrows finished writing and put the diary into his pocket. He clipped the pen to his upper coat pocket.

"Yes. Her husband was my brother."

The youth from the desk at the door walked by, balancing a waste paper basket deftly on his head. Lomax took no notice. "I see."

"I want to find her," Burrows said.

Lomax rose from the desk. "We have the description and the photographs circulated to all the relevant authorities," he said. "We're in touch with the British Consul here in New York and the Embassy in Washington. There's been a detective assigned to investigating the New York end, but apart from the car rental company, he's been out of luck. All we can do is to go on working through our usual channels. We handle thirty thousand cases a year in this office." Burrows remained, hump-shouldered at the desk. Lomax looked down at him sympathetically. "I'd like to spare you this, doctor," he said, "but I'd like you to check some photographs over. Upstairs."

Burrows looked up, puzzled. "What photographs?" he asked.

"Dead people," shrugged Lomax. "They don't always match up with the pictures we get with the descriptions of missing

32

persons. I won't elaborate on that. Every unidentified body that is found is photographed and we keep the prints upstairs. I have to ask you to check through those of females found in the last ten days or so, since Mrs. Burrows and her daughters disappeared."

"But there were *three* of them," mumbled Burrows. "Three. Surely if you found three bodies, you'd realise—" He stopped. "They may have been separated, you mean," he said.

"That could happen. Do you want some more coffee?"

"No. Let's get it done."

Lomax took a bunch of keys from his desk. "Benny," he called to the youth. "Get the phone, okay?"

"Sure thing," replied Benny. He was busy clipping newspapers again. The detective led the way and they mounted echoing concrete steps. Lomax unlocked the door at the top. "We have to keep them locked up," he said in macabre joke, "in case they run away again." He glanced at Burrows. "Sorry," he apologised. "You get into departmental gags. That's one of them."

"I thought it was," replied Burrows.

"You could go crazy," said Lomax continuing the excuse. "This ain't a happy job."

He pushed the door and turned on a rank of neon lights to reveal an immense filing cabinet running the entire length of the room. "We have the description of everybody who's been reported missing in New York City for the past twenty-five years in this collation," he said, his footsteps sounding in the void. Burrows followed him blinking in the bleak light. "And the descriptions and photographs of all those found, alive or dead, who are identified." He leaned against the end cabinet. "Two things I need to ask you," he said. "It's routine."

"What are they?" Burrows was staring at the cabinets as if they might contain not documents, but flesh and blood.

Lomax said, "Have any of these women got any criminal convictions?"

Burrows looked astounded. "Criminal–?"

"We have to ask. I told you, it's routine. It may put a different aspect on the case."

"No," said Burrows bleakly.

"Okay. Had any of them been confined to a mental or psychiatric hospital?"

Burrows shook his head. "Not to my knowledge," he said in a low voice.

Lomax pulled open the first cabinet drawer. "This shouldn't take too long," he promised. "Just look at these mug shots – photographs – and see if you recognise anybody." He brought out a half dozen photographs and then another batch. "It's just as well you're a doctor," he said.

Burrows took the pictures hesitantly and stared at the first one. It was the frontal view of a young girl, dead and lacerated, her eyes staring in final horror. He passed quickly to the next. A woman, her mouth agape, pulled back savagely at the edges as if she had been struck by a wind. The third victim reminded him of a dead stoat he had once seen pinned to a barn door. The fourth, someone of indeterminate age, was swollen and contused. "Drowned, that one," said Lomax. "The first one had her breasts cut off and a toothbrush in her vagina."

"I'd be glad if you'd forego the details," said Burrows.

"Sorry. This is a live one," Lomax went on with some relief. "Aged about seventeen. Found wandering. No recollection of who she is."

Burrows took the picture, "I don't recognise any of these women," he said. "None."

Lomax yawned as he replaced the photographs. "The rest are all men," he said. He closed the cabinet drawer. "Well, your people are not here. That's a start, I guess." He led Burrows onto the staircase, locked the room after them, and went downstairs.

"Dr. Burrows, were you conscious of any other person in her life?"

"There *may* have been someone," agreed Burrows wearily. "There *could* have been, but I doubt it. She was an intelligent and composed woman – she *is* an intelligent and composed woman – and if she had needed to keep secret some emotion she could have done it."

"Right. I'm sorry about all this. What are your plans now?"

"Plans?" answered Burrows. "I'm going to look, that's what I'm going to do, Mr. Lomax. Look for them. After I've had some sleep."

"You're going to look in New York?"

"Everywhere. New York to Charleston."

"That's a lot of country."

"I know. But I've got to try. If *I* don't search, who will?"

Lomax looked down. He looked fatigued too. He took out a card from his wallet. "That's me," he said, handing it to Burrows. "It has my home telephone number as well as the office. If you need somebody anytime, just call."

The Englishman thanked him and took the card.

"Sorry to have given you such a hard time. This is not an easy job."

"No. I understand that."

"I'll get the car to take you to the hotel." He called over his shoulder, "Benny, can I have those pictures?" The youth went out and returned with the envelope. Lomax checked that the photographs were inside and returned them to Burrows.

"Thank you," said Burrows.

Lomax picked up the phone and arranged for the car. "I'll walk you to the lift," he said.

They left the big, stark room. The youth was now cutting paper patterns in the newspapers on his desk. He nodded to Burrows. Burrows said to Lomax, "You have thirty thousand cases a year, you say?"

"Of one sort or another."

"How many do you solve?"

"Ninety-five percent," said Lomax firmly. They had reached the lift and he pushed the button. "You have to hand the badge in on the way down," he said pointing to Burrows' lapel. "At Security."

"Niney-five percent?" queried Burrows. "You *solve*?"

"Cleared up," said Lomax. "Missing persons have a habit of solving themselves."

"They turn up," said Burrows, getting into the lift.

"One way or another," said Lomax. "As a rule something . . . " he hesitated, "something . . . happens to them."

By the time the police car had reached the hotel Burrows was buried in sleep. The two-man crew had to haul him from the back seat, watched by a quickly gathered crowd on the sidewalk. He partially roused and saw the faces watching him through a haze. A cracked-voiced woman was loudly asking if he was a drunk or injured. "What's wrong with the man?" she kept repeating. "What's wrong with the man?"

The night porter got him to his room and without taking off his clothes Burrows lay on the bed which Edith had occupied and descended into a dreadful sleep echoing with cries, howls and running corpses. He woke, frightened, and blinked about him. He had not turned out the lights and they clinically illuminated the interior of the room, like a warm green box built around him. He stared at his watch and saw it was six o'clock. Outside it was dark. For a moment he had a panicky thought that it might be six in the evening, that he had missed an entire day. Going to the window he saw that it was not. The lights of Manhattan were faded, tired; a mist hung about jaded streets and gaunt skyscrapers. Solitary cars were cruising below.

The room felt close. He was still wearing his overcoat and he had sweated in his sleep. There was a sensation of dried mud on his face, so strong that he felt to see what it was. He touched only his unshaven skin. For ten minutes he returned to the bed and lay sprawled, stupidly looking at the ceiling, hopelessness seeping through him. Today he had to begin to look.

Going to the bathroom he used the lavatory and then showered and shaved. He put on a thick golfing sweater under his suit and then pulled the overcoat on again. Feeling to make sure his diary and pen were in his pocket, he left the room and took the lift to the ground floor.

The lobby was occupied only by the porter behind his pulpit desk, a night receptionist feeding accounts through a machine and a black woman polishing the brass handrail of the main staircase. The porter said the coffee shop did not open until seven.

Burrows pulled his collar around his head and went out into the leaden cold of the dark morning. Steam was writhing from manholes in the street as if emitted from some infernal volcano. His feet sounded slyly on the unkempt sidewalk as he went past shops locked and lit. A dustbin man was noisily emptying a bin at the corner. Burrows walked by like a ghost pounding its beat. He had no idea where he was going, nor of his object in trudging the skeleton streets. Ahead he could see the lights of a shop spread out onto the sidewalk as if through an open door. A small man was sweeping along the front of the shop. Two women in abbreviated skirts and short fur coats stood at the corner.

He was still slow and tired and it struck him as being only mildly curious that they should be stationed there, dressed like that, at six-thirty on a January morning. As he shuffled toward them they ceased whatever they were saying and revolved on their elevated shoes until they confronted him. Both smiled barren smiles. "You want a fuck, mister?" one inquired.

Burrows, startled from his dullness, stared at the pair. "No, I don't," he said finally.

"Fuck *off*, then," retorted the first woman. They returned to their conversation, their shoes tapping the cold pavement. The man sweeping in front of the shop twenty yards away laughed through the damp. Burrows approached him, suddenly thinking it might be a coffee shop. When he reached the window he saw how much he was mistaken. It was hung with violent, pornographic magazines. He stared as if his nightmares had followed him from sleep.

"Come on in, mister, look around," suggested the man who was sweeping. He was rheumy and whiskered, his eyes running with water, his mouth collapsed. He gave the surface a final swish with his broom. "Have a job to keep this place clean," he remarked incongruously. "You got any special tastes?"

To his own surprise Burrows had accepted the invitation to step inside the shop. It was as though he needed the warmth of the place. Now he gazed around at the many-coloured racks. The old man hovered expectantly, his broom hooked into cold horny hands.

"Scatology?" remarked Burrows slowly. He stared at the magazine. He felt he had to utter something. The whole rack before him was labelled "Scatology" and adjoining that was "Enema Corner." The next section displayed a notice saying "Restriction and Bondage," and a fourth "Spanking Specials."

"Shit," explained the man with simple logic. "Eating shit and that kind of crap."

"Oh, I see," replied the dumbfounded Burrows as though he conversed about it every day.

"That's a big seller," grinned the man with his bent mouth. "Folks like it. Not as big as enemas though. Bondage and enemas – now that's real big business." He rose on small feet as if eager to please. "You want to buy, or you want to look around?" he asked. "We ain't too busy right now."

"It's a bit early to be open, isn't it?" asked Burrows cautiously. "It's not seven yet."

37

"We never close any time," recited the man quite proudly. "We're real busy until late – like maybe three in the morning and then we got an early clientele, see. Guys on their way to work. It ain't worth closing the joint."

Burrows wanted to get out. He turned and in doing so saw a magazine with a yellow and red cover entitled: *Kidnapped and Raped*. To his own astonishment he found himself reaching for it. On the cover was the photograph of a girl, naked, spreadeagled and tied to a chair. He handed it to the man. "I'll have that," he muttered.

"Okay, sir. That'll be four dollars." He slid it into a brown paper bag and handed it over as if he were serving in a hardware store. "Have a nice day," he said politely. Burrows stumbled out into the still dark street. The two whores were still stamping their feet at the corner. As he shuffled past them, his collar up, one said, "Shithouse." He muttered "Shithouse yourself," in return. At the end of the next block he stopped and took *Kidnapped and Raped* from his pocket. He stared at the posed girl on the front cover. Everything she had was showing. There seemed to be real terror in her eyes. Around him moved the icy American wind. "Jesus Christ," he said to himself, almost as a prayer. "What bloody chance have I got?"

Back at the hotel he had breakfast. He counselled himself that he must eat if he were to be fit enough to pursue his quest. It was difficult, but he had cereal, bacon and eggs, and three cups of good coffee. He was so weary still that it made him nauseous. As he paid at the coffee shop cash desk the girl looked at him with curiosity. They knew who he was. The story had gone around.

He went to the gift shop. A wiry man with a limp was arranging paperback books on a shelf. He looked too insignificant to have ever been a wounded soldier. "Are you Gus?" asked Burrows.

"That's me," answered the man continuing to stack the books. "What's your problem?" He reacted late to the English accent. When he did he looked up hurriedly. "Ah, sure," he said getting up from his crouch. "You're the man from England. I'm sorry about what's happened."

"Thank you. I understand you remember seeing my sister-in-law and her daughters."

38

"I do, indeed, sir," said the man. He went behind his counter as though that were the proper place for him to be. "I didn't know their names but I just served them and we passed the time of day. Same as I do with a whole heap of customers. I find it makes the job better. The days go easier, if you get me."

"They never gave any indication exactly where they were going from here? Where they might stop overnight, for instance?"

He did not pause to ruminate. "Just they was heading south," he shrugged. "Charleston, I think they said. But nothing else, mister. Nothing at all. I've told the manager and I've told the police. There's no more I know."

"Quite. I understand that," nodded Burrows. "It's just I thought there might be *something* you remembered later. Possibly."

Gus's face crumpled in wrinkles. He moved his injured leg with difficulty. "Not a thing. I'd sure like to help. I'm sorry for you, mister." He went over it again in his mind. "They were really disappointed in the weather," he added, 'and I said they should come back in the spring. They all seemed fine and healthy. Sure were pretty females, if you don't mind me saying so. I guess you're worried more on that account."

"What account?"

Gus hesitated, regretting he had said anything. "Females," he said. "Them being females. And . . . pretty."

"Yes, I'm worried on that account. Thank you, anyway. If you think of anything, Gus, no matter how trivial it may seem, ring me. I'm in room 1313."

"Sure thing." Gus moved from behind the counter and limped toward the book rack. "See what people read," he said scornfully. "Sex, killing, more sex. No wonder things happen."

Burrows returned to his room. He intended to call the car rental firm and he sat on the bed by the telephone. But as he undid his overcoat his hand touched the pornographic magazine and he took it from his pocket. He slumped onto the bed and began turning the pages. "Christ almighty," he said to himself. The models were all young girls, trussed and tied, humiliated, and in the apparent process of being raped and beaten. One was tied backward on a rocking chair, an imitation penis thrust into her.

The expression on her teenage face was convincing terror. She could have been Abigail . . . or Kate. He snarled and flung the magazine across the room. "Fucking filth!" he shouted after it. He lay back against the pillow, staring at the ceiling, and dropped abruptly into sleep. When he awoke it was seven o'clock in the evening.

His first annoyance at the waste of the day was tempered by the fact that he felt rested. The magazine was on the floor. He picked it up and put it in the bedside drawer. He would dump it later. He didn't want a chambermaid finding that in his wastepaper basket. He had a bath, shaved, and put on a clean shirt, one of three he had brought in his small case. His suit was crumpled so he took the sports jacket and grey flannels he had packed and wore those.

Then he rang the Missing Person's Bureau. Detective Lomax was not there but they said there were no developments. "The case has been double-marked F.O.A.," said the man on the line.

"What's that?" asked Burrows. "F.O.A.?" In England, he knew, D.O.A. on police records meant "Dead On Arrival." The man said: "F.O.A.? For Other Authorities.' It shows that this department has ordered a double check outside New York. For the car and so on. Maybe we'll get something moving soon. Why don't you call tomorrow?"

"Thanks, I will," said Burrows hollowly. He put the phone down. "Bloody fool," he muttered.

Next he telephoned Andy Curtis in Charleston. "Any news yet, Andy?"

The replying voice sounded flat. "Nothing, Phil. Not a damned thing. I've been to the cops again today. But, Jesus, they're such jerks. You'd think it was a missing cat, not three women. What's happened to you?"

Burrows related his visit to the Police Plaza. He felt more assured now, now that he was active, doing something.

"What do the police think, Phil?" asked Curtis. "What do they really think?"

Burrows waited. It was very clear to him. "They don't commit themselves, Andy," he said. "They can't. But *we've* got to look at this thing logically. It's no use trying to pretend anything to ourselves – that they've had an accident, that they're breezing around America and just haven't bothered to telephone. If they've been kidnapped, for money that is, Andy, then nobody

40

has received a ransom note yet. It seems we've got to face up to three possibilities."

"Yes, I know," Curtis told him sadly. "But tell me anyway."

"The first is that, for reasons we don't know of, Edith has disappeared of her own volition, taking the girls with her. I cannot think why for a moment, but it could be so. It's a possibility. She might be in hiding – perhaps with someone."

"Okay, okay," answered Curtis. "But for Christ's sake, surely she would at least write and tell us there was nothing to worry about."

"That's what I think. That's why I believe it's unlikely. She was not that sort of woman."

"No woman is the sort of woman you think she is," remarked Curtis curiously. "And the other possibilities?"

Burrows drew in his breath. "We know them, Andy. Both of us. Either they've been taken by . . . by some madman for his own purpose . . . or they're dead. In some way, Andy, they're dead."

The bitter silence from Charleston seemed to travel in all its intensity to Burrows in New York. "You've said it now," Curtis said eventually. "What we both know. What Adele knows in her heart as well. But Adele and I, we haven't said anything to each other about that. We just haven't been able to face it."

"It's got to be faced," Burrows told him deliberately. He felt his voice rise with a choking anger. "If some bastard is holding them, Andy, or he's killed them I'm going to *get* him. I'll track him down if it takes the rest of my life. I'll *kill* the swine." His voice shook. He could not control it. "If you'd seen the things I've seen, Andy," he whispered. "At the police headquarters. Christ, photographs, terrible, terrible atrocities . . . I'll find whoever it is. And when I do, Andy, God help him."

Abruptly he realised that he needed a meal and before the meal he needed a drink. He went down in the lift and out into the cold. Across the street a sign said "O'Keefe's Place. Restaurant and Bar." The icy air caught him as he ran across the street, not waiting for the change of lights, dodging through the traffic. A cab driver swore at him and he swore back.

O'Keefe's was warm and animated. It had a red-brick interior with plain white tablecloths. Even at that early time of evening it

41

was crowded. A girl sitting alone at the bar looked at him as he arrived.

"One, sir?" said the waiter at the entrance. He was young but looked like an old-time barber with waxed moustache, shining black hair, and a striped apron. "I was going to have a drink," said Burrows. "First."

"O'Keefe's gets crowded, sir," pointed out the youth. "In a half hour we may not have a table. Why don't you sit down and have a drink while you're looking at the menu?"

"Right," agreed Burrows. For some reason he glanced at the girl again. She was dark and smart, in her early twenties. He thought she must be waiting for a man to return. The waiter led him to a table and he sat down. "I'll have a double scotch," he said, "with no ice, just some water."

The waiter left him and he looked around. The conversational noise of the place was like a busy engine room. Everybody who wasn't eating seemed to be arguing, and those who ate, argued between mouthfuls. Burrows' glance went to the girl again. He felt a sharp annoyance at wanting to look at her. He was in a corner seat and she was at the distant end of the room. Her legs were crossed under the barstool, the points of her shoes caught in the rail. No one had come to sit with her. She laughed at something the barman said, and ordered another drink. The tab was put down in front of her. The waiter returned to Burrows' table. "Are you ready to order, sir?"

He ordered chicken soup, steak, and jacket potato, with salad and a half bottle of Californian burgundy. So crowded had his thoughts been for the past three days that now, all at once, he found himself sitting in a mental vacuum. He could not think about the matter any longer. Not for the present, he told himself. Then he had the sudden thought that Edith and the girls might have come into this restaurant. After all it was just across the street from the hotel, the weather had been poor, and the place had warmth and atmosphere. He took the three photographs from his pocket und put them on the tablecloth before him. Their faces engrossed him once more. The waiter returned with the chicken soup and looked down at the pictures. "Your family?" he asked pleasantly. "They sure look nice."

"Have you ever seen them?" asked Burrows to the youth's intense surprise. "Have they ever been in this place?"

42

"No," said the waiter looking again at the photographs and then uncertainly at Burrows. "I've never seen them. Not as far as I know."

Burrows answered his unasked question: "I'm looking for them," he said. "They're missing."

"Gee, you don't say. Are you from the police?"

"No. I'm just a private individual. I'm from England."

"Sure. Sure you are. I'm sorry, I can't help you, mister." He backed away as if nervous of Burrows. Then he stopped and said, "I can ask the others, if you like. The other staff."

"Yes," agreed Burrows. "Please. That would be a good idea." He picked up the photographs.

The waiter hesitated. "Just hold it while I get your steak," he said. "Then I guess I'd better ask the manager. I haven't been here too long and I don't want to step out of line. I'll ask him."

Putting the photographs back in his pocket, Burrows nodded. He ate the soup. The girl was still alone at the bar. There was an old-fashioned wall mirror in front of her and he could see she was observing people in it. His steak and wine arrived. The young man said, "The boss says that if you like to show the pictures to the staff yourself, that's fine by him. But I'm going to be too busy. Is that okay? I'm sorry."

"Don't worry," said Burrows. "I'll do it when I've eaten."

"Listen," suggested the waiter quietly. "I've had an idea. You see that lady at the bar. Show her. She's in here a lot and she has more time to note people than we do. We just concentrate on our own tables. She's pretty bright too, for a hooker."

"Hooker?"

"A pick-up, you know," replied the waiter, a little embarrassed. "A street lady. Except she works inside. You get me?"

"Oh, I see," said Burrows, genuinely surprised. "I wondered why she was sitting by herself. It didn't occur to me. . . . Well, she seems too . . . smart, clean . . . well, you know. . . . "

"She's a real nice lady," said the youth sincerely. "I like her a lot. If ever I get going with one of those, it'll be her. If I can get the bread together."

He retreated with a diffident smile. Burrows looked again at the girl. She was wearing a circumspect beige silk blouse. There was a short fur over the back of the barstool next to her. He ate his meal and had coffee and another scotch. With an unexpectedly easy confidence he got up and walked over to the bar. "Excuse me, miss," he said when he had reached her side, "I wonder if I could have a word with you."

"Sure," she smiled unhurriedly. "I'm always ready for a word."

"May I sit down?"

"Why not?"

He eased himself onto the seat. As he did so she quickly emptied her glass. "You'd like another drink, I expect," ventured Burrows.

"Wow, you guessed. Vodka on the rocks. What sort of accent is that you've got? You sound like Rex Harrison."

"I live in England. In Northamptonshire."

"That sounds cosy."

The barman arrived and seemed pleased she had found a companion. Burrows ordered her vodka and his own scotch. "The staff in here are very friendly," he said. "The barman, the waiter."

"He's just glad I got somebody to talk to at last," said the woman honestly. "I'm supposed to give people company and the way it works is that these guys come and do me the favour."

Burrows looked at her seriously. She had an unlined face and good teeth. Only her eyes seemed worn. "That's what you do then, is it – give company?"

"It's been called other things," she shrugged and then gave a small laugh. "A lot of other things. What did you want to ask me, or was that your way of getting over my shyness? I guess you did want to ask something. I saw you talking to the waiter."

The drinks arrived and he waited until the barman had served them and moved away. Then he took the three photographs from his pocket and handed them to her one by one. "Have you ever seen any of these people?" he asked. "It's possible they've been in here within the past three weeks." He added, "I'm not a policeman."

"I know all the cops," she said.

He watched her face with care as she studied the pictures. She took it seriously, her expression intent. "I think I would certainly remember," she said. "Very pretty ladies. But I don't. Sorry." She looked up at him and took up her drink at the same time. "Your family?" she said. "She walked out on you?"

44

"It's my sister-in-law and her daughters." He returned thoughtfully to the composed image of Edith. "As for walking out on me, well that is possible. I don't know."

"It sounds complicated," she commented. Her eyes moved to the mirror for the briefest glance. "Could I ask *you* something?" she said quietly to Burrows.

"Yes, of course. It'll be a change."

"You know I'm a business girl. Well, there's a guy who's just walked in, he's one of my regular clients. I don't want to miss him because he's been good to me. He's generous. If you're not interested, would you mind moving away? I'm sorry, but it's my living."

He looked quickly at her. She smiled quizzically. Astonished, he heard himself saying, "Who said I'm not interested?" He leaned forward and she touched his knee with her slim fingers. "You said you sell company," went on Burrows. "I need some company."

"My name is Sharon," she said, taking off her coat in his room.

"I am the Rose of Sharon and the Lily of the Valley," he recited. He was standing on the far side of the bed.

"I know, I know," she smiled. "I've heard that before. You'd be surprised to know how many religious guys I get to screw. One used to go right through the Ten Commandments, you know, saying them. One after the other while he was balling." She paused and said, "It's one hundred dollars by the way. Did I mention that?"

"I've no idea what the going rate is," he said. "It sounds like a lot of money."

"It is," she agreed. "It's expensive. But things are." She had half unbuttoned her silk blouse. "You still want to go on with this?"

He regarded her soberly from the far side of the bed. "Yes I do," he answered. "I need someone like you."

"Fine," she smiled. "I take the money first, as a rule, but you seem like a good guy . . . "

"No," he said hurriedly. "Let me pay now. I want to." He fumbled through his wallet and handed the note across the pillows. He remained looking at her. She undid the buttons on the front of her blouse, without rush, as if he were not present.

45

She unhooked a white brassiere and took it off. Her breasts were modest and firm. She glanced at him. "You look a little nervous," she said.

"Well, I am a bit. I lead a quiet life in England, I'm a doctor in a small place. . . . "

"A doctor?" She ran the palms of her hands over her nipples. "Then this can't be a novelty. Not to you."

"It's different," he said quietly. "And my wife's been dead some time."

She grinned. "Why stand on that side of the bed? Come over here; the light's better."

He obeyed, walking around to where she stood. He stood before her. She took his hands and placed them on her warm breasts. "Feel," she softly suggested. "You're entitled to feel."

Burrows' tired head dropped against her neck. She kissed him chastely on the cheek. "You're right, Doctor," she said. "You need me."

She kicked off her shoes and got out of the rest of her clothes quickly. He began fumbling with his tie. She moved close to him, so that her nipples were touching his waistcoat and her stomach his pelvis. In a few moments she had expertly undressed him. "Now we get into the bed," she joked.

"I seem to remember," he replied. He found himself smiling for the first time in days. Rolling against her he put his arms around her waist. The warmth of the bed and the coolness of her body roused him and he knew he would have no difficulty or fear with her.

Then the telephone rang. He stopped and thrust out his arm to take the receiver. It was easier for her; she reached it first and handed it to him. They were still locked together.

"Mr. Burrows – Dr. Burrows, it's Gus at the gift shop."

"Yes, Gus."

"You said to call if I thought of anything."

"Yes, of course. What is it?"

"Mrs. Burrows and the girls," said the man pedantically. "They *did* say something, now I remember. The weather was so lousy that they couldn't see the sights, in New York I mean. They said they hoped it would be better in Washington so they could look around. I only just remembered them saying that. I thought I'd better call you."

"Washington? Yes, thanks, Gus. I thought they would go there. But thank you anyway."

"All through?" she asked. She replaced the phone for him.

"Sorry," said Burrows. He returned to her. She played him on and they joined easily as if they had known each other a long time. Afterward he lay enjoyably against her, quietly, like a real lover.

"Was that satisfactory?" she inquired. It was a genuinely professional question, as though she were conducting a survey.

"Very much so," he answered. "Are you always like that?"

"Just with people I like," she replied. She eased herself away from him and he thought sadly that she was immediately going. But instead she lit a cigarette. "And with people who like me," she added.

"As I said, I needed you," he said, still lying low in the bed. "I've been having a hell of a depressing time."

"I can just imagine," she said. "Are they American?"

"They're English," he told her. "They came over here on a visit and they've vanished."

"For Christ's sake!" she whistled, suddenly realizing. "You mean that? They've *disappeared*, not just gone away some place?"

"Yes. Disappeared from the face of the earth. They came to this hotel, Edith slept in this very bed, and left for Charleston, South Carolina. After that nothing – and that was two weeks ago."

She turned and regarded his face. "And you're trying to *find* them? How the hell are you going to do that?"

He answered quietly, "The choice is between looking and not looking. And I'm going to look."

Sharon blew some smoke toward the far wall. "She's your sister-in-law?" she asked.

"Yes. But her husband – my brother – is dead. My wife and he were killed in the same car crash." He thought he might as well tell her. "They were going off together."

"Jesus," she breathed. "Things happen in England as well."

"They do."

Sharon said, "Let me take a look at the pictures again." He reached, took them from the pocket of his coat, and gave them to her. "She is different," said the girl. "And the daughters are beautiful, especially the little one. She's cute."

47

"She is," he confirmed. "And I'm afraid."

"I see it all the time," she agreed. "Guys who try to work out their hang-ups on me. The country's loaded with nuts."

He leaned to his side of the bed and took the pornographic magazine from the drawer. "Look at this," he said. "I bought it. Look at this stuff."

The prostitute regarded it casually. "It's all over the place," she shrugged. "Crap like that. I went with a john last week and saw a book called *Multilation* on his dressing table. I didn't stay."

She eased herself from the sheets. Burrows put his hand out and touched her leg. "Thank you," he said. "I enjoyed the company."

"Me too." She went to the bathroom and emerged with a towel about her. "I'll take you downstairs," he said, making to move from the bed.

"Stay there," she advised. "I'm used to ending up alone. Anyway the night's young." She dressed sedately, moved to the bed and kissed him on the cheek. "See you again, maybe," she said. "I'm usually in O'Keefe's."

"Yes, I hope so."

She was at the door now. "I don't know how you're going to do it, but I hope you find them."

"Thank you." He watched her from the bed. He had an odd feeling he was going to miss her. He would be alone again.

"One thing," she said finally. "One piece of advice."

"What's that, Sharon?"

"Get yourself something like this," she said. She felt in her handbag and brought out a gun.

3

At eight o'clock the following morning he was in the office of the Real Value Car Rental Company in Newark, New Jersey. The manager was a small, slim, black man. Despite the time of the year he wore a white, short-sleeved shirt, the name of the company in red across the breast pocket. "Dr. Burrows," he said coming around his desk. "I'm Elliott Jones. I'm the manager here, so they tell me." It was something he obviously always said to customers. Then he remembered Burrows was not a normal customer.

"We've heard all about it from the police, Dr. Burrows," he said. "Anything we can do, you just let us know."

"Do you remember them coming here to hire the car?" asked Burrows at once.

"Sure. I didn't make out the forms for them. Another guy, Lonnie, did all that."

"Is he here now, Lonnie?"

"He's sick right now. I'm sorry. But we've told the police everything we know, everything we can remember. They got the number and description of the rented car. I was sitting right here in the office when they came in. I saw them through that window behind you."

Burrows turned and looked through the partition as if expecting that he might see them too. The front section of the office was occupied only by a small black boy playing with a cat. "That's my son, Philbert," said Jones.

"Did they say anything? What their plans were?" Burrows asked.

"They told Lonnie they was heading south for Charleston. They rented the car for fourteen days which means they were scheduled to be returning it here, let me see . . . "

"Today," Burrows finished for him. "It's January 20 today."

Elliott Jones looked up from the pad on his desk. "Maybe they'll come," he said. "Maybe they'll just come back smiling."

The Englishman shook his head. "Somehow I don't think so," he muttered.

"What are you going to do?" asked the black man sympathetically.

"Look for them," said Burrows. He was tired of answering that question.

"There's only one route," Jones said decisively. "One main route. There ain't a lot to see between here and Washington. Well, Baltimore I guess. But it's straight down Interstate 95. Straight south. You have to search along that road, Doctor."

Burrows smiled shallowly. "You're the first person who thinks I've got a chance of finding them."

"You got to try," shrugged Jones. "Ain't no use sitting on your ass."

"I looked at the map," said Burrows. "They could be anywhere in three or four states."

"Okay, we've got to accept that. But they went heading down the road, down Ninety-five, and that highway is only so wide. There's places you can stop and eat and get gas and stay for the night. You got to try all those places."

Burrows took the three photographs from his wallet and pushed them across the desk. "That's them," he said.

Elliot Jones nodded. "That's them, okay. You just gotta check every gas station, every hamburger place, every motel. If they got off the highway, made a detour or took a trip, then you've got trouble. If they stuck to the road, then you've got a chance."

Burrows regarded the neat black face. "You make it sound possible," he said.

"Sure, it's possible," answered Jones firmly. "One road ain't too wide."

"What do *you* think has happened?" Burrows almost blurted out the question.

Jones looked unsurprised. "I've thought about it, naturally," he said cautiously. "Ever since the cops called. An accident?

Forget it. There's no way that couldn't have been reported. Except maybe they got off the road and somehow drove into a lake or a river or a swamp. There's places like that in Virginia and especially in the Carolinas. Places where a car could sink without trace."

"A taxi driver," remembered Burrows, "told me about the other route from New York, the coast route."

"If they went that way and somehow went into the sea north or south of Norfolk, Virginia, then you can forget it until the spring tides," said Jones spreading his hands. Burrows, who had met few black people, looked at the pale palms. "But if they were heading for Washington – which figures since they're tourists – they just wouldn't go miles out there. Why should they? No, I calculate they went down Ninety-five."

"That leaves the possibility that they've been abducted," said Burrows. "But there's been no demand for money, no ransom note." He said it almost desperately, shying away from the other reason.

It was Jones who said it: "There's other motives besides dough."

"I'm aware of that."

He did not want to go over any more reasons. "I'll be going," he said rising. "Thank you for your help. You've given me the first bit of hope I've had since I arrived here."

They shook hands. "How did you get here from New York?" asked Jones. "Taxi?" Burrows nodded.

"You're going to need a car."

"Yes. I thought I might hire one from you, if you have any available.

The black man laughed. "Right now we got cars up our ass." He picked up his desk telephone.

"I'm used to British cars," Burrows said.

Jones smiled and nodded. "I got you," he said. He spoke into the phone. "Harry, we got that Aspen there? Right, okay, bring it around will you? Thanks." He replaced the phone. "Nice medium car. I'd like you to have it with the company's compliments, but I'm only the manager here. The bosses want to grab every buck. But I can give you a special rate."

A red Aspen rolled up to the front of the building. They shook hands and Jones opened the door for Burrows. "They sure was

51

good lookers," he said. "You've just got to find them, man."

Interstate Highway 95 runs due south through New Jersey into Delaware, Maryland, and on to Washington, D.C., before continuing through the flat country of Virginia and the Carolinas on its journey to the Deep South.

Burrows travelled cautiously, nervously, crouched behind the wheel, at first keeping well below the speed limit. With a perverse sort of hope, at the beginning – a first-time lucky wish – he left the road at every exit, stopping at petrol stations, lunch bars, showing the three photographs to attendants and people serving at tables and behind counters. The only reaction to the smiling pictures was the shaking of heads and shrugging of shoulders. He covered the miles slowly and after three hours he was still only seventy miles south of Newark.

Then he pulled off the highway into a petrol station and saw a police patrol car parked just clear of the pumps. There was a small coffee and hot dog cabin attached to the place and Burrows could see the policeman sitting at the counter. He walked to him and took the next stool. "Officer," he said as soon as he had sat down, "I wonder if you can help me?"

"Only too pleased, if I can," said the patrolman. He was drinking coffee and some was left on his chin as he looked up at Burrows. He wiped it away. The chin was the foundation of a solid face set with flat blue eyes. Burrows wondered if the man had ever drawn his bulky gun meaning business. "I'm from England," Burrows continued.

"I guess I don't need to be a cop to figure that out," agreed the man. "There during the war. Piccadilly, hah, I remember Piccadilly! You could catch anything there from the plague to shrapnel wounds. What a place! Is it just the same now?"

"I don't know," answered Burrows truthfully. "The last time I was there was years ago." The counter attendant arrived slowly and he ordered a cup of coffee. The man came back and refilled the patrolman's cup also.

"I'm John Harrison," said the policeman.

"Philip Burrows,' answered Burrows. They shook hands.

The patrolman's expression altered. "Now, I've heard that name." He jabbed a square finger toward the Englishman. "Right. I got you. You're the guy looking for the three missing females. We got an all cars message about you."

"They haven't . . . they haven't been found, have they?" He spilt coffee on the counter. The attendant wiped it up without expression. "You haven't heard anything?"

"Not a thing," said the policeman. "Not a goddam thing. But we got the first information about them being missing and then, yesterday, about you being on your way to search for them. Listen, you've got a hell of a job."

"I know," nodded Burrows. "But they *must* have come down Interstate Ninety-five. Someone down here *must* have seen them." He took the photographs from his pocket and displayed them to the sleepy man behind the counter. "I don't suppose you've seen these people, have you?" he asked. Wiping his hands on a cloth the man took up the photographs one by one, laying each down before taking up another. "No way," he answered. "I'd remember them. They ain't been here."

"You know the newspapers are looking for them too," said the patrolman. Burrows shook his head. "I didn't," he said. "I didn't know what to do about the papers."

"Hold it a minute," said Harrison. He left the counter and returned to his blue-and-white striped car. He came back unfolding a newspaper. "See here," he said. "They got the pictures and the descriptions, the whole story. And they got a picture of you. Seems like they're hunting for you as well, the press I mean."

He handed the local daily paper to Burrows. The photographs were the originals he had sent by wire to New York. Detective Lomax of the Missing Person's Bureau in Manhattan was quoted on the case. His own picture he recognised as one taken at a shooting club dinner in England. Him posed with his champion marksmanship trophy. He blinked at the photograph as if he could not recognise the man. It seemed a long time ago. "What do you think?" he asked Harrison. "I just didn't know what to do about the newspapers."

"Well, they got the story," shrugged Harrison. "They do. They nearly always do. Ain't no use crying over that. Maybe it'll help to find them. Somebody maybe will recognise them. On the other hand–"

Regarding him steadily, Burrows said, "What's on the other hand?"

Harrison shrugged. "Well, you asked and I'll tell you." His

53

voice became official. "It could provoke maybe somebody who's been holding them against their will. It could cause that person or persons to commit a further crime."

"You mean kill them."

"You asked me and I told you," repeated Harrison holding up his large hand. "I ain't saying it will. God, I hope it don't, but just that it could." His large, hard face was sympathetic. "Do you want the press to find you?"

Burrows twirled the coffee in his cup and watched the brown whirlpool. "Not particularly," he answered. "There's no advantage. In fact I'd just be hampered with a load of reporters dogging my heels."

"Right," nodded Harrison. He looked pensive. "They ain't likely to have needed gas this close to where they picked up the rental car. Where was that? Newark?"

Burrows nodded.

"They would have a full tank, right? When they started. It was a Tempo, if I remember."

"Yes, a red Tempo."

"They wouldn't need to refill much before Washington," said Harrison thoughtfully. "But can you see that lady driving into Washington? What time did she leave Newark?"

"About two in the afternoon."

"She wouldn't be likely to drive into Washington at night. A strange city, a strange car, a strange country, bad weather. No, I figure she would have stopped short. Let's see." He took out a pocket road map. "Somewhere like Emporia . . . or maybe Silver Spring. Just short of Washington. Did she have plenty of dough? What kind of hotel or motel would she head for?"

Burrows said, "She wasn't short of money, but I imagine she wouldn't have been extravagant."

Harrison said, "Maybe like Howard Johnson's. They let kids under eighteen stay for nothing, free, if they're in the same room as the parent. Would that appeal to her?"

"It would," said Burrows. "Yes."

"There's two Howard Johnsons between here and Washington," said Harrison. "I'd head for them. Stay at one tonight, maybe Silver Spring, and get the yellow pages and call all the motels and hotels you can. She'd be using her real name?"

"I don't see any reason why not," said Burrows, surprised.

54

Harrison's pale eyes remained thoughtful. "The car, the Tempo," he added. "To me it don't seem logical that the car ain't been spotted, picked up. This highway is patrolled all the time, and we've got the description and number of the car and yet nothing's showed up. Somebody must be hiding it. Otherwise it don't make any sense at all."

Burrows found himself getting restless. He wanted to get to the Howard Johnson motel and go through the yellow pages. "I must be going," he said. "Otherwise I won't be anywhere at all before it's dark."

"Good luck, mister," said the policeman. "And one more thing—"

Burrows paused as he was getting off the stool. "What is that?" he asked.

"Like when you came in here and you said to Harry here, behind the counter, you said: 'I don't suppose, by any chance, you have seen these people?' And then you took the pictures out. Well, don't do it like that, see. It's negative, if you get what I mean. 'I don't suppose by any chance—' No goddam use at all. Be direct. 'When did you see these people?' See? Hit them between the eyes. Folks get busy and they forget or they haven't got the time. So don't pussyfoot it. Okay?"

"Yes, I see," said Burrows. "I'll remember that."

"You should, buddy; nobody ever got to be a good cop by being a gentleman." He pushed aside his stool, wiped his hand across his mouth, and turned towards the patrol car.

At Silver Spring, ten miles north of Washington, Burrows stopped at a motel and went wearily to his room after producing the photographs for the receptionist and getting the same shake of the head he'd been receiving all day. It was the end of his second day on the highway. He had been to the two Howard Johnson motels and been told no persons of that description or name had registered there during the past three weeks. He went into another dozen similar places but no one had any record or recollection of Edith Burrows and her daughters. It began to rain thickly in the evening and he pulled the car off the road and went tiredly to the motel. He bought a local daily newspaper and saw immediately his own photograph and the other three on the front page. He took it to his room and read the report. There was

55

nothing new in it. He suspected that they would not occupy the front pages, even in these smaller more local papers, for long. At the end of the story was a quote from a police officer which said what he knew they were all thinking: "It's more than possible that this lady and her daughters have gone to some other part of the country without informing anybody. People do that kind of thing when they've had troubles."

He threw the newspaper onto the floor, picked up the telephone, and asked for the Charleston number. Adele Curtis came on the line. "Hello. Oh, it's you Phil." Burrows immediately detected her irritation. "Any news?" she asked as if she did not really care.

"Nothing," he said. "Nothing at all. I'm just outside Washington, at Silver Spring. I'm trying all the hotels and motels. Nothing that end either, I suppose?"

"*Everything* this end," she said bitterly. "Goddam reporters, photographers."

"Oh, I see. I knew the newspapers had got the story."

"*You* didn't tell them?" She sounded as if she did not believe him. "*You* didn't let it out?"

"No, Adele. It must have come out through the police. I've said nothing."

"Well, whoever opened his mouth has not done us any favours here, I can tell you," she said nastily. "There's all hell let loose. You can't have missing females, murdered females maybe, hanging around your neck, not when you're on the fringe of politics like Andy. Not in this country."

Burrows stemmed his anger when it got to his throat. "I see," he said quietly. "I'm sorry." In his mind he was trying to grasp why the disappearance of Edith Burrows should be professionally harmful to Andy Curtis.

"There's no point in *you* being sorry," Adele said, still sharply. "But if that woman gets here, after all, and it turns out she's been sneaking off some place and not told anybody, I'm going to be as mad as hell."

Her voice had risen hysterically. Burrows remained silent. "I want you to understand *that*, Phil Burrows," she went on. "I wish you people had stayed in your own goddam country and left us alone." He could hear she was crying. "Is Andy there?" he asked evenly.

"He's here, but he's asleep," she sniffed. "Shit, it's made me so depressed, so goddam angry."

"I can hear," said Burrows still quietly. "I'll ring off and call him some other time."

"You do that." Then, suddenly, she melted. "Jesus Christ, Phil, you've got no idea what it's been like here. It's been in all the newspapers and my husband was the guy who fell straight down the hole." Her words slowed but then, decisively, she continued, "He was seen with a woman. I knew all about it going on – but some smart guy from the press figured it was Edith. You know how they put things together. God, it was all in the papers. Pictures, everything. This woman was his secretary once, until I made him get rid of her, but he still kept seeing her. And it had to come out like this."

Burrows' chest felt like lead. "I'm sorry, Adele," he said. "I'm really sorry. It's amazing how things happen, one thing after another."

"They certainly do," she answered. He could tell she was crying again. "I'll hang up," she sniffed. "I'll tell Andy you called."

"Thank you. I'll telephone again in a few days. Or if I get any news."

Burrows replaced the phone and sat, hunched on the bed, staring at it. He had never met Adele Curtis. Now he felt he knew everything about her and Andy, an insight into the lives of two strangers. Wearily he opened the yellow pages of the telephone directory and turned to Hotels and Motels. Beginning at Abacus Court he went through the list, ringing each number and asking the same question. After half an hour the receptionist at the Old Hall Motor Court said casually, "Sure, those people were here. I remember them myself. I just now saw the pictures in the newspaper. I thought maybe I ought to call the police."

"Don't," said Burrows his heart leaping. "I'm coming over there immediately."

"Wait a minute, they didn't stay," said the man. "I sent them on to Pine Lodge. We didn't have a vacancy. I guess they stayed there, but I don't know for sure."

"Pine Lodge," repeated Burrows, writing it in his medical diary. "Where's that? Is it far?"

"Not too far from here. Where are you, sir?"

"God, I don't know. Wait. Westland Hotel," he said looking at a pad on the nightstand.

"Pine Lodge is only three blocks away," said the clerk.

"I'll go over there. Then I'll come over to you."

"Are you the police, sir?"

"I'm a relative of Mrs. Burrows. Did they seem all right when they came to you?"

"Why, yes, fine as far as I could tell. They didn't stay long. I just told them to try Pine Lodge. In fact I called Pine Lodge from here to make sure they had rooms."

"They seemed normal?"

"Like I say, just fine. Tired I guess, but otherwise okay. You don't want me to call the police? The newspaper says call the police."

"No, please. Wait until I've come over there."

"Well, it sounds okay, so okay," said the man. "If you say so. You're from England?"

"Yes. I'm Mrs. Burrows' brother-in-law."

"Oh, I get it. Yes, I read about you in the newspaper. Well I'm sorry about this. I'll wait until you get here."

"Thank you very much," said Burrows. He put the phone down, almost missing the cradle of the receiver in his excitement. Pine Lodge. He found the number in the yellow pages, picked up the receiver again and dialled it.

A man's voice answered, weak and sleepy as though it had been roused in the middle of the night. "Pine Lodge. Sorry, no vacancies."

"I don't want a vacancy," said Burrows quickly. "I want to know about a Mrs. Burrows and her two daughters, from England, who stayed there three weeks ago."

"I don't know a thing about that," replied the voice.

"Listen, it's important."

"Sure, sure, but I don't know a thing about it. Like I told you."

Burrows heard his own voice become nasty. "You've got a register, haven't you?" he said. "Look in it. Their names were Burrows."

The man remained unimpressed. "Mrs. Wingate ain't here," he said without interest. "The register is locked away. She always locks it away when she goes to dance class and she's gone to dance class."

"Fuck the dance class," snorted Burrows.

"That's what I say," agreed the sleepy man. "I really don't know why she goes."

To Burrows' amazement and anger the other phone went dead. The Englishman, seething inside, charged out of his room and went to the lobby. "Where's the Pine Lodge?" he said to the girl at the desk.

She looked concerned. "Anything wrong?" she asked nervously.

"Nothing, nothing at all," said Burrows through tight teeth. "I'm just going to strangle somebody, that's all."

"Three blocks to the left," she answered as though the explanation were more than reasonable. "You can't miss it."

A meagre drizzle was falling, but he did not bother with the car. Instead he ran along the sidewalk like a football player, head down, shoulders humped, getting odd glances from the few people who were about. He saw the illuminated sign of the Pine Lodge Motel ahead through the murk, a green outline of a pine tree with the name in red at its centre. By now his heavy breathing had increased his agitation. He pounded straight into the lobby and to the vacant reception desk. There was a bell on the counter and he crashed his fist down on it. A young black head came from beneath the desk. "Was that you calling?" inquired the sleepy voice. It was the same voice that had answered the phone.

Burrows glared at him. When the youth straightened up he was only slightly shorter than Burrows. "Yes, I bloody well was calling," replied the Englishman. "You just put the phone down on me. I want to see that register."

"I just told you, man, I ain't got no—"

Burrows leaned across the desk and caught him by the lapels of his coat. "The register," he said threateningly. "Get the register."

An elderly man and woman appeared from the lift at the other side of the lobby, put their key down on the counter and went out, with hardly more than a mild glance at the large Englishman grasping the black youth.

The boy's eyes widened. "Listen man," he said desperately. "Mrs. Wingate, *she's* got the fucking register. I ain't got it!"

Behind him was an open door to a cloakroom. Burrows' eye

59

suddenly caught something that made him release the clerk and edge quickly around the counter. He moved toward the door and pushed it with his foot. On the floor was a blue canvas bag with a union jack sewn onto its side. The last time he had seen it it was in the hand of twelve-year-old Kate Burrows.

The black youth was regarding him now as he would have regarded a madman. He stood back trembling against the desk. Burrows slowed and almost crept into the cloakroom. It was strewn with pieces of luggage, coats, and packages but he took in nothing but the blue canvas bag. There was no doubt about it. It belonged to Katy. She had written her name in ball-point pen along the side, just above the union jack. "K. Burrows, England." His eyes filled with tears as he picked it up.

There was a trestle table in the narrow room. Gently he lifted the bag, and placed it on the table. Then he unzipped it. He saw the small plastic toilet bag. the bright-covered diary and the pencil, the satin slippers and the miniature teddy bear that she had called her "Good-luck Bruin." One by one he took them from the bag, he could almost feel the girl's young hands guiding him. At the bottom of the bag was something wrapped in a plastic container. Clumsily, almost fearfully, he opened it. Inside was a nylon garment, pink, with embroidery about the neck. Trembling, Burrows took it out. It was a girl's nightdress. His choked reaction suddenly turned to a cry as the garment unrolled. Across the hem were slashes of blood.

"You! You!" he shouted. "You fucker!" He turned toward the door. The boy was desperately looking for something in a cupboard. Burrows rushed toward him and stuffed the night-dress under his nose. "What's *this*?" he demanded furiously. "What d'you think *this* is? I want to know what's been going on here!"

Very frightened, the youth pushed him fiercely away, turned quickly, and picked up something from the cupboard. Burrows found himself looking down the eye of a gun. It trembled in the boy's hand. "Just you stay away from me, mister," whispered the clerk. "You're a crazy man." He reached for the telephone with his free hand, put the receiver on the desk and dialled a single digit. The operator answered. "This is Pine Lodge Motel," said the boy. "On Washington and Almond. I need a cop around here. I got a crazy guy in the place."

"Okay, okay," said the police lieutenant with heavy patience. "So you got wound up. You're plain lucky, mister, you're not stretched out in our morgue. The kid would have shot you if the catch hadn't been on the gun."

Burrows sat like a large untidy bundle on the chair in front of the desk. "My mistake," he said. He rubbed his eyes because they ached.

"It sure wasn't anybody else's," remarked the policeman. "Jesus Christ, *you* ought to know about blood on nightdresses. The girl was growing up. You're supposed to be a doctor."

The Englishman nodded miserably. "I didn't *think*," he admitted. "I've been in a state. I'm worried to death about them."

"Sure, I can understand that," said the policeman more sympathetically. "But you're not a cop, remember? You can't go around just blowing your top, taking the law into your own hands. We don't do things like that here. We don't mean to, anyway." He was silent for a moment, looking across the desk at Burrows. "Could you use a cup of coffee?" he asked.

"Thank you. Yes."

The policeman went outside to a coffee machine leaving Burrows staring at the blue travel bag with its scrawled name "K. Burrows, England" and its contents distributed on the desk. The pink nightdress was in soft folds, the blood marks hidden. He thought he was going to cry.

The lieutenant returned with the coffee in plastic cups. He found Burrows with his head buried in his hands. "Here's your coffee," he said. Burrows looked up and took it. "Didn't it occur to you that the kid might just have left the bag behind?" said the policeman. "If there'd been any criminal activity there, the bag wouldn't have been left lying around."

"I know," nodded Burrows wearily. "I'm not seeing much sense at the moment."

"Have you got a gun?" asked the policeman, returning to his chair behind the desk.

"No, I haven't."

"Good. The way you are, you'd use it and then be on a homicide charge." They drank the coffee in more silence. Then the officer said, "Where are you headed now?"

"South," answered Burrows.

The policeman threw his plastic cup into the bin. "What are you going to do about Washington? It's a big city, Washington. If they're there you're going to have to be real lucky to find them. You never saw Mrs. Wingate who runs the Pine Lodge, did you?"

"She was at her dance class."

"Well, I've got an officer checking with her now about your relatives. Maybe she can give us a lead. Also, I can get the likely hotels and motels in Washington checked for you. It will save you time with the yellow pages."

Burrows looked up. "That's very decent of you," he said.

The policeman had the diary which had been in Kate's bag on the desk before him. He picked it up and ran his thumb along the rim of the pages. "Not a thing in this to help," he said. "And that's a great pity."

Burrows nodded his agreement. The diary had contained a few entries in Katy's firm fresh hand – New York, the rain, the road south – but nothing which would give a clue as to which way the intended journey was eventually to take. The telephone sounded. The policeman picked it up. "Right. What did she say?" He listened, then added, "That's all? Nothing else she can remember? Well, I guess that's something anyway. Right. Anything else, call me." He replaced the receiver and turned to Burrows.

"They were there at the Pine Lodge for four days," he said. "They went out every day to Washington to do some sight-seeing. And one day they went to Gettysburg. But nobody at the motel remembers them saying anything about future plans."

"And they seemed to be all right when they were there?" asked Burrows. "Nothing out of the ordinary?"

"Not that we know. Just three out-of-season tourists looking at the sights. Whatever happened, happened after they left here." As though embarrassed by the final sentence he rose and went across to a long map on the wall. He sniffed at it as if hoping it might give some clue. "Interstate Ninety-five," he muttered. "It goes a long, long way, Doctor."

"I know," sighed Burrows, not leaving his chair. "It's like the small intestine."

The lieutenant smiled sympathetically. "If they left here and drove for a day," he said, "taking time off to eat and to look

62

around at things, they would have got somewhere around here."
He pointed at the map and Burrows got up and went over to him.
"Somewhere about the Virginia-North Carolina state line. The
highway goes through Roanoke Rapids to Rocky Mount, North
Carolina. It quits just north of Rocky Mount and it's just another
road until south of Wilson when it gets back to interstate standard
again. They're working right now on the section in between."

"Roanoke Rapids?" said Burrows slowly. "What's at Roanoke
Rapids?"

"Nothing special. Just the rapids. Where Lake Gaston funnels
into the Roanoke River. The town is just another town."

Half an hour later Burrows was driving south again, toward
Washington and beyond. In his mind the name Roanoke Rapids
recurred. Somewhere and some time, he had heard that name
before.

It was evening, early, cold evening, and Burrows stood staring
down at the rapids. The lake spread like flattened lead into the
early mist with the water suddenly beginning to run and gather-
ing pace as it moved toward the funnel formed by the narrow
river. He felt like some lone Indian standing there at that solitary
hour looking down onto the white tails of spray the water threw
up as it careered over boulders and banks. He still did not know
why he was there.

Then, abruptly, it came to him. Katy and geography! Katy and
school! He stood motionless, outlined against the washy sky,
gazing at the lake as it became a river. A stab of excitement was
sticking in his chest. Yes, it was! He remembered!

Turning from the gorge he rushed heavily down through the
trees to where the car was parked on the road. Excitement
propelled him. He almost shouted as he brushed aside the
branches of the birches, jumping over outcrops of rock pushing
from beneath dull grass. Yes, he knew it! There *was* something
about this place!

Burrows scrambled into the car. Her school – he had to
telephone her school. That's what it was about. He started it
quickly and drove fast along the deserted road and into the small
flat town of Roanoke Rapids where he had arrived that afternoon. He turned the car into the driveway of the motel, parked
outside his room and rushed in. He picked up the telephone.

63

"Give me international directory, please. As quickly as possible."

The clerk caught his sense of excitement and got the number quickly. "I want to obtain the number of a school in England," he said to the telephone operator. "Urgently."

"Give me the name of the school and the address, please."

"It's the Highfield Girls' School, St. Albans, Hertfordshire."

The woman repeated the address. "That sounds nice," she commented kindly. "You sure have some nice-sounding places over there in England."

"Thank you, thank you," said Burrows impatiently. "I'm afraid it's rather urgent."

"Sure. Hold the phone. I'll be right with you." It took her only minutes.

He thanked her and replaced the receiver, picking it up again as soon as the line was cleared. The motel operator came on. Burrows dictated the number to her. He replaced the receiver and waited. It was two summers ago, in the garden at Edith's house. He had hardly seen them since the inquests and he had gone there on a Sunday for tea. It was a warm afternoon and they had been sitting in the garden. Katy had been talking about Roanoke Rapids. He remembered it with such clarity now. They were doing something at school – a play perhaps – that was connected with Roanoke Rapids. This must be the place. He smiled even now, after all this time and all the sadness, at the memory of her young face lit up with the enthusiasm. The phone rang. "Your party is on the line."

Hurriedly he spoke into the phone. "Hello, is that Highfield School England?"

"Yes, and it's three o'clock in the morning."

"Who is that? Is that Matron?"

"Yes. Who is speaking?"

"I'm sorry to disturb you at this hour, Matron. It's Philip Burrows here. Katy Burrows' uncle. I have to speak to the headmistress."

The voice was immediately mollified. "Oh yes, Dr. Burrows. You're in America, are you?"

"Yes. I must speak to Miss Springfield. Could you get her, do you think?"

"Yes, of course, Dr. Burrows. She's been half expecting you

to call. We've heard all about it. Terrible, terrible. I cried so much. It's all been in the newspapers. Oh, I'm so sorry. You – you haven't traced them, have you?"

"Not yet," said Burrows shortly. "Do you think you could get Miss Springfield? And Katy's form mistress. Please get her also."

"Miss Catlin," said the matron. "Yes, I'll call both of them. It will take a few minutes. And it's very expensive, isn't it?"

"Don't worry about that," said Burrows impatiently. "Just rouse them. Please."

The woman went immediately. He waited several minutes and then he heard voices approaching the receiver from the other end. It was picked up. "Dr. Burrows, Miss Springfield here. Sorry to keep you waiting."

"It's nothing," said Burrows. "I'm sorry to get you up in the middle of the night, but it's important."

"You've not found them, I take it."

"No. Sadly not. But I do have something. Miss Springfield, Katy did something at school connected with Roanoke Rapids, here in America. In North Carolina. I'm there now. Do you recall what it was?"

"Roanoke Rapids?" He could tell by the voice that she didn't. "No, Dr. Burrows. I simply don't remember. Wait. Here is Miss Catlin, her form mistress. Perhaps she remembers. I'll put her on."

A younger voice came across the line. "Dr. Burrows, I'm so sorry. Is there anything I can do?"

"Yes, Miss Catlin," he said, glad of her brevity. "I'm at Roanoke Rapids, North Carolina, and I have some idea that Katy did some schoolwork connected with this place. I seem to recall her mentioning it. Do you know what it might have been?"

"Yes," came the immediate reply. "It was the Lost Colony. One of the first settlements in America, in 1582. The colonists just vanished. We did a study in history about it. Katy was fascinated. She loved mysteries. In fact, she told me, I remember this well, when she knew she was going to America, that she wanted to go and see the place."

"Anything in particular that she wanted to see?" asked Burrows breathlessly.

"They have some sort of museum there. And they do a play depicting the early colony. Katy was fascinated by it."

"There's nothing else you can remember?" he asked. He felt deflated. For some reason he had expected more.

"No, I'm sorry. We simply did it in class and she was very interested, that's all. I certainly think she would have visited the place if she had half a chance."

He said good-bye to her and the headmistress and put the telephone down. Then he went out of the room and across a wet lawn to the motel reception desk.

"Where's the Roanoke Museum?" he asked.

The receptionist looked up slowly from the ledger in which she was writing. "Not here," she said.

"What do you mean, not here?"

"This is Roanoke Rapids," she said. "You want the Lost Colony, right?"

"Right."

"The Lost Colony is on Roanoke Island," she said. "A hundred and thirty miles east of here on the coast. It's on Cape Hatteras."

She found he was staring at her. She looked uncomfortable.

"Lots of people make that mistake," she shrugged.

"Thank you," said Burrows. "I'm checking out."

4

Cape Hatteras hangs like a long finger down the eastern seaboard of the United States. It begins a few miles south of Norfolk, Virginia, running down almost the entire flank of North Carolina. The peninsula goes through Kitty Hawk, where the Wright Brothers made their flight; Jockey Ridge; and Kill Devil Hills, where the nation's highest sand dunes rise like yellow mountains; through the summer fishing resort of Nags Head. Here it is joined to the rest of the state by a causeway over the Croaton Sound with the small town of Manteo, on Roanoke Island, at its middle.

Below Nags Head the peninsula becomes wild and narrow. At Oregon Inlet in the extreme south is a small, sheltered habour, and there the three-mile-long Herbert C. Bonner Bridge – an amazing structure in such an isolated place – carries the single windy road over the sea to Hatteras Island. The road runs along the thirty miles of Hatteras Island through the villages of Rodanthe, Waves, Salvo, Avon, Buxton, and Frisco before arriving at the southern harbour of Hatteras. At no point is the island more than half a mile wide, and for most of its length its girth is limited to a few hundred yards; there is no place where it is more than two or three feet above sea level. The wooden houses are built, like spiders, on stilts, to keep them above the reach of winter waves running unchecked from the ocean.

From the harbour of Hatteras there is a forty-five-minute ferry journey further south to Ocracoke Island, another slender slice of lowland, with its only settlement, Ocracoke, at its lower tip. From here to the mainland, just above Wilmington, North

Carolina, is another ferry trip, this one two and three-quarter hours long.

Cape Hatteras remains a remote place, visited by silent fogs, huge storms, and engulfing seas. Game fish, the striped marlin, the swordfish, the fighting tarpon, and the sailfish are taken off these Outer Banks of America. There are marine birds, great flights of duck and honking geese across the low marshes, and wild horses on Ocracoke, the descendants of animals left by the Spaniards in the sixteenth century.

In winter it is a wild and empty place, with silent days of washed skies, and pale light, with mists and winds interspersed with bouts of stupendous fury from the charging ocean.

On Roanoke Island, between the Cape and the rest of North Carolina, are the remnants of the first settlement ever established in the New World by English colonists. Virginia Dare, the first white child born in America, was born here on August 18, 1587. She vanished, together with her parents and the rest of the colonists, leaving a mystery that has never been solved. Just outside the town of Manteo is a museum and exhibition. It was here that Edith Burrows with daughters Abigail and Kate visited on January 13, seven days after they had driven south from Newark, New Jersey.

The family were undecided whether or not to continue their journey across to Cape Hatteras and down the single road that fading winter afternoon or to stay and find accommodation in Manteo or Nags Head. It was Edith Burrows who decided to press on. She felt they had taken too long over the excursion and should continue south. She was worried because she had not called Andy and Adele Curtis. It would have been possible to return inland and drive towards South Carolina on one of several routes, but both girls wanted to savour the wildness of the deserted Cape and she let them have their wish. It was a fatal decision.

They left the museum at three o'clock and went east across the causeway to Nags Head before turning south along the Cape Hatteras seashore. It was a quiet, red afternoon when they began their journey, a sign a local could have told them was a forewarning of an oncoming storm. The land was flat and grey with flights of duck rising from the channels of reeds as their bright car pushed south. Occasionally another vehicle, mostly the sturdy four-wheel-drive Fords and Chevrolets of fishermen, passed in the other direction, but there were few of these. An uneasy dusk began to converge on them quite suddenly as they reached the extreme tip of the mainland peninsula; as they approached the three-mile-long Bonner Bridge, connecting the long arm of Cape Hatteras, with Hatteras Island, rain began to fly in on heavy gusts from the black, open sea. The sun had gone down like a furnace and all was abruptly dark. The rain hit the car with astonishing force, without preliminary spots or drizzle. The Englishwoman slowed, the car crept across the high arched causeway, and her daughters fell anxiously silent. The wind increased as quickly as the rain, as if it had suddenly spotted the lonely automobile and attacked it as an isolated target. As the high concrete bridge curved gradually down toward the island and the villainous sea spread out beneath them, Edith Burrows felt like the pilot of a light aircraft landing in fierce weather.

Both girls shouted with relief as the highway over the lofty bridge eventually flattened out and there was firm land on each flank again. The rain had not diminished, however, and as they drove along the straight road, it charged with renewed violence over the flattened landscape. They passed an indistinct group of two or three houses, some distance off the road, empty and black and standing on their high stilts.

"Perhaps we ought to stop and see if we can shelter in one of those places," suggested Abigail, sitting in the front of the car with her mother.

"They look as if they're all locked up for the winter," said Edith, leaning forward to peer through the deluge. The wind was hitting the car on the left-hand side and pushing it across the awash road. She struggled to keep it straight and tried not to show her anxiety to the girls. "We'll keep going until we see a place with a light. Then we'll stop. It can't be long before we find somewhere."

"The houses are on stilts because the sea comes across here," Katy quietly observed from the back seat. "If you look just across the ground over there, you can see the waves breaking."

"I saw them," said her mother tersely as though she wished it had not been pointed out. Another vehicle appeared travelling towards them, its high headlights blurred by the rain. It went by sending a great bow wave over the smaller car. Edith clenched her teeth and tried to steady the vehicle. "This," she said grimly, "as the Americans say – seemed like a good idea at the time."

It was a deep night now, not merely dark but black, a physical blackness that seemed to heave in the gale. The lights of the car probed pitifully a few yards ahead. There were no lights on the road for as far as they could see. They might have been in a storm on the ocean.

The two sisters sat taut and silent while their mother drove at a creeping pace into the dark rain. The road was difficult to pick out even a few feet ahead. Katy was about to say something and had merely got as far as "Maybe we could–" when the vehicle gave a swift lurch and began skidding along at an angle, almost as if it had lost both wheels on the off-side. They all cried out. They were sliding sideways down a bank. Edith Burrows used every bit of her strength attempting to bring the car onto the highway again, but it was too far gone. It slid and slithered and then the wheels tipped further and it ran along on its belly skimming the wet reedy bank of a deep roadside ditch. Edith braked and the vehicle screeched as if it had been wounded. It cut through a mass of thick growth and stopped. Water came in through the crack of the door. The engine stalled. Edith Burrows rested her head against the wheel. The girls threw their arms around her.

"Are you both all right?" she asked. She turned to them and all three faces were white in the dimness. They replied they were. "I think," said Edith with an attempt at a reassuring joke, "that we are what they call up the creek. Or rather *in* the creek. It looks as if we're going to get wet."

In the shelter of the harbour at Oregon Inlet, almost below the armpit of the Bonner Bridge, joining the peninsula to Hatteras Island, a white thirty-five-foot cruiser called *Canopus Candy*, registered in the Port of New York, rolled uneasily in the rain. The inlet was on the lee side of the Cape but the Atlantic waves, running in below the three-mile-long bridge, fretted the waters in the anchorage.

There were a few other craft in the habour but the *Canopus Candy* was the only vessel showing any lights. They came from the portholes of her main saloon where James Dade, twenty-four, and Candice Broom, twenty-one, both of New York City, lay naked together under a blanket in the double berth. They had been sniffing cocaine. The man was thin, almost stringy, but his sharp features were made remarkable by pale blue eyes of disturbing intensity. The girl was beautiful, her unkempt blonde hair slipping across a delicate face and then over unblemished fawn shoulders and elegant breasts.

Still lying down, James Dade pulled away the small curtain from the port near his head. "Shit, this place knows how to rain," he commented. "Can't even see the shore."

The girl lay against his hard chest. "Tommy's got trouble," she said. "He'll have a job to keep the pick-up on that goddam road."

James grinned. "He's so stupid he won't notice," he forecast. "He'll get here right on schedule."

"Are you going to give him a bad time again tonight?" she inquired with a grin.

"Maybe," he mused. He shook his head against her hair. "Jesus, that was so funny. That ugly bastard really thought we were going to have a threesome."

"Sure it was funny," she said. "But don't push it. He's a big guy. He might take matters into his own hands if we upset him. I don't want him screwing me."

James said, "Nobody rapes Candice Broom unless she wants to be raped."

"Right," she said looking at him sideways. "And especially not Tommy."

"Tommy's one of the world's natural victims," grunted James. "He'd never do that. Some people *do* things, and some get things *done* to them. He's in category two."

"He's an unattractive victim," she said.

"Most victims are. That's part of being one," said James. "It would sure be more fun for the rest of us if, now and again, they were prettier."

"And innocent," she put in. She turned to her side of the berth and lay on her stomach. "Remember I told you about that butch woman cop in L.A.?" she said. "The one who tried to frame me, with the drugs. That was when *I* was innocent. White as a lily. Christ, that dyke, she begged me, begged me, to beat up on her. She was even crying, you know, begging me to do it. Just because I was sixteen." She laughed quietly. "I found it more fun refusing."

"The complete sadist," he murmured. "But if it was *now, today*, and you *had* somebody, you controlled them, you'd *do* it."

"If they had the innocence," she repeated. "Evil's no fun if the victim's evil too."

"Innocence is getting to be a rare commodity," he ruminated. "There's not many virgins left." He eased himself from the berth. "And if there *are* any, my old man gets there first, the bastard." He glanced about the saloon. "I wonder how many he's debauched in here?"

"Of both sexes," she said.

"Yet he wants *me* out of *his* hair," he complained. "One cocaine rap and he wants me out. Worried about *his* reputation. Hypocrite."

Candice smiled. "Wait till he finds the boat's gone."

"I guess he has by now," he replied. "He probably thinks it's a good exchange – his boat for my absence." He pushed his fist against the cabin ceiling just above. "And that suits me. Let's get this baby down to Florida. She's just built for the cocaine trade."

A car horn sounded from the quayside. Then again. Candice looked out. "Tommy," she said. "And the rain's quit for a minute. Let's go now." She began sliding from the berth.

"Like I said, right on time," commented James Dade. "Dumb people take a pride in keeping to schedules. It's usually all they can get right."

It was only minutes after the red Tempo had slewed off the narrow road that James Dade, Candice Broom, and Tommy Earls saw the lights of the car still shining as it lay on its side in the ditch. They were driving south having just crossed the Bonner Bridge to Hatteras Island. The rain had started again and thickened to a deluge but their Ford four-wheel-drive ploughed through the storm like a tank.

James saw the lights first. "Somebody's in the ditch," he said without excitement. He pulled the Ford through the water lying like a river along the road and stopped a few feet short of the half-capsized car. James and Tommy got out.

"There's somebody in there!" shouted Tommy above the howl of the rain. "They're moving!" James leaned over so that his hands rested on the right-angle of the roof and door of the

Tempo. He peered down through the streaming windows at the blurred white faces.

"Pull the door," he ordered Tommy. The youth did so. It was jammed. James took hold of the handle, tried it, then turned it with a fierce, abrupt twist. It opened at once. James Dade looked into the car at Edith Burrows and her two daughters.

"Hi!" he said as if it were a casual meeting. "How ya doing?"

"I think we're all right, thank you," returned Edith Burrows calmly. "Just a little uncomfortable."

Tommy stared at James because of the accent. James leaned further into the car. "Soon have you out of there," he said. "Nobody hurt?"

"No, we're all all right," said Edith. "Just shaken – and getting wet. I couldn't keep the car on the road."

"Okay," said James. "Let's get you out one at a time, hey?" It was Kate, the youngest, who thought there was something strange about his speech and, in the dimness, his eyes. Even at that first moment. He withdrew his head from the cabin and said to his companion "Okay, give a hand, Tommy. Let's get this young lady out first."

Abigail was sitting in the seat nearest to them. She undid the seat belt and allowed them to heave her out. Tommy, who was bigger than James, put his hands underneath her armpits and eased her away from the car. She felt his palms slightly touch the underneath of her breasts and his breath on the back of her neck. James lifted her legs and they set her on the side of the road. She stood up in the buffeting wind and streaming rain.

"Run for the pick-up," said Tommy. The girl turned her wet face and tried to smile. Even at that moment she noticed the poor, wet, moustache he was attempting to grow.

"I'll wait," she shouted through the wind. "I'll wait until my mother and my sister are out."

They extracted Kate next, James picking her easily from the rear seat, having pushed Abigail's seat forward. He lifted her and handed her slight form to Tommy so that he could assist her to the top of the bank. He set her down. She had felt very slender and frail as he carried her.

"Why don't you get out of this rain?" he suggested. Kate, streaming with rain, shook her head as Abigail had done. "I'll wait for my mother," she said. Tommy stared at her voice.

"That sure sounds good, talking that way," he said. She smiled uncertainly through the downpour.

Edith Burrows managed to lever herself halfway out of the car. She was about to take James's offered hands when she turned back. First she took a small suitcase from the rear seat. Then she smiled and turned again. She said, "Mustn't forget to turn the lights off." She switched off the main beams and climbed from the car assisted by James.

"Let's get out of this," said James, leading them toward the big, square Ford. "It's going to be intimate but it'll be dry." He helped them into the truck, Kate last, giving her bottom a casual heave with his hand. She turned. He smiled. "Sorry, miss," he said.

Candice Broom was sitting at the wheel. "I'll take it, James," she said. "You're too slimy to drive." They laughed and Edith Burrows said, "I'm so grateful to you all. We might have been there for hours."

"I don't think so, lady," said Tommy climbing in the crowded vehicle. "A couple of hours and that car is going to be sunk real deep. Maybe down in ten feet of water. It's not the first one to go over the side like that." He glanced around in the dark, pleased they were listening to him. He went on importantly. "Me, I've lived on these Outer Banks seventeen years, all my life, and I know. A little bit at a time they slip and then down they go."

"Oh, but our luggage is in the boot!" exclaimed Edith. "Everything we have."

Candice stopped the engine. "You'd better go and try," she said to James. He glanced at her.

"Okay," he answered. "I guess you can only get a certain amount wet. Come on, Tommy."

The youth sniffed the rain up his nose and turned and went with James. They returned at once.

"Maybe we could open the trunk," said James, "if you have the keys."

"Yes, of course," said Edith. "I took them from the car. I'm so sorry, but it's everything we have."

The two young men went back toward the tipped car. Candice smiled at Edith and her daughters. "Not much of a welcome to Cape Hatteras," she said. Her voice was quiet and measured. In the dim light within the car Edith could see she had a beautiful

74

face and the dashboard lights touched her fair hair. "You're from England, naturally," she said.

"Yes, we are," said Edith. "You've been so kind. I'd better tell you who we are. I'm Edith Burrows and these are my daughters, Abigail and Kate."

"Abigail?" said Candice. "That's a pretty name. I'm Candice Broom. The tall guy is James Dade and the square one is Tommy . . . oh hell . . . what is it? Tommy Earls. James and I come from New York. Abigail? I guess in this country you'd soon be called Abby."

"I am now – in England," laughed Abigail.

"Abigail means a maidservant," added Kate quaintly.

"That's interesting. Ah, they've got the trunk open. I guess your belongings are saved."

The rain had not eased. It was pushed across the flatland by the wind as if before a giant broom. Gusts splattered against the Ford. James and Tommy, running, loaded four suitcases into the vehicle. "Okay?" shouted James above the wind.

"Fine. Thanks you so much," replied Edith. The Americans climbed aboard and Candice started the engine again. "I'm Edith Burrows, this is Abigail and this is Kate. They're my daughters. I know you're James and you're Tommy."

"Great. Nice to meet you," said James. He shook hands with all three, and Tommy, waiting for James to finish, followed him. "It's not the best night to be touring the Cape," said James as the sturdy car pushed into the wind and the stormy rain again. "I suggest you come back in summer. It's nice then, really nice."

"Can we find somewhere for the night?" asked Edith. We'll all be getting pneumonia. So will you."

James Dade waited. It was, Candice thought, a strangely long wait. "We're headed a couple of miles south on this road," he said eventually. "My father owns a motel out here. It's shut for the season but I have a key. We were going anyway. We'll soon get dried out there." Edith glanced at his profile in the semi-dark. She said, "Don't let us put you to any more trouble. You've been kind enough already. Is there anywhere else we could stay?"

"Nowhere," shrugged James. "This place is deserted in the winter. In Manteo there's a couple of motels and at Nags Head. But anyway, that's way back. I think you'd be better coming with us. It's no trouble, Mrs. Burrows. No trouble at all."

They drove for only about five minutes. The storm continued with them, unremitting, throwing rain against the vehicle. Above the wind they could detect a deeper, more threatening sound. "That's the ocean," said Candice quietly. "Sometimes it comes right across the land."

She eased the wheel to the right and the Ford left the road and plunged along a single track, full of holes and water, so that it seemed that they were already in a bumpy sea. The American girl leaned forward, almost against the windshield, intent but not anxious, the side of her cheek, her nose, and her hair caught by the dashboard lights. There was no way they could proceed very far along the track because the island was so narrow. Almost at once they came to a single-storied building, seemingly crouching against the storm. It was in darkness.

"Sweetwater Point Motel," announced James.

He left the Ford and jumped into the rain and mud. They could see his vague form at the door to the motel. He returned quickly.

"Okay, it's open," he said. There seemed to Edith to be a slight change in his manner, almost an assertion of authority. "Come on in," he said.

They climbed down from the pick-up, and Tommy was left to carry the luggage from the back and put it in the small lobby. Candice left the wheel and, covering her hair, ran through the gusting rain to the lit entrance. "Safe," she smiled at the English-woman and her daughters. "Safe at last."

The lobby was small and cold. It was decorated for a summer clientele with blue walls painted with leaping marlin and sword-fish. There was a small reception desk and on it a rack of damp-looking picture postcards.

"Just come in here," said James from the room behind the desk. "We'll get some heat in this place."

"These folks need to change," pointed out Candice. "In fact everybody does, except me. I'm not wet."

"Right," agreed James. "Why don't you just show them along to some rooms? They're all open, I guess. If not, the keys are hanging here. They won't be too warm, but it will be okay for getting into something dry. Tommy will get some coffee going. If he can."

"I can," said Tommy in a hurt way. "Sure I can."

Edith Burrows said. "Thank you. We *would* like to get out of these things. We've got plenty of clothes in the suitcases." She laughed. "Absent-minded Miss Kate here left one of her bags behind near Washington. Fortunately it doesn't matter much."

Candice suddenly smiled at the young girl. "Katy's a forgetter, is she?" she said. The girl flushed at the familiar use of her name "Yes, I am," she admitted shyly.

James led the way from the lobby down the corridor. "My old man owns a whole lot of motels," he said. "But this isn't the choicest. It's only open from Easter through Thanksgiving. Nobody who wasn't crazy would come out here after that."

"I think we've found that out," agreed Edith. She said "Thank you," as he showed her into a room.

"Edith – that's an unusual name these days," he mentioned. "In America anyway."

She laughed. "In England too. I was named after my grandmother. It makes me feel about her age."

He was going to say something else. She could sense that, but he changed his mind. Instead he nodded along the passage. "The girls will have to be down the corridor a little," he said. "There are some rooms due to be renovated next to here and they're not very comfortable."

Edith saw Abigail and Kate shown to two rooms at the far end of the corridor. "They could share," she said. "If there are two beds. We don't want to put you to too much trouble."

"There's no trouble," said James. He smiled with slight familiarity and leaned against the door of her room. "The one thing we got here at Sweetwater Point is room right now," he said. "Where were you headed when you went into the ditch? Did you figure to get the ferry from Hatteras Inlet?"

"Yes," she replied. He stood against the door, so she remained three feet or so inside the room. "We hoped to go from there over to the next island – the one with the strange name."

"Ocracoke," he nodded. "But there's no ferry until tomorrow. You would have had to stay over somewhere. My boat's at Oregon Inlet. Just below the bridge. Well, it's my old man's boat. I'm taking it down to Florida with these other two. Candice and I came down from New York and we picked up the kid here."

"It's a bad time of the year to be taking a boat down to Florida, isn't it?" Edith asked. She wanted to get changed but she did not want to be rude to him. "All these storms."

"No, it's really easy," he smiled. "You can travel the whole way by lakes and canals and sheltered water, like the Roanoke Sound. Right now we're going from Norfolk right down to Wilmington, keeping inside these islands. It's no trouble. You never have to go into the open sea."

"That's amazing," she said. "And very convenient." She smiled politely. "I think I'd better get changed."

"Sure, sure, I'm sorry," said James. He moved away. "Just come out when you're fixed and we'll get some coffee going. I guess you'll all be hungry too."

Edith paused and smiled at his kindness. She felt sorry she did not like him. "We haven't had anything since lunchtime," she said. "Have you got anything here?"

"Sure, there's a freezer and there's some TV dinners or something in there. They're not great, but they're okay."

"Oh, that's wonderful," said Edith. "You're very kind indeed, James. I won't be very long."

"Good," he nodded. "We'll get it all fixed." He was going to go away when he paused. "Did you make a reservation on the ferry? Not the one from Hatteras, the next ferry from Ocracoke to the mainland? That's the long ride, nearly three hours."

"No," she replied. She could hear the shortness in her own voice. "Is that necessary?"

He shrugged. "Oh, not this time of the year, I guess. In the summertime you have to. They keep a record of all the cars going across. But I figure it's okay in January. They don't have a lot of business."

As she shut the door on him Edith Burrows could not help but think what a strange question that had been. She shrugged and opened the suitcase on the bed. She went back quickly to the door and quietly turned the bolt before undressing. She smiled at her own pointless apprehension. She was becoming quite an old maid. Time she married again.

Candice Broom went quietly along the corridor. She paused outside the door of the room she knew they had given to Kate. She waited, still for a moment, and then, with sudden resolve, turned the handle and went into the room. The English girl was standing at the side of the bed wearing only a pair of blue panties.

Her trunk was as white and lean as a fish. Her blunt breasts hardly swelled from her body. When she saw Candice her face flushed, her navel contracted with alarm and she covered her chest.

"Oh, golly me!" exclaimed the American girl. "Oh, Katy, I'm so sorry!"

"That's all right," said the English girl looking straight at her. "I should have locked the door."

"This is the room I usually use when we stay here," said Candice. "I didn't realise that Tommy had shown you in here. I'm sorry. I'd better be going."

"My sister is in next door," said Kate evenly. "Don't make a mistake and go in there."

"I won't, baby," smiled Candice easily. "See you soon. We'll have some coffee and some food ready."

"Thank you," replied Kate. She wanted the woman to shut the door. It seemed a long time before she did, but eventually it closed. The girl stood there feeling cold. Around the roof she could hear the inordinate shrieking of the wind. She felt uneasy. She wondered where this place was.

"Sorry about the junk food," said James Dade pushing a plastic fork against the skin of a resistant steak. "They call these TV dinners."

"They're so bad they take your mind off how lousy the television show is," smiled Candice Broom. The others smiled but only Tommy Earls laughed.

"Just now this tastes like a banquet at the Ritz," answered Edith. Her daughters, pushing plastic forks into the aluminium foil trays, agreed.

"How come you find yourself out here?" asked Tommy. There had been a silence. Again he seemed pleased to have said something uninterrupted. He tugged at his fair, undernourished moustache. "This ain't a great place in the winter. Okay in the summer."

Kate finished her food and set down the tray. "It was me," she sighed. The way she said it, like the young girl she was, with a slight, acted sigh, made Candice smile and nod towards her. Edith noticed but Kate did not. Kate went on. "I wanted to see the Lost Colony at Roanoke," she explained. "Because we did a special study at school about that. We didn't realise it was such a far drive."

"You're right about that," said Edith. "Then the girls wanted to drive down the Cape Hatteras road instead of going back inland and continuing south from there. The guidebooks described it as wild and exciting, and that was right too."

"How about your people in Charleston?" asked James. "Did you let them know about changing your plans? Maybe they'll be worried."

"We didn't let anyone know," Edith said readily. "We just turned off the main road and drove. We ought to telephone soon, though, just to tell them we're all right. They'll start to get anxious. Perhaps I could phone them from here."

"The phone's out," said Candice abruptly. "It's cut off during the winter."

James was about to say something to that. His mouth was open but he slowly shut it. He continued to look at Candice, his face immobile, then he smiled at her, a small sign of incredulity. Edith caught the expression. So did Abigail. The girl glanced at her mother but in a moment James had replaced this mood.

"I guess all we can do, all of us, is to make ourselves comfortable," he said genially. "I don't think this storm will be away before daybreak. And I guess you people are going to need a new automobile."

Edith looked up, startled; the implication of what had happened to the car had not occurred to her before. But James smiled widely. "Don't let that worry you, Edith," he said, using her Christian name for the first time. "All that can be figured out. So they lose a car. They got plenty."

Tommy had been pouring coffee into plastic mugs. Edith drank hers as quickly as she could without burning her mouth. The rain was hitting the windows of the Sweetwater Point Motel like gravel. They could hear the gale travelling furiously across the coast that gave no resistance. "I think," said Edith, putting down the coffee mug, "that we ought to be retiring. We've had a very full day." She stood up and her daughters stood obediently with her. The three Americans regarded them with differing expressions. Candice with a cool smile, James with his pale eyes, Tommy with an idiotic grin. "Good night," continued Edith. Within herself she felt an unease that she sensed would not be settled until she was out of the room, or better still away from the place altogether. "Thank you for your help and your kindness," she continued. Abigail and Kate nodded and smiled in agreement.

"It was nothing," said James easily. "Glad to be of help, Edith. Tomorrow we'll get you to a phone where you can call your people in Charleston and let them know where you are. It worries people when folks vanish."

When the Englishwoman and her daughters had gone, Candice, James, and Tommy remained sitting, not speaking, each of them looking idly towards the door through which the three had walked. Eventually, as if some silent and secret interval of time had passed, James produced a small silver box of cocaine and he and Candice, still unspeaking, sniffed it. Tommy, sullenly excluded, went to the refrigerator and opened a can of Coca-Cola. It had become a joke with the other two, every time they took coke he had a Coke. Now they grinned at each other with spiteful elation, almost childish in its glee.

"You're *not*, you bastard!" Candice said, her voice low and excited. "You're not going to *do* it?"

"Why not? It's the complete opportunity." He grinned wolfishly. "Beautiful innocents."

Tommy did not understand. He sucked at his Coca-Cola. He guessed it was something smutty. He had a feeling it was to do with the Englishwoman and her daughters. Something that he would be left guessing about. James and Candice were like that with him.

Because he had to say something, he said, "Did you see? Did you get the way that woman was looking at me? The mother. Man, I looked at her, you know, I caught hold of her eye and she was looking at me . . . like *that*."

"Like what, Tommy?" inquired Candice mischievously.

"Like she liked you?" suggested James with his sly laugh. "Like she wanted you to get her down and screw her? Like that?"

"That's right," replied the boy defiantly. It came out like an excited grunt. "Like that she wanted me to get her down and roll on her and screw her."

"You ain't never screwed anything 'cept your fist," put in Candice, mimicking the youth's accent wickedly.

81

"And that's just about the prettiest thing you're ever going to screw," added James following the impersonation but not so well.

Tommy looked at them sullenly over the curve of the can. "You two," he snorted. "You two you just use me like shit. You always do. Like shit."

"You're not shit, Tommy," cajoled the girl. "You're a ballsy young guy. Big and strong and great at screwing. Great looking too. Great!" He was so simple that he beamed at what he thought was a compliment until he looked closely and saw that it wasn't.

James came in with the belly punch. "Great looking, apart from the acne and the weepy eyes. Fucking your fist makes you have those eyes, Tommy."

The youth, snarling silently like a hurt tomcat, got to his feet. It was Candice who calmed him. She put her hand on his crotch and stroked it, smiling at him. His anger stopped at once, draining away from his whole body. He looked at her hopefully. She turned on James. "Now you quit, James," she warned with a pretence of seriousness. "Tom's just a kid, only seventeen, and he's got a lot of life to live yet, haven't you, Tommy?"

Mollified, the youth sat down and drank the remainder of the Coke noisily. He wiped his mouth with the back of his hand, as if he thought it looked manly. "A lot," he agreed. "And maybe I ain't from the big city, maybe I just never got out of this goddam place, but that don't mean I'm dumb. No sir, I ain't And I tell you that lady from England *was* looking at me like that. She was for certain. Older women get hooked on young guys like me. After you're twenty it goes. But with young guys it's still there. We had a neighbour who was always trying to get me into her place when her old man was away. She wanted it. She wanted to be screwed. Just like this one does."

It was a long speech for him. Its length more than its sentiments embarrassed him and he sat, head hung, and caressed the Coke can. The others remained in amused silence. Then Candice touched him again, right underneath the parting of the legs of his jeans. He reacted like an animal.

"Don't do that, Candice," he threatened unconvincingly, making a rare use of her name. "I won't be able to help what I do if you go on touching me there."

"You're a big boy," she replied stopping the stroking but

82

keeping her fingers on the place. "A big guy with a lot to offer. You should just get a load of what this kid's got there, James." She grinned at James.

James took another sniff. "No thanks. I guess I can do without that."

The girl returned to Tommy. He was undecided whether to be proud or miserable. He knew she was making fun. Now she approached him and squatted down before him like a mother trying to talk to a dull child. "Tommy," she said, leaving a long pause. The youth could smell her. Her breasts were almost biting him. He badly wanted to touch them but a look sideways at the mean expression on James's face stopped him.

"Yes, Candice?" he replied as coolly as he could.

"Listen, Tommy. That lady, that English lady – she really *liked* you. I could tell. The way she spoke to you. It was different."

Tommy stared at her. "You really think so?" he asked. Her face, directly opposite his, was serious. "You ain't kidding me?"

"Oh, no," she told him softly. "I wouldn't kid about a thing like that. I think maybe you got through to her. Women with daughters have this hang-up about young guys. They have fantasies about young guys screwing them and beating them up – all that stuff."

Tommy's face set. "You figure she'd let me do that . . . like you said. Screw her and–"

"Beat her up," completed Candice quietly, teasingly. "I think that's what she'd really like you to do."

"But she – she didn't seem that kinda type–" argued the youth softly. He was conscious of James's narrow look toward him. "To let a guy, even a young guy, do that sort of thing. Beating up." He waited and dropped his eyes as if he were ashamed. "You don't think she's too old for me? She's got to be older than my ma."

Candice tutted. "Oh no, Tommy. Not that. She's a good looker, slim, and she's nice and swollen and soft up here." She curved her hands over her breasts.

"She looks better than your ma," put in James maliciously. Candice warned him with her glance. James said, "Listen kid, if you don't do it now when are you? It's just a great opportunity. Once in a lifetime. Go on – go and ask her."

"Ask?" said Tommy, his sticky eyes widening. "You mean

83

just *ask* if it's okay? If I can screw her?"

Candice gazed at him like a mother again. "Sure, ask," she said softly. "You don't get a single thing in this life if you don't ask."

Tommy rose from his seat. He crushed the Coke can with one squeeze of his pale fist, a trick he liked doing. He wiped the back of his mouth again. There was a mirror on the wall and he took a moment to straighten his hair. Candice silently warned James not to laugh. The youth looked at them again. "You're not taking me for a ride with this, are you?" he asked. "You two. I mean, if I do and I foul it up, you'll help me, won't you? Like to cover things up with her?"

"Sure, sure," nodded James. "Go on. Go ask her. Do it quiet because you don't want to have the girls hearing. Maybe they'll all want some."

"You're kidding," said Tommy with quiet savagery. "You're fucking me around."

James looked at him with arch steadiness. "No kidding, Tommy," he said.

"No kidding," said Candice. She touched him on the balls again. "Go and ask the lady. Nicely."

He straightened his shirt into his belt and went towards the door. He went out and returned again at once like an actor in a farce. "And if she says nothing doing, what do I do then?" he asked innocently.

"Make her," said James.

"Sure, make her," said Candice.

He walked down the corridor, stood uncertain and tense outside her door for a moment, looked back towards the voices of the others and, knowing how they would ridicule if he returned, he knocked.

"Yes, who is it?" said Edith Burrows. Tommy had never heard a voice like hers before, soft and mature. The English female accent made his blood run to his stomach.

"It's me, Tommy," he said, attempting to sound steady, casual. "Could I have a word with you, please, Mrs. Burrows?"

There was no hesitation. At once he heard the lock begin to turn. She opened the door without caution. He was already smiling when she looked at him. She returned the smile firmly.

"Gee, *of course*, you're unpacking," he said looking down at the open overnight case on the bed, "I'm sorry, you're busy."

84

It sounded so lame that she looked at him oddly. "That's perfectly all right, Tommy," she said. "It's only two or three things."

"Look," he said as though about to blurt a confession. "Can I just come in here a moment – and talk with you?"

She waited, then answered. "Yes, I suppose so. What about?"

He was inside the room now. Edith Burrows experienced the first small, nasty feeling. It was a tight room and he was a big youth. His acne glistened in the reflected light from the dressing table mirror. His smile was bland, almost stupid.

He sat on the edge of the bed and then said, "Is it okay, if I sit here? If I sit on the bed? Is that okay, Mrs. Burrows? Right here."

"Certainly, if you wish," she said. Her apprehension, even while she was telling herself that it was foolish, was growing. The bed took up so much of the room there was not much space to keep her distance from him. She noticed he had sore eyes. The moustache he had attempted was ragged, damp, uneven. He pushed out his large boy's arm and pushed the door firmly enough for it to close. Immediately he glanced at her, at once a warning and an apology.

"I need the door shut," he explained as if he were doing some repair to the room. "I need it that way. Because *they'll* hear us if I don't. Those two. You don't know, Mrs. Burrows, what a real creepy couple those two are."

"James and Candice?" She laughed outright at him. "They seem to be perfectly all right to me."

"But they're *not* to me." he complained. His face curled up into a whine. "They've got *ways*, see. Real nasty *ways*. They try to get *me* involved. Me! In their *ways*. But I won't go along with it."

She looked at him more in curiosity than fear now. His speech was measured, like someone reciting something carefully rehearsed. "Whatever are you talking about?" she asked briskly. She was ready to put him out into the hall again. It abruptly occurred to her that she might be unable to do so. He rubbed his eyes roughly, like a small child. She thought that is why they looked so sore.

"You'll understand. I *think* you'll understand," he said, humping his back. "They're down from New York in their smart boat, which ain't even theirs, it's James's father's. Like this motel is. He

85

has a lot of motels. But me, I'm just from around these parts, and don't they let me know it. See, I don't have any – well, any *experience* of things. I hope you'll be able to appreciate that. It's very difficult to get *experience* in this sort of place. Not like New York or Norfolk, Virginia. You know – wow – you gotta believe this Mrs. Burrows, when they mentioned *coke* to me, I really *thought* they meant Coca-Cola. God help me, so I did. So they think I'm dumb. Maybe I am."

Edith was staring at him. His head was bowed like a man making a penance. "What is it then?" she asked slowly and suspiciously.

"What?" he asked stupidly.

"Coke. What is it if it's not Coca-Cola?"

A huge patronizing grin swallowed the lower half of his unattractive face. "Wow, you too!"

"What is it then?" she repeated. "If it's not Coca-Cola?"

"Cocaine." He said it with an appropriate squeeze of his fingers next to his untidy nostrils. "That's what they meant."

"Oh," she said uneasily. "What does that do to them?"

"Makes 'em high, of course. Higher and higher."

"Are they taking it now?"

"Sure, sure. They do all the time."

"Oh dear."

"I didn't want to get mixed up in it right from the start. Please understand that. You *can* understand that, I know. I have enough in the way of troubles as it is."

She had some vague feeling that she should humour him. If she did that he might just maudle on for a while and then get up and go quietly. "What troubles do you have, Tommy?" she asked. She made the mistake of sitting on the side of the bed. He was still a yard distant but she knew she was in the wrong place. She rose hurriedly and moved away as far as the confined area would allow.

"Aw, you know. The kinda troubles, worries, teenagers get. You know what I mean, when you ain't great looking or good at anything like basketball, or even fishing. And, Jesus, you try to grow a moustache and the goddam thing won't come right."

He tore at his moustache as though he could peel it off. She laughed genuinely. She was off the guard she had begun to keep a few minutes before. She sat down on the bed again, her expression the amused sympathy of a mother for a backward son. It was a mistake that time, too.

"I just don't get any *experience* around here," he repeated, looking down at the floor. "Not with *girls*, you understand, or anything. You got two really sweet girls, Mrs. Burrows." Edith felt herself stiffen inside. "That little one, that Katy, she's *so* neat. And Abigail – wow, what kind of name is that? Like something on TV – Abigail. Now, there's a girl you could be proud of. I mean, I could. Proud of, like to take her out and walk her around the area just to show her off. She has real nice legs, if you don't mind me saying so."

Edith swallowed. "They're very young girls yet," she said inadequately.

"Sure, sure they are. But, you know, girls like that in these parts, in Manteo or Nags Head, or in fact *anywhere* you care to mention, they just ain't like your girls. Do you know, Mrs. Burrows, the first thing I noticed about your girls? About Katy and Abigail. Do you know? Can you guess?"

"No," she answered slowly. She wondered what would happen if she tried to get to the door. She decided to delay trying for a few minutes. "No, what was it?" She had to be calm.

"Teeth," answered the youth with his silly, sly grin. He seemed as pleased as if he had answered some question on a quiz game. "Teeth."

"American girls have teeth," she pointed out slowly and carefully. "Very nice teeth."

"When you can *see* them, Mrs. Burrows. That's the whole goddam point, if you will excuse me using that word: *goddam*."

She smiled bleakly. "It doesn't mean anything very bad in English," she said. He was not mad, she decided, not dangerous. Just retarded. She ought to be able to handle it. He bared his teeth to illustrate his point. "You just never see young girls' teeth in this country," he complained, running a thick thumb along his own. "You can just *never* see them. They always got them in braces. Like having their teeth in cages. It's awful. How anybody can kiss them I just have no idea. All that metal!" The thumb now pointed at her, thrust out like an index finger. "Now, your girls, they got teeth. *And* you can see them. You can even *count* them."

"Tommy," she said, trying to sound kind, motherly. "Did you come in here to talk about teeth? I'm very tired. We've had a very trying day." She was still sitting a yard away from him on the bed. He had not moved during his rambling, and he remained as though buried in thought. "That's a real beautiful ring you have on your finger, Mrs. Burrows," he remarked almost dreamily. "That blue stone–" Then, still looking at the floor, he reached out and placed a large, sweating hand on her leg.

"No!" she barked at him. God, it frightened her. She lifted the paw and removed it as if it were some piece of waste matter. Her fingers shook. "Just you get out of here before I call James."

"James told me to come." His big sore eyes rolled up to her horrified expression. "And Candice. They *dared* me."

This time Edith saw the hand coming at her like a fat, fleshy spider. She would have screamed but his other hand caught her across the mouth and pressed her back across the bed. She was terrified by his strength. He hardly seemed to be leaning on her but she could not move. His thick leg swung over her lap clumsily but lazily as though he were mounting a motorcycle. Then his free hand pulled the buttons away from the throat of her dress. The hand crawled in onto her breast, first rubbing and eagerly fingering the nylon brassiere and then sliding on its own oozing sweat under the material and over the breast itself until it held the nipple. His face turned with an indolent, smashed, sleepy look, as if his thoughts were elsewhere.

She forced her eyes away from that blank face. She couldn't stand it. Jesus Christ, he *was* mad! She tried to shout but it ended as a gurgle in her throat. He held her easily. He was squeezing the breast savagely with one hand and held her with the other across her mouth and his puffy leg across her thighs. She prayed in her whirling mind. Please God, get this monster away from me. Send somebody!

For a moment she thought her prayers had been miraculously and immediately answered. The door was pushed open and in strolled James and Candice. But at once, she knew there was no help.

"Wow, what a technique!" sneered the young man. "Real smooth, hey Candy?"

To Edith's horror she saw that the girl was smiling. "Thought you said you'd *talk* her into it, Tommy?" she remarked. "This is great conversation."

James burst into laughter. The girl touched her finger to her lips and motioned a warning with her blonde hair. That was when Edith began to realize about the girls. She stopped struggling. Tommy turned his head away from her and looked over his shoulder at the others. "I'm doing okay," he said huffily. "This is the way she *wants* it. She likes the rough stuff." He pulled back his hand from her mouth and struck her across the face. The blow almost knocked her out. Her head ran around wildly. She felt blood in her mouth.

"Now, now, Tommy, that is *not* gentlemanly," murmured Candice.

James looked at her because of the tone that had come into her voice. "Gee," he said, almost admiringly. "You turned Candice on at last, Tommy." He remained standing by the door. Then he glanced along the corridor in the direction of the girls' rooms. Nothing was disturbed. He stepped into Edith's room and closed the door behind him.

Now all three of them stood around her. Candice had moved forward. "You made her bleed, Tommy," she admonished. "Christ, you're a clumsy lover." She bent over as though to examine the trapped woman's mouth. Edith stared at her with disbelief and terror. The girl took a pad of cotton wool from her handbag. "Open up," she said leaning forward. She gave Tommy a firm push so that he moved the top of his body away. He kept his leg heavily across the Englishwoman.

"Open your mouth, Edith," she repeated. It was an instruction. Edith let her mouth open, she could feel the salt of the blood on her tongue. "We'll staunch that," murmured Candice. She leaned low and Edith looked straight into the other woman's eyes. They were like a marsh.

The American girl's body was slim and arched. She bent over and positioned the cotton wool. At first she dabbed at the gum where the cut was. Edith had begun to cry when she had recovered from the force of the blow. Candice, with a clever smile, then dabbed at the tears on her cheeks. "You have really nice skin, Edith," she remarked quietly, like a beautician. "I suppose it's that English rain. It's really good skin for a woman of your age." James had moved from the door so he could watch. Tommy was sweating so furiously through his shirt that it seemed someone had thrown a basin of water across his front. His hand remained on Edith's breast. It was thick with sweat in

89

there. Candice cast him a look and pulled the hand out. "Fingers, fingers," she rebuked.

The youth's face dropped. "I *can* have her, though, can't I?" he said anxiously, like a child thinking it was to be denied a promised treat.

"Sure," replied James from behind. "Just take it easy, that's all. There's no hurry."

"There is when it's your first fuck," replied Tommy sulkily. "The first one that's for real."

"Dry up," ordered the girl. She still had the pad of cotton wool and she pushed it now, placed it, into Edith Burrows' mouth. The woman gagged on it. "Easy, boy," the girl admonished Tommy. "Take a little load off." She pushed his leg away. He had an erection thrust right down the leg of his trousers. James and Candice both saw it. James laughed and Candice patted it. "Save it," she said. "It's a goodie."

She turned to Edith. The woman was so weak that she had remained lying flat across the bed, her legs hanging over the side, her eyes moving frantically. The boy held her easily with one hand between her breasts.

"Edith," said Candice quietly. "The one thing you must not do is shout or scream. You have to understand that. If you do kick up a scene, nobody will hear. You must have seen that this place is nowhere and back. There's nobody to listen, you understand, only Katy and Abigail. And you wouldn't want them coming in here and seeing their mommy in this position, now would you? And if they did we would have to do something about them. You understand that too?"

Edith felt sick. She began to heave. Candice put her slender fingers into her mouth and pulled out the cotton wool like a magician performing a simple trick. Edith gulped the air. Then she lay gasping, sweat and tears mixing on her face. Her eyes revolved to each of their faces. "You're mad," she sobbed.

"I have to admit that *is* a possibility," remarked Candice coolly. "But what is done is sure done." She took on an almost businesslike air. She gave Tommy a further insolent push and moved him along so that she could sit on the bed next to the prostrate woman. "We have to come to an understanding," she said.

"An understanding about what?" whispered Edith Burrows.

90

"Our situation. All of us."

James, as though wanting to listen more closely, moved onto the other side of Edith. He sat looking at her dispassionately. Then he leaned forward and put his fingers on her cheek where the boy had struck the blow. "I sure hope you don't bruise there, Edith," he said solicitously. He looked at Tommy. "He's just a dumb, clumsy kid."

"Thanks," sulked the youth. "Thanks a million. I like the way you just take over. It's me – *I* make the first move then *you* take over. Both of you."

Candice glanced toward him. "Shut up, Tommy," she repeated quietly. "I'm trying to talk to Mrs. Burrows." The sulk solidified on the youth's face. He seemed as if he were muttering inside. The girl returned her attention to the Englishwoman.

"We have this situation, right now, as you can appreciate," she said. "Where something has happened which we can't make unhappen. It's not a retrievable matter. So we are in trouble. Assault at the very least. All kinds of other things too. We didn't really mean to go this far, we were only kidding. We didn't think this dumb-cluck kid had enough shit in him to *do* it. But, okay, it turns out he did.

"You know, it's a situation we've talked about between ourselves – me and James. Just kidding. Just a fantasy. Having somebody, or a number of people really *under your control*. To do what you want with them. Lots of people have hang-ups like that. Read the books. But suddenly along comes the opportunity to really *do* this thing. *To make the fantasy come true.* And here we are.

"We didn't bring you along here for this. I mean, when we found you on the road, we only wanted to help. But it's just that the situation developed and – well, Edith, you just have to face it, these things happen."

Edith Burrows felt as if her whole being had solidified. She felt as though a frost had entered her body and frozen it. She stared at the girl. "You ought to get some treatment," she said inadequately.

James laughed. "I think it's you that's getting the treatment, lady," he said. The girl ignored the remark.

‧Instead she leaned down again. "I expect you're worried about your daughters," she said in a low concerned voice. "Frankly, so

91

am I. But we're in this thing now. You have to understand, we're as trapped as you, Edith. We're stuck with the situation."

She gave a thoughtful smile and ran her finger like a lover down the wetness of the older woman's face, from her forehead to her chin. "Tommy wants you," she murmured. "He was first. First come first served, don't they say?"

All three people now looked toward Tommy. Edith closed her eyes with horror. She had thought she was past praying but she prayed now. When she opened her eyes again he was still there. He had a dull shine in his peasant eyes. "Come on, Tommy," whispered Candice. "Do it now."

The result of the invitation was almost laughable. Tommy fumbled with his zip fly and brought out a limp penis. Edith heard James say, "Christ." Candice glanced at James reprovingly. "Give him time, James," she said. She smiled towards Tommy. "You're a little nervous, I guess, Tommy."

The youth gulped like an innocent. "Sure I am," he said. "It gets a whole lot bigger than this. All the time."

Candice now turned her soft smile on Edith. "I'm sure this nice lady will help you, Tommy," she said. Edith felt herself trembling out of control. Candice laid her slender hand on the English-woman's thigh and rubbed against her skirt as if to pacify her. "You'll help him, won't you, Edith?" she asked. "Or maybe I'll get one of the girls to help him."

All Edith could do was to sob. She felt the tears warm on her cheeks as she nodded dumbly. Beguilingly, Candice smiled. "There, I knew you wouldn't mind," she said. Come on Tommy, give what you've got to the.lady."

Tommy, face wide and blank, not blinking, stumbled forward. He stopped at the side of the bed, unmoving, waiting for something to happen, his penis as limp as his expression. Candice took Edith's left hand. "A beautiful ring," she commented almost absently. "And a beautiful hand. Let me help." She eased the hand toward the staring youth. He was standing, stupidly, too far away. The girl flicked her eyes for him to move up but he did not appreciate the signal. He remained mesmerized. "Tommy," said Candice, like a reminder. She touched his sleeve and encouraged him forward. Edith was staring at the youth and he at her, as if they were players in some drama beyond their control.

Candice took Edith's slender hand and eased it towards the

boy. Edith sobbed through her teeth and turned her eyes away. Tommy grunted with sudden pleasure as her fingers touched him. Stepping to the head of the bed Candice briskly turned Edith's face back towards the youth. "Look at him, Edith," she ordered. "Take a little interest. See what you're doing. My God, *look* Edith–"

Tommy was shivering as he moved. Candice could hear James breathing by her neck. She half turned and smiled at him. "James, you're jealous," she reproved. "Jealous of Tommy."

"Yes, I am too," mumbled James. He began to pull at his fly. "I'm real glad she's got another hand," he said. He grinned a bleak grin and moved around the other side of the bed. He picked up Edith Burrows' left hand. His free hand pulled at her clothes, tugging the blouse apart and then tearing the brassiere away. Edith cried out and Candice, swiftly, leaned over and smacked her across the mouth again. Then she put her hand over the trembling lips.

"Come along, Edith," she said. "Don't lose interest now. Don't let the boys do all the work."

Then Candice stood and watched. She had become even more relaxed, efficient almost, like a competent nurse. Suddenly Tommy spat through his teeth and began howling like an animal. He fell forward across the bared breasts of the prostrate Englishwoman. James began to laugh wildly.

"Shut up," said Candice sharply. "You'll wake the children."

"Why don't you guys just go somewhere? Give the lady time to straighten herself out."

They nodded obediently at Candice and followed each other from the room. James was still laughing, but softly, to himself. Tommy turned around at the door and looked back at Edith still lying on the bed. "I still didn't get it," he complained. "Not the real thing."

"Okay, okay, you will," promised Candice almost blithely. "Maybe something even better."

"What do you mean by that?" whispered Edith. "They're not going to touch my girls, are they?"

Candice smiled at her. It was the smile of a grown and knowing daughter for a mother confused by something outside her scope. "Don't you worry, Edith," she said. "I've got every-

93

thing under control with those hulks. Don't you worry about a thing. Now why don't we go and get you cleaned up?"

The Englishwoman obeyed dumbly, getting up from the bed. Disgust consumed her. "God, you're in such a mess," said Candice, as though she were surprised. "That's the trouble with guys. *We* keep our feelings inside, don't we?"

Edith was stumbling towards the bathroom door and she did not answer. Candice moved towards her and caught the end of her torn brassiere. She pulled at it like a mule driver at a halter. Edith turned. "I said we keep our feelings inside us, don't we?" repeated Candice. "But you didn't answer."

Edith's face trembled. "Oh, I see. Yes," she said, trying to sound firm. "I suppose we do. Yes."

"Come on," said Candice pushing her gently into the bathroom. "You'll need a shower. It's cold I'm afraid, because there's been no water heating in this place for months. But it will do. And it will fresh you up. Make you feel good again." She looked at the key in the door, removed it thoughtfully, but then replaced it. "I don't think we need worry about that," she murmured with a slight smile. "I guess you will want a little privacy now and then."

She sat easily on the side of the bath. I could push her now, thought Edith Burrows. Shove her across the bath and bang her head on that wall. I could kill her. She knew she would not and Candice confirmed her thoughts as if they had occurred to her simultaneously. "Don't be crazy, Edith," she remarked. "Just remember that we're in this real deep now. All of us. You too. If you try anything out of line I can't guarantee what that Tommy might be tempted to do with your little Katy. He's a mad boy that one, a mad, mad boy."

Suddenly the Englishwoman slumped onto the bathroom stool, her torn clothes hanging about her. She turned the tap in the wash basin and washed her arms and hands while she remained sitting. Candice handed her a towel. They sat facing each other. "Please," said Edith. "I beg you, don't let that monster touch my Katy. Nor James. Please, Candice."

"Now don't you go worrying your head about possibilities like that," said Candice, patting her knee. "I guess the boys will want to have a little fun with the elder girl, but I won't let them have Katy. I shall look after Katy."

Edith looked up and met the pale eyes. She dropped her head into her hands. "It's a nightmare," she whispered. "Things like this don't happen to people."

Candice laughed. "Well they sure did to you," she said. "You're just plain unlucky. The way it all came about – the car in the ditch and us just happening along like that. And then everything else. Wow, I just can't believe it."

"Nor can I," muttered Edith. "But be sure you'll be caught. Somehow. And you'll pay for this."

"Could be," agreed Candice seriously. "It's a risk we have to take. Like I say, we've got no choice now anyway." She waited, looking, almost examining the other woman. She leaned forward and held one of the breasts in the palm of her hand. "You're really fortunate," she murmured. "I could never grow out of a 34B cup." She took her hand away as though replacing a vegetable on a barrow. "Now why don't you get under that shower? It's cold, but you'll feel invigorated. Here, let me help."

She made the older woman stand and then pulled her clothes away from her briskly. "Tommy was disappointed," she said as she did so. "He wanted the genuine article and all he got was yet another substitute. The story of the kid's life."

Edith said, "I shall vomit if he comes near me again."

Candice pushed her towards the shower cubicle. "You've got a nice neat ass, lady," she commented jokingly as she did so. "Stand still. Just like that."

She reached forward and placed her fingernails down the crease of the buttocks. Then she pushed the other woman into the cubicle and immediately turned on the water. Edith had promised herself that she would not cry out when the cold spray hit her but she couldn't help it. Candice laughed again. "Make you feel good?" she shouted above the noise of the water. She stood and watched. Edith slumped to the floor of the shower so she turned off the water and told her to stand again. Then she turned it on once more. After two minutes she switched it off and allowed Edith to stumble out. She was waiting with a large bath towel. "Just dry on this," she said. "You see how good you feel then." She handed the towel over. "Do you have a nightdress in your valise?" she asked.

Edith, uncontrollably shivering, nodded. She was violently towelling herself. Candice turned and went back into the bedroom. "I'll get it for you," she called back with grotesque cheerfulness. "Don't go away, now." She returned with the coral pink silk nightdress and draped it across the bathstool. She sat down and considered Edith. "You're in great shape," she said, "for a lady of your age. How old are you, Edith?"

"I'm thirty-seven," replied Edith. She had towelled her hair.

"I'll keep Tommy away from you," said Candice like a suddenly decided promise. "He's just too gross. James is nice looking. And he enjoys older women. You'd be really surprised how many young guys do. It's kinda reassuring for us girls, don't you think?"

Edith Burrows dropped her head in her hands again. "Oh God, please God," she muttered pathetically. "Do I have to go through all that again?"

"God's never around when you want Him," smiled Candice. She put the nightdress over Edith's head and helped it slide down the body. "That's nice," she said approvingly. "Don't worry about your hair. James won't mind that."

Edith was sitting on the bed, staring at the wall as though trying to force her very being through it. The storm had abated from its first fury but it coughed and howled in short bursts and the rain continued to agitate against the window. She stood up and walked to the curtains. She pulled them a few inches apart and looked out. At first she thought there was nothing out there, only blackness and sounds. She could hear the sea now as well, drumming against the land, its note distinctive from the blows of the wind. Then she saw that all was not dark. The remote beam of a lighthouse swung abruptly like a white arm through the night and then immediately swung away again. She heard the door open behind her. She was past being shocked now. She turned almost casually. James was leaning indolently against the door-post and watching her with a smirk.

"I was looking at the lighthouse," the Englishwoman said calmly.

"I thought maybe you thought of getting loose," said James. His shirt was open to the waist and a gold chain with a medallion hung like a sign of bravado. "That light is on the mainland, miles away. Too far to shout."

"Don't worry," she replied. "None of us can escape and leave

96

any of the others here. I understand that."

"I'm glad," he sniffed, moving forward. He put his hands on her shoulders and she felt herself contract at the touch. "I wanted you to be in bed, all cosy," he complained. "When I came through the door I wanted you in that bed. Now get in it."

She moved sadly towards the bed. "It was my hair," she said. "I was drying it." She looked at him steadily. "Listen, James," she said. "You've got me. You can do whatever you like but my girls–"

'Sleeping like babies," he said cheerfully. "Curled up, beautiful."

She stared at him. She was on the edge of the bed, having turned the sheet and blankets back. "You've – you've been in their rooms?" she said. "You went in?"

"Ah, we kinda peeked in. Just to see they're okay," he said. "And like I say, they're just fine. Very pretty too."

"Where's Candice?" she asked suddenly.

He was pushing her into the bed like a father. "She's trying to talk some sense into that thick Tommy. Jesus, that guy would do anything if he was given the chance. He's a crazy man."

"She will – she'll be able to – ?"

"Lady," he said firmly. "We've spent the last five minutes talking. Now I've had plenty of talking. I came for something a little different."

"Yes," she said sullenly.

He pulled his shirt from his body, kissed the medallion. "The patron saint of fuckers," he smiled. Then, curiously, he became almost modest. He turned off all the lights except for the one at the bedside and turned away from her while he pulled his jeans over his legs and feet.

She was half sitting up in the bed, her head against the headboard. He pulled her roughly flat on the mattress, then pulled away the nightdress from the top of her body. He eased himself up and looked at her breasts. His hands pushed them together. They he backed away down the bed until he was kneeling between her legs. He took each knee in turn and forced them further apart. First he looked at her in the diffuse light. Edith closed her eyes and lay as though in remote sleep. "Wake up, Edith," he muttered. "I want you to know what's going on here."

She opened her eyes and looked down over her body at him. Her gaze was dull with hate. James lifted the hem of the night-dress from around her thighs. He looked up and then sniffed. He glanced at her again. Her expression remained the same. With an abrupt thrust he threw the nightdress back from her legs and groins. It rested on her pale stomach.

He looked at her and laughed. "How about a little kiss?" he said. "A loving kiss."

James pushed his mouth onto her slack lips. "Come on, lady," he snarled. "I want a kiss. Do it!" She had to. She tightened her lips and he kissed her brutally, at the same time forcing himself within her. She began to cry and continued to weep softly while he raped her. When he had finished, he lay beaten, as good as dead. He slumped across her. She hardly noticed that he had begun to shake. "That was nice, Edith," he trembled. "God, that was terrific. That's the best thing that ever happened to me, baby. The best thing ever."

Candice came through the door and grimaced when she saw them. She moved forward and pulled the sheet over their figures. "Your hairy ass, James," she complained "is not a pretty sight." She sat on the side of the bed. Edith opened her eyes.

"Candice," said Edith, as though speaking to someone she could trust, "where's Tommy? What's he doing?"

"He's okay," replied Candice evenly. "Don't you worry about Tommy. I've had a talk with Tommy. He understands things now. How did it go with you two lovers?"

"I gave her a good time," said James, rolling away from the older woman. "She got hot, didn't you, Edith?" He looked down as if expecting an answer. Edith did not say anything.

"I guess you'd like some coffee, both of you," said Candice as if sitting by a honeymoon couple. "I'll get it." She went from the room again. James got up from the bed and went to the window. "Storm's blown out," he said casually. "I can see the stars. We get some great stars in this area, you know. Pretty as hell. Ah . . . and there's the lighthouse. Those poor bastards in the lighthouse. All the winter. Just like goddam prisoners." He only seemed to realise the significance of the remark when he left the window and looked at her still lying there. "Ha! I guess you know how they feel, Edith," he said. He went into the bathroom and she could hear him urinating forcefully. Candice returned with the coffee on a tray. She poured three cups. James came into the room with a towel about his middle and sat on the side of the bed.

"I'd like to cover myself up, if you don't mind," said Edith.

"Sure, go right ahead. Don't get cold," nodded Candice. She watched as the other woman pulled her nightdress over her shoulders. James drank his coffee. Edith took hers and drank it also. No one said anything until Edith pushed her ragged hair away from her forehead.

"Can I make a suggestion?" she began.

James glanced at Candice. Candice said, "Sure thing. Let's hear it."

"You said that we're all in this now," said the Englishwoman slowly,. "All in it together. There's no escape for any of us."

"That's how I see it," nodded Candice sagely.

Edith looked at her. "Well that's not strictly true, is it?" she began. "Four of us are deep in this matter. But not the two girls. I have an idea – a way out. It will help you to escape without anybody knowing any of this has gone on."

Candice regarded her steadily. She said, "If it lets us off the hook, we're interested." James said nothing. Edith looked to see if Candice was just playing another game. She could not tell.

"Say you just . . . dispose of me," said Edith. "You've had your bit of fun."

James snorted. "Great – that's what they call English under-statement."

"Cut it out, James," said Candice seriously. "I want to hear this."

Edith breathed deeply and continued. Her voice trembled. "You've done what you wanted to do. Now say you just . . . got shot of me. Simply made me vanish. You could take me out and throw me in the sea, couldn't you? That would be easy enough. I might even welcome it."

Candice put her hand on the other woman's wrist. "Go on, Edith," she said seriously. "I'm still with you."

"The girls know nothing of what's gone on," said Edith. "You leave them unharmed. I vanish. I can even leave a suicide note. My body is found floating. You can clear up the evidence here. And that's that. Nobody can blame you, and the girls are safe. They can go back to England. It's just another family tragedy. In time everybody will forget."

James sat staring at her with his coffee halfway to his lips. "She's crazy," he muttered. "Who ever heard of anything so crazy?"

"She's brave," said Candice. "Bravest woman I ever met. She dies, and we all go free as the birds. It's got its attractions, James."

"Can I have another fuck first?" grinned James.

Edith looked straight at them, then turned with pleading seriousness to Candice. "Please," she said. "Please, Candice." At that moment there came a terrified scream from beyond the room, along the corridor. Edith sat up violently in the bed, spilling the coffee over her nightdress.

"Abigail," she whispered in horror. "Abigail."

"Tommy!" snorted Candice. "God, that Tommy."

Edith tried to get from the bed but James pushed her back and held her. She had little strength left. She began to sob again. The scream was uttered again. Candice shook her head as though in sorrow. "There goes the big escape plan," she sighed.

Candice knocked firmly, but oddly politely, on the door. "Tommy, Tommy. What are you doing?" Her tone was soft, persuasive. "I hope you're not doing anything bad."

"Go away, Candice," Tommy called. "Just go away. Come back in three minutes. Just give me three minutes!"

He paused, poised above the girl, listening. An animal caught with its prey. There were no further words from outside the door. Abigail rolled her eyes uncomprehendingly.

"Don't worry about a thing," Tommy said to her, almost comically confiding. "Everything is going to be okay." At once he leaned into her and continued his gross assault. His hands held her slim wrists back against the bedsheet. He came to the conclusion with a schoolboy whoop, collapsing on top of her, his heavy body knocking the breath from her lungs. Now she was all but unconscious. "Great," he whispered. "Oh, that was just great. Wasn't it great, baby?"

His hands went to her breasts, this time tenderly and he stroked them. Her nightdress was half-draped around her, a remnant of pink nylon. He fingered it. "I guess we messed this up," he said. "I'll buy you another one. Honest I will."

There was a knock at the door again. "Three minutes," came the mocking voice of Candice. "Are you all through?"

100

"Hold it a minute," he called. His voice was sure. He withdrew his body from the girl's, and pulled the sheet up around her prostrate, naked frame. Then he went to the bathroom and wrapped a towel around his middle before going to the door. When he opened it Candice was standing there, grinning.

"Ain't nothing to laugh at, Candice," said Tommy. "Maybe you think it's real funny, but not me. I'm serious." Tears gathered in his dumb eyes again. "At last I had somebody to love me."

At four in the morning the wind still cuffed the walls of the Sweetwater Point Motel, but the storm was almost spent, the rain had ceased and stars and ragged clouds covered the Cape. Candice sat alone in the small room just off the lobby of the hotel. The place was silent. Edith Burrows and her daughter Abigail were in sedated sleep, lying alongside their jailers and tormentors, James and Tommy. The blonde girl drank her coffee reflectively. She was pondering the availability of evil.

It was there for all, the devil's own work. All that was needed was the opportunity. That night they had taken theirs. They had debauched and punished two innocent people. The third, the girl Kate, was now lying, as Candice was too well aware, in unknowing sleep at the end of the corridor. She looked at her watch, took the tiny silver spoon from her handbag, and sifted out a small heap of white cocaine from a plastic packet. She did not enjoy sniffing by herself but she did it now. She inhaled and felt it tingle inside her nostrils and around the foundations of her eyes. She always got high very quickly. She smiled at the sensation, like someone unused to alcohol who has become mildly drunk. Another pinch went on the spoon and she sniffed that into her head. The stimulant streamed through her head and her lungs, her stomach. It travelled fast and never failed to turn her on.

She rose carefully and went to the mirror as though she wanted to make sure she was looking right. Pulling her full blonde hair more tightly behind her ears, she wiped the lipstick from her mouth with a tissue. From her handbag she took a pair of precise gold-rimmed glasses in a mother-of-pearl case. She kept them in her hand as she left the room and went slowly down the corridor. At the far end was the room where the young girl slept deeply. Candice tiptoed past the other doors, smiling to herself because of her secret, and arrived at the final door. She was going to knock lightly, but she changed her mind. Instead she put the glasses on her nose in an almost schoolmistress fashion, turned the key in the lock and went into the dim room.

5

It took Burrows all night to drive from Rocky Mount, North Carolina, to Manteo on Roanoke Island. Although the countryside was flat as a pan, the roads were frequently narrow and the night was very dark with intermittent squalls. He drove through small towns where weary, solitary lamps glimmered. At one place he saw two men loitering beneath the overhung roof of a shuttered shop. He thought they might be burglars. There were dogs and cats about but little else. Once a cat appeared in front of the wheels and he swore at it, but hardly swerved. He told himself he was becoming a hard man. In the open country only an occasional light could be seen, like a firefly in the fields.

He realised by now that a fatigued mind was no instrument for making investigations. But as he drove into Manteo, in the opal dawn of another winter's day, he immediately saw a sign pointing down a side turning: "The Lost Colony. Roanoke Island." He turned the car so quickly the tyres squealed, and drove down the indicated way. The gates of the exhibition area were closed but a timetable, squinted at in the uncertain light, told him that opening time in January was nine o'clock. It was now seven-thirty. He returned to the car and turned it back towards Manteo.

An early-morning café was open, its windows steamy and almost obliterated by the back of a big truck parked outside. He pulled the car in behind the truck and walked in rubbing his chin. He needed a shave and he felt tired. A young woman, very bright considering the time of the morning, served him coffee and asked him how he would like his eggs done.

He replied: "Both sides." He was tempted to show her the

photographs of Edith and the girls. She must have been about Abigail's age. Had they been in that locale she might have noticed her. Girls often noticed others, particularly strangers, because of their clothes or their hair. He surprised himself by not producing the photographs and merely accepting the food and another cup of coffee with a tired acknowledgement.

"Been on the road all night?" asked the girl.

He said he had.

"You sure look it," she replied pausing to study him. "Where you from ?"

He wasn't sure whether she meant that night or previously. "England." She did not seem surprised. He thought he would try. "Do you get many English people in these parts?" he asked.

"Oh, England!" she exclaimed. "England. Not *New* England. Well, we have some – in the summer mostly. They come to see the Lost Colony."

"How can you see something that's lost?" He smiled. Indeed, he thought, how *could* you?

"I guess you're right there," she replied. There were only two other people in the place at that hour. She had time to talk. "All that's left there is the traces. Nothing much. You have to use your imagination."

You certainly do, he thought. He began to eat tiredly. Halfway through he idly wiped some of the steam from the window at his elbow. Immediately across the street was an office with the words "County Sheriff" on the window. Beneath it were the words; "Dare County. North Carolina."

He caught the eye of the waitress again. She smiled and went towards him. "This is called Dare County?" he said.

"Sure is. Dare County is Manteo, Raonoke Island, and right down what we call the Outer Banks, over on Cape Hatteras."

"Are you a waitress all the time?" he asked.

"Just now, that's right," she said. "I'm at college. But right now I need a job. So here I am, serving the eggs for Joey – that's my boss."

"Dare County," he repeated. He remembered his telephone call to Kate's school. "Dare. That was the surname of the Roanoke settlers, wasn't it? The people who vanished?"

"One family," she agreed. "Dare. They were the chief family. Virginia Dare was the first white child ever born in America.

They never discovered what happened to her. Some people say she was carried off and one day she became the bride of an Indian chief. But I guess that's just a story."

Burrows looked at his watch. "Is there somewhere I can have a wash?" he asked.

"Sure," she said. "In the back."

"Thank you," he said. He finished his eggs and then his coffee. She was still standing there. He put his hand into his jacket and produced the photographs. "I don't suppose," he said, "that you've ever seen any of these ladies, have you? During the past few weeks?" He handed the pictures to her. As though he needed to say it, he added, "I'm looking for them."

The girl looked at the photographs and shook her head. "Can't help, I'm afraid," she said. "I would have remembered. They're sure pretty."

Burrows was the first visitor at the Lost Colony that day. When he entered a girl in the brown uniform of the National Parks Service was sitting just inside the exhibition hall playing an Elizabethan harpsichord. She glanced up in surprise, played a final chord on the instrument and walked over to the ticket desk. "You're early," she said cheerfully.

He felt tempted to say "No. I'm too late." But he stopped himself. She looked at him a little unsurely. "Do you want to see around the Lost Colony?" she asked before pressing the ticket machine.

"I'd like to look around, certainly," answered Burrows. "But I wonder if you could give me some assistance?"

"You're from England," she smiled as though that made everything all right. "What can I do for you?"

He was getting so used to the routine now that his hand went automatically to the envelope. She looked a little alarmed as though she thought he might produce something unpleasant. He eased the photographs from the envelope. It was getting worn, he noticed. He would need to replace it soon.

"Have you," he said, "ever seen these three people? I think there's a good chance that they came in here to see the Lost Colony. Perhaps two weeks ago."

He watched her intently, as he had learned to do now, but the familiar disappointment was soon pricking him. She had never seen them. He could see that. She shook her head. "Sorry, but no," she said. "I think I would have noticed them."

"They're very noticeable," he agreed. And before she could say it, "The girls are very pretty."

She nodded. "That's just what I was going to say, but also they're English. I would have remembered three English people, certainly at this time of the year. We don't get that many visitors from there, and no way in January. I'm sorry."

He replaced the photographs, tearing the edge of the envelope as he did so. Now he would have to get another. She seemed concerned for him. She could see he was weary.

"Your wife and daughters?" she asked, sensing a story.

"No. But relatives. I seem to have lost . . . touch with them."

"We have other people on duty here," she said. "We take turns. Dennis was on holiday for the whole time since New Year. He's still away in Maine. But the others, Sue and Henry, they might have seen them. Sue's here now and Henry Ballard generally comes in later in the mornings. Hold on." She pressed a telephone button on the desk. It was immediately answered.

"Thank you," said Burrows.

"Sue," said the girl. "Just come through here for a moment, will you? There's a gentleman from England and he needs some help. Okay? Okay."

She replaced the receiver. "She'll be right here," she said. "Maybe she was on duty. You're pretty sure they would have come here?"

"Reasonably sure," he said. "They were driving from New York down to Charleston, South Carolina."

She thought about it. "It's a good distance off the route," she said. "Especially at this season."

"I know," he agreed with feeling. "I drove it last night."

"Ah, here she is," said the girl. Another young woman in the same brown uniform appeared. "Sue," said the first girl. "This is Mr.—"

"Burrows," he said.

"Mr. Burrows," she continued. "He has some pictures of three English women. Well, a woman and two daughters. He's looking for them and he believes there's a chance they may have visited the Colony during the first part of January."

Burrows was already taking the photographs out. He tore the

106

envelope irrevocably as he did so. He screwed it up and threw it in a wastebasket by the desk. "It may have been any time," he corrected. "Since January 10. Would you recognise them?"

She had never seen them. He could detect the expression easily now. "No, I'm sorry, sir," she said formally. "They didn't come to the Lost Colony while I was on duty. I would have recalled them, I'm sure. But there's also Henry – that's Mr. Ballard – he may have seen them. He'll be coming in later. It's his day off, but he usually drops by."

Burrows felt deflated. "I'll come back," he said wearily. "What time?"

"Make it eleven-thirty," suggested the first girl. "Once he gets here we'll stop him going anywhere else. Okay, Sue?"

"Sure thing," agreed Sue. She looked at Burrows. "Is this really a serious matter?" she asked. "Or are you just looking for them?"

He knew the difference. "It's serious," he said. "Well, I think it's serious. They've just vanished. They came on a visit to America and they've disappeared."

The young women glanced at each other. "That's terrible," whispered the first.

Sue said, "Have you been to see the Sheriff?"

"Not yet," Burrows answered. "But I think I will now. There's not much else I can think of."

Stray winter sunlight filtered bleakly through the windows of the Sherriff's Office. Burrows sat in an uncomfortable wooden chair. His bones ached against the arms and the back.

"Okay," nodded the man behind the desk. He got up and went to a map on the wall. It showed the entire length of Cape Hatteras from the uppermost village of Duck and its neighbour, Kitty Hawk, to Ocracoke in the south. The Sheriff was away. The man was one of his deputies. His name was Wheeler.

"Suppose we say they *did* get out here," he said. Burrows rose and went towards the map, peering at it closely as if he expected to see Edith and her daughters depicted on it. "We haven't any evidence that they did. All we're going on is your hunch, okay?"

"Okay," repeated Burrows. "My hunch, as you say."

"If they visited the Lost Colony – and nobody remembers seeing them–"

"There's Henry," put in Burrows firmly. "Henry Ballard. The man from the Parks Service who wasn't there this morning. He might have seen them."

"We'll check that out," said Wheeler. He glanced at Burrows. "We'll check everything out, I promise. Gas stations, hotels, motels. Anything we can do to help. This place is quiet right now so it won't take too long." He returned to the map. "All righty – let's say they came this way from Rocky Mount, North Carolina. After visiting the Lost Colony they either stayed in Manteo or Nags Head and then continued their trip. In that case we have three possibilities – they retraced their route, went back west and then took one of the roads south. In which case we aren't going to find them in Dare Country. If they went across the causeway to the Outer Banks, to the Cape, then they could only go north or south. Going north to Norfolk, Virginia, doesn't make sense. Not if they're still headed for Charleston – due south. If they went south there's just one road. Highway Twelve. That runs from one end of Cape Hatteras to the other. They would have had to take a free ferry across Hatteras Inlet to Ocracoke, and another ferry from Ocracoke back to the mainland."

Burrows looked at him hopefully. "Is the ferry used much this time of the year?" he inquired. "A ferry is the sort of place they might have been noticed."

Wheeler shrugged. "It's the only way out," he agreed. "In winter it's pretty well mostly local folks. Strangers might be noticed. It runs every hour during daylight." He looked thoughtful. "The other ferry, from Ocracoke – now that's something different. Every car is checked out of there. You have to make a reservation – buy a ticket – and the car number is recorded." He reached for the phone. "I can check that right now," he said. He asked for the number then turned to Burrows waiting with sudden new hope. "Like I say, the first ferry across Hatteras Inlet is a free service," he explained. "But the Ocracoke to the mainland takes nearly three hours and you have to pay." He turned his mouth back to the phone. "Hi," he said. "This is Deputy Wheeler at the Sheriff's Office, Manteo. How are ya? I'm fine, just fine. Listen, I have a gentleman from England here looking for some people. Relatives. Yeah, that's right. He has a theory they may have driven down to you sometime around January 10 or 11. Three females."

Burrows found himself again reacting at the law's official description of Edith Burrows and her daughters. "Right," went on Wheeler. "Edith Burrows, thirty-seven, and two young girls, one seventeen, the other a kid of twelve." Wheeler picked up the photographs which Burrows had handed to him earlier. "Real good lookers," he said. Burrows winced. "Driving a red, eighty-four Tempo, New Jersey plate number 345 PZY. Do you have any record of that vehicle riding on the ferry to the mainland? Okay, yes. You'll call me back – right. Thanks."

He replaced the phone. "It should only be a couple of minutes." He moved towards the map again. "*If* they didn't go back west before driving south and *if* they didn't get on the ferry from Ocracoke – then they must be somewhere here, along the Cape." Wheeler ran his finger down the map. "It's pretty difficult to hide on Cape Hatteras," he said. "Especially in winter when there's nobody around. It's a hundred miles long but narrow; you can just about spit from one side to the other. There's nowhere to hide, not unless somebody's hiding you."

Burrows followed the line of the islands to an elbow joint at Cape Hatteras itself, where the land jutted out into the ocean. "It's wider there," he pointed out.

Wheeler nodded. "Buxton and Frisco. It's a mile wide there. Real nice. They even got trees." He looked up and saw that Burrows was not interested in a travelogue. "But it's still no place for anybody to vanish." He leaned forward. "Listen, that car would have been spotted in a day, hours maybe."

"These villages," said Burrows, jabbing the map with his finger. "Frisco, Buxton, Avon, and these, Salvo, Waves, how many inhabitants have they got?"

"They ain't even villages," said Wheeler. "Just places. A few houses, most of them vacation houses. They're empty now. The Cape's no place for sunbathing in winter. We get some out-of-season fishermen here and some folks bringing boats down inside the Cape where it's sheltered; the Croaton Sound, the Roanoke Sound, and the Pamlico Sound. And some bird-watching buffs, but not a lot else."

The telephone rang. Burrows glanced expectantly. The deputy picked it up. "Sherriff's Office, Manteo," he said. "Deputy Wheeler." He listened. Burrows moved towards him unconsciously, trying to listen also. "No trace," muttered Wheeler.

"Not a thing." He looked up at Burrows then returned to the telephone. "There's no way a car could have gone to the mainland without being recorded and ticketed, is there? . . . No, none at all. I thought so. Right, thanks."

He placed the receiver on its cradle. "You heard," he shrugged. "They didn't go thataway."

Burrows sat down heavily. "You want some coffee?" asked Wheeler. He shook his head. "No thanks," he returned. They were always offering him coffee. "I think I'll go back to the Lost Colony. See if this chap Henry has arrived."

Wheeler nodded. He moved towards the door as if he would not be sorry when the Englishman went. "If he comes up with anything, if he remembers them, get over here right away."

"Yes, of course." Burrows got to the door. "Is there any chance that you people might search along the Cape?" he asked.

Wheeler looked amazed. "No chance," he said firmly. "Dr. Burrows, we don't *know* your people were ever within a couple of hundred miles of here. The chances are they weren't. And, in any case, we haven't got the facilities to search like that. The Cape is a hundred miles long. I told you."

"And you can spit from one side to the other," pointed out Burrows.

Wheeler looked annoyed. "Sure. But it's all swamp and lagoons and undergrowth. And deserted houses and motels and hamburger places. All empty. We just don't have the men. I'll ask the routine patrolman to keep a special lookout but over and above that—" He became suddenly more sympathetic. "I told you there's nowhere anybody could *hide*," he said. "But that doesn't mean they'd be easy to *find*. Does that make sense?"

"From your point of view, I suppose it does," said Burrows.

Wheeler opened the door for him and he went out into the street. "You'll see what I mean if you go across that causeway. You'll see what Cape Hatteras is like in winter."

"Listen, mister," said Henry Ballard. He leaned confidingly towards Burrows. "Are you going to be around town tonight?"

Burrows said, "Yes. I'll have to stay somewhere. I'll find a motel."

"Right. The Surf Beach is open. Not many motels open this time of the year."

110

"Thanks," said Burrows. "Why did you ask about tonight?" Ballard was a tall, lean man, riven with dark creases in his face and neck although he could only have been in his forties. His eyes were set back so deep they seemed to be peering from twin tunnels in his thin head. Burrows did not like him. He was languid and casually jokey. He said he had never seen Edith, Abigail, or Kate Burrows but he certainly would have liked to. Burrows put the pictures away quickly. He would have to get a new envelope.

"A few of the boys get together," said Henry. "For a little drinking. It don't make the winter seem so long, if you see what I mean. It's at Herbie's Fishing Tackle place, just along by the causeway. You'd be welcome."

Burrows was about to refuse when Henry said, "It's a good time. You'll enjoy it, mister."

"Are they fishermen and that sort?" asked Burrows on an abrupt thought. "Would they be people who might be familiar with Cape Hatteras?"

"Familiar? Familiar, you say? Wow, these guys know the Outer Banks like I know my own face. Every goddam wrinkle."

Burrows decided he liked him after all. He smiled and nodded. "All right," he agreed. "What time?"

"About nine," said Henry. He leaned closer. "We don't broadcast the information," he said. "Drinking don't go down too well in these parts. We have to keep it quiet. Okay?"

"Yes, all right," nodded Burrows. "Herbie's Fishing Tackle. It's not far, I take it."

"Nowhere's far," said Henry. "It's right on the water. You go to the beginning of the causeway and you see a track going down to the sound. Take that – Herbie's is right there. If I knew where you would be staying for sure, I'd drop by for you."

"Don't worry," said Burrows. "I'll find it. How about the drink? Do I bring a bottle?"

"It's there. At Herbie's," said Henry, secretively winking. "You pay for it there." He paused. "And don't mention it," he said. "To *nobody*."

Burrows left him and went out into the chill town. The small place was hardly moving. The thick rain had ceased, but there was a salty drizzle persisting. He purchased a map of Dare County, the Outer Banks, Cape Hatteras, as it was variously

111

called, then turned up the collar of his coat and went towards the place where he had parked the car that morning. It was two in the afternoon now and he realized he was hungry. The same café where he had eaten breakfast presented its steamy window along the street. He went in. It was just as empty. The same girl, the waitress, was reading a magazine against the lunch counter. She looked up and smiled.

"Have any luck?" she asked.

"No, nothing, I'm afraid."

"Oh, that's too bad."

"I'm getting used to it now," he shrugged. He glanced around. "Is it always as empty as this?"

"This time of the year we have to give the food away," she shrugged. "When you came in first today you got here in time for the morning lull, which is followed right away by the afternoon lull."

"Why keep open?"

"It's warm," she said as though it were as good an explanation as any. "Want to eat? I can get you a good hamburger. They're almost fresh."

Burrows took off his coat. "Good idea," he said. "I'm ready for an almost-fresh hamburger." He sat down at a table. She poured some coffee. "I suppose you don't mind coffee?" she asked, suddenly stopping. "Our tea wouldn't be like you have in England."

"Neither is your coffee – fortunately," he said. "What's your name?"

"Bonnie," she said good-humouredly. "Like all the other girls."

He nodded a smile. The warmth of the place and her cheerfulness made him feel more comfortable. She was busying herself with the hamburger. "What's yours?" she called from across the counter. "Your name?"

"Burrows. Philip Burrows." Then, without knowing why, he added, "I'm a doctor."

"You don't say. Like a doctor-doctor? A real one? Not one of these doctors of this and doctors of that."

"A real one. As far as any of us are real," he said.

"Right," she agreed. "But here in this country we have doctors of almost anything. There are people who just call themselves

112

doctors if they can read and write. You went over to the Sheriff's Office. I saw you from the window."

Burrows stirred the coffee thoughtfully. "To no great effect, I'm afraid," he admitted. "The deputy wasn't very encouraging."

"He didn't have any opinions?"

"Why should he?" sighed Burrows. "I haven't."

She returned with the hamburger and set it down before him with a salad and cole slaw. "Is that okay?" she said. "Or do you want French fries?"

"This is fine," he said. "Thank you, Bonnie."

He spread the map out on the unoccupied part of the table and surveyed it tiredly, the capes and causeways, the islands and inlets – a million hiding places.

Bonnie sat down opposite him and studied him intently. "You look like you could do with a month's sleep," she said frankly. "I hope that doesn't sound too personal, but you do."

"I could," he admitted. "It's difficult to sleep with this on your mind. I've thought of very little else for what seems a very long time. The three photographs I showed you this morning, they're my sister-in-law and her two daughters." He pushed his hand across the map. "They could be anywhere here."

Her eyes were fixed on his face. "You mean they've kind of vanished? It's not that they've just *gone* away?"

"They came from England at the beginning of the month, stayed in New York, and set out by hired car for Charleston, South Carolina. And they haven't been heard of since."

"Jesus," she said. "That's unbelievable. What makes you think they came here? This is way off the route."

"I have a feeling, a hunch," he said. "I think they may have wanted to visit the Lost Colony. But no one there remembers them."

"If there's anything I can do, just mention it," she said genuinely.

"Thank you, Bonnie," he said. He lowered a forkful of hamburger back onto the plate. "That's very friendly of you."

"You seem like you need a friend," she said.

The air became still and cold when the rain ceased that evening, Burrows drove the Aspen to the beginning of the causeway that

113

crossed from Roanoke Island to the black arm of Cape Hatteras. He left the car there and went, as Henry had directed, towards a dirt path that led down to the water's edge. A single, swinging lamp illuminated the entrance to the track. The causeway stretched out, deserted as a disused runway, towards a ragged collection of lights at Nags Head on the Cape. The wind was noisy over the sound.

Burrows had rested, bathed, shaved, and eaten an evening meal at the motel. But he felt uneasy as he went down the steep track to the waterside, a disquiet he could not explain. So a group of local men got together for a few drinks on a night in winter. What could be more ordinary than that? He found Herbie's Fishing Tackle shop easily because there were lights on in the place. But the door was locked. He hesitated, then knocked. Henry Ballard himself came to answer.

"Oh boy, you're here!" Henry exclaimed as if it were some miracle. Burrows guessed that Henry was in his best clothes. He was shining and shaved also, the lights of the place burnishing his prominent chin. Burrows went in as he opened the door wider. There were about fifteen men present, half a dozen of them only teenagers. They sat around a little self-consciously, drinking, as though waiting for something else to happen. There were tables and chairs, apparently brought out especially for the occasion. Displays of fishing equipment and several bulky outboard engines had been pushed back against the walls to make room for the tables. It seemed to Burrows an elaborate arrangement just for the sake of having a drink.

Henry and a cubic man wearing a heavy checked shirt dispensed the drinks, walking around with bottles filling glasses. Henry told Burrows he would have to pay ten dollars. Burrows took the bills from his wallet and put them into the cubic man's spreadeagled hand. They called the man Bern. He had a wide head and an expressionless face. He poured whisky into a glass and gave it to Burrows.

Burrows took a drink. It was rye. Its taste surprised him but he did not dislike it. He looked around the room. He was at a table alone but Henry had pulled back another chair at the same table indicating that he would be sitting there during the times when he was not circulating with the bottle. The sense of formality in the room amused Burrows. There was only minor talk and no raised voices. It was just men sitting heavily at tables and drinking ponderously.

Henry returned and sat beside him. He poured himself a generous measure and drank it at one swallow, refilling the glass for more leisurely consumption.

"Is this it then?" inquired Burrows. "I mean is this all that you do? Just come down here and drink?"

Henry's toothy smile almost severed his thin head. "Weeeel, we take a little drink," he said. "We pass around a little gossip, make a few jokes." He paused. "And later on we have something else. You'll see."

The promise made Burrows' unease return. "Something else?" he asked. "What's the something else?"

"Stick around," promised Henry. "You'll see. I like the look of you, mister. I guessed you'd like to come down here for one of our nights."

"As long as I don't have to sing," ventured Burrows.

"Oh you won't have to do that," Henry assured him seriously. "Ain't no singing to be done."

"Could you show some of these men the photographs?" suggested Burrows. He thought he had better ask before too much rye had gone from the bottles. "The photographs of my sister-in-law and my two nieces," he reminded the man. "The ones I showed to you this afternoon."

Henry slapped his own thin thigh slowly. "Ah, those photographs. Sure, sure," enthused Henry. "Sure the guys would like to see them. Pass them around. But give it time, mister, give it a little time." He poured another measure into Burrows' glass. Burrows sipped it cautiously.

The drinking continued seriously for another half hour. Burrows began to feel the rye going to his head. The talk seemed to be getting louder. A man in the far corner began to play a piano accordion. There was smoke in the room and the smell of the whisky became heavier, but for all that, the evening at Herbie's Fishing Tackle Place had a creaky, old-fashioned sense about it, like a Victorian social. Henry was going around with the bottle again. He saw a movement from the shadows as a second door opened. It was Wheeler, the Sherrif's deputy. He was out of uniform, wearing a heavy fishing jacket. Henry walked over, grinned in the semi-dark and poured him a drink. Burrows stood up shakily and – hardly aware of his actions – he took the photographs from his pocket and went to the middle of the open space in the centre of the room. "Gentlemen," he said. He thought he was holding his speech steady but he felt foggy in the head. The talk ceased immediately and, as if they had been awaiting him, every face was turned on him. The effect was again unsettling. Burrows reached into his pocket. He thought Henry was going to move towards him from the back of the room but apparently thought the better of it because he set his bottle down on a table and leaned against the wall.

"Gentlemen," repeated Burrows. "I want to show you some pictures."

He thought there was some interest. Some men in the front leaned forward in an attempt to glance at the photographs in his hand. He continued: "I have come from England to look for . . . to search . . . for three women."

There was definite reaction to that. One youth at the back of the room emitted a wolfish whoop. Burrows glanced up in embarrassment. "No – it's a bit more serious than that," he explained. "I heard, from our friend Henry, that you know these parts well, especially along the Outer Banks, and I have reason to believe that these ladies, well, an adult woman and two young girls, might be in this district – somewhere. They were in a red Tempo–"

To his amazement one of the men leaning forward in the front row put out his hand and snatched the photographs from him. Not forcibly but firmly. Burrows moved forward. "No – just a moment – I don't have any copies–"

But as if it were some novel game, the men began passing the pictures among themselves. They were soon separated and being circulated in three different parts of the room at once. Burrows pushed his way through the men at the front in an effort to retrieve them. He was rapidly getting angry. The photographs were causing great excitement, wolf whistles and rural whoops. Burrows tried to get one from the hand of a short youth who immediately gave it to a tall man who held it above his head and looked up to view it. "Mister," said Burrows, pushing his way forward. "Would you mind?"

The tall man glanced at him unpleasantly. "I want the picture back," said Burrows evenly. The attention of the room became

116

polarised on them. Somebody laughed but after that, silence settled. "I said I want it back," repeated Burrows. "Now." The man examined the photograph above his head like somebody checking an X ray. Burrows could see it was the photo of Kate. "I tell you somethin'," the man said in a strange high voice. "I would sure like to put my prick into this little rabbit!" There were whoops and howls from all over the room and a scramble to get at the photograph. Burrows at first found himself pushed in the upheaval, but blind fury suddenly seized him and he began throwing men aside, grasping one by the shoulders and thrusting him to the right, shoving two others violently into a table on the left. The table tipped, taking with it the glasses of men sitting there. The howls were filling Burrows' ears. His mouth was agape with fury, his eyes closed to slits. The tall man was still holding the picture above his head tauntingly. He looked very ugly laughing. Burrows hit him with his right fist full on the jaw. He had never hit a man in his life before. The man went over a table in a loop like an eel. Someone grasped Burrows from behind. He shook them off powerfully and went over the wrecked table to retrieve the photograph of Kate. Forcing three or four men aside, he reached the prostrate tall man and took the precious photograph of Kate from his hand. That was all he remembered before a bottle descended on the back of his head.

Burrows felt as though a dull, painful wind was blowing through his brain. He opened his eyes. He was in the Sheriff's Office in Manteo, stretched on a table in one corner. The bars of the single cell were directly ahead of him and for the first moment he thought he might actually be on the wrong side of them. But he wasn't. The deputy, Wheeler, was sitting at the desk. It was dark outside and the light from the desk lamp shone down on some work he was doing. He turned when he heard Burrows stir. Burrows tried to sit up and then felt the concentrated pain at the tail of his scalp. His hand went to the place.

"That was a bottle," mentioned Wheeler.

"Full or empty?" asked Burrows, making himself sit up.

"Don't know. It broke on impact. Jesus, you're looking for trouble, mister, and you're sure finding it."

Burrows remembered the photographs. "What happened to my pictures?" he asked hastily. "You know–"

117

"I have them here," Wheeler assured him. He rose from the desk and took the three photographs from an envelope. He replaced them and returned them to Burrows. "Want some coffee?" he asked.

"Yes, that's just what I do need at the moment. I take it I was rescued by the forces of the law. God, my head. Have I any stitches?"

"Nope. There was only one doctor around at the time and that was you. And you were in no shape to do anything." He brought a paper container of coffee to Burrows. "We had the place under surveillance, Herbie's Fishing Tackle," he said. Burrows drank at the coffee gratefully and Wheeler returned to the desk.

"Thanks for rescuing the photographs," said Burrows. "God knows what I'd have done without them."

"Maybe you would have quit," sighed Wheeler. He had gone back to looking at the papers on his desk. "And that might have been a good thing. You got in some trouble at Silver Spring, didn't you? We got a circulated police report on that. And now this."

"I thought those men at Herbie's might have seen my sister-in-law and the girls," grunted Burrows. "They were supposed to be fishermen and suchlike along the Cape."

"So they are," said Wheeler. "Just that. But they get together down at Herbie's place to drink and they show skin flicks, pornographic movies."

Burrows was amazed. "So that was it. I thought they didn't just go there for a quiet piss-up. Sexy films – who would have thought it?"

"That's why we had the place under observation, luckily for you," said Wheeler. "Otherwise you might have been food for the fishes in Roanoke Sound."

"Is that the sort of thing that happens around here?"

"Not regularly, but it could."

Burrows ruminated as he drained the coffee. "Dirty films," he mused. "And I thought it was all the call of the wild goose and the lonely sea and the sky."

"People like dirty films," shrugged Wheeler. "It helps to pass the winter." He paused. "I'd appreciate it, mister, if you'd start heading west," he said heavily. "There's *no* evidence at all that

118

your people ever came out to Dare County. You have a strange habit of disturbing the peace."

"Especially my own," grumbled Burrows feeling his head. "Can I go now? I'm not under arrest or anything am I?"

"You can go," sighed Wheeler. "In fact I wish you would." He rose from the desk as though he thought Burrows might need some help to the door. "You haven't – arrested or charged anybody with this, have you?" Burrows inquired holding his head. "I wouldn't like–"

"We wouldn't be releasing you if we had," said Wheeler. "Ten men claimed the credit, and we couldn't make up our minds. Nobody's been charged."

"Good. I see. Well, I'll be going then."

"You'll be going back to the motel, I guess?"

"Yes, I think I'd like to have some sleep. Rest this a bit before . . ."

"Before what? Start looking for those women again?"

"That's why I came to America."

"Well, do it somewhere else," said Wheeler ill-temperedly, opening the door. The cold early air came sharply into the office. "Try Colorado."

Burrows went into the hollow street. The early morning sky was hardly pale. He looked at his watch. It was seven-thirty. He had been there twenty-four hours. It seemed like years. Across the street the lights oozed from Joey's café where the girl, Bonnie, worked. He crossed the empty highway and went in. The scene was as it had been when he had first entered. Bonnie came toward him as he walked in the door. "Shit," she said as she saw him.

He moved towards a chair and sat down. "Shit indeed," he agreed. He looked at her. Her face was different.

"I've got something," she said excitedly.

A stab went through him. "What?" he asked. "What is it?"

"I've got a friend who's seen them," she said.

Mary Dodson was twenty-three, a small girl with thick glasses and a lonely life. She shared a room with Bonnie. When Burrows arrived at the house, it was seven-forty-five and she was in pyjamas. She hung a faded patchwork robe about herself and stared with her riveting squint at him.

119

"They certainly came to the Lost Colony," she said firmly.

Burrows sat down slowly in the kitchen and stared at her as though she were a beautiful vision. He touched her hand. The girl was excited by the situation. "You see, sir, I work for the National Parks Service. At Kitty Hawk, at the Wright Brothers exhibit. But on this day I was at the Lost Colony because they were one short on their duty roster. Somebody was away. I was only there for one day and I remember your English lady and the two girls."

He could hardly breathe. "Go on," he whispered. "All you remember."

"That's it really, I guess," she shrugged. "They came in just about one o'clock, maybe a little later. I'd just gotten back from lunch. We didn't have too many people that day and I remember them well."

"Which day was that? Which date?"

"That's easy. January 11. It was the only day I was at the Lost Colony. When Bonnie told me last night about your being here searching for them, I recalled right away. We went straight away over to your motel, but you'd just left and nobody knew where you'd gone." She tapped the photographs with her fingers. "But that's them okay, sure as sure."

Burrows couldn't help it. He stood up and put his arms around her. She stared at him through her glasses. "It means a lot?" she said.

"They're not just lost, they're *missing*," he explained. "Somebody is *keeping* them. And I think they're not very far from here." He released her and sat down in the chair. His head pounded as though it were under a hammer. "Unless they're food for the fishes in Roanoke Sound."

Burrows almost tugged the girl across the street. He went into the Sheriff's Office. Wheeler stood up sharply behind his desk.

"I've got a witness," said Burrows triumphantly.

Wheeler sat down heavily. He looked with a narrow expression at the girl. "She's your witness?" he said caustically.

"She's not my grandmother."

"Okay, let's hear it."

Burrows looked at Mary. She was flushed with nervousness. Her eyes flickered behind her glasses. She reported what she had

120

told Burrows. Wheeler sat back wryly.

"So you saw them?"

"I saw them."

"Wearing those glasses?"

Mary looked at Burrows through the thick lenses before returning to Wheeler. "I always wear them."

"I remember," said Wheeler quizzically. "And your eyesight is good when you're wearing them?"

Burrows saw the girl check. She knew something and Wheeler knew it too. "Most of the time," she stammered.

"You're Mary . . . "

"Dodson," said the girl hurriedly.

"Mary Dodson, right," said Wheeler. "I seem to recall that last summer you were requested to recognize somebody, a suspect in a robbery, okay?"

Mary dropped her chin. "Okay," she said.

"And you couldn't because you couldn't guarantee recognising the man with those glasses. Right?"

"Right," she whispered. She looked up. "But this time–"

Wheeler ignored her. He swung around. "Okay, Burrows," he said. "Let's say we suppose–"

"Doctor Burrows," put in the Englishman.

"Okay, *Doctor* Burrows," said Wheeler, only a little ruffled. "Even if these people came here and were recognised by this young lady, who's all of a sudden able to see real good, who's to know where they went then? I'd say they headed back inland and then went down to Charleston. Logically."

"You won't institute a search?"

"Jesus Christ, I *told* you. We haven't got the men to turn over every blade of goddam grass in Dare County. I'd have to have better reasons than this." He thrust his head towards Mary. "A notoriously unreliable witness. Get her to tell you about that." Burrows said nothing. Wheeler continued in an official voice, "The normal patrols will be told to look out."

Burrows stood firm. "Is there a Sheriff?" he asked doggedly. "I'd like to see him."

"On leave," sighed Wheeler. "He's gone hunting."

"Sounds as though he'd be useful back here," grunted Burrows. Wheeler, he could see, had heard enough. The deputy stood up. "Half the staff are on leave," he said. "It's supposed to be the quiet end of the year. I just have enough men for normal duties."

"Like watching pornographic films," suggested Burrows.

"Blow," said Wheeler angrily. He moved quickly to the door and opened it. "Just blow, mister."

"Doctor," corrected Burrows again as he and the girl went into the street. He turned. Wheeler was still glowering. "See you at Herbie's," said Burrows.

An answering service picked up the call when Burrows rang Charleston. He was referred to another number. He called that.

"Oh, hello, Dr. Burrows," a woman's voice replied. "Mr. Curtis said you might call sometime. I'm his secretary."

"I'm just checking," said Burrows. "To see if he's had any news of Edith and the girls."

"Not a thing," she said. "He's out of town right now."

"Is Adele, Mrs. Curtis, around?"

The pause was almost imperceptible. "No, Mrs. Curtis has gone to Chicago to visit with her parents."

"I see."

"Is there a message you'd like to leave?" she said. Her tone had not changed throughout the conversation. He wondered if this was the secretary with whom Andy had become involved. "Nothing," he said. "Just tell them, him – tell him I'm still looking."

He was in his motel room. He shrugged to himself and began to zip his case. A knock came on the door and he opened it. It was Bonnie.

"Too bad about Mary," she said, walking into the room. "That Wheeler's a shitty guy."

"He tries hard to be," Burrows replied.

"There was this guy," she said awkwardly as if explaining something difficult. "He was in trouble but Mary didn't want to have to recognise him. It was last summer."

"Wheeler recognised *her*," said Burrows. "He's very efficient when it suits him."

She looked at the case. "She certainly saw them," she said reflectively. "She's sure. After the Lost Colony, I wonder what they did?"

Burrows smiled grimly. He looked around the room to make

sure he had left nothing. *What Katy did Next,* he recited. "That's the title of a favourite girls' book in England."

Bonnie smiled at him oddly. "I was raised on *True Confessions,*" she said. "My mother's favourite literature." She walked towards the room door with him. "You – you'll go over to the Cape now?" she asked. "And you'll start looking?"

"That's what I plan to do," he nodded. "Deputy Wheeler can get stuffed."

They reached the door. The chill early air came in like a knife as he opened it. The girl reached up and, to his surprise, kissed him on the cheek. "If you need any help," she said, "you know where to find me. Joey's. Anything."

Burrows looked at her gratefully. "You've been very kind, Bonnie," he said inadequately. "If I need anything, I'll know. It may only be a hamburger, but I'll know where to come."

He hesitated, then returned her kiss, lightly on her cheek, and went out into the morning gloom. The motel had required payment for the room before he moved in, so there was nothing to settle. His car, dripping with moisture, stood with two others in the driveway. A greasy light came from the motel foyer. From somewhere across the distance, morning geese began to honk.

"I think they're calling me," mentioned Burrows wryly. He touched his head. It was throbbing. He kissed the girl again, lightly, and got into the car. "I'll drop you off," he said.

She nodded and got in beside him. They drove in silence towards the reluctantly stirring town. Outside Joey's Café he stopped to let her out. "Don't forget, if you need me – just call," she said as she got out.

"I will," he said. "I promise. What's the phone number here?"

Bonnie went quickly into the café and came out with a piece torn from the top of the menu. "That's it," she said pointing to the number. "I don't have a telephone at my rooming house. Not that I can use. But you can get me here. I don't go many other places."

"Right," he said glancing at the number. "I'll phone you anyway in a few days, Bonnie, or when anything turns up. Just to let you know."

"Thanks," she said. Their hands touched briefly, without emphasis, and she turned and went towards the lit door. He

123

turned the car in the empty street and headed towards the causeway and Cape Hatteras.

The fuel was low. He wondered how many petrol stations there were on the remote Outer Banks. As if resulting from his thoughts, the yellow fist of Shell came into view as he approached the causeway. He drove in. A boy about twelve came from the cabin and unhooked the arm of the pump. He was small and the nozzle was heavy for him, but he got it to the car and inserted it into the petrol tank.

"Going to school today?" said Burrows, just to say something.

"Sure," answered the boy. "There's no way I can't."

"Where do you go?"

"Manteo," sniffed the boy. "Man, I hate it."

"How often do you work here?"

"All the time. My pa runs this place."

Burrows took the three photographs from the envelope. "Ever see these ladies?" he asked. "Well, a lady and two girls."

The boy gave them a single glance. "Sure," he sniffed. "They were here. I gave them some gas."

Sudden fingers of excitement closed around Burrows' heart. "You remember?" he said quietly.

"Sure I remember," said the boy. "They came from England. They had voices like you hear sometimes on TV. Like your voice. They told me they came from England. The lady, the mother, gave me fifty cents. I remember them okay."

Burrows glanced towards the cabin and the office. "Did your father see them?" he asked.

"Nope. I saw them."

"When? Can you remember when?"

The boy shrugged. The tank was full. He withdrew the nozzle and humped it back to the pump. "That's fifteen dollars," he said. "It's getting expensive, this stuff."

Almost in a daze Burrows paid him. He gave him an extra dollar. The boy grinned his pleasure. "I don't remember the days," he said. "They get kinda mixed up, you know."

"A week ago, two weeks ago?" prompted Burrows.

"I don't know, mister. One day is just like another day to me. Except some you go to school and some you don't."

"Listen," said Burrows. "This is important. It really is. When

124

they left here, which way did they go? Straight over the causeway to the Cape?"

The boy nodded. "That's where they were headed when they came in for the gas," he said decidedly. "And that's the way they headed after I gave them the gas. They went straight over. It was a red Tempo. I remember. There was a big storm coming up."

6

"I've come for you again," he said.

"I can see."

"I just suddenly got an appetite."

Edith looked steadily at James from the bed. "This is the fifth time."

"So, who's counting?" He walked from the door.

"I am. I'm counting."

"Listen, lady, you're just lucky I'm a young guy who likes older women. Why not open up and enjoy it?"

"With you!" she laughed icily. "You do it like a mouse. My husband could satisfy me – and another . . . "

He slapped her across the face and she cried out.

"Forget it," he said. "I'm not around to give you satisfaction. It's fun for me."

"When will I see my girls, my daughters?"

"They're okay. Real fine. Maybe tonight. I've got a great idea. We'll all dine together, have some wine, some good conversation. Maybe some dancing. I'd like to dance with you."

"What's happening to them?"

"Well, that jerk Tommy thinks he's in love. With the older one. Kisses her. All that crap."

She closed her eyes so that he would not see the tears but they leaked onto her cheeks anyway. "You foul, foul bastards," she whispered. It was so soft it came out like an endearment.

"And the other," he said slowly, because she had not dared ask. "She's something else. Real cute, that Katy. How old is she?"

She would not answer. He knew. He said, "Twelve years old. Candy likes her. She really does. Young girls turn her on so."

The woman lifted her head, gathered the saliva in her mouth, and spat furiously in his face. He wiped it away. "Don't do that any more," he said. "If you do, little Katy will get the blame. Okay?"

She said nothing. Her face was stiff with hate.

"Okay," he said. "Now turn over, lady. I want your ass."

She obeyed. The pillow beneath her face was quickly wet with her tears. She lay against it sobbing. "Have you no humanity at all?" The words tumbled out.

"I ain't got no time for it," he said, still lying heavily on her back and close to her ear. "I ain't got time for very much, Edith. Maybe you haven't given it a thought but there's no way out of this for me, either."

It took three minutes. Then he pulled himself from her careful-ly, almost gently. He patted her buttocks. "A great ass," he murmured as if to himself. "A real great ass." He walked to the bathroom. Edith remained on the bed. She could feel the sweat turning chilly on her. She opened her eyes and looked towards the bathroom where he was running the water. "If it were not for my girls," she said softly but so that he could hear, "I would kill myself."

"Don't you worry about that, Edith," he said quizzically. He appeared around the bathroom door and grinned in at her. "That little Katy," he gave a low whistle. "Now there's a sweet little ass for you. Like a pretty little apple."

Edith jumped from the bed and stumbled towards him, her bruised body streaming, her eyes bright with hate. "You! You deranged bastard!" Her fingers were clawing towards his face. He whooped like a college boy and closed the door just as she reached it. She could hear him laughing on the other side. "Wow, Edith. Like a tiger!" He laughed uproariously again. "Just like a fucking tiger. Okay, okay, I surrender."

She retreated to the bed and sat down, head bowed, her arms hugged across her own chest. There was a polite knock on the door and it opened. Tommy came in, a look of real concern on his dumb face. Her expression faltered but he approached her with-out malice.

"What's been going on?" he asked stupidly. "Is it that guy?"

127

Edith was beyond speech.

"James," Tommy called toward the bathroom door, "knock it off, will ya?"

The door opened and James's face, now serious, peered around it. "Knock what off?" he asked. "What do I have to knock off?"

Tommy's bravado immediately evaporated. "Candice wants you," he said lamely. "She wants to talk to you."

James went back into the bathroom and returned at once wearing a robe. He walked towards Edith, picked up her limp hand, and kissed it extravagantly. "Tonight, lady," he said. "We're all going to dine. At home, of course. Get to know each other a little better. See you then."

Tommy watched him go. Edith merely stared at the floor. "I hate that guy," muttered Tommy. "Jesus, how I hate him!" He glanced at her, then went over to a chair in the corner and picked up her robe. He walked over and handed it to her. At first she did not react, but slowly she looked up at him, a little smile touching her lips. "You really hate him?" she said. She took the dressing gown from him and put it around herself. Tommy hesitated, then helped her with it.

"Sure I do," he replied. "I hate the goddam bastard. He thinks I'm dumb but I ain't so dumb. Not like he thinks." He looked at her sorrowfully before sitting heavily on the bed. "To tell the truth, Edith, Mrs. Burrows, I'd give anything in this goddam world, anything, I mean it, to make all this . . . well, you know, kind of unhappen. You know, turn back the clocks, like they say. So that none of it happened. I've done terrible things and I guess I deserve all that's coming to me. But that daughter of yours, that Abigail. It's crazy, I know, after all that's happened. But I'm crazy about her. I love her. Goddam it I do. I can *talk* to her."

Edith forced her disgust down. "You didn't hurt her?" she said. "You didn't, did you, Tommy?"

"No, no," he stumbled. "I couldn't hurt any girl like that. I was crazy at first, crazy. Maybe then I didn't know what I was doing. I've got problems, you understand, Mrs. Burrows."

"I remember you telling me," she said calmly. She was desperately trying to act it out now. "You've been led astray, Tommy, that's all," she said.

They said nothing for a few moments. Then she rose. "I've got to have a bath," she said.

128

"I'll be going then," he muttered. "But – don't worry – everything will be okay . . . in the end."

He laid his hand on the satin material of her robe, near her breast. She caught her breath, thinking it was going to happen again. But all she saw in those pathetically sore eyes was sadness. "Will you do just one thing for me?" he asked quietly. "Just one little thing?"

"What is it, Tommy?"

"Will you kiss me? Like real. You know . . . in a real way."

She glanced towards the door. "Shut the door," she whispered.

He grinned foolishly and pushed the door closed. Then he walked towards her and stood awkwardly in front of her: "Now," he said, "will you, Mrs. Burrows?"

She put the soft arms of her robe around his coarse body and eased him to her. His breath smelled as well. She kissed him full and tenderly on the thick lips, withdrew a little and kissed him again. His thick arms went around her and he hugged her fiercely.

"Not *Mrs. Burrows*, Tommy," she said. "Edith. It's Edith."

Candice knocked lightly on Kate's door and went in. The girl was standing on the far side of the bed. Her face tightened at once as Candice moved towards her. Her hands were gripping each other behind her back.

"Now that looks really beautiful," enthused the American, stopping and running her eyes down the blue dress the girl was wearing. "Those clothes from England sure have something about them." She advanced around the bed and knelt by the side of the girl as a mother might. Her hands went below the skirt. "Let's get this underskirt fixed," she murmured. "I don't think you have it quite right."

Katy tried to back away. Candice held her knee strongly. "I put it on right," said the young girl. "I did."

"It's not right, Katy," Candice replied firmly. She manoeuvred the garment with her fingers, still holding the girl's leg.

Kate's eyes were full of fear. Candice let her go and sat up on the bed. "Now look here, young lady," she said, her voice and expression hard. "It's no good you backing off and getting all coltish. Nobody's going to hurt you."

"Am I going to see my mother and my sister today?" asked the girl. "You said I would."

"Sure. That's why we want you looking real nice and pretty. We're all going to have dinner together. You and Abigail and your mother. And Tommy and James and me. It'll be cosy."

The girl stared at her. "Is my mother still alive?" she asked bluntly.

Candice appeared shocked. "Alive! Alive! Well, of course she's alive! What sort of thing is that to say? And you'll be seeing her in no time. No time at all. Okay? That's a promise."

Candice, all at once tense, sat on the bed staring in front of her as though in shock. Her expression unchanged, she spread her hands and smoothed them up the girl's calves, the backs of her knees and her thighs, until they rested on the small buttocks. Like a fainting lover she leaned forward and rested her fair hair against the belly beneath the dress. "You're so beautiful, Katy," she said. "So beautiful. Just put your hands on the back of my neck, baby, just at the back. Katy, do as I say. . . . That's right. You're a lovely kid. Now just rub it softly . . . okay. Gee, that's so good."

The woman began muttering like a prayer: "God, oh Christ and God." She looked up. Katy was staring straight ahead, tears coursing down her pale cheeks. Candice released her.

"Baby, I'm so sorry," she whispered. "It's just I'm so weak when it comes to you."

She straightened up with an apparent effort. Her voice straightened too; she smoothed the girl's dress. "Pretty," she said, "real pretty. Now you're all fixed for the party."

"That's a very nice dress, Abigail," said Tommy. He sat stupidly on the end of the bed in her room. She looked at him with dumb sullenness. "I'd really like to take you out somewhere in that dress," he said. "Just to show you off. Just to walk out with you. Jesus, that would show them. All those fucking girls in these parts. Wow, would you be a sensation."

"Am I really going to see my mother and Katy?" asked the girl. "Or is this another of your games?"

Tommy looked perplexed. "Games? What d'you mean by that? We ain't playing a game, Abigail. We're all in this for real now."

"I know that very well," she returned evenly. "You'll all pay for it too. You just see."

"I guess we will," he admitted dolefully. "Ain't never was nothing as bad as this went without punishment." He looked up at her, his face screwed up with sincerity. "But don't you worry, you're going to see your mum and your little sister today. And don't worry neither about other things. Because I'll see they don't get away with it. I promised your mother."

Abigail had turned her back to him. She kept her face away and carefully thought about what he had just said. Eventually she said, "What did you promise my mother?" She added, as she turned around, "Tommy?"

"These two are shit," he said, dropping his voice with childish drama. "Real, 100 percent shit, James and Candice. But *I* ain't. I was okay before I got mixed up with them. Them and their coke. Yuk, that stuff makes your eyes run. That's why my eyes got so sore, you know, not for any other reason. It's that fucking coke."

Abigail tried smiling at him. "I thought you said you didn't sniff it," she said. "You wouldn't take that sort of thing."

He shrugged what he hoped would be a manly gesture. "I do it to go along with them," he said. "But I ain't hooked on no drugs. Not me. I was raised out here on the Cape. We didn't know anything about these kinda things before these smart-assed people came down. I even used to go fishing, you know. Once, off Salvo, I caught a great goddam fish – a marlin. Just off the beach. I guess I should have stayed with fishing. I could have been really someone at fishing."

"Where's Salvo?" she asked cagily. "Is that near here?"

"Salvo? Oh it's just a place. Just a few houses and a beach. Not many people there in the winter. But in the summer there's quite a few. The girls used to go down to the beach there to swim. I heard that they used to go down naked and swim, but I never saw any like that. Not naked. You know, you may not believe this, and I don't blame you, I don't blame you at all, but you're the first girl I've seen naked, without any clothes at all. I mean except in books and things. I've seen those, and films. Sometimes they show skin-flicks, you know porno movies, over at Manteo, at Herbie's Fishing Tackle place. Not when it's open, of course. At night. I got in there once. Wow, you should see what I saw."

131

Abigail sat carefully on the bed beside him. "I'm the first one?" she said. "Nobody else?"

"Nobody," he confirmed, looking at her seriously. "No girls. I mean, well, I peeped in at my mum once when she was getting out of the tub, but that wasn't no great thrill. No, Abigail, nobody else."

She touched his hand lightly. "I feel very sorry for you, really, Tommy," she said. "I'm beginning to understand."

"I'm feeling very sorry for myself," he said, his head dropping. "I don't see any way out of this for me. Not from this."

She let the incongruity of the remark go without comment. "How far is Manteo?" she said. She tried a small laugh. "I haven't got any idea where we are, you know. No idea at all."

He looked at her seriously. "I mustn't tell you," he said, lowering his voice. "They'd kill me, James and Candice. They would, Abigail. Kill me. You're not supposed to know. Although I don't know what goddam difference it makes. Not now."

They sat side by side for a silent minute. "I feel very sorry for you," she repeated. "I've had such a lot of fun in my life and I'm only seventeen now. We have such a good time in England."

"I'd like to visit there," he said. "England. Sounds great. Can I ask you something about England?"

"Yes, anything, Tommy."

"Do you personally have men there? Like boyfriends?"

"Of course, I do. I'd be very strange if I didn't."

He looked miserable. "Everybody has a good time but me," he complained. "Even around these parts. Still, being a girl and looking like you, I guess you would." He studied the carpet. "Do you let them . . . well . . . play around?"

"Now that would be telling, wouldn't it?"

Childishly he sulked and said, "If you tell me, I'll tell you something."

Abigail forced a smile. "All right. That's fair. Yes, I let the boys play around a bit. But only so far, no further."

"Nobody's got as far as I did, then. I figured that out for myself."

She didn't answer. She thought she was going to be sick but she stemmed the sensation. "Now what were you going to tell me?" she asked quietly.

"You mustn't tell nobody and I mean nobody. Promise?"

"I promise, Tommy."

"Your mother, Edith . . . "

Abigail looked alarmed. "Yes, what?"

"She kissed me. I mean, really and truly kissed me. Without even me asking, or making her, or anything. She just came up and kissed me. On the lips."

Abigail swallowed. "She always did like young men," she said eventually, steadily. She formed a deliberate smile. "But I like you too. I can see that you're different. And, as you say, we're in this together. We need each other, perhaps, Tommy."

"Abigail," he said. "Would you take off your clothes for me? So you're naked?"

Frightened again, she stammered. "But you've seen me, everything."

"But I want *you* to do it," he mumbled. "Without any rough stuff. I don't care for that rough stuff, honest. Will you?"

She forced her laugh again. "But I've just got all dressed," she said. "All ready for this dinner we're going to have."

"I know, but it won't take long. I don't want anything else. Nothing at all. I won't touch you. I just want to look."

"Lock the door, Tommy," she made herself say. "Lock it and just sit there quietly. All right?"

Gratitude flooded his face. "You bet," he said. He got up hurriedly and locked the door. He returned to the bed. "Now," he said. "Do it now."

The girl felt hard inside, cold. She was learning. She moved a couple of paces away from him and towards the full-length mirror in the corner of the room. As she turned she spread a smile across her young face. "All right, Tommy," she said softly. "I've never done anything like this for anybody." She made her eyes so soft. "But I'll do it for you."

The youth stirred. His large, pale body wriggled with anticipation. He sat on the edge of the bed. His tongue travelled across his ugly face. "Start now," he said. "But don't say I made you."

"I'm doing this because I want to," she assured him. It's for you."

Abigail turned her back and unzipped the back of the dress. The zip was caught halfway and Tommy made a rush forward to help her. It quickly released itself but she pretended it had caught

133

again. "Please," she said, half turning. "Give me a hand, Tommy. It's spoiling the show."

"Sure, sure," he said eagerly. He stood up and went to her. Clumsily his fingers fumbled with the zip. It was immediately free. She could feel him standing beside her, his breath on her neck. She closed her eyes and tried to control her stomach. His hand crept around to the front and rested on her stomach. She controlled her revulsion. "Stop it," she bantered. "Or you won't see the show."

Obediently he retreated to his bed. He sat down heavily. "I'm ready again, honey," he said.

She pulled the dress over her shoulders. She allowed it to hang from her waist while she undid the clip of the brassiere. He sucked in his breath at the sight of her naked back and shoulder blades, slender and pale. "Turn around," he breathed. "Turn around now," he breathed. "Turn around now."

She hesitated and then turned slowly. Her breasts were plump and indolent, their nipples sleepy, the lobes slightly hanging. "How's that?" she inquired shakily.

"Great," he breathed. "Oh, great! It's the greatest I've ever seen. Even in books."

Her dress still hung from her waist like a voluminous skirt. "You look like one of them statues," he muttered. "Like they have in Washington and Greece and places."

"Thank you," she said. She remained in the position.

"The rest," he said. "Take the rest off."

"Yes," she replied quietly. "Of course, Tommy. Just wait."

She let the skirt slip from her middle and stepped out of it. She was wearing tights and she peeled these away and finally took off her panties and dropped them negligently onto the dressing table. To her terror he rose from the bed and stepped towards her, his face like a white stone.

"You turn me on so much," he mumbled. "Honest, I've got to have you again. I can't control it, see. I can't keep it."

"No, Tommy, please," she stammered, trying to push him away. "Not now, Tommy. Another time. We're all going to have dinner."

He consulted his watch. "Not yet," he said. "There's time. Come on, my darling."

His big, flat hands went to her hip bones and he guided her

134

forcefully to the bed, turning her like a powerful but inelegant dancer. She had no option but to go with him. Her whole naked frame was trembling. "Tommy, please, no," she whispered. "I'm so sore. I've got so sore because of it. Not now, Tommy."

He did not appear to hear. He eased her down onto the bed. She was weeping again but he took no notice of the tears. For a moment he let her lie naked beneath him then he unbuckled his belt and pulled his jeans away from him. She closed her eyes in fear and shame. The youth lumbered onto the bed and, pushing her legs aside, crawled at her. She felt him enter and tear grossly into her. "I love you, Abigail," he said through his gritted teeth. "I want to take you out some place. Some classy place. You're my girl."

"Okay, everybody," smiled Candice brightly. "Now let's all relax and have a good time. Let's try and forget the situation. It's all been a strain on us. Let's forget it exists." She pointed out the places at the set table. "Right, now Edith, you sit there, right next to James, and Abby, Abigail, you get alongside your friend Tommy, and we'll have young Kate sitting at this end and I'll be right next to her. That's wonderful, that's really wonderful. Pour that duck, James. You're in charge of the wine. Let's all drink. . . . No, wait, first we'll have a toast. . . . "

Edith knew the woman was mad. If she had not been before, she was now. She regarded Candice with stony amazement. "How can you be like this?" she suddenly sobbed. "How–?"

"Now, Edith," remonstrated Candice. "If you can't join in and have a good time in the right spirit, then we'll put you away somewhere dark and just keep the girls here. I'm sure nobody wants a whole lot of dramatics tonight. Okay. Is that agreed?"

Edith Burrows looked with her blackened, hollow eyes at her girls. It was the first time they had been together. They had run to each other, crying, in that room when they were allowed to enter, only to be pulled apart by James and Candice, with Tommy looking on stupidly. "Any more demonstrations like that," Candice had shouted at them, "and we call this whole evening off! *Nobody sees anybody again.*"

At that they had backed fearfully away from each other and stood weeping while she arranged them around the table. Now they sat. Abigail was pink-eyed with crying, Kate was ashen with fear and horror. She could not believe what had happened to her mother and her sister, the welts, the bruises. Her mouth was solidly set. She looked up from the table only to see Candice staring at her. The American woman smiled encouragingly and patted her small hand. "You're lovely," she said softly. "You're just too lovely."

She turned to James. "Don't you think so, James?" she said. "Isn't this kid exquisite?"

James sniffed cocaine from the back of his hand. "Don't ask me, baby," he said. "I haven't had the opportunity of seeing all of her. Not yet."

Candice arrested Edith's alarmed glance. "Don't worry, Edith, baby," she said. "No guy is going to lay a finger on our Katy." She smiled around the table. "Let's have some food," she suggested. "Katy, darling, just bring across those plates, will you? I've prepared the hors d'oeuvres . . . and James – for Christsake get that duck. Let's pour it out."

The duck was an ice-cold white wine. James circulated the table filling the glasses, including Kate's. Edith tried to stop him with her hand but he brushed her fingers aside. He leaned towards her and blatantly laid his hand across her breast. "She's having some," he said. "She's a big girl."

The bizarre meal went on. They sat at one long table in the centre of what was, in summer, the motel dining room. It was threadbare and cold, although they had flanked the table with two electric heaters. The three captors ate heartily, the hors d'oeuvres followed by steaks and French fries. The prisoners picked at the food until Candice, looking up, warned them to eat. "If we don't make this dinner an occasion," she said sternly, "then maybe it won't be repeated. Then you won't see each other at all. So let's eat and enjoy it."

The warning took effect. James opened a second bottle of wine and then a third. The Englishwomen were forced to drink. Kate began to cry softly. Candice, who Edith noted never drank more than half a glass of wine throughout the meal, comforted her. "Let's have a little music," she said. "Tommy, do something useful for once and get some music going."

Tommy, his mouth full, left the table and went towards a tapedeck at the side of the room. "Something nice," James called to him. "None of that fucking punk. Let's have something we can dance to."

James was very drunk. As soon as the music began he reached across to small Kate and lifted her hand. "May I?" he inquired. Edith glanced fearfully and automatically at Candice. "Let him," nodded the American girl. "That guy can hardly stand, let alone screw."

Kate began to laugh in a soft, crazy way. She had been forced to drink the wine and now she knocked her chair over as she got to her feet. Her mother's hollow eyes followed her. "God, oh God," she whispered. Turning to Candice, she held out her hands. "Please, please. She's a child. She's twelve years old!"

Candice smiled at her. "I know," she said softly. "I know, Edith."

James made a little mock bow to the girl and then pulled her slight form to him. His hands went behind her back and at once slid down to her buttocks. Edith turned her face away and dropped her eyes into her hands. Abigail, lolling with the effect of the wine, watched dully. Kate, speechless, staggering, went in the direction James swayed her. She did not appear to see anything in the room. Her eyes were only just open. James pressed his hands into flesh, smoothing them against the buttocks and the backs of her young legs. He grinned his pleasure. "Baby, oh, baby, what a butt," he mumbled.

Such was the difference in size between the man and the girl that he was resting his chin on the flat of her head. He rubbed it into her hair and then pulled her body even harder to his. She emitted a strange, small cry. Candice looked up. "Okay," she said firmly. "Just knock it off, will you, James?"

He ignored her and began to push harder against the reeling Kate. "Quit! I said *quit!*" Candice shouted at him. She rose angrily. "You lousy shithouse, stop it!"

Edith was on her feet, swaying faintly. Tommy stupidly put a protecting arm around the stunned Abigail. Candice moved towards James. "Let her go," she ordered.

"Fuck off," giggled James. "She's enjoying it."

Candice said nothing but turned back towards the table and opened her handbag. The others watched and, with amazement, saw her bring a small silver pistol from it. She cocked it firmly and turned again towards James. He continued to laugh. "So now it's a stick-up!" he said. He suddenly swung Katy in front of his body, so that she became his shield. "Go ahead," he challenged. "Just go ahead and shoot. Let's see you make a hole in the pretty one."

Edith moved tremblingly forward. "Candice–" she began. She did not know what her next words were to be. Nor did she have a chance to utter them. At that moment the bell on the front door of the motel rang with an eerie music. Tommy knocked his chair over as he jumped. James released Kate as if she had suddenly become repulsive to him. Candice still had the gun. She turned it around the room swiftly, taking them all in. "Get back to the rooms," she said swiftly. "Move. Come on." She nodded to Tommy. "Get them in and lock them in," she said. Tommy's face worked with emotion.

Candice moved swiftly to Kate, then turned. "I'll kill her if there's any trouble. Just understand, Edith. If it's the last thing I do, I'll kill her."

Edith said, "We'll go." She and Abigail turned. The door rang again.

"Get it," Candice said to James. "Say something clever, for Christsake." She pushed Kate with the gun. The girl moved dumbly. They went along the corridor. She forced Edith to her room and locked the door on her. "Get with her," she said to Tommy, nodding to Abigail. "Don't forget – it's you or her if we get caught."

"I know," mumbled Tommy. "I know that."

They went into the middle room. Candice pushed Kate in front of her to the final room. She pushed her in. "Now listen, sweetie," she said quietly. "Any trouble and I kill your mother. Got it?"

Kate collapsed on the bed and began to cry into her hands. The woman rushed forward and kissed her on the hair before turning away to return down the corridor. The rooms were silent. In the lobby she could hear James talking with someone. Candice steadied herself and walked towards the sounds.

In the lobby was a single policeman, a patrolman. Outside a car's engine was turning over. The man looked up. James, confusion all over him, stretched out a hand towards Candice. She ran her hands through her hair.

138

"Oh, I see," said the officer as though her presence, her ruffled appearance and her attitude explained everything. "I understand."

"I hope we weren't making too much noise," said Candice disarmingly. "Disturbing the neighbours."

The man grinned sheepishly. "No, not that. Pretty unlikely around here this time of the year. No, lady, I saw the lights and I didn't think this place was open so I came for a look-see."

"It's not open," said Candice. "Not to the public. James's father owns Sweetwater Point–"

"I explained," said James. He had forced himself into some soberness. "I told the man."

"Sure," said the policeman. "I've seen you on the boat down at Oregon Inlet. I know you two."

"We came up here for a change of scene," said Candice. "And a little more room."

"Having a little party, just the two of you," nodded the sheriff's man. "Well, I guess there's no arguing with that. I'll be on my way. I have to check out these things. It's my job."

James nodded agreeably. "Sure it is." He was now steady. He had controlled the drink. Candice inwardly approved.

"Don't you have that kid from Nags Head, Tommy something, with you?" The officer asked suddenly. He had been about to go but he turned back to make the inquiry. A knot tightened a little in Candice's stomach. It was James who answered. He remained assured.

"We did," he said. "He kinda helps out on the boat. But he hightails it off whenever he feels like it. He quit a couple of days ago. We don't worry. He always comes back."

The officer sniffed. "How long do you reckon on being in these parts?" he asked. "Are you taking the boat south?"

Now Candice answered. "That's the general idea," she said. "To Florida."

"We're waiting until the weather improves a little," James said. "It's no fun even on the inland waterway when it's like this."

"You're right," agreed the man. "You're certainly right about that."

He turned. This time he was going. "Well, I'll be hitting the road," he said, touching his cap. "Have a good time." He glanced

139

at the dishevelled girl as he turned and grinned wryly. They watched him go down the short path and out to where his car waited glowing on the road. He scowled to himself as a gust of rain caught him in the face. Jesus, what had those two been doing? They looked screwed out. Sometimes he thought he had been born a generation too early.

In her room, only a shout away, Edith Burrows sat on the bed and listened to the patrolman's car drive off through the rain. She now knew she had a little hope. She pushed her hand beneath the pillow and touched the knife she had taken from the table at the sudden end to the meal. It was an ordinary dinner knife. It would need sharpening.

James and Candice returned to the lobby and sat down. There were tight lines around the woman's mouth. James sat back on one of the cane chairs and laughed wildly. Now the policeman had gone his drunkenness had returned.

"I don't like it when that happens," she said angrily. "For Christsake, stop!"

He stopped laughing. "So we should worry? A stupid cop."

"Stupid they may be, okay, but they have a talent for *arriving*. You know what I mean . . . just *arriving*. They don't know why themselves but they just seem to get to some place you don't want them to be. That's when I get scared. Scared shitless."

He moved across to sit on the chair next to her. He patted her on the shoulder. "You? Not you, scared? I don't believe it."

She removed his hand casually. "There's no way out of this situation, you understand. I mean, you *know*, don't you?"

He leaned back and looked at the ceiling. It needed painting. "There's a way," he said easily. "There's always a way, honey."

Candice said, "The only way that's apparent to me is that we have to kill them."

"You got it. That's the way." The reply was casual. He picked up the bottle of cold duck and emptied it into his glass. There was another full bottle on the table. He pulled the stopper from that and left it there. He drank the wine and then said, "Not *kill* them, exactly. I mean, not strangle them or anything violent like that. We don't kill them ourselves, just arrange that they die."

She could see he wasn't just saying it. He had thought of something.

140

"And how do we do that?" she asked.

He looked around and smirked. He was thin and haggard and drunk. The pale eyes had become slits. She wondered how she had ever thought he looked different. She did not mind so much he was a prize shit but he was so unattractive with it. She thought she would go to California after this, northern California, even up into Oregon. Nobody would find you in Oregon. "You don't know too much about anything," James said. "And especially you don't know too much about this place."

Her eyes narrowed but she did not take up the insult. "Sweetwater Point?" she said. "What about it?"

"When this motel was built," he said. He was meandering, his arms thrown back, one hand holding the glass. "When they built it there was a boat dock here. Right where we are. That was called Sweetwater Dock, and the dock was called Sweetwater because the fucking Indians called it that. There was a stream or a spring here or something."

"Okay," sighed Candice. "Save me the folklore."

James glanced at her insolently. "I figured maybe I'd hand you some education," he remarked. "Anyway, here was the dock. They built this motel almost over the top of it. I remember my old man telling me they put it here because the land and rock or whatever it is in these parts, was good and firm, which it wasn't any other place in the area. It's a freak. Got that much?"

"I'm working on it," she said.

"The old man had some idea of using the boat dock still, so they built the motel partly over it. But it never worked out. He never had enough cash, so it never got used. But it's still down there, under the back section of the building and letting out into the ocean. There's a door and you can get down to it. I remember going down there when I was a kid. I thought it was real creepy. When the tide comes in, it comes in waves right up into the dock. They just fill it up, see. And there's no way out, not unless you figure on swimming the Atlantic."

She was staring at him with dawning admiration. "You mean, you just *put* them down there?"

"Sure. The door, it's right at the end of the building there. You get them down there at the right time with the tide and leave them. They just get drowned. No marks on them except maybe a few cuts from the rocks, so nobody can tell anything. One day

141

somebody's out fishing and they find one of them, or two or maybe three, floating around in the ocean. Another Cape Hatteras tragedy. We'll read it in the papers."

"What about the car?" she asked. She leaned towards him. He wrapped a drunken arm around her shoulders.

"No problem," he said. "No problem at all. That little Pinto's never going to see daylight again. Not unless they get an oil rig or something to get it out of the swamp."

She thought about it. "There'll be investigations," she said. "Like – how did they get out to sea?"

"Who cares? Maybe they went fishing. Maybe they got washed off the beach. That ain't our problem. Let the Coast Guard scratch their asses about it."

"It's good, James," she admitted thoughtfully. "It's very good. Simple, easy . . . clean. What about their bags, their belongings?"

"We've got to be careful about that," he admitted. "It's no good throwing the stuff in after them. Some of it might get caught on the rocks or in all this reed crap around here. That would be too close for comfort. We'll have to take the stuff out in the boat and drop it into the ocean. It'll be okay."

She laughed quietly and shook her head. "Jesus," she said. "I never thought we'd be able to get out of this. But maybe we can. It's brilliant, James." Her face fell solemnly. "When?" she said.

"Soon, I guess," he answered. "I don't like cops poking around any more than you do, baby."

His face took on a different expression, as if he were thinking of something new. "Come on," he said suddenly. "I'll show you."

"What will you show me?"

"The boat dock. You want to see it, don't you?"

She glanced at him. "As long as you're not thinking of trying it on me," she said.

He sighed. "Forget that," he said. "It's got a limited capacity, this idea. We can't have too many bodies floating on the ocean – and especially bodies that can be connected with us. Otherwise we could try it out on the kid, that dumb Tommy." He reached over and ran the flat of his hand across her breast. "Anyway, I like you. I wouldn't do a thing like that to you."

Candice stood. "Okay, show me," she said.

James finished the wine in his glass and took her hand. "No

distance," he said. "Right along the corridor."

They walked the length of the passage, past the rooms of their prisoners. There was silence. James tapped on Abigail's door and called, "Take your prick out of her, Tommy. Give her a break." Tommy's voice growled back through the door. James laughed and walked on with Candice. At the end of the corridor he opened a door leading to an engine house which housed the heating boiler and the water pumps. The ocean winds seeped through the seams of the building. Candice shivered. There was a further door set in the extreme wall. James walked towards this and unlocked it with a key already in place. "The bridal suite," he joked over his shoulder. He turned on a single light bulb. The room was used for storage. Spare and damaged beds and other articles for furniture were piled around. The entire room was wood. It was like standing in a box. Below her feet Candice suddenly heard and felt the great rolling swell of the Atlantic.

"It's right below us," nodded James. He pushed up a light switch. "Take a look." He pulled a panel of plywood clear of the wall and she saw a wooden door. This key too was in the lock. James turned it and pushed the door in with difficulty. A heavy rush of wind and spray rushed in at them. Candice moved forward carefully. She was still not sure she trusted him.

James was standing on a stone step just inside the door. She looked over his shoulder. A bulkhead light he had switched on from the other room was fixed beside the door. Its illumination was lost within a few yards. Candice looked down a flight of rough stone steps that vanished into dimness. Beyond was a cavernous black chamber, shrieking with wind and, far below, long rolling waves like great licking tongues coming directly from the ocean and colliding with the furthest face of rock and concrete. It was not possible to see size, only to feel, to sense, its great depth. She said nothing but stood back nervously and allowed James to follow her back into the storeroom.

"Get that," he said. "Custom made!"

She nodded. "I guess it is, James," she said. "And I don't see any other way out."

"There is none," he said firmly. He had reached the far door. He paused and said, "Like I say, it'll have to be soon."

"That's right," she said. She had an abrupt suspicion that he had planned something. Then she knew she was right. He moved quickly to the outer door. He turned and smiled. "There's one thing I need to do before that," he said. "And there's no time like now." She shouted and swore at him but he had reached the door. He stepped through it and locked it behind him. She was trapped in the wooden room. She banged the door with her fists. "You bastard!" she shouted. "You lousy bastard!"

"I'll be back to let you out later," he called through the door. "Enjoy yourself. I'm going to."

Tears flooded her cheeks. She pounded on the door again. "Leave her!" she screamed. She howled plaintively. "Leave her, you shit! She's mine!"

Laughing to himself like a boy, James went along the corridor to the dining room again and picked up the bottle of cold duck and two glasses. When he returned along the passage his face had changed. It was fixed and serious. He knocked at Katy's door, hardly brushing the woodwork. There was predictably no answer. He opened the door and walked in. The room was in darkness. He stood in the doorway and heard the girl breathing. "Katy," he whispered. "Katy, are you awake?"

She was sleeping deeply. He went to the edge of the bed, set the bottle and glasses on the dressing table and put his hand flat on her stomach. She was still wearing the dress she had worn that evening. His hand caressed the material, feeling the firm skin beneath its rise and fall with her breath. Leaning over to the bedside lamp he switched it on. He stood back to look at her.

The young girl was lying on her back, her hands raised over her head. The unaccustomed wine she had been forced to take had sent her into a deep sleep. One knee was raised and the hem of the blue dress had slid down almost to her thigh. James bent forward again and touched her. "Katy," he repeated. "Katy, baby, wake up. I'm here." Kate opened her eyes wearily. She closed her eyes again. Tears began to seep from beneath the lashes. James sat solicitously on the edge of the bed and wiped them away with the end of the sheet. "Aw, come on, honey," he murmured. "No crying. This is a celebration. Have a little more wine."

She shook her head, but James was already pouring the cold, almost colourless liquid into the second glass. He moved it towards her mouth. She opened her eyes to the expression on his

144

face. It frightened her. She allowed him to move the full glass towards her lips, now regarding him without blinking. He gave it to her like a father giving medicine to his daughter. Katy coughed and choked and he held the glass back for a moment before giving it to her again. "There, now, you certainly enjoyed that," he said softly. "And there's more . . . much more than that."

"Candice," she muttered in a little, drunken voice. "I shall tell Candice what you've done. She told me to tell her if you ever did, if you ever tried. She'll kill you with her gun."

"Candice is in no position to argue about it," he smiled. He put the glasses down on the dressing table again. She was in a half-sitting position, her head against the wall behind the bed. The look between the girl and her oppressor was almost a challenge.

She watched him steadily, the expression verging on indifference. He looked up and saw the face. "Why don't you try praying?" he suggested nastily. "Little girls in your position usually pray, don't they?"

"I've dropped God," she replied, almost conversationally. "He's dropped me, us, so I've dropped Him."

"Sure, why not?" he said, surprising himself by answering. "He's like the cops – never around when you need them. Anyway, I never figured God did anybody any good. You might as well lean back and enjoy yourself." Then, to the man's complete astonishment, the girl began to sing:

> "Within the woodlands, flowery gladed,
>   By the oak tree's mossy moot–"

James backed abruptly away from her. "Shut up!" he bawled angrily in her face. "Shut that fucking goddam racket!"

"It's my school song," Kate announced firmly.

"I don't give a screw if it's the national anthem," he snarled. "Just don't do it."

She looked at him bravely. "We were always advised that we should sing it if ever we were in trouble or danger," she said with a simplicity that she seemed to think he ought to understand. "Sing the school song – and pray. But since praying doesn't seem to work very well it's all I can do." Courageously she launched into it again:

"Within the woodlands, flowery gladed—"

"Knock it off!" James smacked her sharply across the mouth. She stopped, stunned by the blow. Her eyes welled with tears. His hand moved threateningly towards her again. She moved before it touched her. Frozen-faced, she eased herself down into the bed and closed her eyes.

An hour later she lay alone in the darkness again, long past weeping. Again she began to sing:

> ".. . . and there for me, the apple tree,
> Do lean down low in Linden Lea."

The thin, brave voice seeped through the window above the girl's head and wandered over the dark night of Cape Hatteras like the song of a ghost.

7

Burrows drove the car across the windy causeway and, ignoring the shuttered and shrouded settlement of Nags Head wrapped up for the winter, he turned south, the Atlantic to his left, the quieter waters of the Sound to his right. Just beyond the road junction was a turning with the notice: "Cape Hatteras National Seashore. Information. Ferry Reservations." He turned the Aspen off the road and into the parking area, but he did not need to leave the car to see that the wooden building, which catered for summer tourists, would not be open for months. Just as he expected. He moved the car forward and went south again on the solitary road.

It was an abandoned place, desolate, deserted for the winter. Low clouds tore across a low landscape. Frightened by the noise of the car, an echelon of geese took off and headed for the ocean. There were no trees and no houses, just flat, monotonous banks with the sea gnawing at them on either side. His spirit diminished.

The broken sky gave birth to a quick squall and rain rattled against the windscreen of the car. There was only enough room on the road for two vehicles, and then it was close. Since nothing else was in sight, he kept the car in the middle of the road. Then he saw the lighthouse.

It stood like an admonishing finger, grey in the sea mist and the rain, but standing high above everything else. He quickly turned at a stony track leading from the highway. Tall grasses and weeds suddenly closed in around and above the car. A silent heron rose disdainfully and eased itself without hurry into the wind. He rounded a curve in the clattering track. There was the lighthouse.

Burrows could see no one was there. A small tourist bureau was shuttered tightly. The lighthouse stood dead and dumb, a lock on the door. No light had shone from there for a long time. Burrows stopped the car and walked in the damp, clinging air towards the door.

Even before mounting the short flight of exterior stone steps to the door, he could see the lock was hanging loose. He walked up to it, disturbing another flight of petulant seabirds.

As he took the lock in his hands and manoeuvred it from its position, it abruptly occurred to him that here, right inside this single perpendicular tower, might be Edith Burrows and her girls. They *had* to be somewhere. *And wasn't the lock broken*? He breathed carefully and opened the tough wooden door. It moved inward without a creak. Inside was a rounded area with two prison-like windows, and an iron staircase spiralling up.

In contrast to the pervasive dampness everywhere else, it was dry as an eggshell in there, dry and cold and echoing. Each step he took up the staircase sounded above him, up in the hollow tube. He remembered the woman in New York had advised him to get a gun. He clenched his fist inadequately.

His breathing shortened, his eyes stared upwards as he took each step. The curling stairs led to another door. It was not locked. He waited, then pushed it carefully, the first inch or so very carefully, and then firmly for the last two feet. He stood back, waiting. Nothing. He stepped into a dry, drum-like room with a desk and a stool and tourist exhibits stacked and stored around the walls. Across the room there was another door.

Burrows tried the drawers of the desk. They were all empty except one, in which he discovered, to his surprise, a half bottle of bourbon. A month ago he would not have contemplated taking it. Now, casually, he put it in his pocket. He moved towards the door in the far wall. Close beside it was a narrow window and he found himself looking directly out above an ugly sea, grey and rolling, coming in and over the rockless land, pawing it and running back again. He opened the door and went through.

It was a stone landing similar to the one on the ground level. He went as quietly as possible up the steps, although each movement on the spiralled metal raised an echo in the slim, tall chamber of

148

the building. Another door appeared around a bend and he entered this just as prudently. It was an empty chamber, without even a piece of furniture. He grunted and walked across to a farther door which led onto another landing. He opened it and began to climb.

The third and final chamber, at the nose of the stair, led onto the gallery of the lighthouse. There was a wooden ladder to an area above which had, at one time, housed the light itself. The round room was empty except, strangely, for a rocking chair. Its presence surprised him and made him, to his additional surprise, smile. He walked around the high windows with their latticed metalwork, in a slow circle, looking out over the stencilled outline of wintry Cape Hatteras. There was little to see: the land below him bitten by the sullen ocean and, less than a half mile away, the other, inward, coastline of the narrow peninsula; marshes and reeds and the wet, reflecting road, all curtained in fine rain. To the south he thought he could distinguish some low pyramids that could have been the roofs of a settlement. He had purchased a map in Manteo and now he took it from his pocket and checked the location. He decided the roofs were Oregon Inlet. Looking into the indistinct distance again he made out a slender wirelike shape rising like a bowsprit of a ship from the limit of the land. Again he checked the map. That must be the long bridge that rose between the islands. He read the name: The Herbert C. Bonner Bridge.

There was no colour in the entire horizon for as far as he could see. He sat down in the rocking chair and, almost without thinking, opened the half bottle of bourbon. He took a deep swig, feeling the molten warmth run down inside him and flood his gut. "What a bloody terrible place," he said loudly to the walls.

For a half hour he sat there, rocking in the quaint chair, high above the land and the sea, drinking regularly from the bottle, the comfort attempting to push back the frontier of his hopelessness and loneliness. For some reason he had a quick picture of the girl, Bonnie, serving in the steamy hamburger place in Manteo. He was too late for her sympathy and help, he thought. Years too late.

" 'Stuck there in damned England,' " he grumbled to himself. " 'Shooting innocent ducks.' " His repetition of Edith's laughing rebuke was unconscious. "God, no wonder you've never seen anything. Never even *spoken* to anyone. That's you, *Doctor* Burrows: careless." He repeated, "Careless."

He had never thought of drink as his weakness, or even a prospective weakness. At night, in his silent house in England, he had habitually poured himself a generous nightcap because it helped him sleep. But now he looked down at the bourbon bottle and discovered to his genuine astonishment that it was empty. He looked around, foolishly thinking that he might have spilled some. But the floor was stone dry. Christ, he thought, imagine emptying the lot. He looked at his watch. It was only eleven-ten in the morning. And he was drunk. He thought of the curling stairs he would need to negotiate on his descent and grinned stupidly to himself. He rocked the chair and let the motion carry him back and forward. Now that *would* be funny. *That* would give Deputy Wheeler something to wrack his pea-brain about – if he were found dead at the bottom of the lighthouse. They'd probably guess right as soon as they saw the bottle and that would be that. A convenient end for all concerned.

The rocking diminished and he felt his spirit wind down with it. He remembered again why he was there. Where in God's earth could they be? Here, or some other place; some place a thousand miles away? Burrows stood and carefully stemmed the rocking chair's motion with his hand. He made his way with the drunk's pedantic assurance to the glass door giving out onto the open gallery of the lighthouse. As he went through the wet wind struck him in the face. Snorting he pulled the collar of his coat roughly up around his neck. He looked out across the ragged land and the rough sea. God, what a place. Wild and flat and grey. Unsteadily, holding onto the iron guardrail for support, he made his way around the complete perimeter of the open gallery. A cloud of duck came in from the direction of the distant and misty mainland, descending to their marshy home.

Burrows, a wild, wind-blown figure on the high platform, looked out with a strange anger. He felt very drunk. He dared not look immediately down. Instead he drew a deep breath, put his hands like a megaphone to his mouth and shouted, "Edith! Edith Burrows – are you there? Edith, Edith Burrows!"

Only the damp wind answered. He sniffed the dismal air again and turned into the dryness of the gallery room, closing the door

150

behind him. "You're going bloody mad," he said to himself.

Two hours later he awoke startled, cramped in the rocking chair. His jerk of surprise set it moving and he stopped it with his feet. He felt stiff and nauseous and his head ached heavily. A pale sun was sifting through the cold latticed window of the lighthouse. Stiffly he rose from the chair and went to the window. The height and isolation of his perch made him reel. He went back to the chair and sat down. God, what was he doing here?

The empty bourbon bottle was on the clean stone floor beside him. Guiltily he picked it up and put it in his pocket. He went out of the thin door and down the curved stairway, holding nervously to the handrail on the wall. In the lower room he replaced the bottle in the desk drawer from which he had taken it and then thoughtfully put a five-dollar bill underneath it. "Have one on me," he muttered.

Carefully he descended the final steps and then walked out into the damp winter sunlight. It was coming through a long tear in the sky, low and directly in his eyes, reflecting off the wet tangled green of the grasses and rushes all around. He walked the few yards to the car, opened the door, and slumped in the seat. Starting the engine, he eased the car along the rough track until he reached the road again and turned south towards Oregon Inlet.

Ahead he could see that he had been right. The strange slim antenna that he had seen indistinctly from the lighthouse was a long and beautiful bridge arching and dipping over the turgid ocean. He blinked and marvelled that Americans could build such a thing in such a wild, unused place. The car rose on the initial upward stretch, as if heading for the low sun. The elevated sensation elated him. He could see across the flat island ahead. A solitary fishing boat rocked below, and glancing over his shoulder he realised that he had missed the enclosed harbour at Oregon Inlet, tucked in under the wing of the bridge. He would need to go back when he had reached the far side.

It took a long time. The Herbert C. Bonner Bridge curved and ran for three miles before the road gracefully dipped low to the water before running onto the flat of the next land, Hatteras Island. Burrows drove on. Two minutes later he passed the place where Edith Burrows had driven her car off the road. He could not know it then, but the red Tempo lay in twelve feet of brackish water beside the road at the place where he chose to turn the

Aspen and head back over the long bridge to Oregon Inlet. Had he continued instead of turning back, five minutes' driving would have brought him to within fifty yards of the Sweetwater Point Motel.

Burrows found that Oregon Inlet was sheltered from the ocean by an elbow in the land. The waters of Pamlico Sound were surely but nothing compared with the long and powerful waves that came straight from the Atlantic onto the other side of Cape Hatteras. The wonderful bridge took off there and went over the water of the inlet curving through the air like a concrete whip. Burrows got out of the car on the harbour front and stood looking at the structure.

"Herbert C. Bonner Bridge," said an elderly voice behind him. "Three miles long. Ain't she a beauty?"

Burrows turned and registered the man's look of quick surprise. He must have looked bad. "It certainly is," he agreed. The man was more than seventy, small and lithe, with half a mouth of teeth surmounted by an extravagant nose. "How come they built a bridge like that in a place like this?" Burrows asked.

"To get you from one side to the other," replied the old man as if it were the only answer. "You want a cup of coffee, mister? You look like you could use one. Been driving long?"

"Yes," said Burrows. "You could say that."

"Where you from?"

"England."

"That's a long trip."

The old man said his name was Garretty. When they shook hands his fingers felt like wood. He had turned and walked back to a coffee shack with a windblown sign outside its door. The paint was peeling off the woodwork and the door creaked like a winch as he opened it. Then he pulled a scrap of curled and dried paint away from the outer wall, examining it before tossing it away. "Soon as this month's through I'm getting the place painted," he announced. He tried to sound as if he meant it.

It was warm in the cabin. The coffee came from a hot urn and Burrows drank it gratefully. He took out the photographs of Edith, Abigail, and Kate. "Have you ever seen these ladies?" he asked.

Garretty's eyes almost disappeared in wrinkles as he examined the photographs. To Burrows it seemed that he explored every

152

feature of their faces. He rubbed his grey-bristled chin and pursed his dry lips in a silent whistle, which gave the Englishman a moment of hope. It was soon dispelled. "Nope," sad Garretty eventually. "Can't say I ever did. They ain't been in these parts. Not these gals. I would have noticed. Even now I notice."

"So does everybody else," sighed Burrows. "They notice but they never see. Or not often."

"They your kin?" asked the old man. He was filling his own coffee mug a second time. He had refused any money for Burrows' coffee and now he refilled his mug too. Burrows looked down at the circling liquid. "In a way, yes," he said. "They've disappeared. I think they might be out here on Cape Hatteras."

Garretty withdrew his eyes into his folded skin again and looked carefully at Burrows. "Disappeared?" he said. "How'd that happen? Folks don't just disappear. Not three at a time."

"These have," said Burrows. "And I'm pretty sure they came this way. They were at Manteo, at the Lost Colony earlier this month. They were seen there and they got some petrol from a station near the causeway. But since then, nothing."

Garretty's eyes had not come from their holes. "That's Manteo. Why would they want to come out here, to the Cape, for God's sake? In January? There ain't a lot here in January, like you see now, mister." He nodded towards the drab habour with its small boats dragged clear of the water and only two or three riding in the choppy tide.

Burrows drank heavily at the coffee. "I've got a witness – only the kid at the petrol station – but a witness nevertheless, who saw them drive across the causeway from Manteo to Cape Hatteras. The people at the ferry at Ocracoke say they don't have any record of them taking their car back to the mainland that way. So, unless they went north to Norfolk, Virginia, which doesn't seem logical, they're still here."

"What make of car would that be?" asked Garretty.

"A red Tempo."

"Plenty of red Tempos around in the summer, I guess," said the old man. "But I ain't see one that I can recall. Not since Christmas. When everything's grey, like it is out here in winter, a red car kinda shows up. Sometimes when I'm not busy, which is most times, I sit and watch the cars go over the bridge. You get a good view from that window over there. Maybe I saw it and I don't remember, but mister, I don't remember."

Burrows looked out of the other window, towards the anchorage. "Not many people go boating this time of year," he said.

"We get a few. They go out fishing when the weather's okay, but not when it's blowing like this. But you can see most of the boats are laid up for the winter. People come over weekends to tinker with them, you know, patch them up and give them a lick of paint, but even that don't really get going until March, April."

"That boat looks like it's being used now," said Burrows. He indicated the white cruiser rolling with the swell coming from the Pamlico Sound. "They've got some laundry hanging out to dry."

"Won't get very dry," observed Garretty. "Been there for a couple of weeks. They must be ashore. I ain't seen them around since last week sometime."

"Who owns it?" asked Burrows. There was no direct intention in the question. He was tired. He asked almost automatically.

"I don't know. He's a young guy, down from New York. He's with a girl and another young fella. They're probably taking the boat down south, to Florida, along the inland waterway. I guess they're just waiting for the weather to quit. Great looking female, but I don't care too much for the guy. He's a smart-ass. I think the other kid comes from these parts. He's real dumb."

"Mr. Garretty," said Burrows, rising heavily from the stool. "It's been a pleasure. Thanks for the coffee. You sure you won't let me pay?"

"Nothing to pay," said the old man firmly. "Glad of the company. Ain't exactly like Los Angeles living here. Where you headed now?"

"Hatteras Inlet," said Burrows. "I want to check there at the ferry."

The old man opened the door for him and again grimaced at the squeak. He took another piece of peeling paint off and threw it away. A seagull thinking it was a tidbit, swooped, then made off with a disappointed squeal. "I know how he feels," said Burrows wryly. "Thank you again. Good-bye."

They shook hands and again the Englishman was aware of the dry wooden fingers. "I'll wave to you when you cross the bridge," said the old man as though it were a deep promise.

"I like to wave to people up there. Not that they ever wave back. They don't see me waving, I guess. But it passes the time. Nothing much happens around here otherwise."

That flat, cold day he drove the length of the Cape, taking the ferry at the village of Hatteras, a forty-five minute crossing over the bumpy inlet to the island of Ocracoke. Then he drove down the single windy road that sliced the lean neck of land in two like a hot dog. At the Hatteras ferry landing nobody recalled seeing Edith Burrows and her daughters. At that sparse time of the year a red Tempo with three unusual women as passengers would have caused comment. But not one person at the ferry terminals at Hatteras nor at Ocracoke harbour, where the boat went back to the North Carolina mainland, remembered them. Burrows had stopped the car at the small settlements along the ridge of Hatteras Island before reaching the first ferry point – the hamlets of Rodanthe, Waves, Salvo, Buxton, and Frisco. Apart from Buxton, where the island flattened and there were trees and a permanent settlement, there were few winter inhabitants, only the ghostly wooden houses in the Atlantic mist, elevated on stilts above the flat land.

Dispirited, he turned the car at Ocracoke, the most southerly point of his search, and drove north once more as the light dwindled into the evening sea. The sky brightened for a period at sunset as he took the ferry back to Hatteras Island, as if to give some consolation for the dreary day. Yellow rays came across the inland lagoon, giving the island a golden sheen. For a while it looked almost attractive. On Hatteras Island he stopped, on impulse, at Salvo, and wandered in the cold twilight among the strange, lofty deserted homes.

Each one was built of bare, uncompromising, unpainted board, lifted ten to fifteen feet above the marshy ground on its stilts. They were spaced a good distance apart with no particular design or planning in their location. They were ugly. As the darkness took over and the mist returned, they squatted like silent, petrified spiders. Burrows wandered disconsolately between their long legs. He was sober now, aching with fatigue and hopelessness, but the place and his desperation forced an odd madness on him so that he once more began to shout the names of those he sought.

155

"Edith! Edith! Abigail! Kate, Katy–" His voice swirled in the mist and returned to him as a muffled echo. He called again and again but no answer came. Suddenly the black comedy of the situation came home to him. He sat down on the lower steps of one of the houses and began to laugh foolishly. Dear God, why didn't he just pack up and go back to England? Go home!

The mist was cold and thick now and it was as good as night. It cushioned the sound of the sea, rubbing itself against the beach only a hundred yards distant. Nor did he hear the sound of the car on the road, the same distance in the other direction. It stopped in the mist and Burrows, sitting stupidly on the wooden steps, was first aware that he was not alone when a thick figure came through the dimness and walked towards him. He stared because he thought he had begun to imagine things, but the voice was firm and familiar. "Hi! It's me, Dr. Burrows. It's Bonnie."

His heart lifted. He stood and smiled in the gloom. He did not see her grin until she was ten feet away. She wore a huge man's overcoat.

He held out his hands. "What in God's name are you doing? How did you know I was here?"

She took his hands and oddly shook them both at the same time, a half-formal, half-affectionate greeting. She was wearing a heavy fishing sweater and jeans beneath the coat. She carried a voluminous canvas bag. Her face was damp in the mist. "It was easy," she said. "I saw the Aspen by the road. Like we said, if you want to find somebody out here there's not much ground to cover. Unless they're concealed."

"Well, I'm pleased . . . but what made you come out here?"

"It's not exactly Disney World," she agreed. "I figured you'd need company and something to eat. I brought some hot dogs, well cold dogs, but they'll warm up. And some coffee."

He released her hands. He looked around. She smiled again and began mounting the wooden steps to the house on stilts, pulling the coat away from her back as she went. She hung it heavily under her arm. "Don't worry," she said cheerfully. He went up after her and he was aware of her slim buttocks in the jeans just before his eyes. She had reached the platform just in front of the door. To his astonishment she took a short screwdriver from her canvas bag and began to lever the hasp of the padlock away from the wood. "When you're familiar with these parts," she said,

156

without looking around, "you'd be surprised what you can do. And you come prepared. All the kids on the Outer Banks know how to get in these shacks. It's easy. There!"

She moved a pace back and pulled the fixture away from the door. It was free and she opened it easily. "Welcome," she smiled as he stepped in briskly and motioned him to follow.

"Breaking and entering," mentioned Burrows as he went in after her. She went to the far wall and turned on a central light. It worked. "They didn't switch off the mains," she said.

Burrows grinned at her. "I'm gradually getting quite a criminal record," he said.

"Maybe it'll get worse," she forecast. She walked confidently to the far side of the large wooden room and switched on a table lamp and then another. The room was revealed as chill and sparsely furnished, the coldness of disuse on it. There were a table and four camp chairs, a rough rug on the floor, some home-painted sea pictures around the wall, and a bamboo bookshelf containing a dozen curling paperbacks. Bonnie dropped her clumsy coat carelessly to the floor. She opened one of the two doors. The first led to a small kitchen and the second to a bedroom. Burrows could not see what they were like. The girl said casually, "Well, at least we can eat and sleep. And they left the electricity on. Some people are meanies; they switch if off."

He watched her moving briskly around as she talked. She turned and saw his expression. "Don't be afraid," she smiled.

"I'm not afraid," said Burrows. "It's just you. You're amazing, I mean, you've just *materialised*. I don't know what I would have done, where I would have gone tonight. I actually hadn't given it a thought.

"I figured that," she said casually. "That's why I materialised." She went to each window and drew the hessian curtains. She checked each one carefully. "Maybe you'd better not attract any more attention than you already have." Her smile was mischievous. The lamplight touched her pale face giving it a trace of colour. "Are you hungry?"

Burrows suddenly realised he was. And weary. She saw it at once, as soon as it came over him, the realisation, the physical ache. She walked to him and said, "Let's get that coat off. And you take a seat for a while. I'll get some coffee, if I can make the stove work, and I'll warm up the hot dogs. Just sit down."

He did so, still wearing the overcoat. "Maybe, after all, you'd better keep that on," she said. "It's not too warm in here. There's no propane in the cylinder so we're not going to get any heat. Not unless we move to another house. Do you want to move house?"

Burrows smiled at her. He started to climb out of his coat. Curiously she came over to help him, as if he were a very old man. "We can't move house," he said. "We've only just come here."

"Right," she replied. She was standing behind him taking the coat so he could not see her expression. She took it away, and he let her. The room did not seem so chill as it might have felt. The coffee was steaming on the stove. She checked on the hot dogs in the camping oven.

"I'll leave this gadget on," she said, nodding at the stove. "It will warm the place anyway."

"You must have driven twenty miles," he said.

"Twenty-five," she said. "There are mile-posts all the way down the Cape. There's one just here. By the side of the highway. Did you have any luck today?"

"A little," he replied. "The boy at the petrol station saw them. The same day as they were at the Lost Colony. They drove over the causeway."

"That's very good," she said. She poured the coffee and brought it to him in an enamel mug. "That's a real break."

"I talked to the old man at Oregon Inlet," he said, drinking the coffee. "And I even went up the damned lighthouse. But nothing. Not a sign of them." He laughed wryly. "I even tried calling them. Shouting through the fog. Can you imagine that?"

She had poured some coffee for herself and regarded him over the horizon of the mug. "Sure, I can," she answered. "That seems like as good a way as any out here. I wouldn't recommend it for New York City, say, but here it seems like sense." She put the coffee down and went over to the stove. The hot dogs were warmed. She returned with them on one plate and set it between them. "We seem to have spent most of our time, since we met, eating hot dogs," he smiled.

"You've done the eating," she said. "Hamburgers and hot dogs. Me, I get sick to my stomach looking at them. But just now there's nothing else. It was great that kid remembered seeing them. I know him – he's a bright kid."

"I'm sorry I can't take you out to dinner," he said. "I'd like to."

"We could make a reservation," she grinned. "For next summer. Maybe we could get a corner table with a view of the ocean."

"Bonnie," he asked with care, "you're staying here with me?"

She nodded, her mouth full of hot dog. "Sure. There's no way I'm going back tonight. I brought this as well." She delved into her copious canvas bag and brought out a half bottle of bourbon. "I thought it might keep you warm."

They had finished eating. "I think I'll have a drink now," he said.

She handed the bottle across. "I'll just busy myself around the house," she said.

She took the plate and the mugs away.

"This is my second half bottle today," he said. "I found some in the lighthouse and I put that away, too."

"It was probably meant for emergencies like that," Bonnie replied. She had gone to the far side of the room towards the kitchen sink. She looked fragile but assured. "We'll have to sleep in the same bed," she called easily over her shoulder. "There's only one set of blankets. Is that okay?"

He regarded her slim back. "That's okay," he said. He touched her waist and turned her easily around to face him.

"We can keep our clothes on if you prefer it. Keep it decent," she continued.

"I was wondering when something good was going to happen to me," he said pulling her gently towards him. His rough face went tenderly against her hair. Her face turned to him and he kissed her, first on the side of the mouth, then fully on the lips, his arms engulfing her slight form. "I think my luck's changed too," she whispered.

Easing herself from him she turned and walked towards the double bed in the alcove at the far end of the room. She pulled back the blankets and arranged the naked pillows. "I'll get in first," she announced. She laughed blithely and pulled back the blankets for him. "Get in," she said. She dropped her shoes on the floor and he did likewise.

Burrows, watching her face, climbed slowly into the bed beside her. They lay there in their clothes feeling the rough blankets gaining warmth from them and returning it. At first, as

159

though by some unspoken agreement, they lay still, on their backs, their eyes on the dim wooden ceiling.

"Let's have a drink," said Burrows quietly. "To you and to me." The bottle was on the table. He was able to reach for it. She sat up in the bed and drank first straight from the bottle. She handed it to him.

"You know, Dr. Burrows," she said solemnly as he put the bottle to his mouth, "I'm such a mess that when I saw you my heart went out to you. I never saw anybody in a worse state than me before. It was such a relief, I can tell you."

"Thank you," he said with equal solemnity. He looked at her with a brief smile. "I don't think I've ever had a nicer compliment. From a lovelier lady."

"You're a liar too," she grinned. "I guess you're just what I needed. That's why I came out here after you." As she spoke she turned inward, towards him. He turned to look at her. Her face was long and white, a few inches from his. She pushed herself so that they were just touching and kissed his lips. His fingers went to her face and he stoked her chin and her nose. "It's a bit strange, don't you think, with our clothes on?" she mentioned.

"They're going to get in the way," he agreed. He eased himself from the centre of the bed to the side and took off his jacket and then, after a glance at her serious face on the bare pillow, the rest of his clothes except for his shirt. He quickly returned to the blankets. "It's a very cold night," he said.

Immediately he was beside her again. She began to tug at her sweater, pulling it up over the top of her chest until it was rolled beneath her chin. Under it she had a checked shirt. With her eyes resting on his face she undid the half a dozen buttons and pulled it apart. Her small conical breasts stared out at him like white eyes. "Suck them" she suggested steadily. "It will do us both good."

Burrows moved towards her and kissed her lips with tenderness. She reached up with one hand and eased his head down until his mouth enclosed one small medallion on her breast. He sucked it quietly and then moved his lips to the other. He lay feeding against her thin frame, feeling the warmth moving through his tired body. She began to feel warm on the skin of his hands held about her waist. Her small fingers were on his naked hip bones. "I need to get my things off," she whispered. "I feel like I'm gift-wrapped." He released her while she eased herself quickly from her clothes. She left them in the bed around her legs and feet and then moved back to him.

The Englishman rolled against her. His mouth went back to her breasts and he lay there eyes shut, tongue flat against her flesh. Her hands were looser now, still caressing. He went slowly to the parting of her thighs and eased it wider. Her legs were slim. There hardly seemed to be more than a soft swelling at the top. His fingers and then his palms eased themselves under her bottom and he was easily able to take each of the small buttocks in his hands. He massaged them carefully and then pushed his fingers from the back between her legs. He was surprised how easy, how natural it was with her. He did not remember it that way at all. She curled beside him like a possum. He trembled and held her, clasping his hands around her unkempt hair and pushed it against his stomach. He eased her onto her slim back. She slid over like a fish. Her thighs were held like those of an acrobat, wide now, and her thin hands beckoned him. He let out his breath and climbed tenderly between her legs. "Don't keep that thing away from me, Doctor," she whispered.

He moved forward only minutely and then slid into her belly with such a sensation that he thought he might end it almost before it had begun. The girl gasped and bit her mouth. He paused and watched her.

She opened her eyes with a sort of sleepy amazement. "Don't let me stop you," she said, wondering at his hesitation. "What do you want? A letter from my father?"

He laughed outright, and rolled fiercely and happily against her. She pulled the blanket high over their heads. The roughness of the wool rubbed against his backside as he moved more quickly, passionately. It was dark and hot and full of the scent of sex under there in the blanket cave. "Christ, that's wonderful," she whispered. "That's really *fattening* me."

"You're lovely, beautiful," he said. "God, what are you doing to me?" With each thrust he could feel her slim white stomach swelling. She moved her legs even wider, seeking to take in every last measure of it. Her fingers moved down and under from the flanks of his buttocks. She stroked him to his ejaculation, softly at first then with increasing force and urgency as she felt him hurrying. The explosion filled her body. It left him lying against her, still keeping his weight off her chest, sweating and empty.

161

"Jesus Christ, Doctor," she whispered in his ear.

"Jesus Christ, Bonnie," he returned, "had nothing to do with it."

As they lay in the quietest and happiest situation that Burrows had known for a long time, the wind began to thud against the window of the wooden house. The same wind struck the window of Kate's room at the Sweetwater Point Motel as she wept in the demanding arms of Candice. The girl's bed was only three-quarters of a windswept mile from the place where her uncle lay with his young lover.

When Burrows opened his eyes, it was morning and Bonnie was already dressed and busy at the stove. The smell of coffee woke him. He studied her outline against the wan window light of another Cape Hatteras winter day.

The girl turned and saw that he was awake. "About time, too," she called. "You really slept. Maybe I should help you out every night."

"I'm not sure I could stand it, but you could try," he smiled. It still seemed amazing that she should be there with him, more amazing that he should be there at all. England? God, where was England? She walked to the bed with a mug of coffee.

"I seem to recall that this is how we met," she said half seriously. "I have a servile streak in me. You could make me your slave."

"My fancies don't lie in that direction," he said. He kissed her on the face as he took the coffee from her. "Have you been up long?"

"Sure," she replied returning to the stove for her own coffee. "I was up and down there swimming in the ocean. It was wonderful. Freezing cold and rough as hell."

He laughed. "I bet you were," he said. "What are you going to do now? Go back to Manteo?"

She shrugged and sat on the bed. "I guess so," she said. "Unless you're thinking of taking on help."

Burrows regarded her seriously. "You can come with me if you'd like to, Bonnie," he said.

"Sure," she said. "You still think they're here?"

"Where else? What else can I think?"

"There's not much else," she agreed. She hesitated. "That is

162

. . . well, that is unless you're hanging onto a fantasy—" She glanced at him apologetically. "You know what I'm trying to say, Doctor?"

He knew. "It's not an obsession, Bonnie. Not like that." He leaned forward and put his hand on hers. "Listen, they've *got* to be here. That boy at the petrol station saw them heading this way. And they never left on either of the ferries. That means they are still here." His head dropped again for a moment. "I think."

The day was full of high wind on Hatteras Island, speeding mountains of yellow cloud across the Cape, sending waves like clenched fists onto the beaches, and launching gulls gleefully into the Atlantic sky.

They began to search in the south again, returning to the village of Hatteras and working north through Frisco, Buxton, Avon, and Waves, towards Salvo and Sweetwater Point. It was the weekend and there were people working on their boats at Hatteras Inlet. The other villages were almost vacant. Wind sliced through the spaces between the wooden houses on stilts, bearing with it foaming spray that stuck and gathered like snow.

The pair worked with a system. On arrival at each settlement they would split, with Burrows checking one section of houses and other buildings and Bonnie the other. Frisco, Avon, Waves . . . They went almost stealthily, working through the deserted places like the earth's last inhabitants searching for company. Sometimes they called. Seabirds squatting between the houses squealed and jerked into the sky as the intruders appeared. But nowhere did they find a sign or a clue of the three people they sought.

Eventually, in the early afternoon, with the horizon dimming already as though the night could hardly wait, they arrived at the village of Salvo, like all the others stranded on the narrow land between the open ocean and the choppy Pamlico Sound. "It looks like a shipwreck," commented Burrows as they drove towards the elevated wooden buildings on their isthmus between the waters.

"Sure," she agreed. "Like one of those old galleons driven ashore. And that's what happened here in those days. They say that's where the wild horses in these parts come from. They were just marooned."

The smalltalk came as a relief to them both after the intensity

163

and the disappointment of their search. They needed something else. As though to acknowledge that fact, Burrows turned the car down a shingle track, off the central road, and braked almost against the curling ocean. They sat regarding it with wonder. The straight, low coast was strung out for miles on either side, only diminishing from sight when they spray erupted in high explosions. Immediately in front of the car, the Atlantic lunged like a hunter at the final kill, throwing itself on the battered beach with enormous force and passion. Its back broken, the ocean rolled up the shingle, finally spreading itself sedately almost beneath the wheels of the car. He looked once more both ways, at the racing sky and the sea surging and breaking all along the furious coast. "What a beautiful place," he said suddenly and quietly.

"It can grow on you," she smiled, unsurprised at the abrupt calm that had come over him. "If you feel like tearing your hair out, this makes you feel a little inadequate."

"Are you always going to stay here?" he asked. "Won't you go somewhere else, New York or somewhere?"

She laughed easily. "New York would swallow me," she replied. "I'd never be seen again. Here you can be *seen*." She glanced at him, realising what she had said, and added, "Sometimes."

Burrows acknowledged the remark with a tired smile. "I just love this Godawful coast," she went on. "Always have. I've been in cities, in discos and restaurants, or at a party, and suddenly, for no reason at all, I can hear this racket we're hearing right now. And I can taste the spray in whatever I happen to be drinking. I guess I'll always want to come back here, whatever happens."

"I shall certainly miss you when this is over."

"Sure," she said without emphasis. "I'll feel just the same. I feel like I've known you forever."

"Yes," he said simply. "I feel like that too."

There was no change in her position. She said, almost casually, "Do you have a wife in England? I never thought of that. For some reason I never thought of it."

"I *did* have a wife," he corrected. "Not now."

"You're divorced?"

"No, she's dead. I'm what is quaintly called a widower."

"Oh," she said. "There's a lot I don't know about you. I guess

164

we did things the wrong way around. Without proper introductions. Did you have children?"

"No. I regard Kate and Abigail as my children."

"And Edith? What about her?"

"She is conveniently a widow." He stared straight out to sea. "I had asked her to marry me."

"There had to be some reason for the way you feel about finding them . . . I guess I should have guessed."

"Edith was married to my brother," he continued quietly. "He and my wife died in the same car accident. They were going off somewhere – together."

This time she reacted. She sat up straight in the seat. "You mean 'going off' . . . like 'going off'? Like that?"

He nodded and watched a great grey wave galloping towards them. He said nothing more until it had disintegrated over the beach. "As you say – 'Like that,' " he confirmed. "They were lovers."

"Jesus," she breathed. "In England. And I thought it was all those little houses with straw roofs and fog and people who talk slow like you do."

"That sort of thing is international," he smiled.

"Do you feel like taking a walk out of the car?" asked Bonnie. "Because I do."

"Why not?" he said. "All that fresh air might do me some good. I feel as though I haven't breathed for weeks." They opened the doors and stood out on the beach, on opposite sides of the car, both pummelled by the flat wind. He looked at her and saw her straggly hair suddenly fly out behind her like the headdress of an Indian chief. Her nose sniffed the salty air. She called across the car. "Okay? Shall we walk?"

He nodded and went around to her. They began to walk, across the wind, going south along the beach, their heads bent, looking down at the sand and the shells. Burrows had a sudden fantasy that something, something belonging to Edith, a brooch, anything, might be lying in the shingle. He walked more slowly, looking down. She watched him. "Searching for clues?" she said.

He laughed grimly. "It's become a habit," he shrugged. "Maybe one will turn up."

They strolled a little apart, each wrapped in an overcoat, his substantial and English, hers the huge hanging thing that all but dragged along the sand. They walked for perhaps thirty or forty yards, the sky skimming above them, the ocean rolling at their shoulders, then Burrows stepped sideways so that they touched. He put his large arm around her small figure in its huge wrapping. She smiled at him and they continued the walk.

It was this sight that Deputy Sheriff Wheeler witnessed when he pulled his car off the road just short of the village of Salvo. He was alone. He sat in the car watching the huddled pair for a while. He could see Burrows' car parked on the foreshore to his left. They would have to return. He waited.

Eventually the pair turned and walked back along the empty darkening beach. They saw the patrol car when they were almost level. Wheeler got out and went, with some difficulty against the wind, down the shingle towards them. "Hi," he said without friendliness.

"Deputy Wheeler," said Burrows. He kept his arm around the girl. "How nice of you to call. This is . . . Bonnie." He suddenly realised he did not know her surname.

"Sure, I know," answered Wheeler, shouting because he was facing the wind. "She serves me hamburgers sometimes. How y'doing? Find anybody yet?" He glanced at the girl. "Anybody else?" He moved around so that the wind was not in his face. Burrows and the girl wheeled slightly too so that they were all in a line, as though performing a little dance, with their backs against the ocean.

"Not yet," said Burrows, shaking his head. "But I have evidence that they came across here. After going to the Lost Colony."

"You don't say? What evidence?"

"I would have gone back and reported to you, but you don't seem very receptive to my sort of evidence."

"What evidence?" repeated Wheeler slowly.

"The lad at the petrol station just short of the causeway," said Burrows, trying to sound convincing. "He's very bright."

"He's about ten years old," answered Wheeler.

"Twelve," corrected Burrows. "He said he was twelve. Anyway, he saw them coming over here to the Cape."

"Sure," said Wheeler unconvincingly. "But you didn't find them yet?"

"We're still looking."

"And I thought you were beachcombing. Where did you sleep last night, by the way?"

"Sleep?" Burrows said. "At the bloody Hilton Hotel."

"Where?" repeated Wheeler.

"In our cars," said Burrows. "Separately. Me in mine. Her in hers."

"You're not supposed to," said Wheeler. "It's vagrancy."

Burrows held out his wrists. "Is it a handcuffs charge?" he said.

"Not yet," muttered Wheeler. "But don't count on my patience, mister."

"Doctor," Burrows reminded him with a smile.

"I keep forgetting," sniffed the deputy. "We had a report that one of the houses along the coast had been broken into. No felony committed, nothing stolen that is, except the use of a little cooking gas by the look of it. Bed occupied, that sort of thing. Lock busted on the door and a car left on the highway. We're checking that out."

"Oh, dear."

"Sure, oh dear, like you say. And somebody went into the lighthouse yesterday. A fisherman saw this guy right up on the top, on the gallery."

Burrows blinked. "All right, that was me. Sightseeing. No damage. I hope. I didn't cause a shipwreck, did I? The door was unlocked."

"You left it open when you quit. The place is full of seagull shit this morning."

"God, I'm sorry. They shit like mad, don't they? There seems to be a lot of it around here."

Wheeler was going to reply, but he paused and breathed deeply. Then he said carefully, "Look, why don't you folks just get in your car and follow me over to the Sheriff's Office in Manteo? It don't do you a lot of good being over here on a bad day like this."

"Is that an order?" asked Burrows. He felt Bonnie shift against him. She had said nothing but kept her pale face towards the law officer all the time.

"Let's say it's a suggestion," said Wheeler. "A good one."

"All right," sighed Burrows. "I'll come. I wish you were as enthusiastic about finding missing people."

Wheeler said nothing. They turned and went towards the car.

167

Wheeler stopped his car outside his office and Burrows drew up the Aspen behind him. The deputy walked back towards them. He said to Bonnie, "Why don't you go over and cook a few hamburgers, young lady?"

She glanced at Burrows who smiled at her. Then she left the car and walked across the street to Joey's. Burrows got out and went with Wheeler into the Sheriff's Office. The deputy sat down with apparent weariness behind his desk. He motioned to Burrows to take a seat. "Want some coffee?" he asked.

"All right," returned Burrows. "I've had a lot of police coffee recently and I think yours is the best."

Wheeler shrugged off the sarcasm and went out to the coffee machine. He returned with the containers and set them down on the desk. "Listen," he said. "Why don't you just fuck off out of here, Doctor? Like now." There was no heat in the remark.

"You're repeating yourself," said Burrows. "I'm not fucking off for you."

"It's for *everybody's* benefit," sniffed Wheeler. He drank half his coffee at one gulp and leaned back again, wiping his mouth. "You're trouble."

"I came to find three relatives," said Burrows angrily but slowly. He looked down into the swirling coffee as if he thought it might hold the answer to mysteries. "I'm not giving up until I've done so. And I have to do it alone since I obviously can't expect much help from you."

"That girl," said Wheeler nodding over his shoulder. "The girl from the hamburger place. She's under age in this state, you know. I'm not suggesting anything, but I'm just telling you she's under age. In this sort of community it's something that gets frowned on."

Burrows was about to make a retort when Wheeler pushed on. "And I'm not suggesting that you broke into that summer house over on the Cape. Somebody did, and they slept there, but I wouldn't blame you. I don't want you to think that, Doctor. And I'm not suggesting, either, that when you were staggering about on top of the lighthouse that the Coast Guard was called out, or that it was you who drank the emergency bourbon over there . . . "

"All right, I drank the fucking bourbon," put in Burrows

angrily. "I left a five-dollar note in the drawer."

"I said it was *emergency* bourbon," repeated Wheeler. "Just try reviving some half-dead guy with a five-dollar bill."

He performed an exaggerated shrug. "None of those things is exactly a hanging offence, I agree. But in this business you get a sort of sniff of trouble. You know what I mean? A situation, or a person, gets a kind of smell about them. You know that they'll either come to a dirty end or something like that. And I keep getting that feeling, that smell, about you."

"Thanks," muttered Burrows. "There are a few things that smell around here." Wheeler waited, not reacting, and Burrows, glaring at him, rasped, "Three innocent people are being held somewhere out there on the Cape, while you're sitting here on your fat backside!"

"I don't believe that," returned Wheeler easily. "I just don't believe it at all. I think you've just got a hang-up about the whole thing. It's a fantasy. You've let it get hold of you. If those three ladies came this way they went the logical way back – to the west and then south to Charleston. Have you checked they haven't turned up in Charleston?"

Burrows leaned angrily towards him. "They're not in bloody Charleston," he said. "I checked a half dozen times. I don't *need* to check that any more!"

"See what I mean! You've developed a fantasy about the whole goddam thing. You don't even *want* them to be in Charleston."

Burrows looked at him angrily. "I brought a witness over here, the girl from the Lost Colony, and you didn't want to know. And the boy at the petrol station, the gas station, *he* saw them going across to the Cape, across the causeway. What about that?"

"The kid's father was in Herbie's Fishing Tackle that night when you got the bottle over your head," sighed Wheeler. "The kid heard him talking about it, I guess. The women and the red Pinto. He knew who you were, mister. He gave you that story because he knew it was worth a dollar. I know that kid; he even lies about his age. He's always playing hookey."

The deputy threw his coffee container in the waste basket. Burrows flung his after it. "There's also the matter of Herbie's," muttered Wheeler. "The guys who were in there ain't too happy about you. They've got it into their heads that it was you who

169

screwed up their little fun evenings with the pornographic movies. Stick around here and there's a great chance of you getting another bottle over your head."

"Herbie's seems to cause embarrassment all around," suggested Burrows, looking straight at Wheeler. Wheeler turned away.

"You could end up in the Roanoke Sound."

"Food for fishes," put in Burrows. "And that's another mystery you'd never solve."

Wheeler stood up. His expression was tight. "I've got enough on you, Doctor, to make life very difficult. And particularly with regard to the girl across the street. Leading minors astray – that's bad news in these parts. She's kept some strange company in the past too."

"What do you mean?"

"Known thieves, people like that."

Burrows said, "You're a bastard."

Wheeler gave an exaggerated sigh, then said, "I'm making allowances for you, Doctor. I'm making a friendly suggestion. The suggestion is that you get the hell out of here, get clear of Dare County right now, and be over the state line just as quick as you can. Like I said to you before, why don't you go and look in Colorado?"

"You're too kind," gritted Burrows, getting up. His heart was stone.

"As of this moment it's a suggestion – just like I said. But I can soon make it official." He went to the door and opened it. "I don't want any trouble, any *more* trouble with you, Doctor. So beat it while the chance is still there." He let Burrows out into the street. "West is left," he added with a nod. "That's the way to go. Now, go."

Burrows faced him. "With a lot of hard work," he said, "you could become a bloody half-wit."

Burrows drove slowly west keeping pace with a grey rainbelt that was drifting inland from Cape Hatteras. He hardly moved in the driving seat. Hunched over the wheel, he merely turned it a fraction to take the slight bends in the long, flat, straight road. His eyes were solid, almost glazed, as he stared over the rim of the wheel and out at the wet road ahead.

Bonnie had stood in the beginnings of that rain, just as it began to smear Manteo that afternoon, in the street, watching him go. Across on the other side Deputy Wheeler was standing in the window of his office. Burrows had touched the girl on the cheek inadequately, before he climbed into the car. He did not kiss her. Then he turned and made an exaggerated V-sign towards Wheeler's window. He saw Wheeler turn his back. He got into the car and drove away. West.

He drove now, the long straight wintry miles, defeat and despair hanging on him like a shroud. He realised he had to ring Andy Curtis in Charleston. Jesus Christ, Wheeler *could* be right. He was letting the fantasy take over. Forgetting the essentials. He must ring.

But he still kept putting it off. He passed through small towns and villages, each with its drugstore where there would be a telephone, but he drove straight on. Highway 64 stretched on west, and that was the way he was going. At the small town of Williamston he stopped and went into a motel which had a restaurant. He decided he had driven far enough that afternoon. He was not over the state boundary, but that was too bad. Wheeler could go and screw himself.

He checked in and ate a silent, tasteless meal. There were no drinks available so he settled for coffee. Then he rang Charleston. Adele answered.

"Oh, it's you," she said with a sort of resigned nastiness.

"Yes, Adele. Sorry I haven't been in touch. They haven't turned up . . . by any chance?"

"By no chance." Her sniff was audible.

"I've had no luck. Well, I *thought* I'd had some, but everything went wrong."

"Just like this end. Things have gone wrong here too. Very, very wrong."

"Oh, what's happened?"

"Well, like, for instance, Andy's taken his ass off with that woman. The one he promised not to see again—" Her voice began breaking.

Burrows dropped his eyes wearily. "Oh, I'm sorry, Adele," he said in a whisper.

"Shit, so am I!" she replied. "A good marriage destroyed, thrown on the trash heap, and why? Because of all *this*, that's why. Everything got so fouled up. He started thinking about things too much and he just took off in the end. Just went – as easy as that." She was crying now. "Leaving me stranded . . . and I'm forty-seven goddam years old."

"Adele," he said. "What can I say?"

"Nothing," she answered bitterly. "Just don't bother. Everybody's said enough. I don't want to talk any more, Phil, I'm putting the phone down. Good-bye. Write to me sometime in a few years or something."

The phone went dead. Slowly he replaced the receiver. He went out of the restaurant and, taking his key from the desk, started towards his room. On the wall by the desk was a large-scale map of North Carolina. He paused, his eyes going at once towards the east to where Cape Hatteras and its attendant islands hung down the Atlantic seaboard. Waves, Salvo, Frisco. He repeated the names mentally, almost affectionately. He imagined the dark, wet landscape out there now, with the ocean bellowing and the wind leaping. In his mind again he saw the little night scene of domesticity that he had shared with Bonnie. Sadness increased as he thought of the miles now between them. He picked up the phone and called Joey's in Manteo. She answered. "I was waiting for you to call," she said in her matter-of-fact way. "Where are you?"

"Williamston," he said. "The Hunting Lodge Motel."

"I'll be there," she said and put the phone down.

He remained standing, smiling suddenly at the telephone. He went to the coffee shop and had another cup of coffee. Then the thought suddenly came to him that he ought to ring the Missing Person's Bureau in New York. He found the card that Detective Lomax had given to him. On impulse he called the home number. Lomax answered.

"This is Burrows, Philip Burrows," he said.

"Who?"

Burrows swallowed. "Dr. Philip Burrows – from England," he said. "I came to search for Edith Burrows and her daughters . . . you remember."

"Ah, Dr. Burrows, sure. How are you? Where are you now?"

"I'm in Williamston, North Carolina, and I'm having a difficult time. No news your end?"

"Nothing. Sorry, but nothing. I came off duty at five and there'd been nothing. I had a kind of funny thought that if they

172

suddenly got back to New York . . . say they did . . . and got on the plane for England. For some reason . . . We didn't know where you were, so *you'd* then be the Missing Person."

"I hadn't thought of that. But they haven't. I've spoken to the people in Charleston and they've had no news."

"Well, I think we might have got to hear about it," said Lomax with a dry laugh. "How have you been doing?"

"I believe I have traced them to Cape Hatteras," said Burrows bluntly.

"Cape Hatteras? Jeese." Lomax didn't sound as if he believed him.

"The trouble is the law there – the Deputy Sheriff – a man called Wheeler – has just thrown me out of the place. That's why I'm ringing you. Is there anything you can do? I want to go back. I hadn't finished there."

"He threw you out? Why would he do that?"

"Allegations of house-breaking among other things."

"Did you break into a house?"

"A summer place . . . I had to sleep somewhere." He could hear the caution immediately.

"I don't see how I can do anything there," said Lomax. "House-breaking is house-breaking. Didn't you have some trouble at Silver Spring or somewhere? We had a report. A gun was involved."

"I'm afraid so."

"Dr. Burrows, let me give you some advice, as a friend. Don't get outside the law."

"Policemen are always telling me that," mumbled Burrows, remembering Harry Mead in England. Lomax said nothing further. Burrows said, "You can't help then? You couldn't have a word with Wheeler at Manteo?"

"I couldn't," said Lomax.

"I see. Well, sorry to have wasted your time."

"Okay. Don't worry about it."

"Thanks."

"That's okay."

Burrows replaced the phone. He looked at the map once more and found Williamston, where he now stood, on the long stretch of Highway 64. Then he noticed that the town was a road junction, that Highway 17 turned northeast from there, climbing up towards the coast, arriving at Elizabeth City. And from Elizabeth City a secondary road went *south* again and entered Cape Hatteras at its uppermost point. God, *he could go back*, and without going through Manteo and attracting the attention of Wheeler.

He went to his room and lay on the bed. He fell asleep and woke only when it was almost midnight. There was a knocking at the door and there was Bonnie, grinning.

Bonnie lay against him in the early morning. "It's goodbye again," she said. "Back to Joey's."

"Wheeler won't be suspicious that way," he said. "I'll take the long road to the north and down to the Cape. As soon as I can I'll contact you."

She said quietly, "When you find them, what will you do? I mean, are you going to ride away on your white horse and carry Edith back to England and marry her? Great celebrations, end of story?"

He looked at the ceiling. Every motel ceiling was the same. "Motels are wonderful," he said drily. "If you hate waking up in a strange room."

"I asked you a question."

"I know. I don't know the answer. Don't you have any . . . well . . . arrangements?"

"Arrangements!" she laughed. "You English." She turned from him and lay on her back also. "I seem to home in on the difficult cases. Like now. Last summer there was this guy. I got friendly with him, you know. He used to steal things – not things he needed, because he had plenty of money, but just things he took a liking to. And difficult to steal. It was a kind of a hobby with him. He travelled all over doing it. It gave him a charge, I guess."

Burrows said, "Is this the same man Mary knew? The one Wheeler talked about? The one she couldn't, or wouldn't, recognise?"

The girl smiled. "You're certainly improving as a private eye," she said. "The very same guy. You should see the things he had – a lock of Lincoln's hair, some silver made by Paul Revere he picked up in Lexington, and other stuff like that." She paused then continued, "You know, he even had Buffalo Bill's six-

174

shooter, with bullets. He got that from the Cowboy Hall of Fame in Oklahoma City."

"Quite a connoisseur. What was he doing in these parts?"

"He wanted to steal something from the Wright Brothers Museum at Kitty Hawk," she said. "He moved in on Mary as soon as he found out she worked there. And that's how I got to know him."

"He didn't fancy Mary," said Burrows. He surprised himself by the touch of bitterness.

"He played her along because of her job," shrugged Bonnie. "He kidded her. But I didn't know about that. Mary didn't room with me then."

"The plan went wrong."

"It got all screwed up. Mary warned him about the police and he beat it. Wheeler and his boys gave her a hard time and they searched my place, but they didn't find anything."

Bonnie smiled reflectively. "He was a 100 percent golden bastard," she said.

8

"It's tonight," said Tommy. "Okay?"

"What is? What's tonight?"

He rolled his pathetic smile at her. "Our date. Remember, we're dating. I'm taking you to somewhere real special, Abby. A place where they have gracious dining. That's what they say on the notice outside. 'Gracious Dining.' I guess it's just the place for us. I've got a Mustang, you know, a great car. But I'll have to take you in my old Chevy, because the Mustang is being repaired. But I got some great stickers on the Chevy – you know, from all over, Norfolk, Wilmington, everywhere."

Abby did not react at once. She tried to think it out. She was sitting at the small dressing table. He was lying full length on her bed wearing only his shirt and socks. His thick, white legs were thrust out straight in front of him like a corpse. Abby knew that everything had to be thought out carefully now.

"How can we?" she said eventually. "How can you get me out of here?"

He sniffed heartily. She thought for a moment he was going to spit but he seemed to have changed his mind. "There's ways," he said, attempting to sound grand. "Those two, they do just like they want to do. Well, that goes for me, too. For *us*, Abby. I just want to drive you out of here and take you out. I just wish I had my Mustang; you'd flip over that."

He sat up and pushed his legs over the side of the bed, quaintly thrusting his shirt-front between his legs to cover his private parts. His cumbersome eyes were on her. She wanted to pull the robe more closely about her but she resisted the temptation. "How then?" she asked again. "How do we do it?"

"We just go," he shrugged. "Take off." He smiled raggedly. "Gracious dining, here we come. I put a new sticker on the windshield. Just today. From here."

"But we can't, Tommy. What about my mother and Katy? What will *they* do to them when they find we're gone? Tommy . . . they could kill them. You know that."

"They won't," he said, not sounding over-confident in the forecast. "They just wouldn't. They're bluffing. Doing like we've done to people is one thing, killing them is something else." He thought about it. "Anyway, listen, I've got an idea. I'll leave them a note. Tell them we'll be back later."

"What will that do?"

"Listen, baby, we're equal partners in this crime, them and me. If they hurt your ma or your sister, then I give myself up to the cops and spill everything. I'll put that in the letter, okay. Maybe you'd better write it for me, because you could set it down better."

"No," she said decisively. "*You* have to write it. In your handwriting. Otherwise they'll think it's a trick and then they could turn nasty."

She had no plan, no thought, only a vague notion that to get out of that place, even briefly, might present a chance for them. She had no idea how, but there was just a chance that something might occur. There would be no way of escaping completely, not with her mother and Kate still held. She looked at the ugly young man sitting opposite. He was their only hope.

"There's one more thing," he said. "Just one more."

"What's that?"

"The ring. That ring your mum wears. The blue one."

She looked at him blankly. "Yes?"

"I want you to wear it. When we go out together. Okay? I'll ask her. She won't mind when I explain. You'd look great with that blue ring. People will think I bought it for you."

Abigail swallowed. "If that's what you want," she said. "Ask my mother. Tell her I'll look after it."

"Sure," he said. "I'll tell her that. But I really want you to *want* to come. You get me?"

"Let's do it," she said, moving her face towards him and composing a smile. "I would love to just get out of here for a few hours." His face clouded. She added quickly, "With you, Tommy."

177

In her room a few yards along the corridor Edith Burrows was carefully pulling the plywood panel away from the bath. She had taken out the holding screws at one end, using her secreted kitchen knife as a screwdriver. Now she had opened a gap big enough to insert her hand. Listening for any movement from the direction of the bedroom door she pushed her slim hand into the opening she had engineered. Relief crossed her face. At once she knew she had been right. There were pebbles under there. She searched about with her fingers and with a tight feeling of triumph brought out a grey pebble the size of an egg. Slipping it into the pocket of her robe she replaced the bath panel and tightened the screws.

Quickly she put the pebble beneath the cold water tap. Then, turning the water off, she began carefully to draw the knife backwards and forwards across the stone's cold surface. She held it beneath her robe to deaden the scraping sound. After a minute she paused and ran her finger lightly along the edge of the knife. She smiled. Already it was sharp.

"Shit . . . shit, shit, shit!"

"For Christsake, what's the matter?"

"They're gone. That crazy bastard Tommy and the girl."

James saw the lines tighten around her mouth. "Gone?" she asked. "How the fuck are they gone?"

"They just are. He's left a note. . . . Oh, that fucking lunatic! I'll cut his ugly throat when I get hold of him–"

"Give me–" Candice took the note from him. She read, "Abby and me are going out dining. You still have her ma and Kate. I will bring her back okay, and she won't squeal because you have got them. So don't worry. If you do anything with them I'll go to the cops. Okay?"

Candice regained her composure. "What do we do?" she said.

"That mad bastard–" he said. He took the note from her and crumpled it up in rage.

"I think what we do is *nothing* right now."

"I think we get rid of these two and beat it now, quick, while there's time," he snarled.

"Kill them?"

"Sure. I didn't mean anything else." He looked at her narrowly. "Both of them," he said nastily. "Including the girl. Got it, lady? Including the sweetie."

Candice turned away as if he had spat at her. James roughly caught her arm and half turned her back. "I mean it," he snarled. "Listen, you fucking dyke, she's got to get it too. Got me? She's—"

Candice turned and struck him with all her force across the face. The blow was such that it sent him staggering away. When he looked up he saw that she had produced the small gun from her bag. "Don't you call me a fucking dyke," she said in almost a murmur. "You don't have any room to call anybody anything."

"Easy, easy," he said anxiously. "Take it easy. Put that toy away. We're going to get nowhere fast like this. You start using that thing and you'll have more corpses than you can handle."

She knew he was right. She lowered the gun and casually put it back in the bag. "All right," she said. "But just be more careful about the insults. "She looked at him steadily. "We still haven't decided what we have to do."

He sat down. They were in the lobby. Outside the window, far out, the remote lighthouse sent its beam like a white arm across the ocean. "I say we do as I suggested. Listen, Candice, we've got to get rid of these women in the end. There's no way we can get out with them still alive. I think you've got to face that. Go and give her a last screw and then we'll do it."

"Shut up," she said sharply. "You don't think any higher than your balls. We've got to wait until those two get back. We can't have that goddam Tommy on the loose. Even if we did it – okay, *killed them* – and took off, we'd have every cop in the country with a full description and everything. We have to wait until we do something with Tommy too."

"Kill him too?"

"Christ, I don't see how we can," she said. "There's nothing to connect these three women with us, nothing at all. But Tommy, that's different. If we drowned him, or killed him and buried him somewhere, it's still known in these parts that he's been associating with us. His mother might even miss him. The cops would check – and they'd check on us in New York too, and I don't think we ought to encourage that. Once they started looking for Tommy, who knows what they might find?"

"We're stuck with him," he agreed. "*Shit.*"

179

"We always have been. He's been the risky link all along."

James gnawed his fist. "There's got to be some way," he said eventually.

Candice said quietly. "There is. We've got to get him in real deep, deeper than he is now. So he'll never open his mouth." She looked steadily at James and smiled a small, sudden smile. "We've got to get *him* to kill Abigail," she said.

Tommy pulled the old, grey Chevrolet, with its rash of gaudy tourist stickers and slogans, into the parking lot alongside the Cape Hatteras Fishery Restaurant. The lot was right up to the beach. It sloped to the moonlit sand and onto the easy waves of a balmy evening.

"Wow, just like summer!" enthused Tommy. He helped Abigail from the vehicle in the way he imagined a gentleman would, holding the door and then her elbow as she climbed out. " 'Gracious Dining,' " he nodded. "See – it says there. I used to come here some nights and see them going in, two by two, and read those words 'Gracious Dining' to myself. One day, I said to myself, I'm going to have me some of that dining and I'll have a real beautiful chick – a beautiful girl – on my arm. Better than all the crummy chicks with the other guys." He smiled like a tame shark at her. "And now it's come true," he said. He crooked his arm and gave it to her. Inside she shivered, but there also were stirrings of hope. There might be a way. She took the arm and they walked towards the lights and drifting music.

Tommy was wearing a light sports coat with a crooked collared white shirt and a soiled red tie. He had two creases in one leg of his trousers. "Do I look okay?" he asked her.

She made herself look at him. She made some pretence of putting the collar and tie in order and said, "Very handsome." He held her at arms' length, in the way he had seen handsome men do in the movies, and looked her up and down. "Great," he approved. "Just beautiful. Let's go in."

He was about to move through the warmly lit door when he stopped again and looked towards her once more. His expression had altered. "And, don't forget. If you try anything – if anybody gets to know about what's happened . . . then you ain't going to see your mom again. You got that?"

She nodded dumbly. He said, "Okay, but just understand. If

180

we don't get back, that's what's going to happen. That's what we decided, Candice, James, and me."

"I won't cause any trouble," she mumbled. He held her arm, a grip so fierce that she suppressed a squeal. "Let's go now," he said, "and get us some gracious dining."

The restaurant was three-quarters full. The man at the door said, "Do you have a reservation, sir?"

Tommy turned and looked at Abigail. His face tumbled. He turned back to the man. "No . . . well . . . no. But we want to come in. We've *got* to come in. My girl's been looking forward to this–"

"Okay, okay," replied the man. "It's no sweat. There's tables. I just wanted to check if you reserved one, that's all. This way, please."

He glanced at them with some curiosity, taking in the girl's looks, the large ring on her finger and the clumsy dress of her partner. He shrugged. There was no accounting for taste. He led them to a table next to an illuminated fish tank. The fish stared out at them. He handed them a menu. "I'll send the waitress right across," he said. "Maybe you'd like a drink first."

Tommy looked discomfitted, as though this was something he had not planned. "Sure, sure," he said eventually. "We'll have drinks. Huh, two vodkas. On the rocks. Yeah, make it vodka on the rocks."

The man went away and Abby leaned across the table. "I *can't* drink vodka," she said. "I've never drunk it. I might do something."

He smiled apparently regarding it as a point against her. "You have to," he said. "This is the kind of place where you have to. Don't worry, baby, I'll see it don't go to your pretty head."

A band began to mount a rostrum at the far end of the room. It was an old-fashioned assembly, middle-aged and elderly players, with bright blue coats and sparkling silver lapels. They held saxophones and clarinets.

"We're gonna dance," said Tommy. "Right as soon as they start playing."

She did not say anything. She was looking around, her eyes blank like those of a sick person. "Maybe not yet," decided Tommy. "Don't want to get people staring at us." He thought about it. "It's a goddam shame, that is," he decided. "Because I

181

wanted people to look at us together so they'd know you belonged to me. But now I can't. Shit, nothing ever works out."

A young waitress came back with the drinks on a tray. Abigail looked at her almost hungrily. She was about the same age, pretty with long dark hair. "She's free," thought the English girl. "God, she's *free*. When she goes from here tonight she can go home. . . . " The pain and sorrow welled inside her. She dropped her eyes to the tablecloth.

"Are you ready to order now?" asked the waitress. "Or do you want to wait a little?" Abigail saw her glance at the blue ring.

"We'll wait," said Tommy, blurting it out as if he were nervous at having to do it. "Just come back."

"Okayee, I'll do that," replied the girl cheerfully. She put the order pad in her pocket and went to a table a few yards to the left. She spoke to a young man, a fair-haired youth with a clear smile. Abby followed her with her eyes and her glance caught that of the young man. Tommy was engaged in trying to drink the vodka. He was testing it like medicine. He saw Abigail's glance and leaning silently across below the table caught the girl's knee with a steel grip. He squeezed spitefully. Her face contorted as she turned back towards him.

"Don't," he said thickly. "Don't start giving other guys the eye. I don't like that. If you're with me, you stay with me. I had that happen when I took a chick out before. Once. She only went to look at the other guys. I was paying and she was shopping around. Don't do it. Okay?"

She nodded dully.

"Drink your vodka," he said. "It costs a dollar and a half." The vodka had been brought straight. "Could I have something with it?" she asked. "Tonic or lemonade?"

His face was immediately a mass of concern. "Sure, honey," he said. "Gee, I'm sorry. Hi, miss!" The girl was passing and he caught the edge of her skirt with his fingers.

She looked at him sourly. "You wanted something?"

"Sure. Some lemonade for the lady. To mix with her vodka."

"Okay, be right with you. Do you want to order now?"

"Huh, yes. Okay. Just bring the lemonade and then I'll tell you what we're eating."

The waitress glanced at Abby as if she couldn't understand what she was doing there. She went to the bar and returned to the

182

table with the lemonade. Tommy put it in front of Abby to pour herself, then grabbed it clumsily, spilling some, to pour it into her glass. He was getting confused.

"Order?" said the girl. "What are you going to have?"

"Yes . . . sure. The order. Okay. I want a big steak, a real good steak with French fries and everything."

"To start? What will you have to start?"

"Oh, sure." He seemed to be thrown. "Juice. Yes, sure, juice. Like tomato."

"And the lady?" asked the girl pointedly.

Abby tried to reach her with her eyes. Just to let her know something was wrong. Then in her mind she heard the threats once more. "You ain't going to see your mom again. That's what we decided, Candice, James, and me." She looked away. "I'll have the same, but with some salad."

The girl looked at her curiously because of the accent. But she made no comment. "What sort of dressing on the salad?"

"Oh dressing . . . What do you serve?"

"French, Thousand Island, Roquefort . . . "

"French, thank you."

Abigal felt as if the words were floating, as though in a dream, from her. All around now, were the sounds of the place: the conversation, people laughing, the band playing an old-fashioned popular song. And she was in the midst of it, pinned in the middle of a nightmare, while the scene whirled slowly around her. She had an overwhelming urge to stand up and scream. *To do just that — stand up there and then and scream.* Let the horror rush from her body. She looked across at him staring at her with all his neolithic passion and its terrible threat. She closed her mouth and dropped her hands to the table. The girl went away to get the order.

"You don't look like you're enjoying yourself," complained Tommy. "You got to *enjoy* yourself. It ain't no pleasure for me if you don't enjoy it. Give me a smile, will ya? Go on, Abby, smile at me."

She was beyond tears now. The urge to scream was still there, caught in her throat. She smiled a skeletal smile at him.

"Wine," he said. "I guess we got to have wine. Or beer. Do you want beer? No, I guess wine. That cold duck is okay. Like James served. They must have it here."

The place was almost full now. There were a dozen couples on the dance floor. "Now we can dance," he said eagerly, after considering the people.

"Come on, I just want to hold you." He got up and she slowly followed him. "We want some wine," he said to the waitress as she passed them. "That stuff they call cold duck. A whole bottle of it."

The girl nodded. She took another curious glance at Abigail, her figure and her clothes, as she rose from the table to walk towards the dance floor. This time Abigail avoided her expression.

"This is old stuff, this music," said Tommy at the side of the floor. He held out his ugly hands to her. He was sweating. The red tie had worked itself away from the centre of his neck and the creased collar was sticking out of the lapel of the garish sports coat. With a moment's hesitation as if she needed to take a deep breath, she closed with him and felt his groin push into her stomach and his fetid breath on her face. He began to move clumsily to the music. She felt his chest harden as he pushed it into her breasts. He was stiff as wood. To her amazement he began to sing in her ear. The voice was tuneful and soft.

> "Heaven, I'm in heaven,
> And my heart beats so that I can hardly
>   speak. . . . "

Her obvious surprise pleased him. "Get that," he said. "I can sing, huh?"

"Yes," she said slowly, "you can." All the time, she told herself, she would have to feel and probe. There must be a way out of it. Her concern was not to anger or alienate him. She could not see the escape but she hoped desperately it might be presented to her, it might suddenly open up and be there before her, so they could get out. All three together.

"I used to sing," he continued in her ear as they danced, "all those old songs."

"How? Why was that?"

"There was a woman. She lived right next door to my ma's house. Even when I was a little kid she liked me to go in there to dance with her. She'd have the radio playing or a phonograph.

184

She liked old stuff for music. Even though I was only a kid, maybe ten or twelve, she liked to dance with me. Close, like this now, and she used to sing the songs too. That's how I got to know some of the words. I guess she wanted to screw me. But she never did."

He looked up and saw the fair-haired youth who had been at the neighbouring table. He was dancing with his date, close together but his face was towards Abby. Tommy grunted. "That guy is looking at you again. I can't stand it when he does that. I'll pull his fucking eyes out of his head."

"He's *not* looking at me," she whispered.

"Good thing I don't want trouble," grumbled Tommy. "Or I'd kill the jerk. Thinks he can take some other guy's girl. I've seen that goddam smartass type before. Come on, let's eat."

His grip on her arm made her wince. He led her off the floor. The food and the wine were on the table. Tommy poured the cold duck and began to eat immediately, drinking the tomato juice at one gulp and then tearing into the steak with his knife, powerfully chopping it up and sliding it around his plate before stabbing the pieces with sharp jabs of his fork. He spoke with his mouth full. "See how many of these young chicks around here have got braces on their teeth?" he said. "God, I hate that. Imagine putting all that junk in their mouths. Like a bear trap. One of the reasons I really like you a lot, Abby, is your English teeth. You've got good teeth. Let me see them."

She hesitated and then made a grimace across the table. A man with a camera approached them. "You folks want a photograph? Something to remember the evening? I sure think it would be nice with a pretty lady like that." The photographer looked doubtfully at Tommy. "How about it?"

"Take off," muttered Tommy, although he looked as if he wanted to agree. "We don't need that. We got plenty of pictures."

"Okay," said the man easily. "If that's what you want."

He walked to the next table, and then to the adjacent group which included the fair-haired youth. He moved around and took a flashlight picture from the dance floor. "Turn away," grunted Tommy quickly to Abigail. "Get your face this way."

She turned as the flashlight jumped. Her face was white and set. Tommy's expression was stony fear. His eyes filled angrily.

"Shit," he whispered. "Jesus Christ, shit."

"They didn't photograph *us*," she insisted. The trapped sensation overwhelmed her again. *If she could only tell someone.* Help was all around her, she only had to stand up now, this moment, and *scream.* She put her face into her hands.

"Quit," he whispered nastily. "Don't do that. You got to look like you're enjoying yourself. I didn't come here for this scene."

His passion was bubbling. He could not stop himself. His hand came across the table and snapped around her wrist. Abby's fearful face raised itself to his expression of violence. Then she was aware of someone standing beside them. They both looked up. It was the fair-haired youth.

"Would you guys like to come over and join my friends?" he said, looking down on them. Tommy immediately relaxed the grip, withdrew his hand and laid it flat across hers in a pretence of affection. The young man spoke to Abby. "You'd really be welcome." He looked at Tommy evenly.

Abby thought Tommy was going to get up to fight. But he remained seated. "We're okay," he grunted. "We're taking off anyway. Ain't we, baby?"

Abigail thought she was going to burst. The great scream was gathered, straining in her chest. Her mouth seemed full of it. She only had to let it go now. To rush to these young people at the table. Then she would see Tommy making for the door. She had a picture of her mother and sister dead in that terrible place. How long would the police take? How long?

She looked up at the young man and said deliberately, "We have to go."

"Okay," he said uncertainly. He backed away towards his own table.

Abigail closed her eyes and prayed. "Oh, God, please send us help. Send us someone strong to help us." When she opened them she saw that her prayer was immediately answered. There he was – Tommy.

She smiled fondly at him. "Why don't we have another dance before we leave?" she said. "You can sing."

Half an hour later she walked with her arm in his along the beach. Her fear had not dissipated, but the terrible urge to panic had gone, replaced by a strange calculating hardness beneath her

186

suddenly relaxed exterior. She knew what she had to do.

"I'm sorry, Tommy," she said. "I was upset in there. That fellow worried me. I thought he was going to do something. We just can't risk that."

He accepted the plural with a dumb nod of his chin. "I can't believe it," he said. "Walking along like this with you. In the moon, on the beach, it's like a goddam commercial on TV."

She produced a light laugh. "You're funny, you know," she said. "Very funny at times."

"You really like me?" he said, stopping.

She turned towards him. "I don't know why, Tommy," she said, "but I do. I suppose it's because we're the same age and we've been thrown in this together."

He looked at her with pathetic hope.

"How about kissing me?" he asked. "Like in the movies. You know, with the ocean and everything."

"All right," she replied. She closed with him and slid her arms about his thick neck. She could smell his breath and the heat of his face. He tensed and then trembled. "Come on," she encouraged him, "kiss me."

They kissed. Then again. He suddenly lay against her, holding her slight body against his heavy chest. His face dropped against her neck. "Jesus Christ," he muttered. "Is this happening to me?"

She laughed again and put her lips to his neck. He straightened up, his face shaking. "I ain't never going to touch you again," he choked. "Never, not unless you want." Tears started in his eyes. "I just . . . don't know how it's all happened."

His clumsy arm went around her waist and they walked a few more steps through the sand. Abigail looked up at the placid sky and then out to where the moon's path ran smoothly across the sea. "It's amazing how things change," she said. "It's just like summer."

Suddenly he halted. "What can I do?" he growled.

Ingenuously she smiled at him. "I don't know," she said. "What?"

"I've got to do *something*," he said. "Something." He looked at her trustingly. "To make it up to you."

"Listen," she said putting her hands on his waist. "There is a way. We can get them, you and I, Tommy. Both of us."

187

"We just go in and bust them up," he suggested.

"What about the gun? Candice has the gun."

She turned him and they began to walk back to the car. "I'll get that gun," he muttered. "That shouldn't be so difficult. And then I'll shoot the bastards." His mouth trembled. "I will, Abby. I'll get them for what they've done to me."

Abigail swallowed. "You mustn't worry, Tommy," she said soothingly. "You won't be held responsible. I'll see to that."

The youth stopped and regarded her with amazement. "You mean . . . I could get away with it? After all I done?"

"*You* didn't do very much. You're not a villain. It's the others. After all, what's kidnapping these days? Hijacks and sieges and all the rest of it." She was trying desperately to keep up the act. Tommy was staring at her with disbelief and yet, she could see, touched with hope. "Somebody always helps," she said. "Somebody fixes it so the hostages get free. It's just part of life today."

"And the somebody could be me," he said. His eyes went dull with thought. His lips pressed together. She squeezed his arm as they approached the car. Almost blindly as he opened the door for her. In the few seconds he took to stumble around the front of the car to the driver's door Abigail steeled herself, forced herself to retain control. This was the chance. The only one.

Tommy opened the door and sat down heavily. He put the key into the ignition but did not turn it. "But rape," he said. "What I did to you was rape."

"Rape," she sighed. "What's rape? Sex is sex. Even when girls say they've been raped people don't believe them. Not these days. Even in England the police hardly ever believe them. It's a thin line. And if I make no complaint about you, then who's to accuse you?"

Slowly he turned. God, she thought. I'm winning. "You'd do that?" he said. "You wouldn't tell anybody?"

"If it meant we were free," she said. "I wouldn't."

"What about your mother?"

"She kissed you, didn't she?" She leaned forward eagerly. "Listen, Tommy, it's the only thing. For all of us, Tommy. You help us – we'll help you."

His mood changed. "Hah," he grunted. "Then tomorrow when you're out you change your mind and the cops come and get me."

Her eyes widened and she moved her face closer to him. She wished she had used perfume that night. "I've given you my word," she said. "My solemn promise. A promise with an English girl is a promise."

"You'll tell the cops that I'm clean? That I helped you?"

"That's what I said." Her voice dropped. "Let me tell you something else, Tommy. If we don't do something, they'll get *you* too. Just believe me. They can't afford to let *you* go free. In this way you'll be rescuing yourself." She played her final card. "Tommy," she whispered. "You could be a hero."

His expression tightened. "You're goddam right. I've got to do it," he breathed.

She leaned into his face and kissed him on the cheek. "You have."

"But the cops," he said. "They'll have to be there. After we get those two, the cops–"

"Let's *go* to the cops!" she said suddenly. The words came out as soon as the thought struck her. "Go to them *now*. Tell them about the others, James and Candice, and lead them back to Sweetwater Point. You and I go in first, make sure that no harm comes to my mother and Kate, and then the police come in."

"That's not so crazy as it sounds," he said thoughtfully. "The cops could *see* whose side I'm on. They could *see* I'm helping."

She was breathing easier now. She had him. He would do it. Her arms looped around his neck. "And I'd never be able to thank you enough, Tommy," she said.

He smiled like an ugly child at her. His paw-like hand touched her breast but he pulled it away quickly. "I promised I wouldn't do anything like that," he mumbled. Abigail took his hand and replaced it on the warmth of her breast. She made herself smile at him again. Tommy returned the smile, but it solidified on his face. He was staring at something over her shoulder. She turned and saw that the fair-haired youth from the restaurant was standing outside the car. A few yards away were a group of his friends. Abigail's heart dropped. She shook her head violently but the youth opened the car door. He was slightly drunk. A loose smile hung on his face.

He addressed himself to Abigail unsurely, "You sure you don't need any help, miss?"

Abigail felt Tommy grunt angrily and move as if to get out of the door. She pushed her hand back and restrained him. She returned to the youth. He was pushing a piece of paper secretively towards her. She took it and slipped it into her pocket. "I don't need any help, thank you," she said as calmly as she could. "We're just going."

"I'll say we are!" bellowed Tommy. "Get your fucking hands off my car!" He started the engine and the Chevrolet jerked forward almost before she had closed the door.

"Don't worry, Tommy," she tried. But he was driving fast along the single road. In the wide moonlight she could see that tears were coursing down his face. He sniffled and wiped them away with his hand. Abigail began to feel cold. She tried again to speak to him but he did not answer. He shook his head fiercely like a sulky child. Then, as though making a sudden decision, he turned the car swiftly off the main road and along another bumpy approach to the beach. He stopped it at the edge of the sand. There were buildings around them, boarded shadows, all unoccupied.

"Okay," he said nastily, "Give that paper to me."

She felt her heart clench. "What paper?"

He turned fearsomely on her, his features contorted. "Don't kid me," he said. "Don't try to do that. The paper that fucking jerk gave to you." His hand went over her wrist, again like steel. His other hand went into her pocket and brought out the ragged message. "This paper. The asshole." He opened it. He switched the cab light on. The words said, "If in trouble, call me. David Ellison Manteo 287-4352."

"Asshole," said Tommy again.

"How could I help it?" she whispered. She was trembling uncontrollably now. "I didn't ask him to do it."

Tommy pushed his face towards her, his teeth bared. She could smell the wine over his sour breath. "You—" he stumbled. "You and your lies. Trying to kid me. Well, I'm not so dumb, I'm goddam smarter than you think." He crushed his face into hers, pulling her neck fiercely with his hands. "I'll show you, you fucking bitch—"

Abigail attempted to back away but she had no room. "No, Tommy," she tried. "You remember what we said, Tommy." Her voice shook with desperation.

His voice dropped to a growl, almost a drawl. "Like the rest

190

. . . You're like the rest." His eyes hardly seemed to be focusing. He screwed up the piece of paper and threw it on the floor.

"Tommy," she said fearfully. "You've had too much. Too much to drink. Come on, let's get back. Then you can sleep."

"You *would*," he insisted as though he had heard nothing. "You'd double-cross me with the first fucker who came by." She saw there were again tears on his white cheeks. They frightened her more than ever.

"Get out," he snarled. "Go on. There's no difference between you and the rest. Get out of the goddam car."

Shaking with fright she fumbled for the catch of the door and found it. She pressed it and the door swung open. He leaned away from her for a moment and then gave her a violent push that thrust her from the car and sent her sprawling onto the shingle. The fall knocked the breath from her. As she lay she was aware of him coming after her again, a black shape coming around the side of the car, lurching towards her. He threw himself at her, landing across her body with his entire weight. The force crushed her into the beach.

Then she heard herself screaming. It was as if it were another, distant voice. Screaming and screaming. "You stink!" she howled in his face. "God, how you stink!"

Tommy went wild. His hands tore savagely at her clothes, stripping her bosom bare. He spat at her repeatedly. Then, with a savage howl, he put his hands about her neck and began to squeeze. He gripped viciously and squeezed again, turning one hand against the other.

Something stopped him. He eased himself away from her and saw what he had done. "Abby, baby," he whispered. "Are you all right, Abby?" He fell forward, sobbing. "I ain't never going to be no hero."

Candice stood at the hand basin in Kate's bathroom and washed the girl's undergarments and white socks. She held them in her fingers and gently trolled them through the soapy water. Kate was in the bath. She sat stonily watching Candice, her slim hands held across her chest as if in some ceremonial posture. Candice glanced at her and pursed her lips. She said, "It's time you got out of there, young lady."

191

Kate glanced at her. It was almost midnight. Candice nodded briskly. "Out," she repeated.

Kate stood in the bath. She still trembled and the suds slid in clouds down her body. Candice again moved back to her, in her motherly fashion. "Let's get that soap off," she said. "That's no good for a young person's skin." She picked up the shower hose and turned the taps. After testing the temperature of the water she turned the gentle nozzle on the girl's slim body, running it all over.

"You have the sweetest little butt, baby," she murmured, turning the girl around. By now the girl recognised the signs, knew the tone of voice, the lower, almost grating sound that came from the back of the woman's throat. She closed her eyes and choked back the sob that rose in her body.

"Okay," said Candice, her motherly voice returning, "out you come."

Kate climbed from the bath. "Stand there," ordered Candice. "Don't move." The girl obeyed. The woman stood back a pace, so that she was pressed against the hand basin. The girl was glistening, posed, motionless, her hair sticking to her white shoulders, her eyes looking at the floor.

"Look up," said Candice brightly. "Come on now. You're not shy any more."

"I'm not shy," said the girl, raising her eyes. "I'm ashamed."

Candice had picked up a bath towel. "Ashamed?" she echoed, her eyes lighting with amazement. "Why should you be ashamed? Oh, now, come on, Kate, no more of that weeping. You know I hate it when you cry."

She moved towards the girl and put the towel against her stomach. Then she raised the edge and wiped the tears that ran across the face steamy from the bath. "No more," she warned gently. "No more tears."

"What's going to happen?" asked the girl, controlling her voice.

"Happen? Nothing's going to happen. I'm just going to get you into your bed. It's almost midnight."

"To us, I mean. To my mother and my sister and me. You're going to have to kill us, aren't you?"

Candice stared at her as though in shock. "Oh, for goodness sake, Katy, stop it will you!" She began towelling the pale body.

192

"I don't see how you can avoid killing us," pursued the girl. "At sometime you are going to have to get away from this. You can't just leave us – so don't pretend you can."

Candice knelt before her. She pressed her cheek against the damp stomach. "God, baby, what are you saying? How could I let any harm come to you? Nobody's going to kill you."

"How will you get away, then?" asked Kate bluntly.

"This is a big country," murmured Candice. She stood and kissed the child on the cheek. "One great big country. We're just going to vanish. It's not too difficult."

"And just leave us?" The girl tried to sound as if she believed it.

"Sure thing. One morning you're just going to wake up and we'll be gone with the wind. And before long you'll have forgotten everything."

"I shall never forget."

Candice transformed the sentiment. "Nor will I," she breathed, closing her face to the girl's again. "Never, never." Her hands swam around the small form and she held on, at first tenderly, then firmly, and then with increasing and uncontrollable fierceness. "God, you're beautiful, child," she whispered. "So goddam beautiful."

She heard the bedroom door open. "James?" she called immediately. Hurriedly she wrapped the towel around the girl. James crossed the room and walked into the bathroom. "Ha, bath time," he remarked acidly.

"Knock, will you?" said Candice. "Next time, knock."

"They're back," he said, ignoring the remark. "He's just got her back."

Candice stood up sharply. "Okay, I'm coming," she said. She patted Kate's towelled bottom. "Get your nightdress on, baby, and get into bed. I'll come and see you later."

James grimaced. "To kiss you good night."

"Yes, just that," Candice replied sharply. "Come on, for Christsake. Where is that jerk?"

"He was just pulling in." James walked from the room. Candice patted the girl again. "Make sure you're all dry," she said. She followed him out. Kate sat slowly on the side of the bed and buried her young face in her hands. She knew they would kill them.

193

James caught her wrist, almost savagely, as they approached the lobby. Candice pulled herself from the grip.

"Wait," said James. "Just hold on, baby. Don't say too much. Maybe he helped us out."

He was smiling a thin smile and looking through the window. Candice waited as she was told. The door opened with force and, almost comically, Tommy staggered in with the sagging form of Abigail held in both arms, his face riven with fright. "Enter our hero," said Candice.

"She's . . . she's still breathing. Help me, for Christ's sake," jabbered Tommy.

"Take her into the room," said James quietly. He glanced at Candice and smirked. She realised what he was thinking.

"You're a shitty bastard," she said to him. "But lucky."

He grinned openly. Tommy, staggering now, carried the prone girl into her own room. They followed. He laid her on the bed and dropped theatrically at her side, on his knees, his face buried against her side.

"Get up," ordered James. "Get away, you goddam jerk. How come you screw everything up?"

"God, I'm sorry," trembled Tommy. "What the hell, James . . . "

He was moving away, staring at the unconscious form. Candice moved forward, but James's arm once more restrained her. "Easy," he said. "Take it easy."

"She's breathing a little," said Tommy, edging forward. "I can see. Look."

"Get him outside," said James firmly. Candice nodded and took hold of the youth's arm. He was openly weeping now. "I just don't know how it happened," he said. "Some guy in the restaurant started to–"

They both turned. "You took her to a restaurant?" James said for both of them. "Is that what you did?"

"It was okay, I promise," he stammered. "Honest. I just wanted to show her off – you guys don't understand me at all."

"Get him out," snarled James to Candice. "Before I do to him what's he's done to . . . " His voice softened. " . . . to this kid."

A low animal moan came from Tommy. "Beat it," said James fiercely. He was staring at the sprawled form of Abigail. Candice tightened her grip and moved Tommy out the door.

194

They left James standing above the girl. He put his hand on her breasts and felt her shallow breath. He lifted the chin and saw the bruise on her neck growing. He bent over and, taking a pillow from the bed, pressed it carefully and firmly over her face.

He climbed onto the bed and straddled the soft, still stomach of the girl. After three minutes he took the pillow away. She was dead. He felt nothing, only the calmness that is the nature of the born, unthinking killer. Rubbing his hands together as though cleansing them he moved to the door and went out of the room. At the door he bowed his head in pretence. Tommy was standing in the lobby with Candice with her arm about him. The boy could not see the slight smile in her eyes when James appeared. James looked at Tommy. He said bitterly, "She's dead. You killed her."

Tommy howled blatantly. Tears rushed down his taut face. James moved quickly and slapped his hand over Tommy's mouth. "Shut up," he grunted. "Shut up and *think* for once in your fucking life."

The youth subsided and James removed his hand. "You're sure?" said Candice. She caught James's eye again. "You're really sure?"

"Sure I'm sure." He turned on Tommy. "You've got to get rid of her," he said. "And quick. Jesus, you're a crazy man."

"I didn't mean to. . . . I just didn't. It just happened. She got me mad. She said I stunk."

"So you do," returned James bluntly. "You stink like hell."

Tommy's glassy eyes rose at him. "Don't try it with me, Tommy," whispered James. "You need us real bad now. How are you going to get rid of her . . . it?"

The young man collapsed again. "I don't know. Shit, I don't know. You got to help me out. You're in this as well, both of you. You're in it up to your asses."

"We didn't kill anybody yet," pointed out Candice coolly.

Tommy slumped into a chair. "Christ . . . Christ . . . Abby. . . . "

"Okay," said James. "I have an idea."

Tommy's head came up. "What?" he said with quick hope. "What is it?"

"You just go in there and change her clothes," James began. He smiled and added, "Since she's yours."

"Change her clothes?"

"Sure. We don't want those things she's got on being recognised. Put her jeans on her and a sweater. If she's ever washed ashore it will look more convincing than a party dress."

Tommy continued staring at him. "Washed ashore?" he said. "We're going to put her in the sea?"

"*You* are," corrected James. "I'm just coming up with the ideas."

The disorganised face sagged again. "Help me," he said. "You gotta help me."

James glanced at Candice. "Is Momma sleeping?" he asked.

"Sure she is. I gave her something. She won't sleep unless she has a pill. She had two tonight."

"We should increase the dose," he mentioned, glancing at her. "Or maybe we don't have enough time for that." He thought about it, then turned to Tommy. "Get her changed into the other clothes, okay?" he said. "Then maybe we'll help you out."

Candice stopped him with her hand on his arm. The boy turned. "You've done a murder, Tommy," she said solemnly.

His face was white, the thick circles under his eyes black, his mouth and moustache wet. "I know what I've done," he said.

"Right away, after this," she said, "we're going to split up. We'll all go separate ways. The further apart the better."

He looked frightened. "Where can I go?" he whimpered. "I don't know anywhere."

"You stay here," she said firmly. "In this area. Manteo, Nags Head, the usual places. Don't run away or you'll start something. *Don't move.* You understand?"

"Sure I do, Candice, sure. I just stay around like nothing happened."

"And keep your big mouth shut," put in James. "Real tight. If you open it *once*, just once, you could be in the electric chair. They're using that again now."

Tommy dropped his gaze. "I know. I saw it on TV," he mumbled. "I'll be real careful."

James glanced at Candice and she nodded. "We can vanish," said James. "Into thin air. *You* can't. So don't blab."

"I won't," pleaded the youth again. "Thanks a lot." He moved towards the door. "I'll get her fixed up." He walked along the corridor and stopped outside Abigail's door. James saw his

196

hesitation and called after him, "Get going!" He laughed thinly. "You look like you're standing in Death Row." Tommy opened the door and went in. There was a pause and then the door shut softly.

"Masterly," said Candice. "You've got a real talent for this sort of thing, James."

He smiled, accepting the remark as a compliment. "It's no use screwing it up now," he said. "Everything needs to be done with care."

He put his hand in his pocket and took out the ring with the blue stone.

"That's Edith's," said Candice.

"Sure. The girl was wearing it."

"You're keeping it?"

"You must be crazy," he said. "It's going back on Edith's finger. When . . . if . . . she gets washed ashore I want it to be still there. We don't want anyone thinking about nasty motives like robbery. The tide will be high in an hour. Edith and the kid have got to be taken care of soon. If we get them down to the place I showed you within the next half hour, the ebb tide will take them out to sea."

Candice looked at him steadily. He had watched her for any change of expression when he had mentioned Kate, but there was none. She knew he was watching. She asked, "What about things like autopsies? When they're washed up, they'll do that. They find out all sorts of things."

"It's a risk we have to take," he said. "Personally I'm not too worried. The fishes in the ocean are real hungry around these parts. We dress them in the sort of clothes they'd be wearing in a boat or on a beach at this time of year. But I don't think we have too much to worry about. I don't think there'll be a great deal to have an autopsy on."

"You're very reassuring," she said caustically. "A real natural."

"It's good that one of us is," he said. "But don't think you're backing out of any responsibility."

"I told you, I'll see to Katy," she whispered. "I have to. I know that."

The door of Abigail's room opened, slowly at first, and then in a hurry. Tommy stumbled out, holding onto the door frame,

197

197

swinging around it like a distraught child. He folded his thick arms against the wall and pushed his face into them, sobbing. Briskly James stepped to him and turned him sharply from the wall. He was confronted with Tommy's wet and shaking face.

"Stop," sneered James. "D'you hear me? Cut it out."

Candice watched them keenly. There was hate in the youth's spongy eyes but it died to helplessness. "I've done it," sniffed Tommy. "Like you said. I've dressed her."

"Okay," returned James. He moved past Tommy and glanced through the door at the body of Abigail lying on the bed. "Let's get *rid* of it."

"Where? How do we do that, for Christ's sake?" asked Tommy miserably. He made as if to glance into the room himself, but he turned away at the final moment. James produced a bleak smile and put his hand mockingly on the boy's shoulder. "Trust your Uncle Jim," he whispered.

"What do we do, for Christ's sake?" repeated Tommy with pathetic hope.

James regarded him gravely as if undecided whether to impart some serious information. Eventually he said, "Tommy, what we do is to take Abigail's body to a place below this motel. It's a kind of cave. And we put it in the sea. That's what we do."

Candice watched the craven hope grow on the youth's face. "And nobody can find her . . . it?" he said.

Candice put in, "The tide will wash her out to sea. She'll look as if she drowned."

"Wow," whispered Tommy. "You mean we could get away with this after all?"

James caught him by the throat, as he had previously caught Candice. With no pressure. Just the fingers against the skin. Tommy's eyes enlarged with alarm.

"*You* can get away with it," said James menacingly. "*You're* the one who murdered her, remember."

"Sure, sure James. I remember," His expression dropped.

"Don't forget it. We're getting you out of a load of shit. Okay?"

"Okay, James. Just take your fingers off my neck, will you?"

James took the threatening hand aways"Let's get it," he said, moving toward the room.

Tommy pushed in front of him and, looking at the other two

198

as if he feared ridicule, he said, "Let me. I'll carry her. I want to."

"Help yourself," smiled James, moving away. "She's all yours."

Tommy went into the room and emerged carrying the body of Abigail. James moved ahead with an exaggerated sweep of his arm. "This way, sir," he said. Candice looked sharply at him. She let Tommy go ahead and they moved down the corridor. Abigail's hair hung like a curtain over Tommy's arm, her head sagging back. Outside Edith's door, and again outside Kate's, James performed a cruel pantomime of passing on tiptoe. Stupidly Tommy followed suit. Candice grimaced.

James opened the door at the end of the corridor, took them into the engine room and then into the wood-boarded storeroom, switching on the light as he went. "Gee," Tommy breathed, manoeuvring his burden through successive apertures. "I didn't even guess this was here."

"Just forget you ever saw it," warned James.

"Sure will!"

He watched as James pulled the sheet of plywood from the far wall and revealed a further door. He opened it. The drumming of the sea and its salt smell came up to them. "Christ," muttered Tommy. "What a place."

"Forget the commentary," suggested Candice. "Go on, take her in."

The youth hesitated. He wasn't entirely stupid. "How do I know you aren't going to leave *me* down there?" he said. "In the ocean."

James had turned on the bulkhead light. "Because," he sighed. "For once in your life, you'd be missed. And people have seen you with *us*. Okay?"

"Right," said Tommy as if he had known anyway. He carried the girl's body over the threshold, like some grotesque bridegroom. A denim shoe slipped from her foot and Candice bent, picked it up, and curiously replaced it.

"Down the steps," said James nodding at the stone flight leading to the dark water. The waves were large but steady, easing themselves lazily into the cave, booming as they met the rocks. James put out a hand to help him but Tommy grunted and he withdrew it. The youth staggered carefully down the steps. At the bottom, at the water's edge he kissed the cheek of the dead girl

199

and laid her in the sea. A retreating wave immediately caught the body and tugged it out into the dark channel. Tommy let out a tight cry and, turning, came slowly back up the steps.

"Jesus," grinned James. "For a minute I thought he was going to dive in to save her."

9

Bonnie left for Manteo in the morning and Burrows took the tangent road to Elizabeth City. When he reached there he left the Aspen at a petrol station and rented a white Gremlin. Then he took the small road that wandered south along the Atlantic lagoons until it reached the northern end of Cape Hatteras at Kitty Hawk.

Two highways ran along the narrow land here, parallel and within a hundred yards of each other, like veins up an outstretched forearm. Between them sat regular, almost regimented, lines of wooden houses, motels, shops, coffee shops, and petrol stations. In the summer it would have been animated, the beaches on the ocean side peopled with sunbathers and with boats and fishermen on the inlets of the sound.

But now, despite the dampness of the January air, he could almost hear, feel, the dust blowing along the deserted lanes. Sand had crept from the beach, loose clapboard rattled in the maritime wind, the streets were empty and the main highways almost the same. The passing of a car could be heard over the housetops. A dog sat at a door as if waiting for its owner to return with the summer. It wagged its tail modestly at Burrows' approach.

He drove at little more than walking pace, looking from side to side at the ranks of empty buildings. A few people appeared walking at the side of the road. He had a niggling feeling that, at any moment, Deputy Wheeler's car might appear and he kept his head low behind the steering wheel.

At the Wright Brothers Museum at Kitty Hawk, he showed the pictures of Edith and her daughters to the staff. Bonnie's

201

friend, Mary, was having a day off. No one else remembered them. Almost as a duty, he spent fifteen minutes wandering around the buildings and then walked out onto the world's first air-strip. Standing in the open wind and looking about he walked the measured distance shown as the first fragile flights of the pioneers. He returned to the car and, scarcely knowing why he did it, he asked one of the museum attendants if there was anywhere open where he could get some lunch. He did not care about food and the remark was almost in the nature of something to say since the man was opening the next car on the parking lot.

"Not much in the way of eating places open this time of the year," the attendant sniffed. He put his nose to the wind curiously, giving the impression that he was trying to get the scent of food. "Down below Kill Devil Hills," he said eventually. "There's a seafood place there. They might be open. In the evenings they open, I know, but I don't know about the day-time."

Burrows thanked him and waited in his car until the other man had cleared the parking lot. Aimlessly, he started the engine. He drove slowly out onto the highway and turned south. To his right the tall pointed sand dunes of Jockey Ridge rose. They looked like pictures he had seen of the Biblical deserts, high and empty, cone-topped against the sky, with the wind whistling.

Just beyond the sand dunes he saw a signpost on the opposite side of the road with the single word "Pier" clinging to its arm. He indicated left, although there was nothing on the road either behind him or approaching him. The secondary road was brief, as they all were, ending abruptly at the grey sea rolling and roaring up over a scarred beach. There was a wooden fishing pier like an outstretched finger touching the water. The waves were reduced enough today to make it accessible and Burrows left the car and walked out on the wet planks towards the ocean. The wind flew around him and the sky and the sea were scarcely distinguishable one from the other.

Turning and looking back at the crouched land of the Cape he saw that there was a substantial building a hundred yards down the beach, standing out against the low roofs of the wooden houses. Above its roof it had an illuminated sign which, even at this time of the day, was lit and flashing. It said "Cape Hatteras Fishery" and below that "Seafood Restaurant." Even as Burrows looked towards it a man came out and began to wave a white cloth towards him. He could hear his faint shouts on the fresh wind. Burrows walked carefully back along the wooden pier towards the beach and the man who called.

He went with caution because of the slippery boards under his feet. The wind at his back seemed stronger than when he had been facing it. Once it punched him firmly and made him stagger. The man had advanced down the beach. He was a thin man, submerged in a fisherman's jersey many sizes too large. Over his arm he carried the folded tablecloth. His face was slim and only a few fair hairs stood up from his head, waving in the wind as though begging attention.

"See," called the man as Burrows neared and slipped again. "See, that's what I'm trying to tell people." It was as if he were carrying on some previous conversation between them. "I'm always telling folks," he continued. He moved forward on the shingle and helped Burrows down from the wooden pier. "This pier just ain't safe at this time of year," he said. "I tell so many I reckon I ought to be an official lifeguard, paid and everything."

To him it was obviously a familiar joke because he began to laugh even before it was finished. Burrows joined in politely. "Thanks for saving my life," he said. "Is the restaurant open for lunch?"

The man looked so astonished that he stopped in his progress back up the beach. "Lunch? Jesus, lunch! No fear, mister. Open for gourmet dinners Friday and Saturday. Until April, that is. I can fix you a cup of coffee and a crab sandwich if you like. Both fresh."

Burrows accepted the offer. They had walked from the deeper part of the beach to the upper fringes where the sand and shingle were firmer. Burrows looked around. He found himself sniffing like the museum attendant had sniffed. "Not many customers in sight," he agreed. "It's kind of you to go to the trouble."

"It's no trouble," said the man agreeably. They walked into the building. It was almost dark, with a few pale lights illuminating an area displaying a fish tank. The man turned a switch and one section of the room was lit. On the walls, he could now see, were nets and floats and stuffed game fish. "Nice place," Burrows commented politely.

"It is at the right time," said the man. "In the season we're open for gourmet dining every evening. We have a band and every-thing. From Manteo. But now it's just Friday and Saturday nights." He was busy with the coffee and sandwich. Burrows sat at the table with the light. "You from Canada?" asked the man. "I just can't place that accent. We get all sorts of accents in these parts. In the season."

"England," corrected Burrows.

"England, Europe?" said the man. He had stopped fixing the sandwich.

"That's right," said Burrows. He nodded towards the sea. "Right out there, the other side of the Atlantic."

"I should have known," replied the man. He had placed the sandwich on a plate and the coffee was steaming in the cup. He walked towards the table with them. "Sure, I should have known. We don't get many English people in these parts, not generally, but we had a kid in the other night, real sweet, and she talked just like you."

Burrows felt as if someone had struck him with a knife in the chest. He could hardly trust the words from his mouth. "A kid?" he asked slowly. "What sort of kid? How old?"

The man had not been looking at him directly, but his tone made him glance up. He was amazed at Burrows' face. "A girl," he answered hesitantly, almost fearfully. "About eighteen, nine-teen, I guess. She was here with a boy – a young guy from these parts. I've seen him around here."

Burrows' hand shook. It went to his pocket and the man, his eyes now transfixed, followed it as if he expected the Englishman to pull a gun. Instead out came the envelope and from the envelope three photographs. Burrows held out the pictures. "Is she there?" he asked. "One of the two girls?"

Carefully, still wondering what was going on, the man put the sandwich plate and the coffee on the table. He lifted the photo-graphs to where the light was stronger. "You could go blind in this place," he grumbled inconsequentially. "Blind." He looked at the photographs. Burrows could not breathe. He stared at the man's expression and saw a short smile come to the corners of his mouth. "Sure," he answered. "This one." He handed the picture of Abigail back to Burrows. "That's her. I'd know her anywhere. Real pretty."

"Bonnie," he said into the telephone. He tried to keep his voice steady. "Bonnie, I've found something."

"No," he heard her breathe. "What? What is it?"

"I'm at a place between Kill Devil Hills and Nags Head," he said. "Cape Hatteras Fishery. It's a restaurant–"

"I know it," she said.

"The man here says Abigail came in the other night. She was with a youth, someone from these parts. He recognised the photographs."

"Who was the guy? Did he know?"

"He doesn't know his name, but we should be able to trace him. I need your help. Can you come over?"

He sensed her hesitation. "I'll get over a soon as I can," she said. "I can't leave right away. It's busy, for once. I just can't quit on the man."

"No, of course not. Listen, I'm going to do what I can. I'll see you here, at the Fishery, at what time? Can you make it three or four this afternoon?"

"Three," she said decisively. Then, "You're still not going to tell the police?"

The silence was measurable. "No," Burrows replied eventually. "No I'm not. Not yet anyway. Wheeler wouldn't listen."

"Ain't you going to tell the cops?" asked the man when he had replaced the phone. He had not been eavesdropping. It was a natural question. Burrows shook his head.

"Not just yet," he said. "It's a delicate matter – very personal – and I don't think I ought to bring the law in yet. I'd like to find this young man myself." The man was sitting at a table with a sandwich and a pot of coffee. Unconsciously Burrows reversed their roles and poured some coffee for him. The man thanked him.

"I've been thinking," he said through a mouthful of crab sandwich. "About this young guy – wondering how we might find out his location. In the summer, I know, he hangs about up on Jockey Ridge when they're doing that skydiving, what do you call it?"

"Hang gliding," suggested Burrows. "Does he do that?"

"I don't know about doing it. But I fancy he's been around up there. Somebody might know him." He pushed an order pad across the table. "There, I wrote all that I can recall about him.

On this paper. He's one of these spotty kids, not very healthy looking. When they came in I remember wondering what he was doing with a smart little doll like that."

Burrows glanced at the description. "Thanks," he said. "You don't know how much this means. Do you remember anything about her expression? Whether she looked afraid or ill or anything?"

The man at the table ruminated. "I've been going over that too," he said. "In my mind. It's not easy, you understand, because Saturday nights it gets busy for just about the only time in the week. And you have to make a living while you can at this time of the year. So you don't notice that much. Maybe I wouldn't have seen this girl at all if it hadn't been her voice was different, being English. But now I think about it again, there was something . . . "

Burrows leaned forward to urge him. "Yes, what was it?"

"Well it seemed kind of odd. But she didn't look as if she'd bothered to get herself prettied up very much to come out. She was a good looker, right enough, but she was . . . well, careless. Her hair and her lipstick and that sort of thing. Most of the girls who come here on Saturdays get themselves real dressed up for their date. But she looked like she didn't take much trouble. It came to me that maybe this was her way to giving this guy the brush-off."

"Where did they sit?" asked Burrows. The man patted the seat of the table behind them. "Right here," he said.

Burrows stood up and walked the steps to the other table. He sat on the seat. "Here?" he asked quietly.

"Right there," said the man. "The guy sat opposite. Looking right at her."

"Thanks," said Burrows. He got up and ran his hand across the seat. "I must go. Will it be all right if I meet somebody here at three?"

The man nodded. "That'll be fine," he said. "I take a nap in the afternoon, being as there's not much else to do, but I'll be around then. I don't want to miss any of this."

"Right," said Burrows. "Thank you again. You've been a godsend. I don't know your name. Mine's Burrows."

"Funny," said the man.

"What is?"

"That's what everybody says," he grinned. "No, the name's Funny. Common one around these parts. George Funny."

They shook hands. George Funny said, "Any time you feel like a good fish dinner: gourmet eating by the sea."

Burrows smiled and said he would remember. He went out into the wet afternoon.

He drove to the sand dunes at Jockey Ridge, parked the car and wandered among the lower hills, trudging through the clinging surface. Desolate sounds seeped through the high-coned dunes, like cries, he imagined. Once again he was tempted to shout for Edith, but this time he resisted. He came across a long shed, locked, its windows hung with sand as frost hangs in other places. With difficulty he peered through them; there were rolls of material inside and metal spars, the contraptions of the hang-gliding enthusiasts. But no people were about under the damp, darkening day.

At three o'clock he was back on the beach. He left the Gremlin on the road beside the restaurant and walked across the initial stones and pebbles. It was a dark afternoon, almost dusk even at that hour. There was a single light coming from an upstairs window of the Fishery. He had only gone a few steps when he saw the shape of Bonnie, like a ghost in the greyness, coming towards him across the shingle.

"Find anything?" she asked immediately. Their hands touched each other at the elbows but that was the only contact. She was swamped in the huge overcoat, her face poking like a pale bud from the neck.

"Nothing so far," he said. "But this man here, at the restaurant, is sure it was Abigail who came in. This youth she was with shouldn't be all that difficult to trace. A greasy sort of character, pimples, the lot."

"Sounds like a lot of guys around here," nodded Bonnie. Then seriously, "Whatever could she have been doing with a guy like that, for Christ's sake?"

"Not from choice, I bet," muttered Burrows. "And yet, if there was something funny about it, if she were under some sort of pressure, why should he bring her to a place like this, a public place with crowds of people?"

"Guys do strange things," she said with feeling. "I know.

Particularly young guys. And Edith and Kate – they were somewhere else, remember?"

"Hostages," he said miserably.

"Listen," said Bonnie. "You've already faced facts. Somebody is holding them, okay? They're not in this area for their health."

His head dropped and then came up slowly, "That sums it up very well," he said.

A pinched look came to her face as she looked at him. Then the upper window of the restaurant opened briskly and George Funny called out. "Hey there, mister. I got something for you. I had an idea. Come on in, the door's open down there."

Quickly they looked up at him and then made towards the door. By the time they had entered the restaurant, he had descended the stairs and was coming towards them with a white envelope in his hand. He switched on one of the individual lights over the table. It was the same table, the place where he said the couple had sat. He indicated that they should move onto the bench and they did so, leaning forward under the low light. "I had an idea," said George Funny opening the envelope. "Is that your girl?"

Burrows paled as the photograph was passed to him. It was of a nondescript couple raising their glasses to the camera. Disappointment flooded through him, but then, suddenly, he saw what the man really meant. Sitting at the table in the background, unmistakably, was Abigail. Burrows almost choked with emotion.

"Abigail . . . " His whimper trailed away. "Yes, that's Abigail. Oh God . . . " He felt Bonnie's cold, thin hand on his wrist. He took his eyes from the photograph for a moment and then returned them. "No mistaking her," he said.

"We have a guy who comes and takes these pictures of the customers on Saturdays," said George Funny. "He leaves them here so that people can come and buy them if they want. And I just had a notion that he maybe took a picture of them. So I looked through. He didn't – but we got the next best thing."

Burrows patted the man's sleeve. "You're wonderful," he said. He leaned closer. "Let's see how much we can make out of this character," he said.

George rose. "Hold it a minute," he said. "I got a magnifying

208

glass. The cashier don't see too well, would you believe? At least that's her story."

He went over to the cash desk and opened a drawer. He returned with the magnifying glass. Burrows took it from him and let it hover over the photograph. Abigail was half profile to the camera, as if she had been looking in that direction but had turned away at the final moment. The face was not distinct enough to detect any expression, but it was undoubtedly her. She had tied her hair back in a graceless pigtail.

Her companion was leaning forward as though saying something to her. His heavy forearms and hands were on the table. Burrows surveyed him carefully, now, making himself calm, holding the photograph very still. The image was blurred but the impression of heaviness, thickness was there. "Small eyes, some sort of straggly moustache," he muttered. "Dark hair, looks as though he's tried to make himself pretty; it's sort of smarmed down with something." He turned to the silent Bonnie. "What do you think?" he asked.

"I think I know him," she said simply. Burrows felt himself tremble. "You *know* him?" he said. "You really–?"

"I think," she repeated. "I said 'I think.' I've seen him around. Manteo, Nags Head. He's the sort of guy who's just *around*, you know, at street corners or in coffee shops or doing odd jobs. I'm certain I've seen him in this area, and this last summer."

"You'd know him again. You'd recognise him?" Burrows leaned towards her.

"If it's the guy I think," she nodded. "I don't know his name or anything. I've just seen him around. We could look for him."

Burrows stared again at the photograph. "George," he asked. "Could I borrow this picture? I'd like to take it with me. It could be a great help."

"Sure thing," replied George. "But let me have it back." He indicated the couple in the foreground. "Maybe these people will want to buy it."

His concern for priorities made Burrows smile. "I promise," he said. He put the photograph in the envelope with the others and looked at Bonnie. "We could start now," he suggested. "Right away."

"Sure," she agreed with a shrug. "Joey's getting used to me not being there. I'll just call him."

"I'm sorry," said Burrows. "Listen, I'll make it up to you, Bonnie, with your job and everything. It's just that if I don't find . . ."

"It's no trouble," she said quietly. She got up and went toward the telephone, calling back, "We're not exactly swamped with business at the moment. He might be glad."

George Funny watched her go and turned quizzically to Burrows. "That's a real nice girl you got there," he mused. "Neat too. How come you find a girl like that? Here's me, I been here all my life and I can't remember that I've seen her before. And you come in and find her – just like that? Maybe you got the talent for it."

Burrows smiled seriously at him. "You're not in trouble, George," he said. "I am. She likes people in trouble, I think."

"Maybe I could just find me some trouble," ruminated George, getting up from the table. He turned back. "You got any place to stay?" he asked. "If you're not accommodated, you could stay here. We got empty rooms. Plenty. And the food's good."

"Gourmet dining," nodded Burrows. He smiled. "I'd like to. I don't know how long I'm going to be around; it depends on how long it takes me – this business."

"Sure, I understand," said George. "Well maybe you could pay a few days in advance and then if one day you don't come back the company won't be out of pocket. Will the lady stay too?"

Burrows glanced at him and answered, "I don't think so. She has a place in Manteo."

"Oh, sure. Right. Well, I'll show you the room."

Burrows left the table. "I'll get my bag from the car," he said. He went outside and returned with the suitcase. "You travel light," said George as he led the way up the stairs.

"My luggage is the easiest weight on me," said Burrows. He followed the man into the room. "Twelve dollars a night," said George. He looked apologetic. "On account of the season. In summer it's expensive."

"A week in advance," suggested Burrows, taking the bills from his wallet.

"You sure you'll be around that long?"

"I hope not," said Burrows seriously. "If I am, it's probably going to be too late."

"There was something else," said George thoughtfully. "About them. It just came to mind. The girl–"

Burrows turned quickly, "Yes? What?"

"It's not something I'd notice. Not generally. But they seemed so strange together and so I did notice. When they were leaving."

"For God's sake, George–"

"She was wearing a great big ring. Like a sapphire. Blue anyway. But big. Very big for a young girl."

"That's right," said Burrows quietly. "It belongs to her mother."

At night, Nags Head and the wooden settlements about Kill Devil Hills and north as far as Kitty Hawk were outlined by a meagre criss-cross of street lamps and an occasional fuller light where there was a winter outpost of people. Burrows sat in the car and waited for Bonnie to come out of the McDonald's. The yellow lights of the place oozed through its steamy windows. A few shadows passed across the glass but he could see the place was all but empty. The door opened and Bonnie, hung with her huge coat, came out. She ducked her head against the evening drizzle and hurried towards the car. "Nothing," she said as she got in. "Not a thing."

"Where now?" he asked. "There can't be many places left."

"Right," she sighed. "One more. There's a coffee shop a mile up the highway. After that I haven't got a single bright idea short of knocking on doors. Not one."

They drove silently along the black road. The lights along the highway ceased and there was only the smearing rain drifting across the headlights. Ahead, like a glowing space-station moving through endless night, the coffee shop appeared. It looked solitary and uninhabited. "Business looks great all over," Bonnie said. He eased the car to a stop. They had agreed that she should make the inquiries. Now she got out and hurried towards the garish door. Burrows sat hunched in the car, staring at the damp darkness ahead and wondering, as he had wondered so often, how far away Edith and her girls were at this moment.

Bonnie was longer than she had been at the other places. When she came through the door he could see there was a hurry about her. He opened the door quickly. "Got something," she breathed as she entered the car.

"What? What is it?"

"The guy's called Tommy something. There's a girl serving in there who knows him. She recognised the picture."

"Tommy," repeated Burrows as if it were a password. "Nothing else?"

"He's not the sort of person that people get to know his other name. Nobody cares to get that friendly with him. Just Tommy. But his mother lives in Manteo. I know the place."

He turned the car in the road, bumping over sand and pebbles as the wheels ran out of tarmac. They headed south again. "I'll go in with you this time," said Burrows. "Or better still, I'll go by myself."

"Forget it." He sensed her smile in the dark. "You'll blow the whole thing. If he's at home you'll grab him and scare the shit out of him so that we'll never get anything. If he's not there you'll do the same for his mother. You stay in the car. If there's trouble, I'll scream."

"All right," he said. "Thanks, Bonnie."

"It's nothing. I just have a kindly nature."

"I've noticed that." He felt her small hand touch his overcoat sleeve and a moment later the head touched his shoulder like a sigh. He rubbed his chin into her hair.

"We turn off over the causeway here, don't we?" he said.

"Sure. Take the right bend. The street is almost out of town the other side."

"Almost by the Lost Colony," he remarked.

"Wrong side of the tracks," she corrected. "You'll see."

The car ran onto the causeway. The wind was sharper there, but not fierce. It cuffed the side of the car. The rain thickened on the windscreen. Ahead they saw the lights of Manteo. "There's the swinging city," she murmured.

They bumped over the last yards of causeway and drove into the main street. It was wide and almost deserted. A few cars meandered as though looking for somewhere to go; a clutch of youths were hanging out under a dripping roof. As they went by Joey's, Bonnie said, "He's still open. Always the optimist." She peered through the windscreen. "Take it easy along here, Doctor. Yes, I guess it's the next one. Make a left."

He turned the Gremlin. The dark side street seemed to swallow it. "I don't know the number of the house," said Bonnie. She sensed the excitement in him. "Take it easy," she said. "Just drop me here. I'll ask."

"Now you're sure?" he asked as she prepared to leave the car. "I'll come with you if you like."

"Stay there," she said. "I'll be fine."

She leaned back and towards him so that her face, a pale oval, looked directly up at him. He leaned down and kissed her. "Thanks," he said. "You're a lovely girl."

"Sure," she replied, opening the door and getting out into the drizzle. "They all say that." He smiled as he watched her go towards a low house, a solitary outside lantern shining on what in summer would be a full trailing plant hanging against the dull white wall. His heart was tight. He felt he ought to be with her. She looked very small in the outsized coat as she waited at the door under the pale yellow of the light. It opened cautiously at first, then wider. He watched her head tilt as she asked the question. Eventually she turned and walked towards the road again. He leaned towards the window. "Move up about fifty yards," she called to him softly. "It's along on this side."

He started the engine and eased the car forward along the street. A dog began to bark but ceased as the vehicle moved on. He saw Bonnie wait at a low gate – a hesitation, he thought. Looking carefully he saw that the house was almost covered with growth. It seemed to hang low under the weight. A single bulb glowed in one of the windows. "Are you home, Tommy?" said Burrows under his breath. "Come on out."

Bonnie went down the path and he heard her knock. She was almost indistinguishable in the gloom. After two or three minutes and several further knocks, he saw a timid light appear in the porch. He could hear the voices. The rain had ceased and it seemed to clear the air. He strained to listen. Bonnie remained at the door and then turned and walked toward him.

"What happened?" he asked eagerly as she got into the car. He was watching the house too, and he saw the light of the single bulb blotted out as if someone were standing at the window looking out at them.

"That was Mom," she said. He started the car and pulled slowly away. "I can see where our Tommy gets his good looks.

213

Jesus, is that lady a mess! She's fat but she looks half-starved, if you get what I mean."

"Where's Tommy? Does she know?"

"Sorry. No, she doesn't. It seems he hasn't been around for some time – until yesterday."

"Oh?"

"He arrived in the afternoon, took some of his things and beat it again. He also took twenty dollars from her pocketbook. She says she doesn't know where he is or where he's been. And she doesn't care, either."

"Tommy doesn't seem to be popular with anybody," said Burrows.

They turned two left corners and drove back into the town again. "Do you want me to take you home?" he said.

She nodded. "Sure. But just drop me around to Joey's first, will you? Just for a couple of minutes. I feel a little guilty about missing so much work."

"Of course," he said. There was a silence between them as he drove. "I'm very grateful to you, Bonnie," he said eventually.

"Don't mention it," she said. "I'm a lovely girl." They were on the pavement outside the place where she worked. The windows were forlornly steamed up. She left the car and went in. A moment later the door opened again and she returned to him, her face transformed. "He's inside," she said, "eating a hamburger."

"Who?" he asked stupidly.

"Tommy," she said.

Bonnie went back into the hamburger bar. She called to Joey, the owner, and he called back through the steam of the coffee machine. "You back to work, or you just paying a social call?"

She laughed and hoped it sounded right. She was so tense her ribs ached; her mouth had dried. The laugh, she thought, sounded like a cackle. Glancing across to the corner where Tommy sat she saw that he was looking at her now with interest, not suspicion. She controlled herself. "Hi," she called across. "Haven't seen you around lately."

His wide pale face took on a look of surprise that she had spoken. "Me? Oh, I've been around. But busy. I've been real busy. You know, doing things."

214

Bonnie felt her legs grow weak as she walked across to where he sat, a drained coffee cup in front of him, the ketchup from a devoured hamburger wiped across the plate and hanging on the ends of his weedy moustache, like drops of blood. He looked astonished, then pleased, then smug as she sat down opposite. His acne cast small shadows across his chin neck. "Mind if I sit down?" she said.

"Sure." He stared at her, unable to believe his luck. Clumsily he moved the plate away from her side of the table and ran his thumb through the smeared ketchup. He put the thumb in his mouth. Bonnie was aware of Joey watching her advance with astonishment through his perpetual curtain of steam. He shrugged and went back to cleaning knives and forks. He saw an outline of a man standing outside and looking through the vapour-clouded window.

Burrows was watching. He took in the thick, folded figure of Tommy, and the slim back of Bonnie. There he was. The bastard. Burrows' face solidified as he watched. He pulled himself away from the window and returned to the car parked a block away on the other side of the street. He waited, his skin twitching.

Inside the close room Bonnie smiled encouragingly at the youth. "You want another cup of coffee?" she asked. "I work here. I can get it. You don't have to pay."

Her attention astonished him, but his ego soon absorbed it. "Sure," he grinned grotesquely. "I'll have a cup of coffee with you."

She got up and walked across the floor to the coffee machine. Joey watched her with increasing curiosity, but her face remained collected. She helped herself to two coffees. "Put them on my account, will you?" she said to Joey. He laughed a reply. Tommy watched her return. She placed the coffee on the plastic table and then pulled the great coat from her shoulders and back across the chair. The youth stared at her modest chest as if she had exposed it nakedly. "You looking for company?" he said, sucking at the coffee. "Not much around this time of the year."

"You been with many girls around here?" she asked. She let her eyes remain down and then flicked them up at his at the end of the sentence.

"Yeah. Too many," he shrugged boastfully. "I don't rate the

215

girls in these parts. I'm going to Norfolk soon, maybe New York. It's too goddam small around here."

She sighed. "That's what I want," she replied. "New York. Jesus, I just wish I could be there now. Have you been?"

"Oh, sure, quite a few times," he lied. "I know it real good. People from there are lots of laughs. I know. I got some friends from New York down here right now." He drank the coffee noisily. "I'll be in Florida soon. I'd be there now, lying in the sun, sniffing coke. But I got hung up on something."

"Like what?" she asked cautiously.

"Oh, just things. I can't tell you about that. Just things happened, that's all. Like they happen all the time to me. I guess I'm just one of those people things happen to." He looked at her steadily. "You really looking for company?" he said.

"Sure," she said, keeping her tone flat. "It gets lonely here. Maybe we could take a ride to the beach. You got a car?"

He nodded. "That old Chevy outside," he said. "It's my spare car, see. I'm just driving it while my Mustang is fixed. I've had trouble. I'd sure like to take you in that Mustang. That's classy. . . ."

"The Chevy will do," she said. "Why don't we get out of here?"

Tommy was looking at her with unconcealed amazement and dawning triumph. "I guess some women just take to me," he muttered, as though to explain it to himself. He drained the coffee, apparently unwilling to leave anything free. She got up and called good night to Joey. He stared at her and said a diminished good night. Bonnie pulled her coat about her and went out the door. Wiping his mouth with the back of his hand and then attempting to arrange the wet ends of his moustache, Tommy followed, almost stumbling in his eagerness.

"Is that the car?" she called over her shoulder.

"Sure," he said. "You ought to see my Mustang. Red. Man, that's some mean car."

"This'll be okay," she said airily. She glanced up the street. Burrows' car was squatting dark and silent. She controlled the trembling in her lungs. Tommy caught up with her. He wrapped a heavy arm around her and tried to touch her breast. "Take it easy," she warned, "We ain't at the beach yet."

They got into the old Chevrolet. The windscreen was decorated with coloured stickers. "See," he pointed. "I been all these places."

"I think the moon's coming out," she said as he started the engine. "That'll be great. I'm crazy about the waves by moonlight."

"You won't be watching the waves," he promised in the darkness beside her. "Boy, have you got some surprises coming."

"So have you," she said carefully.

Burrows gave the Chevrolet several hundred yards' start before he moved after it in the Gremlin. He left as much distance as he thought prudent between the cars although he feared he might lose it in the dark and the rain even on those vacant roads. It took off towards the causeway and he drove carefully, keeping its rear lights within sight. It turned left at Nags Head and drove north towards the sand dunes at Jockey Ridge.

Tommy had turned the radio on loudly in the Chevy and Bonnie made herself sing to the music. She tried, without success, to prevent herself from glancing in the mirror for the reassurance of the headlights following in the distance. When they reached Nags Head and turned left, the car behind was lost and she waited anxiously while it turned the bend behind them and continued the trail.

"I'd sure like my friends from New York to meet you," Tommy said. He lounged against the wheel and pretended to chew gum, although he didn't have any. He was all nonchalance. "But they're busy. We all been busy." He giggled. "Between doing other things like sniffing cocaine and junk like that."

"They sound like cool people," she said in the darkness. She was getting his smell, a heavy sweat smell. She shuddered.

"But they're fixed," he continued. "Sometimes I screw the girl, but mostly I go on the hunt on my own. I like to pick my own grapes, see."

The lump in her throat was so extended that she could not speak, only nod. She made herself keep her eyes from his mirror. Then, abruptly and with what he obviously hoped sounded like a dare-devil laugh, the youth swung the car off the road and onto the sandy soil beside it. The moon outlined the sand dunes in front of them making them heave like mountains. "I thought we said we'd go to the beach," said Bonnie.

217

"This is fine," he answered blandly. "We can have a good time here, just as well. Sometimes on that beach you get those assholes who fish all night. Jesus, fancy fishing all night." He made a sudden clumsy lunge at her. Involuntarily she jumped away, only just stifling a scream. His ugly face sulked.

"Come on, baby," he said. "What you holding out for? This was your idea."

Bonnie tried to stop herself shaking. His breath was worse than his body smell. "Sure, sure," she heard herself saying. "But take it easy. Don't you have any class?"

Tommy paused, apparently astounded. "Class? Class?" he said. "Jesus Christ, have I got class! Listen, baby, I been screwing a real looker. Foreign, too. She loved it, I can tell you. Come on, let me give you what I got."

Bonnie half closed her eyes. God, where was Burrows? She had a sudden fear that he had missed the place where they had turned off. Tommy grabbed her violently and kissed her. It was like being kissed by a pig. She almost gagged. Then she felt her hand being taken and she felt it being guided. He forced it onto the naked hot head of his cock. "Don't that feel nice?" he inquired.

She nodded blindly. "You're scared," he said in surprise. "Scared as shit. Listen honey, I ain't got nothing to lose, believe me. Just believe me, will you? You got me out here and you ain't changing your mind now – because I ain't changing mine." His hands, like a pair of crabs, went for her breasts. She would have screamed out then but she saw something move outside the window, behind his back. "Come on," he demanded again. "Why you holding out on me?"

Burrows opened the car door behind Tommy. "I think she's waiting for me," he said grimly. He reached in with both hands and caught the youth around the throat. He pulled him back savagely so that he fell out of the car and onto the sand almost at Burrows' feet. He lay there staring up comically at the Englishman, his penis still poking out of the front of his pants.

"I ain't got nothing," he whined from the ground. "You can't rob me. I ain't got nothing."

Bonnie was getting slowly from the car. She remained close against the side of the vehicle, her face ashen in the moon. Tommy stared at her. "A trap . . . a fucking trap," he whimpered.

218

"And you're going to open *your* trap," said Burrows. He leaned towards the postrate youth, "Where's Edith Burrows Where are the girls?"

Tommy couldn't take it in. He stared up at him uncomprehendingly for a moment. Burrows had a sudden terrible thought that, after all, he was wrong. Then the expression changed; Burrows saw it clearly in the light coming from the interior of the car. It became the look of incredulity, fright, finally dissolving into a mask of unconvincing innocence.

"I don't know what you mean, sir," the voice was hardly more than a whisper. Then suddenly he began shouting: "Help! Help!" Burrows made the mistake of leaning forward to catch him by the lapels of his coat. As he did so the youth's heavy head came up and rammed like a mallet into his face. He cried out and stumbled back against the car. Bonnie backed away helplessly. Tommy got to his feet and hit her with the back of his fist sending her sprawling on top of Burrows. At first he was going to run off, but he saw Burrows' car standing on the highway only a hundred yards away. He staggered through the sand towards it. Burrows forced himself to his feet and went after him, his heavy coat holding him back. Tommy reached the car.

Burrows realised he had left the keys in it. He shouted desperately, "Hard luck, son. I've got the keys."

The youth turned and rushed towards him, running back in the direction of his own car. He swerved like a footballer in the sand to avoid the Englishman and was almost by, but Burrows threw himself sideways and caught his foot at the final moment. Tommy stumbled a few yards then lost the attempt and fell forward making a furrow in the sand. Burrows, legs apart and arms pawing the air, went after him and fell with all his weight on top of him. He heard the breath ooze out of the youth's body. He eased back, turned him over, face up, and looked down at him. "All right, Tommy," he said almost kindly. "Where are they?"

Tommy opened his eyes. They were encrusted with sand and there was sand up his nose and like a rind across his lips. "I don't know what the fucking hell you're talking about," he pleaded.

Burrows grabbed his ears and pulled his face up towards him. "You're lying, son," he muttered. "Lying. If you don't tell me I'm going to knock three buckets of shit out of you."

The young man's face broke up. Tears, mingling strangely

219

with the sand, poured over his face. "It wasn't me, mister," he said.

"You were with Abigail!" Burrows shouted. "In the restaurant. "What's happened to them? Where are they?" He was amazed at the control in his own voice. His whole inside, his guts, seemed to be shaking, within that outer shell of calm. He was conscious of Bonnie standing almost at his shoulder as he kneeled across the youth's torso. "Where?" he repeated. Suddenly and fiercely he grabbed the boy's ears again and forced his head back into the sand. His fingers found the thick throat. "Tell me, quick," he snarled. "Before I squeeze the bloody life out of you, you slimy bastard."

"She was just around," trembled the youth. "I just picked her up. Down at Frisco." His eyes were watering. "There ain't nothing against that. No law."

"I don't believe you," Burrows said, pushing his face closer. The putrid breath hit him. He backed his face away and relaxed his grip.

Tommy moved his head abruptly and bit viciously into Burrows' left hand. Burrows shouted, and jerked back. Tommy used the movement as the opportunity to heave his body up. He was still powerful and the effort threw Burrows sideways onto the sand. The youth scrambled to his knees, then to his feet. He gave Bonnie a fierce punch as she ran forward and then turned to Burrows and kicked him in the ribs. The next kick was meant for the jaw, but Burrows' arm got in the way and it landed just short of his elbow. He was retching, bent over from the first kick, when another landed on his hip. The night seemed to revolve around his head. Tommy ran towards his car.

He gunned the engine. The old Chevrolet jerked forward and he spun it around the small sand dune immediately ahead. The surface held until he was at the far side, then the wheels ploughed to the axles and the car churned into the sand. The boy was thrown forward against the windscreen, but not heavily. He rushed from the door, thought about going back towards Burrows and the Gremlin, but chickened out and ran instead towards the rising dunes. As he ran through the difficult sand he heard Burrows staggering after him. In the winter moonlight he saw the bulky figure just rounding the flank of his stranded car. He ran towards the slopes of the dunes.

"Bastard!" Burrows shouted from below, as if it would do some harm. A wild laugh floated back. "You bastard," repeated Burrows, this time as a sob to himself. He began to force himself across the deepening sand, taking the rising track towards the valley up which Tommy was still moving.

It was impossible. He was twice the age of the youth. He stumbled and sank down, rose and fell again. Two hundred yards in front, and fifty feet higher, the youth looked around and saw that Burrows was finished. His sweating face hardened. He turned and ambled almost lazily down the slope towards the black figure curled forward onto the sand as though in prayer. Ten feet away he increased speed and then launching himself like a skier he landed with both feet on Burrows' bent back. Tommy tumbled on. He went through the sand with exaggerated hops as if his boots were weighted. Bonnie ran towards Burrows. She lifted his head. His face was creased and ashen in the moonlight.

"Get him," he managed to gasp. "Don't let the bastard go."

But Tommy had reached the Gremlin. They heard the engine start and looked up despairingly to see the car turn a tight half circle on the highway and roar away south.

"Not now," wheezed Burrows, taking in great gulps of air. "We can't lose him now." He crawled to his feet and Bonnie held him upright, rubbing his stomach as he leaned over her. She staggered with his weight. Gradually he was able to stand. "His car," he said. "We've got to get it out of the sand."

Burrows lumbered down towards the Chevrolet, its wheels wedged in the dune, Bonnie slithering through the sand behind him. "Use our coats," grunted Burrows. "Take your coat off. Under the back wheels."

They got out of their overcoats and like two burrowing animals scooped the loose sand from beneath the rear wheels. They jammed the coats down as far as they would go then arranged them to lie flat on the upward slope of the sand. Burrows leaned his head against the hubcap. Every rib felt as if it were sticking into his lungs. He coughed and gasped. Bonnie ran to him and kneeled down.

"Let me call the Sheriff," she said. "I'll *make* him listen."

Burrows shook his head brokenly. "No good," he said. "If that dolt knew I was back here he'd put me straight behind bars."

"Get the man from the restaurant, then," she urged. "He's got *evidence*. He *saw* Abigail."

"Let's get this thing out," he gasped. He staggered to the front of the car. "Get in and start it," he told her. "I'll shove."

Bonnie started the engine and Burrows went to the front of the vehicle. She put it into reverse gear and with every last ounce of strength he could gather, he pushed. The sand came from the wheels in two spurting waves each side of him. He clenched his teeth and heaved and heaved again. He felt it shift. With his face twisted with pain and effort he got his shoulder against the grille and put every pound he could into the action. The rear wheels bit into the coats and suddenly the car was running backward leaving Burrows sprawling like a clown.

Bonnie, not wanting to risk the vehicle sinking in another place, turned it right back to the road. She got out there and ran back toward Burrows. He was on all fours like a man looking for something lost. She pulled him to his feet and they climbed through the sand towards the road.

"I'll drive," said Bonnie.

Burrows slumped into the seat beside her. He leaned over, touched the steering wheel. "His car," he muttered. "Abigail was in this. Right here. And now we've lost the bloody swine."

"We've just *got* to call the Sheriff's Office," she repeated. "Wheeler's *got* to listen. Maybe the Sheriff's back now."

"Just drive," he insisted. "We've got to try and *think* as we go. Christ I feel like a steamroller's hit me. That pig . . . And to think we had him." He clenched his fist. She started the car and began to go south. "He could be anywhere," he acknowledged, shaking his head. "You can bet he's headed straight back to wherever they've got them . . . or they've had them. Once he opens his mouth they've got no chance, even if they're still alive now. Oh, Jesus."

"That's why we need the law," she urged him determinedly. "We want the goddam National Guard out searching."

He shook his head again. "Even if Wheeler listened, there's *no time*," he said. "Did that monster say anything, anything at all to you? Anything to give us a clue."

"Christ, yes, now, wait a minute," she said, staring at the road ahead. "Some New Yorkers. His friends from New York. There can't be that many. . . . "

"Oregon Inlet," said Burrows slowly and triumphantly. "The old man said there were two people from New York. A man and girl. Let's get there, Bonnie. Edith could be on that boat."

James sat easily on the reception desk in the lobby. "Seems like we're getting to the end of the story," he murmured.

Candice said, "That's how it looks."

"Edith's next," he said. He looked at her languidly. "And it's your turn."

"I thought you'd say that."

"I just said it."

Candice went towards the cupboard behind the desk. She took down a phial of tablets. "I thought it might by your ambition to do it while you were screwing her," she said caustically. "That sounds like your style."

"Her attraction is waning," he said easily. "She's aged. You do it."

"All right. I won't chicken out of my share, don't worry your gut." She shut the cupboard and walked around the desk until she faced him only a foot away. "But listen, you evil shit, don't you . . ."

"I know, I know," He grinned fiercely in her face. "Don't lay my dirty hands on Goldilocks. Momma Bear will do that."

"You're such a lousy shithouse."

"So you keep reminding me." He pushed his pale, tight face closer towards her. "But Momma Bear had better make it quick."

"When I'm ready."

"I want to get all their belongings down to the boat," he told her. "I want to be good and sure they end up at the bottom of the ocean. Seems like I have to think for everybody." He got up from the desk and went to the window. He pulled the blind apart and looked out. "I'm still not sure we did the right thing letting that mad, fucking kid go loose."

"He thinks he's done a murder," she shrugged. "He won't blab to anybody. If we'd got rid of him then somebody sooner or later would have traced him to us."

James had turned slowly from the window and was staring at her. "What did you say?" The voice was low and nasty. He walked towards her and put his hand around her throat, lightly,

223

hardly touching her. Her eyes widened with apprehension. "What did you say – he *thinks* he's done a murder? Listen lady, as far as anybody knows he fucking well *has* done a murder. You just remember that, okay?"

"Okay," she muttered. He took his fingers from her neck. She turned away quickly and went to the bar, taking a glass from the shelf.

"What are you giving her?"

"Edith? A double dose of sedatives. Then when she's out we get her down to the cave. Right?"

"Make it a triple dose," he said.

"She'll notice. She's not stupid."

"Fix it so she doesn't notice," he rasped. "And see she swallows it. Get it done."

"I will." Candice took two more tablets from the phial and dropped them into the glass. "She's pretty dopey anyway," she said as she went towards the corridor. "It won't take much to put her flat out."

"Just do it," he repeated. "Me, I'm getting tired of this game."

Edith lay in her robe, her eyes closed to slits, but far from drowsy. On the last two occasions Candice had fed her sedatives she had secreted the tablets beneath her tongue and spat them out at the first opportunity. Now she lay listening. The knife, as sharp as it would ever be, was beneath the pillow. Alongside it was the bathroom key. Now was the time.

A vehicle had driven off and she guessed it was Tommy. She knew the sound of his car now and he always left in a juvenile roar and rush. The other two must be in the lobby area. Edith was amazed at the cool hardness that had come over her, both her mind and her body. Nothing worse could happen to her now. She had wanted to save her girls and herself; now she wanted something more. Revenge.

She realised with something of a shock that she wanted *that* more than anything else. For herself, even more than rescue. She was broken and abused. She wanted to take something back for that. As she lay there it was the dream that kept her cool and sane. She, Edith Burrows, the gentle, assured, good-natured woman from an English village, wanted to, needed to, kill these creatures who had harmed her and her daughters.

She caught her breath as she heard Candice's sharp footsteps along the corridor. It had to be now. Before it was altogether too late. Her hand went below the pillow for the knife. She had rationalized that it would be no good killing the woman first; she would need to immobilise her and to get James while she was still strong enough and while he was unsuspecting. Closing her eyes, she relaxed against the pillow. Candice opened the door.

"Wake up, Edith," she said briskly. "Time to take your tablets."

Edith pretended to stir. The opportunity came as simply as she had dared to hope. Candice hardly glanced at her on the bed before turning off to the bathroom where she began to fill the glass with water. Edith rolled quickly and silently to her feet and moving to the door inserted the key and turned it.

In two steps she was back to the bed. The metal of the table knife felt warm when she brought it from beneath the pillow. The edge was like a razor. She almost laughed. She heard Candice try the bathroom door. She would need to be swift. Out in the corridor she locked the door and then ran silently on her bare feet to the room where she knew they had kept Abigail.

At that moment, in the lobby area, James turned on the radio. A rock 'n roll record was playing and he did not turn the volume down. He would not hear any noise Candice was making.

Edith arrived at Abigail's door. To her surprise it was not locked. She pushed it open. Her hand went to her mouth. The bed had been stripped and Abigail's case was standing, open and clumsily packed, on the floor. She choked back a sound. Swiftly she went into the room and to the bathroom. That was empty too.

"Abby," she said quietly to herself. "Oh, Abby . . . Abby." There were no tears now. She had cried them all. Instead a cold fury rose within her. She gripped the knife savagely and turned back into the corridor. Then she paused, and put the knife under her robe. She walked quietly into the lobby area. James was just turning into the room after staring from the window.

"What are you doing out?" he said. "Candice is–"

"Where's Abigail?" she said strangely, and with a shock she saw herself in the wall mirror. Wild and unkempt, her hair straggling, her face white and crazed. Even frightening. "What have you done with my daughter?"

225

James Dade laughed nastily. "She had to leave," he said. "No time to say good-bye." He moved forward toward her without hurry, like a keeper about to take a wandering animal back to its pen. "You'll be joining her again soon."

One more step and Edith suddenly brought the knife up in a great half circle. The power it gave rushed through her hardened body. She felt it was like a sword. His mouth dropped, his tongue fell forward and his thin pale hands went up to protect himself. He stepped, then half stumbled away. Edith screamed weirdly and rushed at him bringing the knife down in a great vengeful swoop from above her head. She felt it cut into him but then fall away again. The force of her assault sent her staggering on top of him. She could see she had cut a huge gash across his cheek. Blood was streaming over his jawbone. His face was stark with fear. But she was off balance now. She tried to strike him again with the knife, but he caught her wrist and forced it away. He brought up his other hand and pushed it flat into her face, ramming her head back. The blow sent her rolling away from him, across the room. The knife was on the floor, on the square of carpet beneath the low reception desk.

James was laughing like a madman now. His face a red waterfall, his eyes staring through his blood-soaked hair. The radio still blared pop music. Frantically Edith reached for the first movable object at hand. It was the half-empty rack of postcards. It was thin tubular metal and she swung it with all her force catching him on the shoulder. She was screaming like a witch now. "You foul, filthy bastard! My girls. That little girl! I'll kill you for my girls!" Her voice howled over the noise of the radio. Barbra Streisand was singing "Don't Rain on My Parade."

She tried to get to the knife again, but he threw her out of the way. The card rack was bent almost double by the force of the blow she had struck with it, but James had taken the weight on his shoulder. It lay like a crashed zeppelin between them on the floor. James swung his foot at it and it flew at her, striking her chest and sending her sprawling. Now he had her. She lay against the wall, watching, trapped and doomed. James got to his knees and fumbled under the low clearance of the desk for the knife. Then the outside door opened letting in a dark night wind and there stood Tommy.

He was wild and bruised. Almost incoherent. "There's a

226

guy—" he began. He stopped and looked at the scene in front of him.

Edith stared at him pleadingly. "Tommy," she whispered. She pointed at James. "He killed Abigail."

Tommy stopped. His face seemed to expand. James still hadn't reach the knife. He looked up at Tommy.

"Don't be goddam stupid, Tommy," he muttered. "*You* killed her. *You* know that."

The boy's face was illuminated with sweat. He screwed up his ugly eyes and great tears rolled from them. "I *don't* know that," he repeated. "I don't know that, James. *You* told me I killed her. It was *you* who told *me*."

"He killed her!" screamed Edith from the wall. "He told me he killed her!" The radio disc jockey announced another request and put on another record.

The big youth began to tremble. He looked around him as though seeking some weapon. The tears cascaded. "You fucking junkie," he said. "You fucking, fucking junkie I believed you." He ran straight at James and bringing up his boot kicked him with tremendous force in the ribs. James cried, his chest heaved as he heeled over. But the blow was ungainly. It sent the boy tumbling forward with his own velocity. He sprawled and his shoulder hit the reception desk. James suddenly saw the tortured face almost in front of his own. He jammed his thumbs into the streaming eyes. Tommy screeched. Edith crawled across the floor and in a moment of near comedy managed to lever Tommy's leg out of the way so that she could reach the knife. The boy was clumsily getting to his feet, his hands across his eyes. He used the desk as a lever and stood up. Edith handed him the knife.

"Kill him, Tommy," she instructed coldly and clearly. "He's done it to *all* of us. He killed your Abigail."

Bemused, Tommy took the knife. Oddly, he wiped the blood from the blade onto his jeans, then moved over and turned off the radio. James was helpless now. A silence dropped over the deadly little scene. Then Edith heard the splintering of wood from down the corridor. Candice was breaking through the door panels. "Hurry, Tommy," she whispered. "Kill him. Kill him now, Tommy."

She was like someone holding the two broken ends of a rope. Watching Tommy's wrecked face, urging him to do it, and now

227

watching the door as well. Candice did not appear. Tommy moved like a flabby monster. James crouched away from him, his face working with sweat, a croak cackling from his throat.

"You did, you fucker," said Tommy. "You killed my Abby. And you blamed *me*."

He would have killed him then. But almost casually, the front door opened and Candice stood there, ice-faced, the small pistol in her hand. Tommy looked up just as she fired. The bullet hit him in the chest and he folded forward on his face. Horrified Edith fell on her knees. "Tommy! Tommy!" Her cries were like the cries of a raven. Candice fired another shot. It killed the Englishwoman instantly. She tipped forward, her left arm thrusting out and ending, like a comforting hug, around Tommy's thick waist.

Candice looked at James with a steady disgust. He was trying to wipe the blood from his face. "And that's the last goodam thing I'm going to do for you," she said.

"But not the last I'll do for you," he answered. "For example, I'm going to help you get your victims down to the fishes' cave. Don't forget *I* haven't killed anybody yet. And there's only one left, baby, and you know what we've decided about that one."

The girl's face was as tight as drawn satin. She fingered the gun. He saw it and smiled. "You're going to have a hell of a job moving everybody by yourself," he said. "Let's get on with it."

"All right, James," she said suddenly. She put the gun in her handbag. James moved towards Edith's body.

"Come on Edith, dear," he said. "Time to go." He glanced up at Candice. She moved forward as he pulled Edith's arm from Tommy's body. James turned the dead woman over, onto her back, and put his arms beneath her armpits. Staring at the horrified countenance, the English woman's dying expression, Candice caught hold of her legs and lifted her as James lifted her top. She was surprisingly light.

They went along the corridor, Candice turning her eyes away, anywhere, from that final face and the wound the gun had made in her breast. James opened the doors to the engine house and then to the storeroom. They set the body down while he pulled the hiding plywood from the final door and opened the entrance to the cavern. Again the salt and the resouding waves eddied out. Without speaking he turned on the dim bulkhead light and then came back to the body. They went carefully down the slimy steps. The sea was much higher, much rougher than before. They were soaked to the knees and all but knocked sideways by the top layer of a wave running over the rocks and the steps.

James looked up at Candice. "Now," he said breathlessly. Together they threw the body into the darkness and the water. They stumbled back and then climbed halfway back up the steps. Pausing, Candice looked back and saw the dim patch of material rolling on the water. James glanced back also. "Bon voyage, Edith," he said. Then to Candice, "Let's go and get her travelling companion."

10

James took the small suitcase and threw it into the back of the pick-up, with the cans of fuel for the boat. It was a dark night; the lights of the vehicle cut through the rain outside Sweetwater Point. He walked back to the motel and went into the lobby. Candice was standing wearing a robe. He never remembered seeing her look so bad. He was glad he was getting out.

"I'll get this stuff down to the boat," he said. "That case of the kid's should have been dumped at the same time as the others."

"She needed the things," said Candice quietly. "You can drop it in the ocean now."

He half turned towards the vehicle. "I'm coming back," he said. "I don't want you left here. As soon as it's light I'll get you to the bus stop in Manteo."

"That's unusually gallant. I thought you were sailing for Florida. I thought this was the big good-bye. You go your way, I go mine." She regarded him coolly.

"Not until you do what you have to do," he answered. "I don't want that kid left alive."

"She won't be."

"If I find you haven't done it, I'll do it myself."

"You won't ever put your hands on her again," she said. "If somebody's got to kill her it will be me. I wouldn't give you the pleasure of doing it, you lousy bastard."

"Okay, please yourself. Just do it." He glanced at the suitcase again.

"That's everything, okay?" he said. "In the case. I mean *everything*."

"Yes," she replied sharply. "Everything but the nightdress she has on right now – and the clothes . . . she has to wear."

"What about the nightdress? What happens to that?"

"I'll look after it."

James laughed sardonically. "A touching memento," he sneered "A little keepsake."

Her eyes hardened, then dropped. "I said I'll look after it," she repeated. "Don't shit, there's nothing that's ever going to connect you with it. If I get back to New York, maybe I'll just drop it off the Brooklyn Bridge."

"See if you can arrange to be wearing it at the time."

He turned and walked out again. Her lip curled as she made a snarl at his back. Her face went into her hands and she turned into the dining room and poured herself some black coffee. Her hands shook and her lip trembled at the rim of the cup when she began to drink it. "Christ," she muttered. "Oh, Christ."

When she had finished the coffee she went slowly along the corridor to Kate's room at the far end. She knocked before immediately going in. The girl's head jerked upright from the bed. "It's me, baby," said Candice. "Don't be afraid."

"What's happening?" said Kate. Her eyes seemed to have receded into her head. Her skin was like ash. "I want to see my mother, Candice."

"Soon, real soon," assured Candice. She sat on the side of the bed and ran her fingers through the girl's hair. "That's beautiful," she said. "That's what I shall always remember about you, your hair."

"What's happening?" asked the girl again. "Is it day or is it night?"

"It's still night. It sounds like there's a storm coming up. We get storms all the time, don't we? It sounds like a biggie." She stood and went to the window. She opened the blind. "It's so different here in the summer, you know, Kate. This is a real beautiful place. The sky always looks so enormous, so wide. It's because there are no mountains, you see, everything except for the dunes is flat as can be, just land and ocean. And the kids have a fine time. There's even a special beach where they build the biggest sand castles you ever did see. Everybody joins in, parents and kids, everybody. I used to come down here from New York when I was at school, and that's the part I loved most of all. We

231

used to go fishing and boating and swimming and all those things, but building the sand castles was the greatest. They give prizes too. One year my father helped me and we won a prize."

She was talking to herself. Kate watched her. The girl was drowsy and aching. They always gave her something to make her sleep. It made her ache.

Candice returned to the bedside. "I wish we could have been the same age, then, Katy," she said. "We could have built those sand castles together. And maybe we could have tried to ride the wild horses. Do you ride horses in England, Kate? You yourself?"

Kate nodded. "At school," she said.

"That would have been terrific fun. The horses are on Ocracoke. People say they're descended from horses brought here by the Spaniards."

"When can I see my mother?" asked Kate again. "Where's Abigail?"

"Very soon," reassured Candice. "We're quitting. Tommy has already gone and James is ready to go. I shall be leaving today. As soon as it's light."

The girl stared at her. "You're going? You're honestly going and leaving us? Honestly?"

Candice smiled at her voice. "Sure. I always said we would. I promised. We plan to be a long way off before night."

Kate asked, "How are you going to leave us? How do you know we won't be out of here as soon as you've gone? The police would be right after you, Candice."

Candice laughed. "Thanks for telling me. Now I know."

"What are you going to do?"

The woman sighed. "The simple thing. Give you one more sleeping pill than usual. You and your mother and your sister. That ought to keep you quiet for quite a few hours." She bit her lip. "That's what I've come for now, Kate. To say good-bye."

She leaned forward and, putting her arms about the girl, crushed her to her breasts. She kissed the child's neck and stroked her hair. "Hug me, Katy," she trembled. "Hug me back – just this once."

Kate tightened her arms around the woman's slim body and felt the vibration of the sobs running through her chest. She released her and Candice got up and walked away into the bathroom. Kate watched the door. She returned with a glass of water and the familiar pill. "I think one will be enough for you, baby," she said quietly. "Two would be dangerous."

Obediently Kate swallowed the pill and drank the water. Candice regarded her with tearful eyes. She bent and kissed her on the lips and then went from the room, locking the door behind her.

She returned a half hour later. Even as she walked, she trembled. She went into the room. The storm was moving along the coast. She could hear its rumbling. The room was dim and silent. The girl was sleeping.

Candice went to the bedside and lay down quietly beside the child, embracing her tenderly.

Suddenly, after half an hour, she felt very cold. The time had come. She dressed the sleeping figure in underwear, socks, jeans, sweater and shoes. Then she took the pillow and held it above the girl's face. Tears were coursing down her own cheeks. She could feel them salt in her mouth. Looking down in the dim room she was in time to see Kate smile blissfully in her sleep. She dropped the pillow. "No," she said. "No, my love."

Bending she carefully picked up the warm, limp child and carried her from the door towards the engine room at the back of the building. She took her through into the storeroom and finally into the resounding cave below.

Waves, pushed before the approaching storm, were rolling into the cavern. Candice switched on the bulkhead light. It was half-tide. Soon the place would be full of the sea as it had been when they disposed of Edith and Abigail Burrows. Sadly she carried her burden down the concrete steps and carefully laid the child on a platform of rock just above the running of the sea.

Once more she kissed the little girl and then, climbing the concrete stairs, weeping, she reached the door and got out.

Burrows and Bonnie drove along Cape Hatteras, south through the ragged and deserted night towards Oregon Inlet. They were silent for several miles. Then Burrows said, "Can you imagine Abigail letting that stinking creature pick her up?"

"It's difficult," she said. "If she's like you say."

233

"She's like I say she is," he replied quietly. "I hope to God we're not too late."

Bonnie glanced at his hard profile, the chin pushed forward, the eyes glinting in the dimness. Rain began to splatter against the windscreen. She felt in her voluminous bag and to his astonishment brought out a heavy colt revolver. "Maybe you need this," she said in a monotone. "It belonged to Buffalo Bill. My friend the thief left it with me."

He stared at the gun. "It came from the Cowboy Hall of Fame in Oklahoma City," she continued. "It's got six bullets."

"I could have done with that a few minutes ago," muttered Burrows reproachfully. "He wouldn't have got away then."

She sighed in the dark. "I didn't want you killing anybody," she said. "But now, I figure you'd better have it."

Burrows almost missed the Oregon Inlet turn-off, but he saw it just in time and swung the car swiftly off the road and down the track towards the darkened water.

Three lanterns, wide spaces between them, glowed sombrely around the haven. He narrowed his eyes to see across the harbour, but there were no lights on the boats moored in the central water. Outside the coffee shop of Garretty, the old man, a smaller lantern gleamed tiredly. There were no other lights.

"We'll have to wake him," said Burrows. "He won't mind." He held out his hand and she handed him the gun. He put it in his coat pocket.

Leaving Bonnie in the car, he went through the thinning rain towards the door of the small building and knocked firmly. There was no reaction until he had knocked twice more. Then a wavering light appeared and a thin voice of protest came through the wooden walls. The door opened with the same scraping squeak as it had done before. The old man looked through carefully, but without fear.

"Who the hell is it?" he asked. "What d'you want?"

"It's me, the Englishman," said Burrows. "I was here the other day, Mr. Garretty, remember?"

"Naturally I remember," replied Garretty. "We ain't overloaded with your sort." He opened the door. "I'm going to fix that," he said, nodding towards the squeak.

"I was looking for those Englishwomen, the woman and the two girls," said Burrows urgently.

234

"Naturally I remember," said the old man again. "I don't hear stories like that every day, neither. . . . You found them?"

"I think they could be out there," said Burrows nodding across the harbour. "On the boat that belongs to the New Yorkers. I'm going over to see."

Garretty seemed unexcited at the information. Instead he looked at him closely in the lantern light. "Your face is a mess," he commented without emphasis. "You been fighting?"

"A little," said Burrows. "I'm all right." He leaned towards the car and called to Bonnie. She got out and hurried towards the door.

Garretty put the lights on inside the place. He glanced up at Bonnie. "You lost three women," he commented without sarcasm, "but you found one. That's life."

Burrows tried to grin. He leaned towards the old man eagerly. "You know the two who have the boat out there," he said. "The New Yorkers, a man and a girl. And they had a youth with them – from this area."

"Sure," said the old man. He looked steadily at Burrows. "You think your people maybe are out there?"

"I think they might be," said Burrows.

"I ain't seen much of her, as I can recall, or the kid, but I got a sight of him yesterday," said Garretty. "Taking something over in the dinghy. Then the cruiser put out to sea. But she came back . . ."

Burrows' throat was dry. "He took something out to the boat?" he said. "Did you see what?"

"No, I didn't. I guess I just noticed he was loading something. Then he got the anchor up and went out under the bridge and, I reckoned, out to sea. It was no day for fishing, so I thought he was just trying to test out something, like they had a new part for the motor. But he came back quick. I thought maybe it was too rough for him."

"Do you think there's anybody there now?" Burrows asked.

"It's possible," he said. "I don't miss much in this harbour, but some things I do. I ain't got eyes in the back of my head. They could be over there. You any good in a boat? Or do you reckon on swimming? There's a dinghy down by the steps."

"I'll go over with you," said Bonnie. "I can handle that."

"Good, thanks, love," he replied.

235

"With Buffalo Bill?" she suggested.

Garretty looked curious but asked no questions. Burrows said, "Yes, I think I'll take Buffalo Bill with me. He may come in handy. Come on."

She pulled her huge coat around her and followed Burrows towards the edge of the quay. The old man watched them go. He tested the squeak of the door several times and shook his head sorrowfully.

The dinghy was bobbing listlessly against the habour wall. Bonnie went down first and Burrows, awkwardly, after her. She tried to steady the boat against a wooden pile as he stepped in and got his balance.

Bonnie had begun to pull the boat away from the side with unaccustomed use of the oars. The splashes echoed around the harbour like the threshings of a whale. Burrows glanced anxiously toward the moored cruiser. It lay like a ghost. He returned to the heavy revolver and opened the chamber. It was fully loaded. He prudently laid the weapon down on the seat beside him and, turning, surveyed the low hull of the white cruiser getting closer with each pull of the oars. On her stern he could make out the letters *Canopus Candy, Port of New York*. Dark water creaked against the side. He signalled Bonnie to ease off with the oars and the small boat bumped softly alongside. Burrows grasped a fender and waited for any reaction. None came. Inelegantly he climbed aboard the cruiser, leaving the gun on the seat of the dinghy. Gingerly Bonnie picked it up and handed it to him sideways, the muzzle pointing away. He nodded his thanks. He turned on the deck and went with studied steps towards the hatchway.

The door was unlocked. He eased it open. All was darkness within. He tried to control his breathing. The gun was pointing into the darkness. With his other hand he found a light switch and gently dropped it. Two bulkhead lights flooded the cabin. There was no one there. It had a double bunk on one bulkhead and a single bunk above that. The other side of the saloon was taken up with a table and a bench seat.

He looked around again. He realised the saloon light had been on too long. There was another door leading forward. Quickly he went towards it and pushed it open with his foot while keeping the gun half-tipped in that direction. There was a galley full of bottles and cans, and beyond that a store compartment. There was nobody abroad. Burrows closed the door carefully and, walking towards the main exit to the saloon, turned out the light. He went back out onto the deck. Bonnie was hovering nervously just off the stern of the cruiser. She hissed at him.

"Somebody's coming," she whispered from the dinghy. "Somebody's just leaving the shore."

His heart tightened. "Can you get out of the way?" he asked. He looked quickly around in the dimness. The sky was just getting a touch light. "Over there," he said pointing to a trio of moored boats. "Can you get behind them?"

"I'll try."

"And be quiet," he warned.

She pushed away, awkwardly, but silently enough, and edged the dinghy towards the three hulls. Very soon Burrows could not see her. But from the dockside came a regular splash of oars. He went below, through the cabin and the galley and then into the store compartment beyond that. He sat on a bucket trying not to tremble. He took Buffalo Bill's revolver from his pocket and rested it on his knees. In that close compartment he felt he could hardly breathe.

A solid thud came from the hull and then the sound of someone climbing aboard. He listened for voices but none came. He moved an inch sideways on the uncomfortable bucket and waited. God, he hoped he was right. He *had* to be right. There was nothing else left. He heard the door to the saloon open and then the inner door to the galley. Tension tightened in him. He stared at the partition ahead, waiting for it to open. It didn't. The newcomer retreated from the galley and there was a silence lasting two or three minutes. Burrows worried that the person had gone away again. Then he heard the start of the boat's engine and the warm vibration of the hull. Footsteps sounded above him on the deck and he heard the rub of the chain as the anchor was taken aboard. Then the steps retreated to the stern again. Disconcerted, Burrows felt the vessel moving.

Soon he began to feel the slap of heavier waves against the hull and he guessed they were within touching distance of the open sea. He sat, without any plan, wondering whether he should make a move. He held the big butt of the gun firmly in his fist. The move was settled for him. He heard the footsteps return to the galley and then the door in front of him rattled and opened. By the time James Dade bent and looked into the storage space, Burrows had the gun in both hands and was pointing it towards his face. He saw the lines stretch in the young man's creased expression as he reacted to the sight, the jaw fell and the eyes stretched. He had a strap of sticking plaster down his cheek. "Jesus Christ," said James Dade. Burrows got up and pushed him back into the galley.

"Wrong," said Burrows grimly. Dade was against the far door, but it opened inward. "Not Jesus Christ." He paused and breathed in deeply. "My name is Burrows. I'm looking for Edith, Abigail, and Kate Burrows and I have reason to think you know where they are."

He thought Dade was going to faint. He sagged against the wall. "Stand up or I'll shoot you," said Burrows, then quaintly. "This gun belonged to Buffalo Bill. And it works."

"Man, you're crazy," said Dade. He had stood up at the threat and he was trying to get his reactions organised. "The wheel," he said quickly. "I've got to get back to the wheel. This thing will turn over if I don't."

Burrows regarded him stonily. He looked at the thin New Yorker. What a mess, he thought, what a bloody mess. He nudged the gun at him. "Go on, Popeye," he said. "Get on the wheel." Dade went out through the saloon and onto the open deck. Burrows, following him, saw that he had deposited a suitcase in the saloon. He tried to recognise it but he was unsure. He picked it up as he passed and nudged Dade ahead.

"Get this thing back to the harbour," ordered Burrows. "Turn it around – and quick." He pushed Dade ahead to the deck.

Dade muttered, "You're bananas, man, fucking bananas."

It was cold but comparatively calm when they reached the open deck. Burrows saw that they were still within the lee of Cape Hatteras and that the rolling he had felt was when the vessel had been in the path of the longer rollers coming from the ocean. Now they had drifted clear of that tide.

"All right," he said, giving the younger man a jab with the big revolver. "Where are they? With his free hand he was attempting to open the suitcase. He opened one lock.

"That's laundry," insisted Dade. "Mister, I don't know what the hell you're talking about."

"Put your hands behind your back," Burrows ordered abruptly. He nudged forward with the gun again. Dade's expression hardened as he slowly obeyed. Burrows patted the pockets of his denim jacket and his jeans. He felt nothing. "Who did that to your face?" he demanded.

"Fishing," replied Dade. "An accident. With a gutting knife." They fixed each other with their eyes. "You're a crazy man," muttered Dade again.

"And you're a liar," answered Burrows. He opened the second lock of the piece of luggage. The case sagged like a jaw. A jumble of clothes fell out. He bent and picked up a girl's white blouse, his fingers shaking. He stared at the label. As he did so a sharp roll of the boat threw him off balance, and he allowed the nose of the gun to drop a fraction.

Dade saw it and swung the wheel swiftly. A roller coming in from the ocean hit the bow and the vessel heaved like a horse. Burrows went backwards across the pitching boards of the cockpit. The impact swung Dade away from the wheel, but he was prepared for it. As the boat righted he turned and picked up a wrench which had been lying on the shelf next to the wheel. His face taut, he raised it and went towards the sprawled Burrows. Burrows brought the gun up but Dade swung the wrench and struck him across the wrist. He shouted with pain but managed to hold onto the weapon.

The boat jumped again and Dade fell on top of Burrows. They rolled, fighting, with the vessel the friend and enemy of both. Burrows had a hand on the wrench and with his superior weight he was forcing it backwards away from the younger man's grasp. He panted and heaved. Dade spat in his face and tried to bite his nose. Burrows hit him with his free fist.

Another tip of the boat parted them. Dade regained the wrench and brought it down again on the hand that held the gun. The revolver fell from Burrows' grasp and slithered across the floor of the cockpit. Burrows grabbed the wrench again with his other hand. He could feel blood pouring across his face. Then there came a crunch and a grinding noise. Both men paused, as though in truce, and looked up. The boat was striking itself against the base of one of the pillars of the high Herbert C. Bonner Bridge which soared above them like a concrete rainbow. Dade stumbled to his feet and aimed a kick at Burrows which caught him on the shoulder. The younger man glanced towards the gun. It had slid behind a coil of rope and into a recess in the deck. He couldn't reach it.

The boat was now rubbing itself almost affectionately against the concrete and metal legs of the bridge. The foot of a maintenance ladder was only six feet higher than the deck. Dade made for the side of the boat, clambered up and jumped for the lower rungs. He made it by inches, hanging on and swinging violently against the metal. The effort and the collision knocked the breath from him but he sucked in the air and then heaved himself up the rungs.

Below him Burrows swore and forced himself heavily to his feet. The cruiser pitched irritably and threw him sideways again. His head struck the bulwark and he rolled across the boards of the cockpit. As though to revive him, a cold wave came over the side and hit him in the face. He got to his knees and crawled across the boards to where the revolver was wedged in the indent of the deck. He extracted it with difficulty. His hands were bleeding, wet, and icy. He had to crouch for several seconds to get his breath. Then, with an effort that he would have thought beyond him, he reached the side of the boat and, waiting for the next wave to lift the hull, he jumped and caught the same rung of the iron ladder that James Dade had grasped.

His body banged against the metal like the clapper of a bell. Blood was coursing down his face now from cuts on his forehead. Heavily he clambered up the ladder, the wind blowing about him. Breathless, he reached the top and was confronted with the amazing spectacle of the great, curving three-mile-bridge, empty of traffic, and like a solitary runner on a wide track was the escaping Dade.

"Stop!" shouted Burrows. "Stop, you bastard, or I'll shoot you!" Even the effort of shouting made him heave.

Dade was still only a hundred yards away. Burrows, hardly knowing what he was about, grasped the revolver with both hands and bent at the knee. He pulled the trigger. The gun rocked in his hand. The chamber spun. The smell hit his nostrils. He fired again. Dade swerved towards the side of the bridge. Burrows, crouching lower, fired again. He had never fired a weapon like this before. It jumped like an animal in his hands. Again he missed, but Dade, tripping, sprawled face-forward in the road.

Burrows, panting fiercely, ran towards him. Dade got to his feet and staggered along the line of the bridge railings. Abruptly he turned to his left and with difficulty climbed over the rail. Burrows ran to the side and saw that there was a fishing catwalk below, running ten feet lower than the parapet of the bridge. He cursed and ran along the road to the spot where Dade had jumped over. He halted and listened. In the deserted morning silence he could hear steps on the planks of the fishing deck. He ran another fifty yards and leaned over again. Dade was almost directly beneath him. Burrows aimed the gun. "Stop!" he howled. "Stop or I'll blow your fucking head off."

The other man looked up and accelerated. There was criss-cross ironwork between Burrows and his quarry. The English-man levelled the gun, then lowered it. He panted along the road. Ten feet below Dade cursed as he realised that there was a break in the catwalk ahead where one of the main legs of the bridge intruded. He crouched back so that the overhang above sheltered him. He listened but he could not hear Burrows. Quietly he began to retrace his steps along the boarded deck, heading back the way he had already run.

Burrows had lost him. On the bridge above the Englishman kept leaning over but he could not see him. He cursed silently and moved on, the gun at the ready.

Then, thirty yards behind him he heard the sudden squawk of disturbed gulls and turned around to see a dozen birds flap into the air from beneath the bridge. Burrows grimaced. He went back. A trembling excitement had caught hold of him now. He had never felt like this in his life. He ran as silently as he could, almost on tiptoe. After a hundred yards he cautiously looked over, hardly allowing the top of his head to clear the parapet. He smiled. Dade was creeping towards him, as fast as he dared without the loose boards of the catwalk sounding under his feet.

Burrows let him go by, then climbed the ironwork and dropped heavily onto the boards only ten feet behind Dade. The American swung around. "Got you," grunted Burrows, getting to his feet and rushing at him in one movement. He clasped Dade like a beserk bear.

Dade stumbled back against the rail, pinned there by the sheer weight of the assault. Burrows grasped him by the throat against an upright stanchion and brought the revolver up so it was pointing up his nose. "Now," he panted. "Where are they? Where is Edith? Where are those kids?"

"Fuck you," snorted Dade. "You've got the wrong guy. I don't–"

"You do," grunted Burrows fiercely. "You *do*, you bastard. Edith's clothes were in that suitcase. Unless you shop at Marks and bleeding Spencers!"

Abruptly he lost control. He brought the muzzle of the gun around and smashed it across Dade's perspiring face. Then he brought it back the other way and hit him again. He was screaming into that face as the blood flooded down the nose and again from the great gash in the cheek as it reopened beneath the plaster dressing. "Fishing, eh?" he yelled at him. His voice howled metallically under the structure of the bridge. "I *bet* you were fishing!"

Dade controlled his voice. "Listen, mister," he said, licking the blood away from his lips. "You've got it all wrong. Edith's okay. And the girls. Boy, have you got it wrong, though. Jesus, you'll go to jail for this."

Triumph burned like a sudden flame in Burrows' chest. "Get me to them," he said. "Let's go now." He jabbed Dade with the gun. "Move your arse."

He moved a few inches to allow Dade to lead the way. The younger man was staggering. Burrows was breathing like a man with asthma. Both had fought with Tommy within the past few hours. They went towards a flight of iron steps that led from the fishing deck to the upper bridge. As they ascended, both spent and stumbling, Dade bent foward and began to cough violently. He leaned down and for a moment Burrows stepped back. Dade lay against the iron rail. "Give me a break," he panted. "One lousy minute."

Burrows was himself glad to stop. He stood on the stairs behind Dade. The young man was still leaning to one side, holding his ribs. Burrows had no view of his right hand which went into a fisherman's rubbish bin fixed to the railing. He brought out a pint-sized bottle. He half turned towards Burrows as if to say something and then whirled the second part of the turn bringing the bottle with all his strength aiming for Burrows' forehead. The Englishman instinctively raised his arm and the green glass broke across his elbow. Burrows cried out and, losing

242

his balance, fell down the flight of stairs landing in a heap on the catwalk below. Dade laughed crazily and ran up the stairs.

It took Burrows twenty seconds to get up and stumble to the top of the stairs. Once more he had the strange sight of Dade running along the wide and empty bridge, almost one hundred yards ahead now. Burrows gulped in a lungful of air and went after him.

Although Dade was younger, he was not fit. He began to stagger again. Burrows found some last adrenalin from somewhere and pounded after him. A yard at a time he gained on Dade but he knew he could not run much further. His legs felt like cardboard. When he was fifty yards distant he bawled: "Stop – or I'll shoot you."

Dade actually stopped. Burrows could see him heaving for breath. Then he turned and ran on, stumbling like a drunk. Burrows dropped to his knees. He brought the sights of the old gun into line, allowed for the swaying of the target and fired. He had aimed for the lower half of the man, and prayed he would get him, but the shot was not good enough. It struck James Dade between the shouder blades and he fell as though kicked from behind.

Burrows emitted a strange sob. It was the first time he had ever killed anybody. He remained on his knees staring along the great empty bridge to the sprawled form before groping his way to his feet and slowly limping towards the lonely lying figure.

When he got there James Dade was not dead. Not quite. He went on his knees and felt the heartbeat. Dade opened his eyes and stared at him as though he could not believe he was real. "Where are they?" asked Burrows, almost sobbing. "Where's Edith?" It sounded like an appeal for sportsmanship.

"Go get fucked," breathed Dade. "Asshole."

They were inelegant last words. His head dropped back and his eyes dulled to pebbles. Burrows became aware of some seabirds circling above like vultures. Then he heard a car. He stood up and waited. It came over the horizon of the bridge, Tommy's Chevrolet with Bonnie driving and Garretty beside her. They pulled up ten yards away. Bonnie got out, staring at the crumpled man in the road. The old man, mouth awry, followed her. They both walked forward slowly, almost on tiptoe. "Jesus Christ," muttered Bonnie. "You shot him."

Garretty was staring at the blood and the body on the road. His old eyes were wide, pushing back the creases of skin. He licked his lips and smiled. "I hope nothing illegal's been going on," he said softly.

Burrows said, "I still don't know where they are." He staggered forward towards Bonnie.

Then, all at once, he knew where they were. It was staring him in the face.

"Bonnie," he muttered, moving towards Tommy's car. "Look. Look at this. Right in front of our eyes!"

Among all the old, grimy stickers on the windshield, was one that had every appearance of being new. It was black and yellow and showed a hovering gull above the words: *Sweetwater Point Motel. Cape Hatteras.*

"It's three miles south," said Bonnie, getting into the car.

Burrows was suddenly aware of Garretty, bemused, standing there alone on the bridge. "You coming?" he called urgently.

"You bet," muttered Garretty, moving towards the car. "I ain't staying here with no corpse."

An enormous thunderstorm which had been congregating on the Atlantic horizon broke over Cape Hatteras as they drove. It was eight-thirty. The sky was like night, the rain began in cold blobs and thickened until, within a minute, he could hardly see through the windscreen of the car. Thunder clattered behind him and lightning struck the sea with vivid explosions. Burrows hardly noticed it.

Bonnie sat mutely beside him. She did not like the storm. Garretty, eyes rolling, sat in the back. Their faces were white and set. Burrows had washed the blood from his head and face but he ached from every bruise and injury. There were two bullets left in the six-shooter.

The land of the Cape thinned and they could see the dull white explosions of the sea on the low beach on either flank. "It's a mile ahead," muttered Bonnie. "Down the dirt road on the left."

Burrows wearily nodded. The fire inside him was almost quenched now, doused by a cold fear that everything had been for nothing. By now, they might well be dead. Poor little Katy.

"Here," said the girl. "Down here." He turned the car off the swamped road and into a trough of stones and sand. Immediately ahead were yellow squares in the storm darkness. "Sweetwater Point," said Bonnie.

Burrows eased the car into a space between high, swaying reeds. It was a firm, stoney area, used by fishermen to park their vehicles in summer. "Wait here, Bonnie," he said. "I'm going."

"What do I do?"

"Just stay," he said. He hesitated. "After that, I don't know. I can't think." He glanced at the old man, stiff with apprehension in the rear seat. "Garretty'll look after you," he grunted.

"Thanks," she answered drily. "Good luck."

"Yes," he muttered strangely. "I hope so."

She bent sideways in an attempt to kiss him on the cheek but he was already getting out of the door. He leaned back and switched the lights off. His features were like tangled string. "Just wait," he said again quietly before he turned and ran at a crouch through the threshing reeds. Bonnie stared after him, the rain soon blotting out her view. She moved across to the driving seat and bent her forehead forward until it lay against the rim of the wheel.

Burrows ploughed through the sand and mud and stiff vegetation. He slowed as he reached the open area in front of the building. The unlit sign read "Sweetwater Point Motel." He moved forward carefully and reached one of the illuminated windows. He edged his eye around the frame. It was the empty lobby of the motel. His temptation was to rush into the place but he stopped himself. Tommy and the girl must be inside, he thought. Instead he moved carefully around the flank of the building. As he turned the corner the wind and the rain engulfed him. A line of lightning cut across the sea and the thunder clap followed. It seemed to be almost in his ear. There, parked against the high reeds, almost on the beach, he saw his Gremlin. Tommy must be there.

He crouched against another lit window, then eased himself up. A blind was pulled almost to the bottom, but not quite. There was an aperture an inch wide. He looked through the gap and directly into a bedroom where a slim woman, with her back to him, pushed clothes into a suitcase. She wore blue jeans and a white woollen sweater. Her blonde hair was piled behind her head. He strained his neck and swivelled his eyes to see if anyone else was in the room. There was no one. As far as he could see she was alone. Burrows lowered his head.

He moved around the side of the motel. There was scarcely need for silence because of the noise of the storm. The rear of the building faced onto the open beach where the waves rose like grey walls before avalanching onto the shingle. There was no line between stormy sea and stormy sky.

The fury of the onslaught caught him bodily and almost flung him against the wooden walls of the buildings. He flattened himself and moved along to a rear door. It was locked. He returned to the front and, feeling for the gun in his pocket, opened the main door and walked in. Behind the empty reception desk, there was a collection of fuse boxes and a handle which he guessed was the main switch for the motel's power. He moved to it and pushed it up. The lights went out. From the room along the corridor he heard the woman shout, "Shit!"

Burrows stood back against the wall, behind the reception counter. She came stumbling along the dim passage, still cursing.

"*Now*. Why, for Christ's sake, *now*?" she muttered.

She was talking to herself. "Where's the goddam flashlight? Shit and shit again."

He shuffled. Just enough for her to hear him. He knew she had. She stopped.

"Who's that?" she said. Her voice faltered. "Who is it?" she said. "I know somebody's there."

Burrows was trembling all through his body. His lips shook as he opened his mouth. He let off a small dry laugh. Even at this distance he heard her stiffen. "James," she ventured. "James, you bastard, it's you. For Christ's sake, quit."

"James is dead," said Burrows quietly. "Dead as dead."

She sucked in her breath. He heard her move quickly across the floor towards the door. She had just opened it with the storm shrieking outside. Burrows rushed across the lobby and slammed it closed again. She cried out. He caught her around the neck.

"What have you done with them?" he snarled. "Where is Edith Burrows?"

Still holding her he moved, pulling her with him, across the lobby again. He reached for the main switch and turned it on. Candice rolled her eyes around and saw his ashen, scarred, bloodied face.

"You're crazy," she said. "You don't know what you're saying."

"Crazy I may be," he admitted. "But I *do* know what I'm saying. Where are they?"

"Not here," she said. He eased his arm from her neck and turned her around. His eyes went to the breasts below the sweater. He could see what a striking girl she was. "What did you say – James is dead?" She laughed in disbelief. "How do you know? Who the hell are you anyway?"

"I *know* he's dead," he said, easing her into the chair behind the desk. He smiled whitely at her. "Because I killed him. And as for who I am, I am Edith Burrows' brother-in-law." He put his hand on the side of her neck again. "Where are they?"

Candice regarded him incredulously. But she was remarkable. And cool. Cooler than he was. Burrows was aware that it was he who was trembling. She did not miss the signs. "No shit," she remarked easily. "Edith's brother-in-law. All the way from England?"

"All the way," he repeated. Her attitude threw him. Suddenly he began to hope that they might be alive. "Where are they?" he said.

She let out a studied laugh. "They're not here, mister," she answered. She got up from the chair and he did not stop her. "Just take a look around. They quit. They all went away with James. Like a harem."

"You're lying," he accused hoarsely. "You kept them here against their will. You've had them prisoners."

She sighed. "I don't know what kind of fairy stories you've been reading, over there in England," she said. "But mister, you'd better change the book. Sure they *were* here. Christ, I couldn't get them out of the place. They were James's guests, not mine. Your sister-in-law was just crazy for him."

"She . . . w . . . wouldn't." He had to stop himself stammering, something he had not done since he was at school. "I don't believe they chose to stay here. And not let anyone know. I d . . . don't believe it."

Candice was smiling at him. "You didn't *really* kill James," she laughed. "For Christ's sake, I nearly *believed* you! You sounded for real."

His mouth dropped as he realised the situation. *God, suppose he had been wrong!* Suppose Tommy had told the truth. Suppose he had merely panicked – and run! Suppose James was innocent.

Suppose he was only trying to escape from a man he thought was mad. Burrows had made mistakes before. Having Edith's suitcase aboard the boat didn't make James guilty. Perhaps he *was* her lover. A terrible sensation seized him. Christ, no it wasn't possible. He looked up and saw her grinning, open-faced, at him.

Burrows stared at her like a man afraid. "I want to look around this place," he said inadequately. "I want to look in every room."

Candice spread her hands. Now she was well in control. "Help yourself," she said. "Go take a look."

"I want you with me," he said. "Right with me."

"Okay, if that's what you want." She revolved on him. Her eyes had narrowed. "But listen, mister, don't you lay one little pinky on me. Okay? I think you're some kind of crazy man and if you touch me with those English hands, just take it from me, you won't hear the last of it. I'll holler for the police louder than all that crap sounding outside right now."

"I won't touch you," he said. God, he *could* be wrong. No, he *couldn't*. Not about Edith. Could he? "Lead the way," he said to Candice. "I want to see every room."

She picked up her handbag from the reception desk and they walked along the central corridor. Echoing through his mind he could hear that official police voice. "*Maybe she went off with somebody of her own free will.*" No, surely not. Not Edith.

The American woman was unlocking the room nearest the lobby. It was clean and empty. The bed, the dressing table, the closet and the bathroom, bare and clean. They went to the next room. "Edith slept here," mentioned Candice casually. "With James. When he wasn't wandering about elsewhere."

He pretended not to hear the remark. "These rooms have recently been cleaned?" he said. He wasn't certain. It was more a question than a statement.

"Sure. Edith and the girls set about it like the Seven Dwarfs before they went. She'll make somebody a good housewife."

Each of the eight rooms along the corridor was identically clean and vacant. Burrows' spirit was dropping, a hollow wind seemed to blow through his body. No, it wasn't possible. It *wasn't* a mistake. Something *had* happened to them. Christ, it *had* to have happened! Otherwise he had been responsible for a man's death – for *nothing*! He pulled himself up abruptly as he realised the strange circle his mind had taken.

The final room was the one in which he had seen her through the window. On the bed was her open suitcase. Beside, laid across the quilt, was a small white nightdress. Burrows picked it up. "Is this yours?" he said. He looked at the label; it answered the question. "St. Michael. Marks & Spencer."

"It's Kate's," she said coolly. "She left it. I'm afraid she was a little forgetful."

Yes. He remembered the case left at Silver Spring.

Burrows went back into the corridor again. She followed him, watching him carefully, guarding her face and her breathing. He looked along the length of the passage. "What's that?" he asked abruptly, pointing to a low door at the end.

Had he been watching closely he would have known he was right. She steadied herself. "There's just an engine room down there," she replied slowly. "For the hot water and the heating, that sort of stuff."

"I want to see," he said.

"Okay, but you're wasting your time, mister. I'll show you."

She opened the door and led him into the room. He looked around. It was as she had described. Then he saw the door in the far wall. "What about that?" he said sharply.

"Storage," she shrugged. "All sorts of junk. That's all."

"I want to see," he said again.

Candice kept her nerve. "Okay," she sighed. "But you don't have to be Sherlock Holmes to see there's nothing in there. It needs a key."

"Get the key," he said, at the same time trying the door handle. It opened readily. He glanced at her. "It doesn't," he said. She shrugged and smiled tightly. "My error," she said. She went in ahead of him and turned on the light. He saw the room was lined with almost new wood, piled with spare beds, bedding and household implements. She sat down on a bed. "You look like you need some rest," she said to him.

"Right," he said hollowly. Defeat engulfed him. What *had* he done, for God's sake! "I'm tired. I also think I'm going mad." He was staring at her sweater.

She smiled and said, "Let's get out of here." He sat heavily on the bed beside her. "Christ, you have *no idea*," he mumbled. "I can't believe what's happened."

"Listen," Candice said patiently. "I don't know what your

story is, mister, but all I know is that James met Edith in Manteo – at the Lost Colony. She came here with him, and the girls with her. They've been here ever since. I'm sorry they didn't let you know."

"So am I," he whispered. A terrible sensation flooded him. He looked at her from beneath his eyelids.

"What about Tommy?" he tried.

Her eyes narrowed a little. "Tommy? What about him? He's a kid that's been helping on the boat. You've really been playing detective."

"He brought that car, the Gremlin, that's parked behind this place. I know, it's my car."

She shrugged. "I've never seen it," she said. "But I haven't been out too much. I haven't seen Tommy for a couple of days."

"What about *their* car?" he said. "Edith's."

"What about it? It's been here. They left in it yesterday, the red Tempo. They said they were going to Charleston and then onto Fort Lauderdale to meet up with James when he got down there with the boat. That was the plan. Don't ask *me* too much, I was just an innocent bystander."

He stammered. "I . . . I . . . I can't believe it. Edith. . . . Not . . . I . . . letting anybody know."

She smiled at him. "People change. They do crazy things. Edith completely altered even while she was here. She was besotted with James. She seemed to go right overboard – for some reason I didn't know."

"I think I do," he whispered. "You have . . . you have no idea . . . what I've done because of this. God . . . What *have* I done?" He looked at her, suddenly tight-eyed again. This is his last throw, she thought. "What about you and James?" he asked. "Your relationship?"

Candice laughed confidently. "I'm his sister," she said.

His expression fell again. But, at that moment," he heard the sound. A cry like a kitten. His head and his eyes came up.

"What was that?" he said. "That noise?"

He could see she had heard it. "I didn't hear anything," she said. She suddenly moved towards him along the bed. "Listen," she whispered quickly. "This sort of excitement turns me on, you know." Her hand touched his cheek.

"It *was* a noise," he said, not so surely this time but ignoring

250

her touch. He could not make any more mistakes. "I'm almost certain."

"There's plenty of noises," she pointed out. "That storm isn't exactly silent." He was staring at her again. "Things turn me on," she repeated, her voice low. "Funny things." She smiled surely and reached for the bottom of her white woollen sweater and pulled it up almost to her neck. She was naked underneath.

Her fawn breasts, with their pale irises, confronted him. He raised his eyes from them to her eyes. "Let's get out of here," she smiled. "I'm just in the mood for a guy as tired as you. Let's go. I've been lonesome . . . waiting for somebody. . . ."

He gaped at her helplessly. She had half-risen and was reaching out her hand to him. At that moment, the sound came again. The mewing. Burrows' face hardened. "There *is* a noise," he said firmly but quietly. "I heard it again."

He produced the heavy revolver from his pocket and pointed it at her. "You're a crazy fucking nut!" she cried abruptly. "Crazy." His answer was to push the muzzle against her left nipple, not forcefully, but just touching the ruffled skin. Its point was covered by the hole of the gun.

"Evil can be very contagious," Burrows said to her. "I can be as evil as anyone. Where are they?"

Candice backed away from him towards the wall. Once she had made some space between them she pulled her sweater down over her body. "Get out of here, you madman," she muttered. "Get out quick and beat it."

Burrows' eyes were moving around the walls of the room. He reached and pulled away an oblong of plywood leaning against the wall. There was a wooden door. "It goes underneath this place," she said, without his asking. "It's just the sea under there. It used to be a boat dock."

"Thank you," he replied politely. Excitement was rising like a tide in his chest. He reached for the door, turned the handle and pushed. It resisted at first but then swung inward. Inside was a great chamber clanging with the sound of the storm. Burrows turned to the girl. "You're coming too," he said.

"It's terrible down there in this weather," she protested, backing away. "Christ, we'll be drowned."

"You're coming," he said. He nodded at her and turned the gun. "I mean it," he said. Slowly she went towards the door. He pushed her ahead. "I want to keep an eye on you."

They went through the aperture. In a moment they were in the cave, booming from the storm, water rushing through below their feet and washing violently, unseen in the distant void. They were on a set of slippery concrete steps. All around was darkness. "I told you," she said. "There's nothing in here. Nothing but the sea."

The cry sounded again. This time he *was* sure. *It was someone trying to sing*.

"Katy," he whispered, then shouted. "Katy! Katy! Katy!" He had turned his head towards the sound. A wave rushed below. Candice moved swiftly sideways and pushed him. With a cry he hurtled down the concrete steps, rolling and shouting to the bottom where he clutched at and hung onto a metal stanchion and somehow pulled himself clear of a wave advancing like a great, dark tongue through the tunnel. The Buffalo Bill revolver fell onto the stone step, clear of the water.

The force of the push had caused Candice herself to stumble down three or four steps. She steadied herself and turned back towards the top. When she reached there she looked around again and in the dimness saw Burrows rolling like a drunk about at the bottom, half in and half out of the sea.

She stood, as calm as she knew she had to be now. From her handbag she took the silver pistol, aimed and fired. The explosion shattered through the cave. Burrows was saved by the on-rush of a wave that caught him and rolled him to one side. Candice thought she had hit him. She stared down in the meagre light needing to be sure.

His hand moved through the frothing water to the revolver still on the steps. He brought it up and fired in one movement. He thought he had missed also. But he saw her young figure stiffen. She suddenly choked and then screamed, "No! Please – no!" like a plea to God, before pitching forward, rolling acrobatically down the stone steps until her body tumbled into the sea. For some reason he reached out to try and stop it, but his action was too late. A new wave caught it and pushed it violently against the rock like so much debris.

Burrows fell forward, his face against the cold, sea-weeded steps, panting and wracked. Then, again, came the small, insistent sound. It *was* singing.

252

The Englishman heaved himself to his knees. Throwing the old revolver aside he began to stagger up the steps once more. On the transom above he could now distinguish a white square. It was a light switch. He reached for it and pushed it up. A dim lamp illuminated the cave. Carefully he looked around. Something was washing about in the sea down there. At first he thought it was the body of Candice, but then he saw that it was trapped by the rocks at the base of the steps. Slowly he descended again and painfully manoeuvred around the fringe of the rushing water. There *was* a body rolling about in the wash. He heard himself give a small cry. Moving forward again he reached out for it. Even before he touched it he knew it was Edith.

Gasping and sobbing, he pulled the head and shoulders clear of the sea. He stared down at the face. It was only just recognisable as Edith Burrows. Nausea engulfed him as he bent, tears and sickness rising together. Then, again, there came the tight little cry.

"Katy," he muttered quietly. Then, once more, it blurted out like a howl. "Kate . . . Kate!" It echoed through the cavern. He stumbled towards it, his heart banging. Along the ledge he found her. She was sprawled, soaked, scarcely conscious, her clothes clinging around her thin body, in the rotted hull of a small boat pulled up onto a natural platform clear of the pounding sea.

Burrows scrambled like an ape towards her. He cried, "It's me, Katy – it's me, darling!" When he reached her, she hardly opened her eyes. When she saw him it was as an hallucination because she did nothing but begin, once more, to sing.

"Within the woodlands, flowery gladed,
By the oak tree's mossy moot . . ."

Trembling, his face running with tears, he bent and picked up the small, wrecked figure. She fully opened her eyes and recognised him then. "Phil," she said quite clearly. "Uncle Phil. I knew somebody would come."

"Katy, Katy," he wept repeating as he stumbled with her up the stairs towards the wooden door again. The waves were groaning below, the wind flew through the cavern. He reached the top of the steps and pushed the door open with his foot.

He stepped out and carried the girl through the storeroom and into the outer engine room before bending through the door which opened out into the corridor of the motel. Immediately, he saw Bonnie, a thin, hesitant frame, standing in the lobby at the distant end.

The American girl suddenly shouted and rushed towards him. He stumbled and she tried to take some of the weight of the young girl he was carrying. "Bonnie," he croaked in a grotesque introduction. "It's Katy."

As they reached the outer lobby police sirens sounded ghostily over the flat landscape. Bonnie said, "I sent Garretty to call the police."

As they reached the court of the Sweetwater Point Motel the front two patrol cars came swerving through the sand. Deputy Sheriff Wheeler, gun theatrically at the ready, got out of the second car. Burrows, battered, bleeding, soaked, and staggering, fixed him with a look. "I found her," he grunted. "I told you so." He nodded at Wheeler's gun. "You can put that away," he said. "You're too late."

Wheeler called to the man in the second car, "Get this kid to the hospital."

They moved forward but Burrows shrugged them aside. He carried Katy to the police car and one of the officers opened the rear door so that he could lay her on the back seat.

"You'd better go too," muttered Wheeler.

Burrows managed a wry grin from his battered face. "Try and stop me," he said.

Wheeler glanced at Bonnie. Burrows caught the look. He put his arm around the girl and she smiled at him. Burrows moved towards the car with her. "She's staying with me," he grunted. "You can go and screw yourself."

He attempted to help Bonnie into the seat next to the driver. Then he climbed into the rear of the car with Katy. He was shaking. Bonnie half turned and put her fingers lightly on his wrist.

"You ready to go?" asked the driver.

"More than ready," grunted Burrows. Katy had collapsed against him. He put his arm around her. The car moved away.

Burrows stared straight ahead, his eyes unseeing, leaving the Sweetwater Point Motel to Deputy Sheriff Wheeler and the wild weather of the Cape.